THE SECRET CLUB

NAUGHTINESS HIDING IN PLAIN SIGHT

THE CLARENDON PLAYMATES KINK SERIES
BOOK 1

RUBY SKYE

INTRODUCTION

If you love to read scenes with relatable characters doing dark, filthy and quite simply delectably dirty things. You are in good company.

However, look after yourself. Here are some triggers you should take into account before reading.

Anal, Branding, BDSM, Breeding, Captivity, Deep Throat, Doctor, Dom/Sub, Double Penetration, Feeding, Gangbang, Impact play, Pet Play, Shaving, Sploshing, Somnophilia, Stretching, Voyeurism.

PROLOGUE

"Rosie, something has to give. We either sell up and move somewhere more affordable or one of us needs to get another job." My husband's words pull on my heart strings.

I love this house, I love this cul-de-sac, I love this area, and I love the kids' schools. The last thing I want to do is sell up and move somewhere more affordable. My husband works full time, I work part time for my own business. We need extra money because of the rising costs of life—our mortgage, food, bills, just about everything has gone up. And wouldn't it be nice to afford the nicer things in life? Family holidays being the top of my wish list.

James already works every available hour in his job, so Ubering is out for him. I don't even like to drive somewhere I don't know so it's a hard no from me. I also don't want to give up my beloved little business. So it's up to me to find a supplementary income. For my family. I'm 35 years old, when did things get so tough? I thought life was meant to get easier as you got older? Shouldn't we have our shit sorted out by now?

There's been a niggle at the back of my brain since James told me a few months back about a friend of a friend's golf pro buddy being flown out to Singapore to help a golf club member take part in a golf weekend away. It made me wonder about who plays golf at the prestigious Clarendon Club, how they can afford the annual fees and what else goes on there when they can literally pay to fly golfing experts out to their sporting holidays.

Opening my laptop in bed I look up the Clarendon Golf Club and am greeted with a beautiful website showcasing inside a modern clubhouse and beautiful pristine landscapes and greens. I know nothing about golf, have never set foot in a golf club, watched it on tv or desired anything about it. I don't even care for miniature golf. But something is pulling on my desire to reach out to the owners for a job. I have bar and café experience, surely these well to do golfers need some coffee to fuel them around hectares of grass all day. Or a beer to celebrate a successful day of golfing? Do they even call it golfing? And would they drink a nice chardonnay instead of a beer?

Taking a sip of my Pinot Noir for dutch courage, I write what I hope is my most flattering but not desperate email asking to be a part of Clarendon Golf Club in any capacity they might need. Once that's done I shut my laptop and try to sleep. What would it be like working for someone else again? It's been eight years already working for myself. Can I even work for someone else?

The next morning to my utter surprise there is a reply waiting.

Nervously, I click on the email and read to my amazement

Dear Rosie,

Thank you for reaching out overnight. You have actually caught us in a moment of need and we would love to arrange a meeting for Tuesday morning. Please let me know if 10am suits you for an interview at our in house café/bar the Marion.

I look forward to meeting you, Sandy.

1

———

Buttering sandwiches for the kids' lunches, James comes up behind me—his bulk pushing into the back of my body, pushing me into the stone top counter, one hand snakes around my slender waist as it dips down to rest just in front of my pussy. The other hand pulls my long brown hair to the side to expose the side of my neck as he leans in close to whisper, "You're going to smash it this morning," in my ear.

His freshly showered, clean sandalwood scent fills my senses and his close breath sends a shiver down my spine before he nips at my ear lobe and all too soon he's pulling away leaving fluttering in the pit of my stomach. What this man does to me, even after 15 years together...

I turn to meet his playful smile and light blue eyes twinkling back at me. This man knows how to leave me in a puddle and he's doing it on purpose.

"Seriously, Rosie, go smash it. Be yourself, they won't be able to resist you. We don't need the money *that much* if you hate anyone or anything about The Clarendon. I've been to Golf Clubs like this one, they'll just expect things done in a certain way and that is nothing you can't do. Just flash them that beautiful smile, push your shoulders back and keep your chin held high. Yes, we do need money, but, in my opinion they cannot afford to not give you a chance. Go get them tiger."

And with that, my mountain of a man bends down to land a kiss that doesn't last long enough on my lips and pats my bottom goodbye. That goofball of a man is always touching me in some shape or form.

Thirty minutes later, I've packed the kids into the car, dropped them off at school and am making the twenty-minute drive to The Clarendon. Turns out where we live in Melbourne there are plenty of golf courses to choose from. The Clarendon is however the most exclusive and desired of them all. It certainly attracts the highest annual fees of $54k a year or thereabouts. To me, that is someone's actual annual salary. What kind of people can afford to pay that for a hobby?

Nerves start to bubble inside of me as I drive through black iron gates, entering the estate's property in good time for my interview. I follow the palm tree lined driveway a kilometre before it opens out to a stunning white horse fountain in the middle of a roundabout with a backdrop of the most—what I can only describe as a castle manor type building. Not at all what I was expecting. When I was on the website, only the inside and golf grounds were shown in all their verdant glory.

I drive past the fountain and building, the road leading to a carpark on the right. There are only a handful of cars currently parked. All are black, have blacked out windows, are shiny and look expensive. Not quite the grey Volvo I've just pulled in with. I check myself in the mirror before forcing myself out of the car. This is a lot more regal than I had imagined. In fact, this is nothing like I had imagined. I almost kick myself, what on earth was I thinking? Why would they hire someone like me?

I'm wearing the only black pair of heels I own, which I paired with a black pencil skirt and cream blouse. I'm hoping it gives me an air of sophistication, but tottering along the gravel driveway, I'm not sure what I look like just trying to stay upright. Heels are not my usual daytime attire. Working for myself, I wear whatever the heck I like and most often that's comfy leggings and a sweater and Converse.

When I get to the giant double door, I wonder if I should push through or ring a bell. Looking up, I can see a camera and try and hold myself back from giving a little wave. I decide on the doorbell seeing as the door is closed. I press once and wait a mere second before the heavy door is swung open slowly and a petite blonde lady is waiting on the other side.

"Hi Rosie, I'm Sandy."

Sandy reaches out her dainty hand and gives me a firm but gentle shake. It's been a long time since I even had to shake someone's hand. Come on Rosie, pull yourself together now. It's game time.

"Really lovely to meet you Sandy, thank you so much for seeing me today," I say earnestly. I hope that didn't come across as too desperate already. I smile brightly and hope that takes the edge off my nervousness.

Sandy is wearing a cream skirt suit, her blond hair neatly curved into a bob that touches her shoulders. She must be in her 50s and is certainly under my 5'5". "Follow me Rosie, I realised you wouldn't know where our meeting point is so let me take you there now."

Sandy leads me through the foyer that is large, open with shiny parquet wooden floors, a grand chandelier, wooden benches below huge windows adorned with pretty pastel flowers. The room has an old world feeling that speaks of class and money. At the back of the foyer room, we turn right and I take in a breath. In complete contrast to the front of the building, this room has floor to ceiling windows that look out onto the endless greenery of the golf range. The room feels light and airy and reminds me of the wineries I've visited in the Yarra Valley.

Sandy leads us past the bar that is all black, with back lighting on all the wines and spirits they clearly stock. Sandy shows me to a seat by the window overlooking the grounds in the right corner. Before my bottom hits the plush black chair, a pretty tall waitress in her mid 30s is by our side.

"Hi Sandy, will it be your regular for this morning?"

"Yes please Sophie. Rosie, what would you like?"

"A black tea please." I smile shyly up at the beautiful auburn-haired lady.

"Rosie, your email came at the exact time I was about to put a new job description together. I think the universe was giving me a gift, especially as you have bar and café experience, albeit a few years ago now. What made you reach out to us?" Sandy is direct but her brown eyes are warm.

"This sounds strange, but I've had this feeling for a little while now about the Clarendon, like a niggle in the back of my mind that I'd like to work for you. I have been working for myself for the past eight years which has done me well but, in all honesty, I'm looking for some additional work and shifts to boost my income while things are a bit slow." I watch Sandy's face intently. Was that too much information? Am I being too honest? It's been such a long time since I've interviewed for anything. I pass Sandy the resume I hastily put together yesterday.

"Is that so..." Sandy nods and takes the resume.

Sandy takes out a pair of Prada reading glasses and runs her eyes over my work history. It's not long before she's folding it back up and looking intently at me. Like she's sizing me up— looks, body and all. I flush a bit under the scrutiny of her gaze and the silent seconds leave me wondering if I should fill them.

"Rosie, we are looking for an all-rounder to be part of our team. A Jack, or Jill should I say, of all trades. Someone who can pitch in wherever is needed. Someone who has a good work ethic and is up for any challenge or request that is thrown their way. Could this type of role suit you?" Sandy's eyes are now piercing. Like she's looking into my soul to see if she can get the answers just by looking into my eyes.

"Absolutely. I am really hard working; I aim to please and do whatever is needed. When I was a PA I was used to taking care of all of my Directors' needs and whims. And since working for myself, I am no stranger to a challenge and doing what is necessary to get the job done," I answer earnestly, hoping I sound confident and competent.

Sandy seems pleased with my response. She nods and replies, "In addition to working hard, we expect complete confidentiality and we ask all our staff and golf club members to sign a non-disclosure agreement. Will that be a problem for you?"

"Oh no, no problem at all. I am not a gossip and take my work very seriously. What kind of work do you have in mind?" Strange though I think. How many jobs ask you to sign a non-disclosure agreement? What kind of role do they need filing here? Heck, what even goes on here if you aren't allowed to tell anyone about it?

"I like that you have café and bar experience, we will of course show you the ropes on our coffee machine and drinks selection at the bar. You'll also be shown reception and the golf buggy hire. We like our staff to be able to cover each other. Most of our staff work part time shifts and we are flexible on scheduling in order for our staff to work the hours they choose. It works quite well, and morale is pretty high, especially once our staff hit the six month mark. Speaking of which: we have a six-month trial period, mainly to see if we're both a good fit for each other—The Clarendon and yourself I mean. Does that sound reasonable to you?"

"Yes, of course. In fact, the whole job sounds really reasonable. I love that you offer so much flexibility and there is so much variety within the roles. Do you need to see references or anything from me?"

"We like to be our own references. We will know within the first six months if we're compatible. One thing I do need to tell you is, at The Clarendon we pride ourselves on customer service and confidentiality. Nothing comes before these two. We look after our staff and our customers with equal care. The first thing anyone who joins our club does—whether they are a club member or staff—is choose an alias." Sandy said that last part as if it's the most normal thing in the world.

"Do you mean everyone here does not use their real name? Even Sandy is not your real name?"

"Yes, that's correct." Sandy smiles, probably at the astonishment on my face. "We have a few strict rules and one of those is anonymity and we request that no one ask or give their actual names."

"No problem. I can certainly abide by those rules."

"Great. I think you'll fit in with our team really well Roxy. Training starts whenever you would like to start. Would Wednesday morning work?" Sandy winks at me and I grin wide. I'm guessing I'll be known as Roxy then. And I got the job?

Trying to hold a shrill of joy inside my head, I keep my hands on my lap to grip my thighs rather than clap with glee. Considering I was so nervous, that was the easiest and most relaxed interview I've ever had. What is it about this job and place that is drawing me in? Why does it feel like it's meant to be?

Sandy starts to stand.

"Roxy, I'll show you out. When I'm back at my desk later today, I'll send you a form to complete and a contract to sign. I'm looking forward to working with you, I really do think you'll make a wonderful addition to the team." There is an odd twinkle in Sandy's eyes. I can't put my finger on it but I'm sure there is something she's trying to say but without words. Or maybe it's in my head.

I follow Sandy out of the Marion Cafe, noting that I can see two or three golf carts driving across the grounds now. She walks me back to the lavish entrance and holds her hand out.

"It's been a pleasure, Roxy. See you tomorrow."

2

___

I get into the car and clap my hands with glee, turn the car on and phone James.

"I got the job!" I squeal as soon as he answers.

"Amazing, I knew they'd love you. So, what *is* the job?"

I proceed to tell James about the building, the café/bar, Sandy, the type of role being offered, the non-disclosure agreement and my new name, nearly all whilst not taking a breath.

"Are you happy?" James asks with a smile in his tone.

"Yes. This is just what I needed. A role that works around us, the family and my business. But also integrates me back into a team to work around people after working for myself for so long. Funny about the name thing, isn't it? Have you ever heard of everyone—members and staff—having aliases in a golf club before?"

"No, never." James sounds intrigued. And I am too.

"Sandy is going to send me the contract and all the details later this afternoon. I start tomorrow morning!"

"Did you like her? Did you meet anyone else there?" James asks.

"Yes, I think so. She seemed nice. Motherly but firm if that makes sense. I believe she liked me. I guess she did if she offered me the job straight away? I only saw one other person, the waitress in the Marion Cafe. She looked just a little younger than me actually."

"Congratulations. I'm pleased for you. Hey, I've got to go, I've got someone calling on the other line that I need to speak to. I'll pick up the kids from school. See you tonight."

"Thanks, ok, no worries. See you tonight." The car falls silent, and I make my way to my office. My head is whirling full of The Clarendon. What will it be like? I hope the other staff members like me. How long has it been since I made a barrister coffee? Will I enjoy it? Can we now afford a nice holiday away this year? I hope I make it to my six-month probationary period.

Brushing my teeth in our ensuite later that night, James comes in to tell me the kids are both asleep. He's wearing only grey track pants slung low on his hips. A sight that never doesn't make my insides go giddy. What is it about men in low track pants? James is 6'5" and works out only enough to keep his dad body in check. He is graced with genes that keep heavy weight from his tall, lean figure and a full head of tousled blond hair. With his track pants low, I can see the hint of a V that draws my eye line down to the precious goods hidden beneath the fabric. James bends low to nuzzle my neck while I'm still in full teeth brushing motion. He angles his mouth close to my ear and mutters, "Congratulations Rosie, I couldn't be more proud of you."

I'm wearing my cream silk camisole nightdress so James begins to slowly tease my spaghetti strap down one shoulder, exposing the curve of my bare pale shoulder. Gently, he begins to sprinkle a dusting of barely there kisses from my ear, down my neck and across my shoulder. I stand still like a statue enjoying every light kiss he feathers across my heating skin. James presses into my back against the sink and I can feel the hardness of his erection digging into the centre of my back. Slowly he wraps his left hand around my waist and up towards my pebbling nipple. He lightly runs two fingers across the hard nub in gentle circles and I begin to feel my body melt into him.

I don't want to break the spell, but I need to spit the toothpaste out and turn around. Once I wipe my mouth, I turn to James, who lifts me up with ease and places my bottom on the edge of the sink pulling my legs wide open and moving in between my thighs. He takes one hand and lifts my chin, so my eyes meet his. He uses his other to draw my neck close to his face. Looking deep into my eyes, without a word he moves his head close to mine and runs his tongue along the seam of my lips. I let out a small moan and open my lips only the slightest amount, an opportunity James doesn't hesitate to take. With another swipe of his tongue, he brushes past my parted lips and enters my mouth, moving deliciously with my tongue.

Both hands are now cradling the base of my head, holding my head in place so that James can devour my tongue. He moves in closer to deepen the kiss and my body is pulled closer so that my nipples brush up against his naked chest. I bring my legs up around James's waist and hook my ankles around his bottom bringing him in tight to rub up against my naked pussy. James drops one hand from around my neck and moves it along my thighs, edging painfully slow towards the apex of my centre. Once his fingers have climbed to the edge of my pussy he lets out a low groan as he realises I'm bare. Touching his forehead to mine, he mutters in a dangerously low husk, "Are you feeling naughty tonight my little Rose Petal?"

I can feel liquid heat pool at my centre.

"Yes," I reply just before he takes my lips again, delving deeper, making the kiss hungrier and moving with more force against my tongue. Using his thumb, James gently brings it up and down my seam, barely touching my pussy lips but sending electricity through my entire body. I crave for him to touch me there more. Touch me harder, faster, reach for my clit, anything —but James is a master of command, he often teases me to the edge of insanity and now is no different.

I tip my hips so that his thumb is closer and I have more contact with the pleasure I know it can bring. He glides that one finger through my pussy lips, slowly up and down until it's slick with my arousal, with each swipe getting closer and closer to that one spot I need him to touch. And then he's there, that first initial touch setting off sparks deep within me. My clit is throbbing for more but James knows how to play my body. Grabbing my neck with one hand to bring my face closer to his, he dips two fingers inside of me while stroking his thumb against my clit. I shudder at the sudden intrusion, my body feeling limp to James' whims. He nibbles on my bottom lip, watching my face as I begin to feel that welcome spark building inside of me.

"I want your arse tonight, Rose Petal, I want to turn you around and watch your face in the mirror as I push past your tight muscles and slip deep into this perfect arse right up to my balls. Will you give me all of your arse tonight, Rose, will you take my big aching cock like a good little girl, or would you like to take it hard like a naughty slut? Make me punish you for looking so sexy in that pencil skirt you wore, showing off your arse so well today?"

His filthy words are all I need to feel the scales of pleasure tip over. Ecstasy courses through my body as James' curved fingers continue pumping inside of me and his thumb keeps stroking, drawing out every delightful pulse of my climax until I'm shuddering from the sensitivity. Withdrawing his fingers, I watch with hooded eyes as he brings his fingers up and wipes them across my mouth before leaning in to lick up the juices from my lips.

In a flash, James pulls me down from the countertop and bends me over between the two sinks facing directly towards the mirror. He reaches over to the drawers on the right and pulls out a bottle of lube. In seconds, he's pulled his track pants just below his groin and although I can't see his cock, I can feel the heat of it as it springs free and the tip rests on my arse.

"Which will it be Rose Petal, want me to fuck you like a good girl or a naughty slut?" James asks darkly, his voice has grown husky. Heat is radiating off his hard body, yet I need to feel him closer.

I stare at him in the mirror, his movements are dominating my every thought and move. There's something dark in there, I can see it bubbling just under the surface. I can feel it and I love the way he takes from me. I want him to take it all. I want to please him.

"I'm your naughty girl, James," I croak out. "Give it to me like you want to."

James's eyes flash at mine in the mirror as he pushes one lubed finger into my arse and I groan, "Yes," bracing my head onto my forearms. I feel another one enter me as James leans his body over mine, his cock pushed down between our bodies as he kisses along my shoulder.

"You like that don't you. Letting me loosen up this dirty hole, before I'm going to drive what you really want deep inside you."

My clit sparks again at his filthy words as he pulls away from my shoulder. Looking into my eyes through the mirror, James removes his fingers from my body, grabs the lube and rubs it down the length of him. Without breaking eye contact through the mirror, James lines up his thick cock and pushes.

My eyes go wide at the intrusion, I try and relax the muscle currently tightening around the head of James' cock. He bends over my back once again, lacing his hand around the front of me and finding my clit. Rubbing the bud in circles with two fingers helps me relax my muscles and loosen up completely allowing James to push forward until he's fully seated in my arse. The corner of his lips curve and lust enters his eyes. In a heartbeat his eyes darken and he mutters, "There's my girl. Taking me so good. Are you ready for your arse to be filled up? Are you ready for it to be punished? Are you ready to take my cum so deep, right here?" He pulls out a little before pushing the full force of his body up into mine. I scream out at the fullness and how deep his cock is.

I look up at James through the mirror and know that my screams spur him on. I reach one hand down and start to rub my clit to the rhythm of James' thrusts. I can feel the sparks building up through my core. Watching James begin to unravel, his eyes are trained on mine. He's looking like he wants to break me as his thrusts become harder and then more erratic. Holding both my hips as he thrusts chasing his climax, he leans over me and bites into my shoulder, hard. Pain ripples through my body and tips me over the edge of another climax. My arse muscles tense and quiver with the full force of my climax, tipping James over into his. His eyes roll to the back of his head and he holds his body so close to mine, his cock is fully seated to the hilt in my arse as he unloads.

I don't know why the dirtiness of his cum being deep inside my arse turns me on so much, but I'm glad James enjoys giving it to me. Slowly, ever so gently, he slides himself out and grabs a washcloth from the shelf. Running it under the tap, before running it over my hole and cleaning me up. He does the same for his cock before pulling his track pants back up. I turn around, pulling my nightie back down over my waist and look up. Words are spoken between our looks, I smile sleepily and he pulls me in for a tight hug.

"Let's get you into bed my naughty girl," James murmurs into my hair.

3

____

It's Friday and I start the day like every other weekday. I drop the kids off to before school care and then make my way over to The Clarendon. It's been six months of making fresh coffees, helping golf club members, making friends and getting to know the running of the golf club. I haven't taken an afternoon shift yet, but that's because this job is supplementing my income and I work in my own business each afternoon. Weekends I spend with my family and the kids' sports.

Having this new experience has been a brilliant learning curve, a real confidence building journey, and I've loved every minute of it. I've done everything that has been asked of me— even helped unblock a toilet and ran errands when the occasions arose. No job is below me; no problem can go unsolved. I'm praying my can-do energy has secured my place here for longer than six months. I've enjoyed being a part of a team again.

"Hey, you need to relax, Sandy is not going to let a hot little firecracker like you go. All hell will need to freeze over before that happens. So just chill, and please, for the love of god, stop pulling at your hair, there won't be any left and then Sandy won't want to keep your sorry bald arse around." Sophie elbows me in the side. I'm glad she's on shift with me today as she's been my partner in crime here in the café.

Pretty Sophie has been with The Clarendon for over a year now and appears to love it. She was the girl who served me when I had my interview here with Sandy. I say pretty because with auburn hair, fiery light golden-brown eyes and a dusting of freckles across her nose and cheeks, and the cutest, upturned button nose—she reminds me of an exotic pixie.

Sophie is actually a similar age to me being in her thirties—strangely like many of the staff here. I was expecting to be surrounded by students or Uni grads but I have been surprisingly taken aback by the amount of staff here that are a similar age to myself or slightly older. Most have been here longer than Sophie, it appears they don't have a huge turnover of staff, everyone must be happy. I guess the flexibility works great for everyone. Management seems to actually care about its staff too. I've felt more welcome here than in any employment other than working for myself. *Now that boss is a real slave driver,* I think to myself with a smirk.

I'm assuming all the staff enjoy the benefits from working here whatever they might be. Not as if I know what the benefits are other than a decent salary. Sophie has alluded to the fact there are actual benefits once you finish your six month probation but has refused to give me any kind of hint as to what they might be. I'm really hoping it's not a golf membership. I don't want to be ungrateful—although I have enjoyed working at the golf course, I still don't feel the inclination to play the sport. Thanks, but no thanks.

"It's time, good luck. Let's grab lunch before you head off to your other work. We have lots to chat about," Sophie says while hustling me out of the café/bar area and pushing me towards the grand staircase leading up to Sandy's office.

"Do we?" I ask, wondering why we have lots to chat about

considering we've just been chatting all morning between making coffees and looking after the cafe.

"We will," Sophie promises in an 'I know what you don't know' way. My stomach sinks a little. Does she know something I don't? Clearly, she does. What if she knows I've not made the cut and knows I'll need to talk to someone straight after my meeting. There is clearly a reason why it's being held 30 minutes before my shift ends.

Heart thumping in my chest, I walk out of the Marion cafe and up the grand staircase to Sandy's office. After knocking lightly, Sandy calls out, "Come in Roxy." Taking a deep steadying breath, I push on the handle and let myself into Sandy's light filled office overlooking the golf course.

"Hi Sandy," I say as brightly as my nerves will allow it. I feel way more nervous now than I did six months ago when I first met Sandy. Back then I didn't know what the job or extra money would do for me and how much I'd enjoy it. Now that I know, I don't want to lose it.

"Hi Roxy, please take a seat on the sofa, I'll make us a drink and come over." Sandy stands from her desk and moves over to the boiling kettle. Pouring into two mugs with tea bags, she brings the hot brews of green tea over to us.

"How have you found the past six months here with us Roxy?" Sandy turns and looks straight in my eyes for her answer. Unnerving.

I stutter, "Iiiit's been great, really great. I've enjoyed almost every moment of being here. Learning and getting to know everyone. It's even made me question keeping my own business that I run in the afternoons seeing as I enjoy my time here so much."

Nodding, Sandy says, "I'm really pleased to hear that Roxy, management and myself have enjoyed watching you blossom into the role. It feels like you have been with us longer than six months and that is a credit to you and your work ethic and attitude. None of us would like to see you go and to be honest, there are a fair few staff and members who have become quite attached to you."

I blush at her words but also glow with pride. I have enjoyed my time here and I'm glad it showed.

"We would like to invite you to be a permanent employee of The Clarendon. This will result in an updated contract, a slightly higher wage and another perk."

I nod and sip my tea trying to tame down the glee I can feel trying to escape my body. Keeping a fixed smile, I ask Sandy, "Oh what is the other perk?"

"That my dear is something you may not be expecting. It's another way to make some extra money outside of your current shift hours. You see, we have a certain type of member here at the club. Our members enjoy their time on the greens. They also have specialised interests in things we help to accommodate here via our staff. Different tastes that they might not be able to cater to outside of our organisation."

"What kind of interests do you mean?" I raise an uncertain eyebrow.

Sandy searches my eyes to see if I know even a hint of what she's talking about. What she must see reflected in my wide eyes is a complete unawareness of what she's talking about.

"Kinks my dear. We cater to our guests every type of sexual kink and sexual fantasy."

Shock paints my face. I did not see that coming. Not at all.

"Really?" I reply, stupidly. I feel like maybe I'm being punked. But deep down I know that's not the case. I can see it on Sandy's face. I know her demeanour by now, and Sandy doesn't joke around.

A few things start to slot into place in my mind. The non-disclosure agreements, the aliases for everyone. The rooms spotted around the building seemingly locked at all times.

"How?" It seems I can only speak one-word questions at the moment.

"We have an online portal that members can post 'jobs' on and each of our staff have their own profile and can apply for the jobs. The members can read the applications and choose the one they believe will suit their kink fantasy the most. Each job will give a full description of what it will entail, the time frame, and payment offered. We operate with a traffic light system: Green is standard kinks, Amber is a touch more unusual and finally Red is on the more extreme end of the spectrum of kinks." Sandy is looking at me all serious like she's just reciting the rules of a game.

"I'm married," I splutter.

"Indeed, you are. As are half our staff members and they are either in an open relationship or haven't told their partners the type of work they are paid to do."

"Oh."

"When you reached out to us, I had a feeling deep down you were looking for something far beyond meeting new people and working for the extra money. It was why I took you on to begin with. Your eagerness to work hard and please. There is something very submissive and endearing about you Roxy. Something I know our clients would enjoy. Something you would enjoy."

Now all I can do is simply nod my head with my eyes bulging out of my head. Sandy carries on.

"Every member is vetted. We have strict rules and procedures in place. Our team members are also vetted, medically safe and on birth control. Every job that is agreed upon goes through me first. We send our staff with drivers to their offsite jobs, our drivers text to confirm pick up times with our playmates on the day so they know in advance how long the journey will be and then return them home safely after the job is complete. Our rules are simply that they must wear a blindfold within the cars. You may not speak of where you are going or have been. Our members demand a superior level of confidentiality and we guarantee it. In return, we guarantee the confidentiality of our staff, their safety and their earnings. In my ten years of running Clarendon's Playmates, not once has anything gone wrong. Our club's safe word is always Neptune. No member oversteps even a toe outside of our rules or risks their membership being terminated."

I blow out a breath. This is a lot to take in. I was not expecting anything at all like this...was I? Something that seems a lot like excitement bubbles in my core. I cross my legs to curb the flutter I can feel between my legs. Shifting nervously on the sofa I try and speak, my mouth becoming very dry.

"I-I," I stammer. "Don't know. That's a lot to take in Sandy. Does anyone else ever know about this extracurricular service The Clarendon offers?"

"No, no one ever does. We've done extremely well at keeping it under wraps. Only members."

"Does everyone who works here also work as a Playmate?" Now my brain is kicking in. Go brain, it took you some time.

"Yes they do. Each to their own levels and interests. Some do it weekly and some do it much less frequently. Most enjoy the 'extra' salary this line of work offers. There is a lot of money being offered and it is very hard to pass up. As a sweetener, we cover your side of the income tax. So the amounts you see offered for a job, are the amounts you take home."

"Why did you think I would be interested in being a part of this other side of your business?" Curiosity is now beating any other sane question coming to my brain.

"There is something about you Roxy, something untapped brewing under the surface. I can feel it. Call it intuition. I haven't been wrong about an employee yet. And like I say, you are beautifully submissive, a trait favoured in our members community."

I take a deep breath. "Can I think about it?"

"Absolutely. I will send you a login for the Playmate Portal and you can review the job board and see for yourself. My advice would be, if you do decide to be a part of it, to take it slow and edge into the salacious world of kinks. I think you'll find, once you've tried a few, you might discover there is more that you're open to than you first considered.

"Go to lunch with Sophie. She will tell you her experience before you go home to your husband. Think very carefully before discussing it with him. You may decide not to tell him at all. Some of our staff don't tell their spouses. That is entirely up to you.

"And Roxy, whether you decide to be a part of Clarendon Playmates or not, please can you sign our contract over the weekend and the new non-disclosure I'm emailing to you. Either way, it will be lovely to continue our working relationship no matter what you decide to do."

And with that, Sandy is standing and showing me to the door. In a daze of thoughts and questions, I walk out of her office, down the stairs and to the front door where Sophie has a shit eating grin across her face. She grabs my elbow and tugs me out of the foyer and into the car park. "Oh boy, your face. This lunch is going to be fun!"

Getting into Sophie's Land Rover it makes sense why she can even afford such a deluxe car now. All I can muster is a, "What the fuck Sophie?"

Sophie's eyes sparkle with mischievous glee. "So Sandy told you about the Clarendon Playmates job board then? You're at least staying on with Clarendon though, right?" Sophie asks, suddenly worried I was in too much shock to accept the permanent position.

"No, I mean yes, I accepted the position. I don't want to

leave. But how come I didn't know or even pick up on the slightest tell that Clarendon was running some kooky underground kink fest and everyone working around me for the past six months has been in on it but I've had no clue?"

Sophie cackles. I raise an eyebrow at her.

"It's the confidentiality agreement. We don't gossip or talk about any of the members, especially not at work around members. Sandy would have our arses for sure."

"Gosh, you guys really do nail it on the confidentiality then. Pulled the wool over my eyes. So, tell me. What are these jobs like? How many have you done? How much can you earn for each job?"

"Wooowow. One question at a time," Sophie jibes. "You know we haven't meant to keep you in the dark, it's just how they do things here. Feel the new staff out and see if they could be the right fit. And you, sexy lady, are what they are looking for." Sophie shoots me a wink before turning her attention back to the road.

"I have done a fair amount of jobs now, yes. How do you think I could afford Betty here?" Sophie smiles.

"Your car you mean?"

"Yes, my car. I love her. Don't you?"

"Erm sure, I guess." I shrug. "So how many are we talking?" I push.

"I don't know exactly but I'd say on average one a week. Sometimes I do a couple a week and then I don't do any for a few weeks."

"And you're paid for doing weird kinky shit with strangers?" I ask.

"Yes, I get paid very well for doing weird kinky shit with strangers. And you will too. I know you will. It is not a bad gig at all. The money is excellent. And the jobs, some of the jobs— they blow my mind. And my body. And my mind again." Laughing she pulls into a car park of a café we know well that has a garden out the back with heaters. I know Sophie has taken us here because we're guaranteed to have privacy in the garden while it's chilly out this time of year.

Ordering at the counter before settling down at a table, I'm ready for my next question.

"Go on then. How much? How much for one kinky job?"

"Well..." she says taking her time extending the suspense.

"Sophie!" I growl.

"Stop, Roxy, you are too much fun right now. Ok, ok. Jobs can range from $1,000 to $20,000 and some I've heard of giving $50k+. I know, I know. It's A LOT of MONEY. And we all know what makes the world go 'round?"

"Money," I laugh holding my hand over my mouth at the scale of the payments. "What have you had to do for so much money?"

"Ah well, now that would be telling." She does a key and lock motion with her hands against her lips. I throw a napkin at her.

"Tell me!"

"The range of jobs is huge. You'll see for yourself. I go for ones depending on my mood in all honesty. Sometimes I click on Green which is your standard lists of kinks—think BDSM dominating guy bossing you around and doing whatever the heck he wants to your body."

I like the sound of that, I think to myself but don't dare say a word out loud.

"Amber is a little more of an unusual flavour of kink. Most of the job posts I'd never heard of nor considered before. I'm not sure if you're a pain slut or have even messed around in this scene, it can be painful and pleasurable with the right member... Then there is Red which is all kinds of fucked up fun. You're guaranteed not to have any long term injuries but still. Anal Fisting is the only one I've glimpsed and didn't even bother looking after that." Sophie shudders like a breeze just went down her spine. It makes me cringe too. I don't mind some anal pleasure, but that does not even sound possible. "But I do enjoy some jobs on there, I just avoid most." She trails off.

We both sit in silence finishing up our food. How do you follow up after that image anyway?

2pm rolls around all too quickly and I have to grab my car and go to my own business and try and work while my head is near exploding with so many unanswered questions. I just need to log into the Playmate Portal and see for myself. I am curious after all. Not just my brain judging by the tingles in my knickers. What is happening in my life right now?

4

———

After dinner I open my laptop and check to see if Sandy has sent me the new contract and login details. I haven't mentioned anything to James yet, I just want to see it with my own eyes. Opening the email, I copy the password and click on the link to the Playmates Portal. I'm greeted with a black screen with a username and password box. Logging in the screen changes into three circles: the traffic light colours. I click on the green circle and sure enough I'm taken to a job board with a short list of 'jobs'. I scroll down the list...

Friday, 8pm - 3hrs, MM/FP, Bondage, $2,750

Saturday, 6pm, 2hrs, FM/FP, Impact Play, $2,000

Thursday 2pm, 1.5hrs, Anal Play, MM/MP, $1,000

Sunday 7pm, 2hr, Breast Worship, MM/FP, $2,000

I noticed there seemed to be a similar fee and timeframe for each of the Green jobs posted. I'm guessing each session was an average of 2hrs and the going rate $2,000. A thousand dollars an hour.

Now my brain is going to the Amber job board and wondering what the timeframes and base payments for those kinks could be?

I click on the Breast Worship job post for further details.
Breast Worship, Sunday 7pm,
Member 805, Male (MM/FP)

'Looking for a lady with cup size c or bigger breasts that I can squeeze, massage, ice, lick, bite, suck, beat and tie up. I would like to spend the entire time worshiping your voluminous breasts. I would like them to end with beautiful purple love bites and bruises. I would like to photograph them at each angle as a keepsake. Before the end of the session, I would like to fuck you whilst admiring my work on your skin'
  Time - 2hrs
  Payment - $2,000

Yikes, this guy really likes to hurt breasts. Liquid heat starts to pool at my core. This is the kind of kink I'm into and would never admit out loud to anyone. What would it be like? What would the stranger be like? Does this make him some kind of psycho? Does this make me some kind of psycho? $2,000 sounds like a great deal of money for 2 hours work and to get enjoyment out of it at the same time. Would I enjoy it? Could I?

I think I'm keen, like really keen. I haven't even read the other jobs and already feel a wave of pure unadulterated excitement. Like I've been let into a secret club and it could be all my wildest fantasies and more. I guess that is exactly what it is—my fantasies could now become an actual reality.

James walks past behind me and pops his head over my shoulder.

"What are you up to, working?"

I shut the laptop with a fright. My face must have been a picture, James narrows his eyes at me as he pulls up a chair at our table placing two cups of tea between us.

"Some secret business I can see," he says with bemusement on his face, one eyebrow quirked up. I blush. I feel like I was just caught with my fingers in the candy jar. Or down my pants would be the more appropriate analogy.

"Ah yeah. Something like that actually." I grimace and blush an even deeper shade of red. "Something happened today, at work. It was my six-month probation meeting, and I passed."

"Of course you did, there would be no question!" James, always my cheerleader, reaches out and squeezes my shoulder. We have no secrets and I'm not about to keep this as one. We can discuss the Clarendon Playmates and decide together as adults—partners, what to do.

"There was something else that came out in the meeting. A revelation of sorts."

"Oh yeah? Spill? Are you now able to see the real names of the members or something? Got any famous people there I might know?"

"Well, no, that is not it. But good guess though. To be honest, you'd never guess it. Heck I didn't guess it. I thought they'd give me a discounted golf membership or something—I was dreading having to look excited about that." I let out a short awkward laugh at the thought of it. James looks at me intently, waiting.

"They have an underground kink club. It's why I had to sign all those non-disclosures and take an alias." I hold in a breath and watch for James' reaction. He does not disappoint. His face screws up as if trying to decide whether he heard me right or whether I'm shitting him.

"A kink club..." he says at last. "Okay. How does that affect you; they need you to bartend or something. Is it on the property or on the grounds or something?"

"Ha." I blow out in a nervous breath. "Not quite like that, no."

I explain the job posts and the traffic light system for the kinks and how the employees double as 'paid for hire sex workers'. James looks stunned. I'm probably looking at my own reaction on his face now.

"And they want you to be a sex worker? They hired you to serve coffee and your pussy?"

"I guess... That's what I'm trying to get my head around. I don't know what they saw in me. It all feels like a lot to take in right now."

"You told them you're married right?"

"Yes, of course they know I'm married. Turns out, most of the staff are either in a relationship or married. I'm surprised about everything."

James sits down in the chair next to me and runs his hand through his hair a few times processing what I've just told him. He looks up.

"You're considering it aren't you?"

"Well, no. I haven't given it much thought. I've literally just logged on to see the kinds of job posts and money. It's a lot of money James. I had no idea."

"Do we need more money now you have this part time job?"

"Well no, we don't need more money. We can now pay our current bills which is a good start. But for 2 hours work, we could be an extra $2k up, that's my entire weekly salary from my own business."

"So these people are basically paying a lot of money for their kinky fantasies and to fuck other peoples' wives?"

"Yeah, that is kind of the gist as far as I can see..." I'm trying to read James' reaction as I'm sure he's trying to read mine. I feel like I'm suddenly thrown into a game of poker trying to pick up a tell of his face but also hide my own. Am I trying to convince James to let me do it? Am I trying to convince myself?

"Show me the job posts," he demands, leaning forward.

I open my laptop and he reads the headings of the few

current job posts in the Green section. Using the mouse, he clicks out of it and clicks onto the amber circle. A restricted notice comes up saying I do not have access to this level. I almost breathe out a sigh of relief. The Green was plenty for a taster.

James clicks back to the Green job board and then clicks on each of the full job descriptions reading every last detail. I scoot my chair over to sit closer next to him and read the job posts too, each one making me feel hotter than the previous one. When James pulls up the final post, he side eyes me.

"You like this one don't you. It interests you." James knows me too well, well of course he does, he's my husband.

"You want some rich guy tying up your tits and beating them black and blue." His voice is deep and rich. There is something that flashes in his eyes. Heat? Lust? Does he want me to do it?

I clear my throat. "You know I like this shit, James. I don't know how I feel about strangers doing it to me. But yes, I do like the sound of it." I feel edgy, embarrassed. Both from talking out loud what my sexual fantasies are and also guilty that I am even considering entertaining this idea of strangers paying for sex amongst other things. "Tell me what you are thinking James."

James has his elbows on the table and both his hands are running through his hair.

"I don't know what to think. You're my wife. I didn't sign up to share you. You are mine. I own you." The heat burning from James' eyes, this look makes my toes curl and my pussy flutter. "Yet the thought of strangers doing things to you, to my wife, turns me on. What's wrong with me?"

"It turns you on?" I whisper in surprise.

"Yes. I want to see what they do to your body. I want to do the same. If they mark you, I want to mark you. If they fuck you, I want to fuck you in the same way."

I bite my lip trying to take in what James is telling me. Is he giving his blessing to take a job?

"You're ok for me to apply for these jobs, like really?"

James stares at me, really stares right into my eyes.

"No I'm not ok, but I think *I will be* ok. I think for the money, we could afford to take the kids to Japan or go back to the UK for Christmas. I'm not even saying do it for the money. I don't want you to do it for the money. I want you to do it only if it's something you want to do? Is it something you *want* to do?"

"Yes and no if I'm honest. I didn't think fantasies came true. I thought they always stayed as just that—fantasies which is why I've never given it any thought, least of all from a stranger. I feel funny thinking about a stranger touching me. But it's the way they want to touch me that makes me feel hot, like a craving. I want to see what sort of a person wants to do these things to me. I want to see their eyes and watch them move." I take in a breath and before James can reply I continue, "James. If this was the other way around, I'm not sure I could cope with you fucking other women. This is really hypocritical of me. I don't want anything to come between us. I don't want to share you."

"I have no interest in any women other than you Rosie. You're my one. I trust you. This is work with a little bit of pleasure thrown in. And some pain by the sounds of it. I am possessive of my things, of you. But I also feel something I've never felt before about you with other men. A desire to share in a depraved way. I like the thought of strangers paying to use your body."

"So, we're doing it. I'll apply for a job and see if I get it?"

"Let's take it one job at a time. See how you feel after the first one. Are you sure you're going to be ok actually doing this? This is your body. And their body. And them touching you, fucking you. Have you considered how this will make you feel there and also after?"

"Not really. But I think I can deal with it. It's 2 hours of my life. I can do this for $2,000. I want to be able to do this for us."

"What are the next steps?"

"I guess I apply. Then book in on Monday for the in-house medical. Sandy's email said everyone is to be tested each week for a clean bill of health. No STDs. Actually, first I need to set up my profile."

"Okay, so apply. I know the one you want. Do it. I'm going to do an hour's work and then call it a night. I'll see you upstairs in a bit."

"Oh gosh, what do I even say in my application... Not to worry, I can work it out. Be up once I've stewed on my job application and profile."

Once I'm 80% happy with my profile and sorted through thousands of photos on my phone to upload just one, I write my reply to the job post.

Hi Member 805,

I would like to apply for your Sunday evening of breast worship. My breasts are 34D and I think you'll enjoy them as much as I will enjoy everything you have planned for me and them if you choose me. I'm sure it's not applicable if it's my kink or not, but as it so happens, what you would like to do to me, is exactly what I would love for you to do to me.

I hope you choose me, Roxy.

Ten minutes later I receive a notification to login to the Playmate Portal.

Job **ACCEPTED.**

THE GREEN JOB BOARD

5

Monday morning at The Clarendon I look around with new eyes. I'm looking at everyone, both staff and members, in a new way. All these people know. The staff sell their bodies. The members buy their bodies. Everyone looks just the same as last week, yet I'm looking at them and wondering what kinks are bought and sold. None of the staff are younger than 30. Club members range from mid twenties to late seventies. Are the members here for the golf or the underground kink club?

To my delight Sophie is working today and although we can't discuss anything playmate related, she covers me when I have a quick medical and we leave for lunch together.

"Listen, here is my number. I'm your Playmate mentor. If you need anything or someone to talk to, I'm your girl," Sophie says, passing me her mobile number when we get into her car. "Call me any day or time, I'm here for you."

"Thanks Sophie, I'm really grateful. I have so many questions, I don't even know where to start. Does your partner know what you do?"

"Yes, Sam knows. He's chill about it. I told him right from

the start. He doesn't know where or any details about the club. He knows not to ask me but we make it work. It's a different kind of lifestyle but we're comfortable with it. Sam isn't worried about sharing, he's been on the swinging scene before, he's good."

"Do you like being a playmate? Is it even safe?" I force myself to end at two questions before ten spill out at once…

"Sure, I like it. I enjoy it I should say, and the money makes it a whole next level of worth it. Plus, I only go for the jobs that spike my interest. But be warned Roxy, while you might start off thinking kinks are not your cup of tea and you're not too interested. You start to change when you dive in. New kinks become more appealing the more you're exposed to them. I'm not saying you'll gain a whole bunch. I'm saying you won't be so opposed to them in a few months. This gig changes you. Opens your eyes and your mind and it takes you places you had no idea you wanted to go. Oh, and yep. Safe as houses. I've been a playmate for over a year and have never had a problem with any of the members. A car always drops me off and picks me up to deliver me home. Nothing that has ever been done to my body has scarred or injured me. That's the rules."

"I had a look at the portal, I only have access to the Green kinks, do you have access to more?"

"Yes, they ease you into this world. I figure they don't want to scare you off before you've even started. Sandy will review how your first few sessions go before opening up the Amber jobs board to you—likely in a few months' time. Are you considering doing it, becoming a playmate?"

Now I blush. "Yes," I admit, biting my lip. It feels like a naughty confession.

"And your husband is on board with it?" Sophie's eyebrows are raised.

"Kind of. I think it turns him on. We're going to keep things fluid and see how the first one goes. I've not been near anyone else in over 15 years, even I am having trouble getting my head around it, let alone James."

"So tell me, what job has caught your eye?" Sophie smirks at me coyly.

Saying it out loud makes it feel real, but also like I'm sharing a piece of myself I haven't done with anyone else, even James. I blush an even deeper red and try to string the words together. "I got the breast worship job for Sunday," I say looking at Sophie to see her reaction.

Sophie nods enthusiastically. "Oh boy you're starting off with a banger. After a while you get to know the members and their kinks. Mind you, there are so many members—most of whom have never set foot on the golf course I'm sure. From looking at the job posts you may never quite know for sure who you're getting but from the wording, sometimes I can work out if I've seen them before. Not very often though, as other members cut and paste previous job postings for their own. Nice little element of surprise when you arrive to see someone different than who you were expecting."

"Yikes, ok. How many staff are there?"

"Last I checked there were 50+ working at the club, male and female. All over the age of 30, had you noticed?"

"Yes, I had! Is it hard getting the jobs? I mean, if there are 50 staff, does everyone apply for the jobs on the jobs board?"

"No, 50 isn't actually that many. Most people only take one or two jobs a week depending on their schedules. And also, not everyone does everything. Some stick to the Green jobs, others just the Red. I'm pretty sure there are over 200 club members. They are busy too and have to fit their 'extracurricular' activities around their commitments in their real lives."

"Do you think some people have families and wives like us? That is a silly question, I bet they do."

"Yes, in a way, they're just like us. But with more money!" Sophie laughs at her own joke. My lips turn up in a grin too.

When we arrive at our favourite café we order some lunch and sit in our usual spot out back.

"So, Sunday, you're going to be okay on your first job? Nervous? I was my first time, but honestly after a few, you wonder why you were so nervous. Deep breaths ok, long breaths in and out. Take your mind away until the minute you are standing on their doorstep. Then once you're inside, your mind is going to focus on what is happening and the time will go by in the blink of an eye."

"Really, do you really think that?"

"Absolutely. I've done it at least 50 times by now. You'll have to come around to my apartment so I can show you where all the money has been going." Sophie winks at me.

"I just want to be able to take the kids away on holidays. I can't even think about spending the money right now. I need to just get Sunday done and see how I feel about it all."

"Call me, if not that night then the next day. It's important to talk in this line of work. And you'll need to. Even now, I call my playmate mentor to share how I'm feeling. It's cathartic. And your mental health comes first."

"I will, I don't know what state I'll be in but I'll phone you when I can. I am excited a little. My mind keeps circling back to the member. Who they are and what they look like..."

"The funny thing about this line of work is, you may never ever see them again. Or you may have served them coffee the day before. I love all the guessing and build up. The anticipation is one of my favourite elements of being a playmate."

Once we've eaten and Sophie has dropped me back at my car. I don't see Sophie again until Friday where she squeezes me tight and wishes me good luck. Sunday couldn't come soon enough.

6

————

I shave and wax everywhere. I blow-dry my long brown hair into soft waves that reach my mid back. I look into my full size mirror and stare back at myself wearing a little black dress paired with the only black heels I own. I've done my makeup to near perfection and I'm now looking at my body double checking my tiny black thong can't be noticed nor my strapless bra. The reflection that looks back at me I'm pleased with.

Prior to working at The Clarendon I had decided to get my health and fitness back on track the previous year and starting those habits has certainly paid off. My legs and arms are fit, my stomach is the most toned it has ever been since having the kids. I really should give myself a high five.

With five minutes to go, I give my lips a final swish of the lip gloss, pick up my bag and phone and head downstairs. I kiss the top of the heads of both kids while they're engrossed on their iPads and say goodnight.

James is in the kitchen clearing up after dinner. I could barely eat. I walk in and he looks up, his eyes giving my body a full up and down appraisal.

I feel excited like I'm going to a fabulous event. But also

guilty for leaving James at home. And nervous for what to expect. There are so many emotions flooding my bloodstream, I don't know which one I feel the most.

"You look stunning, Rosie." James walks over to me, slides both hands around my waist and presses his growing cock into me. "You look so good; I want to keep you to myself and take you right here, right now."

My eyes crinkle at the sides and I smile up at him warmly. I don't know what to say so I kiss him lightly on the lips.

"What is your safe word, Rose Petal?" James asks, pulling back and looking more serious now.

"Neptune." I giggle.

"You use Neptune the second you need to tap out. We don't need the money. Not this kind of money. You tap out whenever you need."

I nod my head earnestly. "I will, I promise."

James draws my hands together in his and squeezes them, my palms are already beginning to sweat. "You're going to do amazing. I think you're really going to enjoy this."

Heat flashes in his eyes. "And I'm going to enjoy your body the minute you walk into this house. That rich stranger might have you for two hours, but I'm going to fuck him out of you when you return."

My clit sparks at his words and the way he's looking at me. Something dark is brewing in his eyes and mind. I can see it. This new job might be unlocking this strange opportunity for me, but it is also unlocking something in James. Something darker that has always been hidden just under the surface.

James blinks his expression clear, kisses my lips, swings me around and taps me on my bottom. My driver is here, my phone just pinged. I say goodbye as I shut the door and open the blacked out BMW car door and take a seat. I smile nervously at the driver who points to the blindfold on the seat and asks me to put it on.

"I'm Frank, Roxy, I am going to be your driver today. It's going to be a 30 minute drive but I'll put the radio on for you. Just relax and we'll be there in no time."

I take a deep breath, slide into the comfy leather seats a bit deeper and try to work on my breathing.

About 30 minutes later I can feel the car turn onto a gravelly road and I suspect we have arrived. The car stops and Frank tells me to take my blindfold off.

Blinking for a few moments, I look out of the window to see we are at the back entrance of a large old house. It's dark but I can see there is a driveway circling the house with trees and lawn for as far as I can see. Frank nods for me to go up to the door. "I'll be right here at 9pm," he assures me. And with that he's back in his car.

My palms are sweating, I'm almost wobbling on my heels like the first time I had my interview with Sandy. Six months of wearing these heels and I don't even recognise the person I am now and what I'm about to do. I try and suck in deep breaths to fill up my lungs. I can do this, I repeat to myself. I want this. I want to be here, I want to play.

The door creaks open and standing before me is a man more attractive than I was expecting. Why I thought people with kinks would look unattractive is beyond me. He's tall, built shoulders with light brown hair, slicked over to one side. Not in a geeky kind of way, more a classy, rich kind of way. He's wearing black rimmed glasses and a light blue striped Ralph Lauren shirt tucked into trousers that look more designer than high street. A brown leather belt is around his slim waist and he smells fresh and clean, like he's fresh from a shower. I'm horrible at guessing ages, but my money is on mid-forties.

"Hi," I manage to squeak out as my eyes meet his. They're green from where I'm standing and he's looking at me like he's measuring me up before his chin dips a little, his eyes clouding with lust.

"Roxy?"

I nod, smiling hopefully. Should I offer my hand, do people shake in these situations? I decide to keep my hands to myself seeing they're damp from nerves.

"Please come in Roxy, I'm Greg." Greg stands to the side and gestures for me to come in.

I step into what looks like a larder. I'm guessing my entering through the front entrance would have raised some eyebrows. I wonder if anyone else is in this house currently. I'm not going to ask that though. Instead, I look expectedly at him.

"Thanks for coming, Roxy. If you'll follow me, I have a room set up for us upstairs."

To the right I can see a staircase, it's narrow and if I were to guess it would lead to staff quarters if they actually have any. I follow Greg across the tiles and up the old creaky stairs that lead to a small corridor. Greg pushes open the first door on the left and I follow him in.

Inside is a double bed facing the window, made up in clean white sheets. Under the window is a wooden table with a camera on it. There are bedside tables on each side with lamps that give off a warm inviting glow like I've just walked into a guest room in a B&B not a little sex room ready for some kink fantasy.

Greg closes the door behind me. I stand in the middle of the room, waiting for instructions. I dare not speak. What would I say?

He walks up to me, bringing his right hand to touch my chin, looking into my eyes. Lust fills his green eyes looking down at me. He slowly moves his hand down my neck and fans it out across my upper chest. "Stunning," he mutters to himself in a low whisper. A slight shudder runs across my body as I feel electricity radiate across my chest from the path of this hand.

His hand dips down under the top of my dress and his fingers graze the top of my strapless bra. The bra seems to displease him. He takes his eyes from my chest, pulls his hand out and orders, "Take off your dress and bra please."

I nod my head, shimmy the bottom of the dress up over my hips and then over my breasts and shoulders. Greg takes a step back, his eyes glued to my breasts. I reach behind me and unclip my bra. My breasts drop out from the cups and I smile shyly at the man looking so intently at them.

He walks straight up to me and with his thumb and fore-finger he pinches my pebbling nipples to form stiff peaks under his touch and gaze. There is something fascinating about watching and waiting to see what he'll do next. My body is solely here for his purpose, his enjoyment. The thought gives me butterflies of lust swirling in my core. I want him to touch me more. I want to be his plaything and let him do things to my breasts that have never been done before.

Pinching my nipples with both hands now, Greg pulls them out stretching them as far as they'll go, squeezing them hard to pull them further out. Then he lets them go and watches them drop. He does this a few times before slapping my right breast with so much force I gasp and stumble back. Then he's rubbing the red splotches where he hit me. I'm slightly more prepared when his left hand—palm open wide—collides with my left breast, even harsher than his right. Again, he rubs the spot while simultaneously pinching my right nipple.

If this is what he does in our first few minutes together, my pussy is throbbing anticipating where the next two hours will take us.

"Lie on the bed," Greg instructs. I can tell already that Greg is a man of very few words.

I step backwards a few steps, then pull myself onto the bed, all the way up near the pillows.

"Lie down. Hands behind your head. Rest your head on your forearms. Do not move from this position unless I give you permission to."

I lie down. I watch as Greg grabs a bowl I hadn't noticed on the bedside unit. He gets onto the bed with the bowl, lies down next to me on my right side putting the bowl down between my ribcage and his. Leaning on one arm, the other reaches inside the bowl where he picks up an ice cube and holds it on my right nipple. The cold is biting. My body recoils naturally from the frigid touch. Greg sits up a bit, holds my right breast tight in one hand, then holds the ice cube firmly over the nipple with his other.

It's cold. Like really cold. He keeps it right there, the ice melting and running tiny rivers down my chest and across my ribcage, finding its way down onto the bed.

Greg flicks his gaze up to my face and is now watching me to see my reaction as the ice against my nipple is becoming painful. I squirm—not trying to get away, just unable to remain still against the onslaught of sensation. He seems to like that reaction; I can feel the length of his cock rub up against my hip in his trousers.

"Good girl," he coos. Those words spark my clit and instantly my worries drop. All I want is to please him and hear him say it again. The first ice cube is almost melted so he lifts it off, drops it back into the bowl and picks up another one, placing it back over my painfully cold nipple. Again, his eyes are back on mine. It's hurting and he knows it. I start to breathe through it. I feel the pressure to move become almost too much when he lifts the cube and replaces it with his hot mouth. Sharp pain is then followed by glorious warmth and then pressure. He sucks with such a force, I'm sure my nipple hits the back of his mouth. He sucks and sucks until I hear a pop where he's released my now puffy red nipple. Greg smiles down at my breast, he looks pleased with how it looks. He shifts and moves to the other side of the bed to do the same with the other nipple. Every touch of Greg's hand or mouth builds within me, the ecstasy rising as

I watch him enjoying himself, enjoying my body, enjoying his control over me.

When my left nipple is as puffy and red as my right, Greg pulls back and places the bowl back on the bedside table. He picks up his camera and takes a photo of my breasts. One front on from the end of the bed, and then one from each side. I can't even imagine what my face looks like, high on pain and lust, so I'm glad to know he's not allowed to include that in the photos.

I watch as Greg opens a drawer on the bedside unit and pulls out what look like cable ties and a pair of safety scissors. My heart starts to beat a little faster now. I've seen these used in porn, but never imagined them on myself. I don't know what they will feel like, but it won't be long until I find out.

"Sit up and drop your arms, come sit here on the edge of the bed," Greg instructs, pointing in front of him. He kneels down in front of me and proceeds to hold one breast while hooking and tightening the cable tie around it. Once he has both ties on, he takes it in turns to pull the ties tighter, squeezing around my breasts a bit further so that my breasts are now two balls of flesh. Right now the ties are tight, but not uncomfortable.

Greg sits back on his heels to admire his work. In a flash he's raining open hand slaps on my breasts. One, two, three, four. The breath is knocked out of me, but I stay as still as I possibly can. Greg's eyes meet mine, he leans forward and pulls the ties tighter. Much tighter. He sits back again and watches as my breasts begin to bulge and are turning purple in colour. Looking me straight in the eyes, he slaps my breasts in tandem one after the other. He's observing and delighting in my reactions at his hands beating down on me. Greg is hurting me and it's quite clear he's enjoying doing it. As for myself, I am loving watching the beast within him come out to play. For me, it's watching that unravelling and being at his mercy that is the biggest turn on.

Stopping the slapping, Greg leans over my right nipple and sucks it deep into his mouth and stays there sucking. My breasts are now throbbing from their restriction in addition to the slaps. Simply sucking my nipple is now making beads of sweat form on my forehead. This feels wrong and right all at the same time. I moan. Greg bites. I scream.

Greg moves over to my left nipple and sucks it just as hard while pulling at the increasingly tender nipple on my right breast. The tug on the nipple in his mouth has me reaching my fingers down to my clit. My body is thrumming with a need for a release, this desire is building out of control—I need to come right now. Greg notices the movement and doesn't stop me. Just a couple of strokes is all I need before I'm unravelling, my climax tearing through my body like nothing before.

Greg continues sucking until my quivers have subsided. He releases my nipple looking up at me in awe. "You meant what you said about enjoying this."

"Yes," I breathe out. "You have no idea what you are doing to me."

"You have no idea how much I am enjoying your body already. Oh the things I'm going to do to you..." Greg whispers in my ear, his breath sending waves of pleasure down my skin.

Standing up, Greg walks over to the bedside table and pulls out two clothes pegs. When he's back kneeling in front of me I notice my breasts are now a deep angry purple. He pinches at my nipples, trying to pull them into peaks and places one peg on each nipple. Mother of God, the bite is extreme. I begin to whimper. Greg runs a hand down the side of my face.

"Shhh little one. There is my good girl. You can take it. I know you can. Look how beautiful your breasts are. Stunning."

Tears build in my eyes until they start to leak at the edges. Greg leans down and sucks at the side of my bulging purple breast. He sucks deep and I know he's leaving me a hickey. Around he moves, below and over the top of each breast, sucking eye-waveringly hard and leaving his marks as he goes. When enough of each breast is covered in his marks, he releases the clothes pegs and I breathe the deepest sigh of relief. Suddenly, his mouth is back over each one, sucking and I shriek as the pain and the blood flow seep back into my nipples.

Greg picks up the camera again and once again takes photos from the front and sides of my throbbing breasts. Setting down the camera, he reaches under the bed and pulls out a cane.

My eyes bulge at what he has in his hands. I've never been caned before, but I'm pretty sure whatever Greg has planned will hurt beyond anything I've ever felt, especially while my breasts are still tied up like they are.

"A couple of taps for you Roxy. You are being my most favoured muse. Would you like to take this one small punishment for me?"

I move my head hesitantly and nod. I'm nervous, my blood pumping loud in my ears. I don't really want to hurt even more than I do right now, but I do want to please Greg. I want to please Greg so much, I'll do anything. He smiles at me like I've just given the right answer.

"I'm going to give you two strikes on each breast, Roxy. I want you to count with me. Use your safe word whenever you need. Hands behind your back. Hold each elbow tight. Do not let go, there will be an extra tap for each disobedience." He pauses for a moment to ensure I understand the instructions and have moved my arms behind my back. After my nod he pulls the cane back.

Neptune, Neptune, Neptune. I chant in my head. I can do this.

"One," I gasp as the cane cracks down on my left breast. My body doubles over in agony. Fire is burning in a path across my skin, a white hot line of fury where the cane hit. Stars are blinking behind my eyes as they fill with pools of water. If I thought my breast was throbbing before, that was nothing to the pulses that are emanating now.

Greg waits and watches me. I'm still bent over, careful to not touch my breasts to my knees so as not to cause even more pain. I breathe deeply. My body has started to shake, tears have erupted down my cheeks. Slowly I rise again until I'm sitting up on the bed and my back is straight. Meeting Greg's eyes, I give him permission with them for the next so-called 'tap.'

"Two," I wail as the whoosh of the cane hits my right breast. Another shot of searing pain and I fold into myself again. Full body shudders encase me. I force my hands to stay on my elbows by pure determination alone. I stay bent over for longer than the first time, quivering and chanting *I can do this, I can do this* in my head. I wait until I can catch my breath and my shudders subside to quivers. I suddenly feel like I'm freezing and burning up at the same time. My body feels cold but heat is radiating from my breasts like pure lava.

Finally, I unfold myself and I'm back to sitting up straight but no longer still. My eyes meet Greg's again bolstered by the strength of lust I can see in his eyes. I give the smallest nod and he extends his hand out again with the cane.

"Three," I whisper just before it hits square on my left nipple. I let out a loud sob. My right hand almost unclasping my elbow to move in front of my chest and soothe my burning skin. I find myself looking down to see if the nipple is still there as the fury of the pain emanating from its location is almost unbearable.

Greg is smiling wider now, the bulge of his hard cock obscene in his trousers. He's enjoying the show I am putting on for him, he's revelling in my suffering. "One more my beautiful muse. Now don't move those arms or it'll be two." His voice is deep and rough, and though the words seem benign his tone is cruel almost, like he's hoping I'll fail and he can give me an extra strike.

I'm ugly crying now, tears flow down my face in rivers, but I try to keep my facial expressions in check. I want to do this, I can do this. For him. I want to finish this for him. I sit back up straight, tighten my grasp on my elbows, and take my time moving my eyes back up to meet Greg's.

"Four," I croak out as it hits straight across my right nipple and I black out for a moment.

Greg drops the cane, catching me before my body hits the floor, the pain becoming too much for my body to handle. He starts kissing the side of my neck and mutters soothingly, "There's my good girl, you've taken your punishment so very well. Such a good girl. I can't wait for you to see the beautiful lines you have across your perfect breasts."

I'm shaking, full body sobbing at the pain still pulsing from my chest to the rest of my body.

Greg lifts me up, cradling me to his chest like a precious China doll. He's peppering the side of my face and neck with kisses, whispering his praise over and over again. Lying me on my back on the bed with my head resting against the pillows. He reaches for his camera and once again takes photos of my brutalised breasts, now covered in red angry stripes. Greg reaches for the safety scissors waiting on the bedside table and cuts through the ties releasing the blood flow back to my breasts. He holds a small tub of some cream, pops the lid and scoops some out, massaging it into my breast. He's not soft and his rubbing and squeezing is making the cane marks sing, the tenderness of the return of blood flow intensifying every sensation.

Greg might be massaging me but he's certainly savouring the ability to prolong the torment. Tipping my chin, I can see the red streak marks from the cane and purple blotches covering my entire breasts. They are entirely fucked up. Greg seems to be enthralled.

Once he's satisfied that he's massaged my breasts enough,

every inch glimmering in the light reflecting off the cream. He climbs off the bed, undoes his belt buckle and removes his trousers, shirt and pants. His large cock hangs down heavy and painfully erect. Pre-come is dripping from its tip.

Greg climbs back onto the bed, tucks his fingers under the side of my thong at my hips and pulls it down my legs.

"So delicious," Greg murmurs as he looks at my bare pussy for the first time. He runs his fingers through my folds, pulling back to see them glistening in the lamplight. "You are so wet Roxy. Are you wet for what I have done to you or wet for my cock?"

"Both," I croak out. My voice has turned husky since crying so hard.

Greg lowers his head so his nose brushes my pussy and inhales while looking directly into my eyes. His lips curve up and he runs his tongue through my centre as my legs quiver with need. I arch up as his tongue reaches my clit where he circles for blissful seconds.

"Greg," I moan. Pushing aside the thought that this is the first person's name I've moaned since James.

Teasing me some more with his tongue, I can feel liquid heat pooling at my core. I want him, I need him. Pulling away, Greg lines the huge meaty head of his cock up to my entrance and thrusts inside to the hilt with one push. I gasp at his intrusion. Nothing gentle about him. His eyes dart between my battered breasts and my eyes, shining with pleasure and satisfaction.

After a few thrusts I can feel my own climax building as I watch Greg head towards his. "More," I stammer, and he adjusts his angle and hits that sweet spot inside me, thrusting deeper and more vigorously. My nerve endings electrify and I come undone. Screaming out his name, my climax takes over me. Greg's thrusts start to become urgent and more frequent and just before he's about to come, he pulls out and moves higher up above me, angling his cock at my chest so his long ropes of silky white come drizzle across my breasts.

Greg, breathing heavily, lowers to my side and runs a hand through his hair. "That was everything."

I smile back at him, glowing from his words. "That was… incredible." And I mean it. I enjoyed almost every minute of it and orgasmed twice. I was paid to orgasm. I'm almost delirious at the thought. Yes I knew I was selling my body tonight, but not once did I even consider I would enjoy it so much I would come too. I was literally paid to live out my own fantasy. What kind of parallel universe have I stumbled into? How can any job ever beat this one?

"Stay there." Greg moves off the bed. He grabs his camera and snaps his final photos of my come soaked breasts before grabbing a cloth and wiping me down.

"If you'd like to get dressed, I know your ride is waiting for you."

Has it been two hours already? I'm startled by how quickly the time has flown. How can this be work?

I shuffle to the side of the bed, reach for my clothes and start to dress, flinching as the strapless bra comes into contact with my sore breasts. I watch as Greg gets dressed too. Once we're both clothed, he leads me down the stairs and back to the larder.

"Thank you for the perfect night, Roxy."

I smile brightly at Greg. This feels weird. I've just had possibly the most exhilarating two hours of my life. I'm not ready to never see Greg again. But I can't say that. I can't say anything without sounding like a clinger. I am also not allowed to. So, I muster the first thing that comes to me.

"As first times as a playmate goes, I've had a really special one. Thank you." I resist the urge to touch or kiss Greg good-bye. It doesn't feel appropriate. He doesn't move to do anything either, he seems a bit surprised that it was my first time but also really relaxed like he just lived out his favourite fantasy. A job well done.

I open the back door and find Frank waiting for me in the blacked-out car. I say hi as I climb in. Once I'm seated, I put the blindfold back on and Frank pulls away. I put my head back against the seat and wonder how I'm going to return to real life in thirty short minutes. What just happened to me? I just cheated on my husband. Well, it's not actually cheating if he knows about it right? And I enjoyed it. What I feel right now is such a high, I imagine it is what drug addicts feel. I want more. But how can I have more? What will James say? How is he going to react?

7

———————

I pull the blindfold off when Frank says I can, noting it's exactly 9:30pm. I look up at my house. My kids will be fast asleep, but I can see the light on in my bedroom knowing James is waiting up for me. I climb out of the car and let myself into my home. I kick off my shoes, pour myself a glass of water and climb the stairs to a waiting James.

James is sitting on the edge of the bed. He's in his usual grey track pants and no top with the lamp light casting low shadows across our bedroom floor. He looks up at me. His face is full of expectation and nerves, there is a heaviness from the worry in his eyes but also something else—lust? "I heard the car pull up. Are you ok?"

"Yes," I nod, trying to tame down the excitement pulsing through me.

"You enjoyed yourself." It's a statement not a question. James' eyes burn into me. I can see the outline of his hard cock as he looks up at me.

Without any more questions James simply says, "Strip for me."

I pull down each strap of my dress, then shimmy it down

my body. I then unclip my bra from the back, like I'd done over two hours earlier for Greg. James sucks in a breath. But he doesn't look horrified. He looks hungry.

"Come here," he commands and I walk in between his waiting legs. He cups both hands around my tender breasts and then strokes them. They're each covered in purplish hickies and two red angry lines. Leaning forward he licks up over my right nipple. Squeezing it, he then does the same with the left. Then he bites down hard, sending heat pulsing to my core.

"James," I moan.

His name is all it takes for James to turn feral. He picks me up and throws me back onto the bed. He crawls over me and starts licking and sucking at the sensitive spot on my neck. I know he's marking me. I know he's claiming me as his.

His lips travel down to my breasts and I'm confused when he holds one hand over my mouth—until his teeth bite into the skin of my left breast. I scream in surprise and pain. James lifts his head and he's not the James I've known for fifteen years. This is another James, an animalistic version. He moves to the other side of my body, holding me down with his hand over my mouth as he bites again and then claws at my thong until it rips straight off me.

He pushes two fingers into my centre and then he moans. I know I'm wet for him, he doesn't need to say anything. He pushes another finger in and stretches my pussy as his thumb begins rough circles around my clit. "I own you, this cunt is mine. Who do you belong to Rosie?"

"You!" I exclaim as I can feel the sparks of an orgasm begin to build.

"And your cunt, who does that belong to? Say it."

"My cunt belongs to you, James."

"Did you enjoy letting me share you with someone else tonight?" James curves his fingers inside of me and I move my hips to match his rhythm.

"Yes I did," I answer honestly. I feel coy about sharing the truth but at the same time I want him to know that I have no regrets. This answer seems to please him judging by the way his eyes darken.

"You enjoyed someone else's cock did you? Who do you have to thank for that?"

"You," I breathe. "Thank you James." I'm panting and yearning for him to tip me over the edge and into oblivion.

"I'm going to fuck him out of you so that all you will remember is my cock." And with that James pulls his fingers out from inside me, pulls down his track pants, flips me over onto my front and making me internally squeal at the pain emanating from my beaten breasts as he pulls up my hips so they're level with his cock. Lining himself up, he pushes deep inside of me in one long, slick thrust. Then he fucks me like a man possessed. His fingers dig deep into the tissue around my hips as he holds me up and ruts into me.

"James!" I cry as he hits so deep, pleasure is building and although he seems lost to his own desires, he reaches around and starts circling my clit. It's the exact thing I needed and a climax rips through my body as James keeps pounding into me, drawing out the pleasure for what feels like hours until I hear James roar and he stills his throbbing cock inside me, pouring his seed deep into my womb.

And then the spell is broken. James hugs my back tight. When he pulls away, he rolls me back under him so he can look into my eyes. I know that look, he's checking to see if he hurt me.

I smile back at him and mutter, "Wow." He gives me a sheepish grin and there is the James I know so well. But now I see another side to him and I'm totally ok with that one too.

"I'm sorry if I was a bit rough, Rose. I couldn't control myself. Seeing what another guy did to you made me want to prove you belong to me."

James might sound like an Alphahole right now, but it kind of turns me on. I love it when he speaks so possessively of me. I want to be claimed and owned. I want to be fucked by a feral hungry man. And if that just happens to be my husband—I've done something right.

I smile warmly back up at him. "I enjoyed every second of whatever just came over you James." I know he's looking for reassurance and I want to give that to him.

Looking shy again, James blushes at his actions. "Let me help you up and into a bath young lady. You look fucked." Quite literally I'm sure.

The next day I wake to sore nipples, sore breasts and a sore pussy. I also have a selection of hickies on my neck and heat pulses to my clit just thinking of how hot last night was with my husband. I cover them as best I can with makeup. I text Sophie to see if she's on shift today. Sadly she replies that she's not but phones me soon after knowing I'm in the car driving to The Clarendon.

"Sooooo. How was it? Are you ok?"

"Oh my goodness Sophie. It was incredible!" I squeal. "I don't even know where to start."

"It's next level being a playmate isn't it?" Sophie laughs out loud.

"I know I'm not in love but at the same time, I don't know what I am feeling. The experience was mind-blowing, life changing!"

"I know right? Can you see why hardly anyone leaves who joins the Clarendon and becomes a playmate."

"Yes I can! But now I feel sad that I may never see my stranger from last night again or experience anything like it again."

"Ah yes, the come down is a real bitch. It sucks, especially when you did enjoy yourself."

"How do I not feel like I'm grieving? I'm so confused. What do I do?"

"Oh that's easy. You hop back online and apply for another job."

"Really?"

"Yup. The best way to get over one cock is to get under another."

"Sophie!"

"It's true Roxy. It was the advice my mentor gave me, and it's the advice I am so wisely passing on to you my friend."

"Okay... Well, sure. I'll have a look later on today. See if anything takes my fancy."

"Ha, you'll find something, I know that for sure."

"Thanks for calling and checking in on me. I feel good. More than good, I feel, like, alive."

"Welcome to the Clarendon Playmates Roxy. Where fantasies come alive, and dreams come true."

8

It's been a week since my first job as a playmate for the curious Greg. The cane lines, hickies and bites have dulled down to light yellow bruises on my breasts. The only thing left is the memory and reliving the experience with my vibrator. That fantasy-turned-reality-turned-back-to-fantasy was a job I lucked out on. Not only was I accepted on my very first Green playmate job, but I was also lucky enough to enjoy it as it's my kink too, although much more to the extreme than I'd ever experienced. Being paid $2,000 for something I've fantasised about feels too good to be true. But it wasn't, it happened and now I'm spending this week coming down from the incredible high of the experience.

It was time to get under another cock to get over the last one, as my mentor Sophie had so wisely advised.

Opening my laptop, I log in and go to the Green playmate job page. Once again a bit relieved that I don't have access to

Amber or Red yet. Reading through the titles I came across the heading *Stretching* amongst others such as Voyeurism, Choking, Body Worship and Foot Fetish. Feeling the pull of curiosity, I click on the Stretching job post for more details, my heart starts thumping. It feels like spying on someone else's fantasy. Which is ludicrous because it's a job post.

Stretching, Pussy & Anal, Wednesday, 7pm
   Member 204, Male (MM/FP)

I would like to play with different sized dildos and plugs with your pussy and your arsehole. I enjoy watching you stretch around each one. I would like to take the time and watch as you take a bigger dildo or butt plug each time, eventually taking the biggest ones and filling both your holes up together. When you're full with both of my biggest toys, I would like to fill your mouth with my cock as I come deep in your throat. This will be filmed for my personal use only.

Time - 3hrs
   Payment - $3,000

There was a reason why I clicked on this job post, that reason was making my panties wet. I'd never done anything like this with James before, but my interest is piqued nevertheless. How big could the dildos be? Can I stretch enough to take them? And my butt, sure we've tried butt plugs a few times in the bedroom, but never at the same time as a dildo. What would it feel like to be stuffed with two sex toys at the same time?

·   ·   ·

As if on cue, James enters the lounge and slumps down next to me on the sofa.

"Whatcha looking up? Some new minxy Roxy job?" Of course he knows. This man can read me like a book.

"Uh huh." I nod and smile coyly back at him.

"Seen something you like then?"

"Uh huh. Wanna see?"

"Oh baby, I want to do more than see," he says cheekily. "Come on, pass over the laptop."

I slide the laptop across to his lap and then watch his face as he reads the job description. The sides of his lips turn up and one eyebrow shoots straight up towards his dirty blond hairline.

"Stretching. Interesting. Hot. I'm going to have a lot of fun seeing how stretched my wife has become when she gets home."

"You don't mind this one?"

. . .

"I don't mind at all. I want to see you stretched out with my own eyes."

I smile widely at him. I want to do this one for the club member and also for James. And myself if I can be honest.

"When is the job for?"

"Wednesday evening if I get it. I'll apply now. $3,000 is so much money!"

"You might well earn it depending on the size of the dildos and butt plugs this sick fuck wants to shove up you."

"Ouch, you're right." I laugh and screw up my face. "He does say he's going to build me up to it though. Hopefully with a vat load of lube..."

I apply for the role.

Dear Member 204,

I would like to offer myself over to your use on Wednesday evening. I think you'll enjoy stretching my pussy and arsehole to their very limits. I want to feel those dildos up in my stomach. I want to feel the stretch of those butt plugs for days after. Please will you fuck my face whilst stuffed with your favourite toys and give me the pleasure of drinking your come?

Yours, Roxy

I giggle to myself. I wonder how other playmates apply for jobs? I need to remember to ask Sophie. Is that too much? I do want to get the job; $3,000 would make such a difference to us.

Before I've even closed the laptop, a notification flashes up on screen.

ACCEPTED

I clap my hands in a burst of excitement. Clearly Member 204 liked my naughty words. I don't even speak dirty to James, I'm not sure how I managed to write it. Roxy is becoming my alter ego as well as my alias at the club. She is getting out of control! I kind of like her though. She sounds confident and sexy. I want to be confident and sexy.

I phone Sophie, she answers on the first ring. Sophie is not her real name like Roxy is not mine and occasionally I wonder what hers is. I hear Sophie's sunny voice, "Hey Roxy. How are you?"

. . .

"Hi Sophie, I'm doing well thank you. Are you working this week?"

"Yes I'm working the café Tuesday, Thursday this week and then the bar Friday. I'll see you tomorrow?"

Sophie knows I just work mornings 9-1pm to accommodate my own business, which ironically is looking less and less appealing by the day. I love my little business but if making $3,000 in three hours is possible for me, I'm not sure I'm going to need to run it for much longer.

"Yep I'll be there tomorrow. I've just been accepted for a new job. It's for pussy and anal stretching. Have you done anything like that before?"

"Oh sure, nice. It'll be an experience, but you can handle it, I know it. You've pushed two kids out so it's just your butt that might need to relax. Remember, deep breaths, breathe through it. Play with your clit, it makes relaxing much easier."

"Thanks, I will do that. What do you have on this week, playmate jobs I mean?"

"I'm getting ready for a job right now actually. It's Electrostimulation. Don't freak out. I'm not getting electro-cuted. Well, I am, but not fried."

· · ·

"Wow and ouch? How does that even work? What job board is that?"

"It's basically an electro sex toy. I've played with this guy before, if it is who I think it is. He's real naughty. Likes to blindfold me so I don't know where he's going to touch me. He builds up the intensity as the time goes by. He likes to hear me scream, especially when he zaps my clit. It's from the Amber board by the way. You wouldn't have seen it. But all good, you'll get to play with the Electro Kinkers one day soon."

"Ouch, I think I need to build up to that one. Do you like it?"

"I love it. The anticipation of the zaps and giving over complete control and freedom of my body... I could come just thinking about what this member will do to me."

"Good luck with that one. I take it, it doesn't leave any marks or burns."

"Oh god no. Nothing is allowed to be done to us that will permanently mark us. Although I did hear that one playmate was offered more money than they could ever refuse to have a surprise session on the Red list. I don't know what was done but I know there were a few permanent reminders. This one club member and job received special permission to take place. Sandy told me once that each Red job is authorised on a case-by-case basis. I guess if I looked on the Red list maybe I might see more. But I'm happy sticking to Green and Amber, I can always find a job that I can't resist. And that's enough money for me."

"Wow, I wonder what was done to her and how much she was paid..." I muse.

"Don't stress about it. You can see for yourself soon enough. First things first, you need to survive your first stretching job. You'll be fine though; I'm just fucking with you."

"I'm kind of looking forward to it."

"Good, you should be. Enjoy it. Just lie back and think of the money! And on that note, I need to fly. Catch you tomorrow my friend."

"See you tomorrow, enjoy your job you little minx!"

Ending the call I muse about the Red list. I'm so curious to see what is on there. Certainly, I won't be able to guess. I'm already googling what kinks are even out there—the majority I've never even heard of. How much money could they offer for unrestrained access? My pussy flutters at the thought. What would I be open to allow for the right price? What even is the right price? If I make it to the Red jobs list, will it enable me to start paying off our mortgage, not just the interest?

·　·　·

My daydream of a mortgage free life is interrupted by a sleepy little angel who has woken up and needs a glass of water and to be put back to bed. Being a playmate and a mum is worlds apart yet I'm doing them both. It's my life. The confidentiality of the Clarendon Club gives me a sense of security that neither side of my life will ever cross paths. At least, I pray I can always keep them totally separate.

After putting my youngest back to bed I do all the usual things that a mum does. I tidy away the day in the kitchen and dining room, put another load of washing on and fold the one that has been sitting in the dryer for a few days now. Before my playmate days I would listen to endless audiobooks to fill my head with stories and spice whilst doing chores. Now I find I don't need either, I have so many thoughts rolling through my mind and imagination. Becoming a playmate has turned my real life spice up to a five-out-of-five chilli rating on the spicy scale and that's just with my husband. Including the jobs, it blows my mind how this is my life, and it is happening to me. And there are two of me, Rosie the mum and wife—hard working, normal and friendly. Then there is Roxy: playmate, confident and willing submissive for a fee. I catch myself laughing out loud. What is happening to my life?

9

F rank picks me up at 6:35pm precisely and drives me blindfolded the 25 minutes to my next mystery club member's location. I have no idea what direction we even started in, I'm listening to the radio and taking deep breaths. I'm nervous, just as nervous as I was on my first job. No amount of shaving, waxing, lotions, make up, blow-dry and new clothes is helping. I'm still going to an unknown address, with a complete stranger. Will they hurt me? Of course they will. But will it be unbearable? Will I have to use my safeword? I really hope I don't, I want to be able to submit and please Member 204, show him I'm a good girl and worth the money he's paying me.

When the car pulls to a stop, Frank lets me know I can take my blindfold off. I blink as I adjust my eyes to the dim light of a lamp light in front of a winding path. I say thank you to Frank and he lets me know he'll be right there in three hours to collect me. I open the blacked-out BMW door and climb out of the car, closing the door as carefully as possible so as to not draw any attention. The house I've just been dropped off to is a big double story detached house in a long street of detached houses with neighbours.

I hurry up the pathway through a manicured garden of shrubs and bushes. Once I'm at the big green door I wait and wonder if I should knock when I glance up to see a motion camera. I have no doubt that whoever is behind this door knows I have arrived. In a moment of uncertainty, I wonder what kind of a person lives here. The door makes an unlatching noise from a lock and a man stands in the doorway, light streaming in behind him so I can only see his outline. "Please come in," he murmurs in a low, quiet voice. I move my feet quickly inside and the door is closed swiftly behind me.

I turn to face the stranger in the light and can see he's almost 6 foot, has a buzz cut of dark greying hair and is built like a tank. I think my reference to the tank is also because he looks like he just walked out of the army. His eyes are grey and they look menacing. I almost take a step back.

"Roxy," he states. I nod. "I'm Henry." Reaching out his arm, I shake his hand. His giant hand almost engulfs my tiny one and I wonder if my fingers will survive the crush of his hand.

"Follow me."

It's then that I take in my surroundings. The interior of the house has crisp white walls and dark wooden flooring. Black frames adorn the entranceway walls showcasing black and white photos of different landscapes and countries. They're beautiful photos and I wonder for a moment if Henry is a photographer. More photos line the stairway that I glance over as I follow Henry up the stairs. He leads me down a hallway lined with closed doors on either side of me until we stop at the last one on the right. When Henry opens the door I almost gasp. Inside there looks to be a hospital bed in the centre of the room with lighting set up around it and a camera angled on a pole towards the end of the bed. I shudder, it looks like a medical theatre on set at a tv station.

As room set ups go, I was not expecting this one to look like this. I'm not sure if it looks more like a medical examining room or a serial killer's room who enjoys dismembering his victims. There is no plastic on the floors which I take as a good sign. To the side, where you'd expect the medical instruments to be lined up on a side table, there *is* a heavily laden small trolley but the instruments are of the dildo variety. I almost let out a sigh of relief. No knives.

Taking in the rest of the room, it's white like the entrance and hallway but has dark grey fluffy carpet. There is a black velvet sofa in the corner and a drinks trolley where Henry waits.

"Can I offer you a drink, Roxy? I am going to pour myself a whisky. I have Champagne on ice."

Grateful for the offer, I reply quickly, "Champagne would be lovely, thank you Henry." His eyes darken at me using his name. I wonder if it's his actual real name rather than the alias he's supposed to use. I watch as he pours himself two fingers of amber liquid. Then he uncorks a Dom Perignon bottle and pours out a flute for me.

"Thank you." I smile as Henry hands me the flute, I take a sip and the delicious bubbling liquid slides down my throat like honey. I take a few more sips in quick succession before Henry speaks again. He's looking at me intently, darkly. His eyes are burning into me and making the hairs stand up on the back of my neck. My instincts are firing, wary of this solid man of muscle. He's wearing black jeans and a white t-shirt fitted tight across his huge chest. His forearms are massive, big veins prominent against his bulging muscles. This man looks like he could tear me in half with his bare hands. Maybe just the one hand to break my neck. I blanch at these thoughts invading my mind.

"Drink up Roxy, I would like you to be nice and relaxed for

me," Henry instructs as he tips his own glass back in one gulp. "Come, sit down on the sofa for a minute."

He doesn't have to ask me twice; I've already sipped half the glass—the second half doesn't take me long whilst I'm seated on his lovely posh velvet sofa. The bubbles are going straight to my head, and I encourage the heady feeling of being tipsy and relax back a little.

"Have you been stretched before Roxy?"

"No, I-I haven't. This is my first time."

"Excellent. That is music to my ears Roxy. I want to be the first person to fill up your beautiful holes to their maximum capacity. Then I want to watch you gape for me."

I let out a nervous laugh. I don't know what to say in reply. This man is slightly scaring me; my brain is telling me to run. But his words are turning me on and the intention set in his eyes is sparking a light within my core.

"It's time to get you undressed, Roxy."

"Would you like me to take my shoes off?" I don't know why I am asking this, he must want me to. I kick myself for asking a stupid question. It must be the wine loosening my lips.

"Yes please."

I remove my shoes before pulling the straps of my black minidress down each shoulder and arm and then past my braless breasts. There is one hickey on my left breast that James gave me last night. It seems he's taken to branding me to stake his ownership over me. That makes my pussy flutter thinking of his possessiveness.

I stand, letting the fabric fall to the floor before stepping out of it. Henry moves close on the sofa, wrapping one meaty arm around my body to pull me closer to him. "Allow me." He gradually, slowly lowers my black thong down my hips like he's opening a Christmas gift. Seeing my bare pussy he breathes in.

"Turn around and bend over—put your arms onto the bed, let me see all of you."

Blushing, I do as he asks. Naked and tipsy I rest my fore-arms and head on the hospital looking bed that doesn't have any side bars.

"Spread your legs. Wider." He kicks my feet apart expectantly to his desired position. I feel wholly exposed. What is he going to do to me now?

With both hands Henry parts my arse cheeks as wide as they will go. Is he trying to open up my tight back hole? Then he spits and rubs his fingers from my arsehole to my pussy. I almost moan at his touch. My body is responding to his touch before my brain can keep up. I want him to stop at my clit and he reads my mind. He does pause at my sensitive bud, circling his fingers as I bare down on him. It feels good, he's helping me relax.

"You remember your safe word?"

"Yes," I reply.

"And that is?" Henry asks sternly.

"Neptune," I reply.

"Excellent. Climb onto the bed, Roxy. My cock is leaking to see how much you can take."

I straighten up and awkwardly climb onto the bed. It's on wheels and has a controller to raise or lower the bed. Where did he even get one of these?

"Put your head on the two pillows there and lift your bum please." I do as I'm told. Then Henry picks up a cylindrical cushion and slides it under my bottom. He picks up both my feet, bends my legs at the knees and places my feet down flat either side of my knees. At this angle he has a perfect view of everything. Thank goodness I had that glass of Champagne, I'm not sure I would have been able to relax at this much open exposure.

"Let's begin the show, Roxy." A true smile grows across his face, it would be beautiful if his eyes didn't look so menacing. My heart rate increases. What is about to happen?

Henry turns on the camera and the lighting. I feel like I'm about to have a surgical procedure but instead Henry picks up a rather small butt plug and a tube of lube. I watch as he rubs the lube over the plug and then squirts a drop on my back hole. The cool gel is welcome against my heated skin.

I watch like an out of body experience as he nudges my arsehole gently, much more careful than I had anticipated. I had expected him to be rough and forceful but in actual fact his movements are softer and gentle.

"Relax for me Roxy, there's a good girl. You can touch yourself if that helps." I preen, what is it with these men and their praise... I can't get enough.

I'm relieved. I do touch myself and it's heaven. My clit is sparking while I'm watching this man with fascination. I'm enjoying watching him push a plug into my body. I loosen up with each circle of my fingers around my clit helping the largest part of the plug to enter my tight ring of muscle. Once it's passed, it's sucked in and stops. "Beautiful Roxy, it looks stunning." I flush at his words. "Let me give you a sip of champagne as a reward." Henry stands, picks up my glass, tops it up and saunters over to me. "Open your mouth for me, Roxy." I do as he says and he pours champagne into my mouth, only a tiny bit slips past my lips and rolls down my chin.

"Thank you," I say with my words and my eyes. That champagne is really something.

"Deep breaths, let's pull this plug out of you." And with that, he's back at the end of the bed and nudges the plug, my body tries to keep a hold of it but he keeps the pressure and my back hole releases it. "Good girl." He puts the plug onto the trolly and picks up a large dildo.

Rubbing lube onto the large phallus, he goes to insert it but before he does he runs a finger through my folds. "You're dripping Roxy. You're enjoying yourself?" It's a question as well as a statement.

"Yes," I breathe. And watch as he lines up the dildo to my entrance, pushing slowly, he slides it in incrementally allowing my body to expand around it and accept it. After only a few seconds he pushes the dildo all the way to the hilt. "Excellent, this is the baby one Roxy, you take it nice and easy. Here let me reward my good girl." Henry stands up and pours the champagne into my mouth. I take a small mouthful, I love how it makes me feel, the alcohol now coursing through my veins, making me hornier by the minute.

The next plug he takes from the tray is almost double the first but still smaller than my husband's cock, so I know I can take it. He adds more lube to the toy, gently fingers my fluttering hole, and then pushes this one back in. The base is a bit larger than the first and I can feel the stretch even after the widest bulb is fully seated. I assume he will remove this one like he did the first but he simply reaches over to grab the next dildo. I've never had toys fill both holes at once and I find myself rather eager to experience it.

"Rub that clit for me Roxy," he reminds me as I'd paused in contemplation of this new sensation. I rub harder and can almost feel my pussy opening to him as he slides the next dildo in. The combination of pressure from front and back is intense, and as he moves the dildo in and out a few times I am acutely aware of how thin the membrane is between the two.

"Be a good girl and hold this in for me, won't you?" he requests and I'm a bit flummoxed for a moment before I realise he wants me to hold the dildo in while he increases the butt plug. It takes me a moment to respond but I silently reach my hand down to hold the base of the silicone dildo while his hand moves to the plug.

The plug feels so much wider as he pulls it out achingly slowly and I struggle to maintain my grip on the dildo. "Such a pretty hole you have here, Roxy. I can see it fluttering now, empty... Don't worry, we're nowhere close to done yet," he coos, his voice somehow simultaneously soothing and threatening.

I wonder if he's going to make me wait while he enjoys the view but only moments later I feel yet another plug touching my hole, this one I didn't get to see but I can already tell is almost double the size of the first, certainly at least as large as James now. I subconsciously tense my body and clench my back hole. Not knowing the size that is about to enter me is thrilling but also daunting. Henry responds by pausing his initial pressure at my back hole and looking up at me. I look back giving him a shy nervous smile.

"Let go of the dildo, I've got that, rub your clit as we stretch your arsehole open some more. Can you do that for me, Roxy?"

I bite my lower lip and nod my agreement. I want to do that for him. I let go of the dildo I've been holding in place and resume a slow and steady rub over my clit. It works to relax my tensing and allows Henry to press the large plug further and further inside of me. This bulb feels huge, I'm not even sure my body will allow it to enter me but Henry maintains the pressure he's been applying and I feel my tight ring stretch and then release as the bulb is suctioned inside of me.

I let out a breath I hadn't realised I had been holding. The fullness is a pleasure I hadn't been expecting. It's like nothing else I have felt before. The depravity of watching this man pushing large plugs and dildos into me, his look of intent, the ways his face lights up when my body takes a dildo bigger than the one before or a plug twice the size of the previous one.

Henry looks up at me watching him. I wonder if he feels my eyes on him. I wonder if it bothers him. But his eyes tell me he's enjoying both me watching him and me knowing what he's doing to my body. I'm not sure if I should be unnerved or turned on. My brain signals to be unnerved but my body releases a hot trickle of liquid as he keeps our eye contact.

Henry's lip curls up, "You stretch so beautifully. Here, let me get you your champagne."

My eyes follow Henry as he picks up my glass and dribbles more champagne into my open waiting mouth. I'm enjoying Henry's rewards. I've not had even half the second glass of champagne but I am enjoying every drip he's offering me.

"I'm looking forward to watching you release these two now, Roxy. Are you going to lay back and relax for me, let me do all the work?"

"Yes," I breathe and he smiles back, appreciatively, enjoying my obedience.

Slowly I watch as Henry twists the dildo and with the combination of how watching him makes me feel and all the lubrication my body has been creating, the dildo slides out of me in a rush.

"Look at you," Henry appraises. "The more I give you, the wetter you become. Your body is gagging for me to give you more."

I flush at his appraisal. I do want him to give me more, I am enjoying the way he's using my body.

I can feel the liquid heat trickle down to my arsehole that is currently being held full with the large plug.

"Let's pull this one out and see you gape. Hold your cheeks open for me."

I reach my hands down between my feet and body and pull the cheeks apart even more. Henry begins to pull at the plug and I try my best to relax as the large girth stretches me wide once again as it tries to be released from behind my ring of muscle. Ever so slowly I feel the bulbs building pressure release and the widest girth pops out.

God, the pleasure on Henry's face as he watches my back hole open so wide for him... I know he's getting what he's paying for. I wish I could see what my hole might look like. "Magnificent my darling Roxy, you are coming along nicely."

I glow at his words. This big, scary beast of a man knows how to make me feel good inside and out. I don't know what he does outside of our encounter but he has perfected the art of getting what he wants by reinforcing good behaviours with words of affirmation.

Then shit starts to get real. I look over and notice he's used every toy on his trolley so I let out a sigh of relief, assuming we were finished. But instead he walks over to a drawer and pulls out two objects: the biggest dildo and butt plug I've ever seen. The dildo might be the size of my forearm and is bright green silicone. There's no way that's going to fit. The butt plug looks to be almost twice the size of the last one that was just pulled out of me, and it no longer has the iconic butt plug shape as the base is only slightly thinner than the bulb. My eyes bulge and Henry doesn't miss the look on my face.

"No fear Miss Roxy, you are going to enjoy these two my girl, every last inch of them. This time I would like you to kneel on all fours. Can you flip over for me? That's it, good girl." His words send a tingle straight to my core.

I glance over my shoulder to see him rubbing lube on the large plug before he lines it up to my back hole. "Rub that pretty clit of yours Roxy, think of the delicious full feeling you're going to have."

"Is this the biggest one?" I ask warily and he nods. I reposition myself so I'm resting on my elbow and my right hand can reach my clit, my arse thrust high in the air.

"Yes Roxy, this is the last one that is going up your arse tonight. Deep breaths, here we go."

With my butt in the air, I rest my head on the pillow, reach my arm under myself and rub at my clit. How I'd managed to hold onto my building orgasm all night I didn't know. I was trying to relax but this butt plug was massive. I start to whimper as he pushes the tip past my still tight ring of muscle.

"There's my good girl, you're taking it, you're going to take it all."

I focus on rubbing circles on my clit, taking deep breaths and let the champagne do its magic. Deeper he pushes into my arse and I keep taking it. The stretch burns and the girth around the bulb feels like a ring of fire as it moves inside of me but my body allows it passage. I'm honestly a bit surprised how easily I have managed to take it—the previous ones must have loosened me up to get to this point. "There we go, nice and full Roxy."

The base on the plug is so wide there is no relief when I reach it, no chance for my poor arsehole to tighten around it. So when he releases it the plug begins to move out on its own. I flush with embarrassment at the feeling but he seems to have expected it as he immediately pushes it back in then maintains pressure against it.

Holding the plug deep in my arse with his forearm, he picks up the giant green dildo, rubs lube all over it and edges it slowly into my pussy. I don't think I could take this size on its own, let alone with what's already in my arsehole. I already feel so full. Twisting the dildo gently, Henry continues to push. Further and further, my breathing becomes rapid along with my fingers thrumming back and forth over my clit. There is not enough room for the two of them yet my body is opening wide enough to accommodate them together. How is this possible?

My orgasm is building with the fullness I've never felt before. I am being stretched to my ultimate capacity when the green dildo hits my cervix.

"The most beautiful sight I've ever laid eyes on. You are perfect Roxy, your hungry holes taking everything I have pushed into you. I love how much you have been able to take. I'm going to love even more watching them come out of you and gape for me. But first your mouth needs to suck my cock."

Those filthy words send waves of ecstasy through my body.

Reading my trembling body Henry pushes both large objects into my holes in tandem pushing my climax to a mind altering level until it explodes and floods all my senses. My whole body shakes from the intensity and its waves flow over me for what feels like minutes. I can barely hold myself up, pulling my hand off my clit to catch myself before I fall on my face. As I begin to come down, Henry releases the pressure of holding them inside of me and walks around to the head of the bed. I'm worried the plug will fall out again but my orgasm must have tightened me up enough that it stays put, or maybe it's the giant dildo that's holding it in. Either way, I'm pleasantly surprised that neither starts to move as while I can't wait for them to be out I know Henry is eagerly anticipating removing them—after I suck his cock.

Unzipping his jeans, his cock springs free. It is just as thick as the rest of his muscly body—he wasn't wearing any under-wear. "Open up Roxy."

In this position my head is aligned perfectly to his crotch at the end of the bed. I open my mouth and he pushes in hitting the back of my throat in one deep thrust. "I want you to touch yourself again, Roxy."

Moaning around his cock, I do as he asks, resting my weight on my left forearm again and snaking my right arm underneath me. The initial sensitivity subsides as new sparks began to light as Henry holds my head and starts to fuck into my face. I can't believe I have all three holes completely filled, it's such a filthy and yet arousing fact.

"Your throat is divine, so tight, wet and ready for my come. You are going to drink me up Roxy, this is your final reward. The best one of them all. I want you to suck my come straight from my balls down your throat and straight into your stomach."

His words are driving me out of my mind. I can barely breathe through my nose as I can feel his orgasm building. His body is beginning to shake, he's chasing his climax with my throat. Now he's holding my head still and thrusting faster and deeper with bruising force hitting the back of my throat. Saliva is sliding down my chin and onto the bed.

With a roar his body stiffens after one full thrust, almost choking me when I feel the salty liquid hit the back of my throat. The taste of his release pushes my second climax to the surface and takes a hold of my body—just the thought that I was drinking this stranger's come has set me alight. I did this to him and he did this to me. This complete stranger who has spent the evening stuffing and stretching my holes with toys.

My body starts to go limp and he can sense I'm becoming boneless so he pulls out from my mouth.

"Let me help you down Roxy. Here, lie down on your front, put your head on the pillow. Good girl." He retrieves a cloth from a drawer and walks back over to me and cleans the drool from my face. He then wipes up his cock before pushing it down back into his jeans and doing up his zip.

"And now for the finale. Here we go, let's turn you over onto your back. Lift your bottom up and let me slide the pillow back underneath you." I do as he asks, my body feeling like jelly.

"Pussy first, here we go, ah gorgeous." Henry twists out the giant dildo. "Look at that stunning gape." I feel a rush of warm liquid slide too which can only be from my two orgasms. "Now, last one Roxy"

I take a deep breath as he nudges out the final plug from my arsehole. "That's it, give it a push—perfect, your arse is so perfect Roxy. I wish I could have my whole fist up there."

I shudder. I'm sure that would never fit even with two glasses of champagne inside of me but I don't say anything.

Henry bends down to ram his tongue straight into my arsehole. He pushes deep and I quiver. Watching him with hazy eyes it looks like he's feasting on his favourite dessert. When he pulls out, he licks his lips and turns his grey, heavy-lidded eyes up to mine and mutters in a low husky voice, "Thank you for letting me taste you, that was more than I could ask."

And with that, he straightens and takes a long slow look up my body until our gazes meet. Does he look bashful? I'm not sure, but I can also see gratitude shining back at me. I attempt to convey the same with my eyes because this may be a job but I came twice and enjoyed every minute with this man.

"Let me grab your clothes." Henry moves around the room collecting my panties, dress and shoes. He then helps me off the bed allowing me to get dressed. Once I'm fully clothed again, he leads me back down the stairs stopping at the front door where I entered. Holding out his hand, I shake it. "Thank you for applying for my job Roxy, it's been one of the best nights of my life."

Filled with gratitude, I reply, "Thank you for accepting my application, I've had a wonderful time with you Henry."

"Goodbye Roxy."

"Goodbye Henry."

And with that, Henry opens the door, I walk outside, back down the pathway and climb straight into Frank's awaiting car. I can't help a wince when sitting pulls on my recently stretched muscles and the door has closed before I turn to look back up at the house. I re-tie the blindfold and Frank pulls away.

I take a deep long breath and let out a big sigh. That was an experience I won't forget in a hurry. Henry wasn't someone I was likely to forget and most certainly don't want to forget. For three hours I was all his and he too was all mine. There was that sadness again for knowing that I may never see Henry again. I know I can't get attached, I'm going home to my husband and children right now. But sharing such an intimate experience, it means something. A connection. We may not have chatted; I know absolutely nothing about the man. I wish I did though, even some small detail about his personality. But that is the job. It's exactly that, a job. I am not paid to ask questions and get to know my clients, instead they are paying me for not knowing, no strings attached confidentiality. And they are paying me well for it. I turn my mind to the money: $3,000—what was I going to do with that?

The rest of the journey is taken up by my imaginary allocations of the $3,000 in the areas we need to for the house and expenses. Maybe the next job I do I'll spend a little on myself. I'll get the boring bills paid and make way for some fun.

10

———

Frank stops outside my house and lets me know I can take the blindfold off. I wish him a goodnight, climb out of the car and look up to see my bedroom light is on. As expected, James is waiting up for me. I open the front door, kick my shoes off, walk into the kitchen and down a glass of water. I'm still a little giddy from the two glasses of champagne I'd enjoyed earlier.

I climb the stairs, peek into each sleeping child's bedroom to check on them and walk into my bedroom. James is sitting up in bed watching something on his phone.

"How was your evening?"

"Surprising. But good. How was yours?"

"It was not surprising but also good. Just the usual Tuesday evening for us here." Running his gaze up and down my body, he continues, "I want to see my wife's stretched holes though. I've been thinking of that kinky bastard all night and the things he was doing to you. Show me." He smiles wickedly, placing his phone on the bedside table.

I smile back, looking him dead in the eyes and peel off my dress, then I lower my thong to the floor and walk over to the bed. James throws off the covers, climbs out of bed and pushes me back onto it. Pulling me into position on my back, he bends my knees so they're wide open and places my feet on either side of my knees. "I want to look at you." And then he stares at my splayed-out pussy.

James pushes two fingers inside of me and I'm wet. I'm wet watching my husband drink in his used wife. Heat is coiling in my core at the intensity in his eyes. "How big was the dildo that went into here? Bigger than two fingers?"

I nod and breathe out a "Yes."

"Bigger than three fingers?" James adds another finger and I can feel the stretch now.

"Yes," I answer again.

"Bigger than four fingers?" James adds another finger up to his knuckle. He's stuffing me full; I can feel the stretch burn and it ignites the soreness from earlier tonight.

"I think that is the size of the biggest dildo he used on me," I manage to say as James pumps his hand in and out.

"And what about this hole?" he points at my back entrance.

"What about that hole?"

"How much did you take up there?"

"I took a huge butt plug, bigger than any I've ever seen before."

"Did it feel good?"

"Yes."

"Did you gape for him?"

"Yes." I can feel my cheeks growing warm as I remember the look in Henry's eyes as he stared at my stretched arse.

"Did he fuck your mouth?" James moves his thumb up to bump my clit on every thrust of his hand.

"Yes."

"Hard?" James emphasises this with a particularly rough thrust making me gasp before I manage to respond.

"Yes."

"And he came down your pretty throat?"

"Yes." I moan remembering the massive orgasm that hit me as he filled my throat.

"Anything else I should know?"

"He stuck his tongue deep into my arsehole."

James' eyes become alight. Like those final words just flicked a switch inside of him. He looks feral. Withdrawing his hand from my aching pussy, he pulls his track pants down and ploughs straight into me. No easing in, no gentleness, only pure need to consume. To own.

Bending across my body, his weight falls heavy onto mine. One hand is roaming furiously over my body and squeezes my breast whilst he bites and sucks at my neck like an animal. Seeing and feeling James lose control is my undoing. I love to see him like this, over me. I love that I am doing this to him, that my new job is bringing out this feral beast in him. My beast.

He pulls away from my neck, his lips all puffy and red. Looking down at me, he realigns himself, hitting that sweet spot deep inside. Thrusting with his full body weight, he's hurting and making me feel good at the same time. I like the pain with my pleasure. I like him causing pain for me, I like knowing he is doing it on purpose.

"I want this to hurt you Rosie, feel you stretch around my cock like that member did to you. I want you to feel all of me and more. I want this pussy that I own to be sore from me, not from that other bastard. You only think of my cock and no one else's. It will be my cock that stretches your pussy and your arsehole. I'm going to destroy your arse and come deep inside, marking my territory and no one else's."

That's all I need to hear for my climax to rip through me. Pleasure ripples through my body as James continues to plough deep inside of me. When I've stopped quivering and pulsing around his cock, he pulls out, flips me onto all fours and pushes his cock into my arse using only my own come to lubricate his cock. I scream as with one hard thrust he bottoms out and is fully seated in my sore, stretched arse. In a repeat of my earlier position I reach back under me to once more rub my clit, letting my head hang down.

"I bet you enjoyed this little hole being stretched in preparation for my dick. I bet you took everything he gave you like the good little girl you are. Knowing it would be me he was making you loose for. I wish I could have watched him plough your arse with those toys. I would have liked to have joined in. But better yet I get to stick the real thing inside my favourite hole."

I moan as he talks dirty to me through his own growls, and I can tell he's getting close. Heat starts to bloom in my core, my arse completely impaled on his cock. My clit is sensitive from its use all evening, but it doesn't fail to alight at the thought of James' come filling me up. Wrapping one hand around my neck he squeezes and stills his cock deep inside me to unload with a roar. I come as I start to see black stars behind my eyes, the climax igniting electricity through my veins. My arms wobble and nearly collapse on me, James catches my torso before I land face first into the bed. "Easy tiger," he whispers in my hair, so caring and gentle. He pulls out slowly and asks, "Was I too rough?"

"No," I answer honestly, "I liked it." Relief washes over his beautiful face, not a hint of the animal that was bursting out of him just a few minutes ago.

James picks me up cradled to his chest and carries me into our ensuite. Placing me on the top of the toilet lid, he turns on the hot water in our shower. When it's warm enough he pulls off his sweatpants and holds out a hand to me. Taking it, I stand on shaky legs and walk into the shower, the heat feeling glorious washing over my body.

James lathers my floral body wash and carefully runs his

hands across my chest, around my neck and shoulders and along my arms. He's washing me like I'm the most precious person in the world to him, moving his hands in slow circles. He moves down my stomach and carefully cleans between my legs, nothing sexual as his fingers glide between my folds, but I don't miss the twitch of his cock as it begins to rise again. Going down onto his knees, he moves his soapy hands down each leg to my toes. Standing again, he squeezes my shampoo into his hands, turns me around and lathers my hair. The pressure of his hands massaging my head makes me groan in pure bliss. A different kind from what I've enjoyed this evening. I begin to sway as I relax into his movements.

James tilts my head back under the water and lets the rain-fall shower wash away the suds before running conditioner through the ends of my hair and rinsing that off too.

Turning the shower off, he grabs a large towel off the hook and wraps me like a burrito. Grabbing a smaller towel, he rubs it gently over my hair. He is dripping, gloriously naked in front of me. When he's finished with my hair, he unwraps and pats me dry before pulling my nightie over my head.

This man. My man. I couldn't love him any more than right at this very moment. He points to the sink and I automatically move to brush my teeth whilst he gets dry and back into his track pants. I gladly climb into bed and snuggle in close to James, resting my head on his pillow as he wraps his body around mine. Sleep finds me quickly.

11

———————

I wake up late at 7:30am to an empty bed. My head is heavy and I can feel the repercussions of my stretching job yesterday. And my husband's pounding too, let's be honest.

I go downstairs to find breakfast is in full swing, James already has the kids dressed in school uniforms and eating whilst he is making lunches. I smile lovingly at the sight. My beautiful family. *How did I get so lucky I wonder.* James passes me a cup of black tea and I take it gratefully.

"Morning handsome."

"Morning Rose Petal." He gives me a kiss on the cheek, adding, "I'll drop the kids this morning, you take your time and get yourself ready for work."

"Thank you, I am feeling slow this morning."

I make myself some toast and slide in between my two kids both eating and doing something on an iPad.

An hour and a half later I'm in Café Marion serving coffees, cleaning tables and waiting for Sophie to arrive. I get on with everyone who works at The Clarendon but Sophie is my work wife, we just gel together and I love our chats and our lunches.

"Hey Roxy," Sophie says breezily with a warm smile as she slides in behind the coffee counter.

"Hey Sophie," I reply brightly, looking up over the coffee machine. "How are you feeling this morning?" I say with a wink.

"Oh you know, toasty." Sophie winks back. We giggle in a shared unspoken joke bumping shoulders. Then we straighten up, remembering where we are, we put back on our professional faces and demeanours and begin our shift together.

The morning passes like any other Monday until noon brings in the early risers who have just finished the circuit of 18 holes of golf. I am busy restocking the shelves with teas and fresh coffee beans, Sophie is at the till. I'm not looking but see the men who have just saddled up to the counter in my periphery.

"Flat white and two cappuccinos please Sophie," a sexily husky voice requests.

"Flat white and two caps coming up. I'll bring them over, please take a seat," Sophie purrs in reply. My head shoots up, and I side eye Sophie and then look at the man who is ordering. He's tall and pleasant looking but I've never seen him before. Maybe he visits after my shifts usually or on the weekends?

Turning my attention back to Sophie, she runs up the order in the till and begins to make the gentlemen's coffees. She's going through the usual motions to make the coffees, but she has a slight tremor about her. Like she's been caught off balance. I move across to stand next to her and hand her another two cups for the cappuccinos. "Everything ok?" I ask quietly, genuinely intrigued. I'm trying to work out if Sophie is happy about this man being here or is unnerved.

"Everything is fine," Sophie chirps in a high pitch tone. The bright reply is in contrast to her lowered chin and mischievous sparkling eyes.

"Ok," I say, convinced she is fine but also well aware I'm reading something going on between the lines. "Lunch at 1?"

"Perfect." Sophie grins at me with a wicked smile that does not show her teeth.

I watch as she sashays over to the table with her tray of drinks. Placing them on the table in front of each of the men, they all give her their attention. I can see them speaking and joking around with her and she laughs along with them before sashaying back over to the counter. The devilish look she gives me has me wanting time to speed up an hour so we can leave, and I can find out who that man is. The last hour is painful as I watch each minute of the clock, dying to ask questions but knowing that I need to uphold the professional expectation (and confidentiality agreement) of no gossiping at work.

I keep peeking at the men. All are attractive in their own way and in their mid thirties, all wearing wedding bands. The one who ordered has long blond hair tied back in a slick ponytail. Easy for me to spot if I see him again but I'm sure I haven't seen him before.

Thirty minutes later the men stand up and start heading out. Blondy strolls over to the counter where Sophie is trying to look busy. She looks up as he gets closer to her and whispers in her ear. Sophie blushes, narrows her eyes at him with a coy smile. He looks equally coy as he dips his head in a nod, which I can only assume is a confirmation or a goodbye. Gahh I need to get out of here now and find out who this man is. My imagination is going wild. He must be a member who has booked Sophie, but for what? And when?

Once the men have left and are out of sight, Sophie turns to me and bends over fanning her face. I've never seen her look so flustered. Raising my eyebrow at her when she catches my eye I give her a look that I hope says 'you're going to tell me every last detail at lunch.'

Thomas and Ava arrive just before 1pm, and I couldn't be

happier to see them. I thread my arm through Sophie's and pull her out of Café Marion and then out of the golf club leading her firmly towards her car. It's only when we're safely inside that I turn to her and say, "So! Tell Me! I'm dying right now Sophie!"

Sophie lets out a breath and sighs. "Where to start?" She puts her head back on the seat's headrest. I'm bemused, but I hold in the urge to shake her and ask her to hurry up with the story, I'm dying to know!

"You remember when I said it's hard to know who each job is for when posting because club members have access and can see the jobs posted and often cut and paste a listing? Each time they post a job they are allocated a new one off member number, only management knows who they are when they post a job."

Yes…"

"Well that was Kieran. I haven't mentioned him because it's been a few months. He is my one."

"Your one?" I ask, wondering if she means the one she wants to marry.

"He's the one who got under my skin. He's the one that I hope I get every time I take a certain type of job. He's the one that I shouldn't want or like or enjoy. But I can't help it."

"You have feelings for him?" I ask curiously.

"Yes and no. He's just the one who gives me butterflies. Makes my knees weak and turns my world upside down after a job booking. I've decided not to fight it, just enjoy it now."

"What is his kink?" I ask. It's such a shame you can't look at someone and know. But then that goes both ways and I'd prefer if no one looked at me and knew mine.

"CNC."

"Which is?"

"Consensual non-consent."

"Which is…?"

"He likes to run after me in a balaclava in the dark, he likes me to fight when he captures me and fucks me."

"Oh right." I'm surprised. I have never heard of this before. I assumed there was only the black and white, consent or non-consent. But it sounds interesting, from the way my body is reacting it sounds like something I'd be interested in trying. "And I'm guessing you enjoy this kink? Or is it mostly him?"

"I didn't know I liked CNC until I tried it and it turns out, I love it. But what makes it better? Him."

"How so?"

"He's rough, throws my body around like a rag doll. He loves it when I fight back so he can hold me down harder. His body is strong and he likes control."

"Sounds hot. What did he whisper to you before he left?"

"He said he was posting a job tonight on the Red job board and to look out for it."

"Wow, so he clearly wants you to apply for the job then. He likes playing with you too."

"Yes he does." Sophie smiles at me. "I don't see him often but when he plays golf, he often seeks me out and lets me know he's posting a job."

"Do you know anything about him?" I wonder, I don't know anything about any members other than clues from a wedding band.

"No, I know nothing like everyone else. He doesn't speak a word about his life or ask about mine. He sticks to the confidentiality agreement, only bending it a smidge to seek me out. I know getting attached to one member is not ideal, but I enjoy the jobs I work with him, they're incredible. As long as I don't develop feelings for him I can keep our relationship strictly business. Which is what I've managed to do but I can't keep my body's reaction to him under control when I see him."

I eye Sophie. This is dangerous territory. Catching feelings is the downside to this job. I really hope for her sake she can keep the line strictly business between work and want. Falling in love can surely only lead to hurt and pain.

When we arrive at our favourite café our conversation over lunch is on much lighter topics such as new shoes and holidays, basically everything I haven't been able to afford in a long while. After saying goodbye once Sophie has dropped me back at my car, I muse over our conversation about her Blondy the rest of the day at my other 'day job'. This playmates job is risky when it comes to your heart. Many of the members are seriously attractive and wealthy. It must be easy for any of us—playmates or club members —to fall in love. Just because I hadn't met someone who gives me butterflies, doesn't mean it might not happen. I have my husband and he is more than enough for little ol' me.

My afternoon orders are slow so I click onto the jobs portal and see if any new Green jobs have been posted that might be of interest. Scrolling down the list my eyes fall on the heading 'Submissive for my every whim.' This piques my interest, I love being submissive in the bedroom with James but I've never been an actual submissive in a Dom/sub setting. I click on the job post.

Submissive for my every whim, Friday 9am

Member 975, Male (MM/FP)

On Friday morning I would like to have a playmate to submit to my every request. I will be working in my office and will give you orders to follow my every command. I will use toys, handcuffs and spanking between my day to day working duties. I expect deep throat & to fuck you when I please. Expect some degradation. Most of all, I would like a good little playmate who seeks to please above all else.

Time - 4hrs

Payment - $3,500

My body heats. I call James. "Hi, I've just looked on the

playmate job board and there is a job I find appealing. Are you free to talk right now?"

"Hold on two minutes, I'll just head into a meeting room," James replies and I can hear him breathing as he makes his way out of his open plan office space and into one of the many meeting rooms they have lining the office. I hear the door close behind him as he says, "What is the job?"

I read out the job description and payment. James blows out a breath. "That sounds right up your alley Rose. I bet you'd pay $3k to do it?"

I giggle in response. "You don't mind if I apply for it then?"

"Go for it. Who am I to stop you. I would like you to indulge in your fantasies."

"Thank you, thank you."

"What about working at the club on Friday?"

"If I am successful in my application, I'll let Sandy know and see if she can get cover for me. I know for a fact being a playmate takes priority over my standard job at the club so I don't feel bad at least."

"Ok, will you be ok to run your business after?"

"Yeah I think so, it's a morning thing so I don't think any alcohol will be involved. I'm not sure what to expect, but that's the fun of it."

"Apply and let me know when you get home if you get it. I've got a hard-on just thinking about what he might ask you to do, I'm going to have to wait in this office until it goes down."

"Oh no James, think of boring bills or work or something. Not my work!" I giggle. "See you soon. Love you."

"Love you too. Bye."

My heart fluttering, I end the call. I love this man. I love how supportive he is and how much pleasure he gets out of my new job. I begin to write my application.

Dear Member 975,

I would like to put myself forward for your Friday morning of obedience and control. I would like nothing more than to please you in any way you see fit. It would be my honour to provide any sexual pleasure you desire and would accept any of you or your toys within any part of my body. I am submissive by nature but also particularly enjoy being submissive in the bedroom.

I hope to be of service to you.

Roxy

I press send and wait. I leave my laptop open whilst I pack my final orders for my online business until I hear a ping. Looking back at the screen I can see the word:

Job: **ACCEPTED**

I clap my hands with glee. Another job, another $3,500 and another experience I can add under my belt.

12

———————

I wake with a start, sure it's too early to be morning yet. Why am I awake? I open my eyes to see two legs straddling my neck, one thigh on either side of my face. Pointing down, hanging low and hard so it almost touches my lips is James' cock. I raise my eyes up to find James looking straight down at me.

"Open for me Rose Petal, be a good girl." I'll do anything to be James' good girl. I begin to open my mouth.

"Nice and wide, there we go," James soothes as he lowers himself down and edges the head of his velvety cock between my lips. I curl my lips around the tip and draw just the head into my mouth. I suck greedily and hear James let out a deep groan as he steadies himself on the bed's headboard behind my head.

I let go of the suction with a pop and allow James to feed his cock lower into my mouth. James slides himself down lower slowly until the head of his cock taps the back of my throat, then eases back up a little. He does it again and again and I suck him down deep.

"Fuckkkk," James groans as he lowers deeper, making me gag from being filled to choking.

I move my hands up to massage his balls as he continues to drive in and out of my mouth. Then I begin to rub one finger along his taint and he begins to shudder. I see for myself as his balls begin to draw up whilst he continues the assault on my throat. I'm making gurgling noises right now, trying to suck him down whilst sucking in air through my nose.

James' thighs are quivering around my ears as he begins to offer praise above my head. "You suck me down so well Rose, you are going to suck my seed right down the back of your throat like a good whore. That's what you are going to be for someone else tomorrow, so that is what you are going to be for me this morning. Suck me dry Rose, take every last drop of me so I can brand you as mine so the kinky fucker knows you belong to me tomorrow."

James' words make me reach down and start to stroke my clit whilst the other continues to massage his taint, I can feel the heat building in my core and this one touch is going to push me over the edge any second. James has never woken me up like this, it's hot and I love the surprise and the dominance. I want to be branded and to show the stranger who I belong to tomorrow.

James pushes himself in and out of my mouth, fucking my face like I'm his good little whore. "You're milking me Rose, you're fucking taking it so well. Open wide now, take it all." James' naked body above me stills as he pushes his full length deep down, hitting the back of my throat. I try to relax my throat and resist gagging as I can feel his hot seed sink down it and I do my best not to choke. His orgasm triggers mine knowing I'm drinking his come like the good little whore he wants me to be. James starts to withdraw himself from my mouth whilst I ride through my climax and he watches me until I float back down to earth.

"Good morning Rose Petal. It's early, we can go back to sleep."

"What time is it?"

"5am. Here, have this." James passes me a glass of water. I sit up and drink it down gratefully, the cool liquid soothing the tender part of my throat where James has just been. Once I've had a couple of gulps, I pass it back to him and snuggle back down under the covers. James puts the glass back on the bedside unit and lies down, he reaches out to me and I shuffle closer so our heads are touching and our bodies are curled in towards each other. James wraps an arm around me.

"Go to sleep now baby. I'll wake us before 7am."

Sleepily I close my eyes and let the weight of James' arm cocoon me and the floaty feeling of my orgasm takes me back under. Today is going to be a lovely day.

13

———

The next morning, I wake up earlier than usual for a weekday. I climb out of bed quietly trying not to wake James. I creep into our ensuite and start the shower. I shave and scrub and wash all over from head to toe. When I get out, I dry and cover myself in shea butter body lotion and comb my wet hair.

I pull on my dressing gown and open the bathroom door to see James sitting up in bed looking at something on his phone. He looks up at me and then says, "Good morning. Getting ready for your job this morning?"

"Good morning husband. Yes I sure am."

"Come here," James instructs. I raise an eyebrow but walk over to him. He puts his phone down and then reaches inside my dressing gown and pulls out both my breasts so they're on display for him. Squeezing them with both hands, he looks at me and says, "These are mine. And I'm going to make sure the member today is fully aware they belong to me." Pulling me closer by my breasts, he bends his head and sucks on the side of my right nipple hard. I know what he's doing, he's branding me. After a minute he stops the suction and my breast pops out of his mouth. Moving back he looks at his handy work and looks smug. There is now a purple hickey where his mouth just was.

"You're mine, these are mine. And now he will know."

Liquid heat is pooling between my legs but I don't have time to do anything about it. I bring my face close to him and mutter the words, "I'm all yours James, you can brand me whenever and however you want. I belong to you."

His lips find mine and they kiss me hungrily, his tongue finding mine and lapping together as he pulls me into him. I put both my hands around his head and kiss him back. I wish I could continue but I still have breakfast and my makeup to do before Frank picks me up at 8:30am.

I pull away and say breathily, "James, I have to be ready by 8:30, I can't stay and play this morning."

"I know, go eat. I just needed to do that first."

"I know you did and I would stay if I didn't have the clock against me right now."

James nods and I walk out of the bedroom deciding to eat breakfast before getting dressed. I contemplate my job for the morning over my cereal. What will he be like, what will he want me to do? I'm nervous but with two playmates jobs under my belt now, I'm not so nervous I can't eat. Plus, I seriously don't want my stomach to growl whilst I'm there.

After brushing my teeth and painting my makeup on to perfection, I pull on a pastel blue, short sleeved shirt with a pretty collar and blue buttons and pair it with a black pencil skirt and black heels. I pull on a deeper blue cardigan and tie up my hair. My reflection says cute secretary which is exactly what I was aiming for.

Still standing in front of the mirror, James walks up behind me and checks me out from behind.

"I'd do you," mutters James.

"I know you would," I reply with a grin. "Do I look ok? Is it right for my job this morning?"

"You look ok for any job this morning. He won't be able to resist you," says my always supportive husband.

"I'm nervous a little. What if I am not a good enough submissive for him? I'm afraid he'll tell Sandy I'm not very good."

"You have nothing to worry about Rose Petal." James snakes his arm around my waist and spins me to face him. "You were a born submissive. Go to this kinky fucker, do whatever he says like a good little girl. Then come home, tell me what he wanted you to do and we can re-enact it another time if you enjoy it. Which I know you will."

"And *you* will enjoy it." I smile up at him with a knowing grin. Despite James never wanting to share before, he's found he loves it. He loves me bringing home new ideas and experiences for us to try. He loves just the thought of me being with someone else. I wonder if he'd like to actually watch me with someone else. That is a question for another day.

Just as that thought flashes through my mind. My phone alarm goes off. My 5 minute alarm. I set it so I'd have enough time to say goodbye to the kids on my way out. James pulls me into a bear hug and kisses the top of my head. "You're going to knock his socks off. Go enjoy yourself because I know he will."

I pull away and look up at him. I rise up on my tiptoes to lightly brush my lips onto his. "Thank you. Despite my nerves, I am looking forward to it."

"Of course you are, you little minx."

I pull away and blow him another kiss. "Goodbye husband."

"Goodbye Rose Petal. Text me when you're back at your office."

I nod and walk out of our bedroom and into each of my children's. Giving them both a kiss on their heads and telling them to have a lovely day at school. Both break out in big conversations as I'm rushing to leave, and I make a note to do an earlier alarm to give me more time to say goodbye to them next time. Just the way it is; kids don't have anything to say when you ask them about their day but have heaps to say when they're in bed supposed to be going to sleep or when you're in a rush to leave the house.

I hurry down the stairs and see Frank's blacked out BMW waiting for me at the end of my driveway. I climb in, say a friendly hello to Frank and tie the blindfold around my eyes—happy that none of my neighbours can see into the car windows to see what exactly I'm doing. I have no doubt my neighbours have noticed by now a blacked-out BMW collecting me, but none have mentioned it so far. I really need to get my story straight about why I'm getting picked up in this way before I'm asked on the spot and I'm not ready.

Frank turns up the radio so I can listen to his channel of choice—Smooth FM—as he drives us around the Melbourne streets towards who knows where. For all I know we could be driving around in circles but hopefully not. It would not be ideal for me to find myself with a local school parent. Now that would make an interesting school fundraiser or parents' evening...

14

———

Frank slows and I know we must be close. I hear him roll down his window and say into an intercom, "I have Roxy." Before rolling up his window. I hear what sounds like gates opening and he drives slowly before stopping and telling me to unfasten the blindfold.

I remove the blindfold and blink into the morning sun. I look up at a dainty brick house that has black timber lining it and black shutters surrounding each window. This house looks like it belongs in the English countryside. There is an orange tree growing to the left and over a black shiny door. Quaint, I really like the look of this house. I open the car door and close it quietly, waving goodbye to Frank,

I walk up to the front door, and it swings open. I'm greeted by a tall, slim man with chestnut hair, a moustache and a stern look on his rather handsome slim face. He's wearing a crisp white shirt, a black blazer and dark jeans.

"Hello Roxy," says his deep intimidating voice. I cringe on the inside, he looks like he could be a school teacher at a private school and I'm getting naughty school girl vibes from him.

"Hi," I answer brightly, giving him my warmest smile. I'm not sure if I should reach out my hand or not but seeing as he doesn't and I don't know his name, I wait to see what he does next.

The man ushers me inside and closes the door behind me. Inside is just as lovely as the outside. Black beams and white walls. I can see down the hallway but not much more than that. There's not much time to take in my surroundings.

"I'm Aaron but you can call me Sir or Master."

Wide eyed I nod. "Absolutely Sir." I shouldn't sound so eager, should I sound more demure? I kick myself for not phoning Sophie to get some tips on how to be a good submissive.

"Have you been a submissive before?" Aaron asks me.

"No Sir, I have not. But I'm eager to please. I'll do whatever you ask of me."

"Excellent. I can see for myself. Let's get a few rules for the morning sorted now." Aaron speaks with an authoritative tone. "You will not speak unless spoken to. You know how to address me when you are spoken to. Any disobedience will require a punishment. When I ask you to do something, you do it until I tell you otherwise. You stay where I tell you to stay. You move when I tell you to move. Do I make myself clear?"

"Yes Master," I breathe out. This man is bossy, he knows what he wants, and he is not shy in the slightest about it. I'm in awe of such a strong man. And already a little bit turned on. What is he going to ask me to do? I don't have to wait long to find out. I look up into his brown honeyed eyes. He's at least Jame's height or above at 6' 5".

"I will lead the way into my office. I have work to do as mentioned. You will assist when required."

Assist? I wonder. *How?*

Aaron turns on his matte black loafers. Down the hallway and to the right up the staircase and into the first bedroom on the left. I say bedroom but it's a really large room with a four poster bed against the back wall opposite the door but also a large wooden regal desk on an angle to the right of the four poster. The desk is angled so that whoever sits at it has a direct view of the bed to its right and the window to the left. Seems strange, especially as the desk is not against a wall or under the window. Closing the door behind me he says one word. "Strip."

Walking over to his desk, he folds his long arms across his chest and perches his bum on the desk which only holds a laptop and his mobile phone.

I don't want to hesitate and get into trouble, so I slowly pull my arms out of the cardigan and fold it over an armchair just to the right of me. I unbutton the top button of my blouse watching how Aaron eyes follow my fingers to each of the next buttons. He looks raptured. When I get to the bottom, I edge it off my shoulders and place it on the chair exposing my pretty cream lace push up bra.

I then reach behind me and undo the zip on my pencil skirt. I shimmy it down over my thighs and step out of it before bending down and picking it up for the chair. Standing in my heels and lacy cream thong and bra, I certainly feel like I'm giving a strip show.

I reach around my back and unclip my bra and let my breasts fall down heavy and full. I stare at Aaron whilst he stares back at my body, I notice a large bulge in his jeans down his leg. I'm pleasing him. That is a relief. Finally, I dip my thumbs into my tiny lace cream thong and shimmy the small piece of lace down my legs and step out of them still in my high black patent heels. Before I can place the thong onto the pile of my clothes Aaron speaks.

"Put them in your teeth and crawl over to me." Heat flushes my cheeks and pools in my core.

"Yes Sir," I answer dutifully before lowering to my knees. I put my thong in my teeth before placing my hands onto the plush light grey carpet and crawl slowly across the floor to his feet. I raise back onto my heels looking up at him with the lace between my teeth. Never in my life had I been asked to crawl. I feel a mix of embarrassment and horniness.

"Good," he says. He reaches out his hand and takes the thong from my teeth and puts it down next to his laptop. Then he reaches down and rubs his thumb down my jawline and under my chin. The stroke feels like a reward, I almost preen for his touch. Up close, his eyes are honey pools and his pointed, stern face looks softer. He looks younger than I initially thought but still in his mid-forties.

Holding my chin so I can only look directly into his honey eyes he instructs, "Lick my right shoe."

Confusion flickers in my eyes before understanding and then compliance. "Yes Master," I reply and he lets go of my chin, nothing has changed in his voice or his eyes. He just watches. I feel horrified and horny all at the same time. What is this man doing to me? Embarrassment encases me, why would he want me to do this?

I lower my head down, incidentally raising my bum in the air. My face is almost as low as my knees as I draw closer to his left shoe. I tentatively reach out my tongue and touch the tip to the side of his shoe. It doesn't taste bad, if anything it tastes like new leather. In fact they do seem to be brand new loafers. I flatten my tongue a bit more and lick again. *How much of this shoe does he want me to lick?*

I am not allowed to speak so all I can do is continue licking around the ankle and towards the front of the shoe. The longer I do it, the flatter and longer the strokes of my tongue become. I'm now lapping up at the shoe, I want to do a good job and please him, Aaron, my Master.

"Good." Is all he says as he strokes my hair. That is all the reward I need to lap around to the other side of the shoe. "Now do my right."

I move across and lap from the heel of his left shoe all the way around to the other side. I hope Master is enjoying the show because he's certainly letting me do it for some time.

"Now stop. Look back up at me." I do exactly what he says immediately and return to my kneeling with my weight on my heels looking up at him for my next instructions.

Master strokes his hand down my face, the touch feeling so intimate I don't want him to take his hand away from my face. "Well done, you looked good licking my shoes. I enjoyed watching your tongue work and your arse in the air.

"Take off your heels and crawl over to that spot there to the left of my desk, just in front of the door." Aaron points to the spot in the light filled room on the carpet. "When you get there, I want you to sit like you are now but with your knees spread wide apart and your hands on your thighs. Can you do that for me?"

"Yes Master." I nod in response. I slide off my shoes and leave them where I was sitting before crawling across the soft, light grey carpet. Getting into position I watch as Aaron moves around his desk and sits down on his chair. Where he is sitting, he has a perfect view of me to his left, my nakedness and my open pussy. I'm completely exposed.

"Lower your gaze. And now stay there." I lower my gaze to the sides of the desk and carpet.

I don't know how long I kneel there but it feels like an age. The anticipation of how long I will stay seated and what he might do next is flooding my senses. I can hear him typing and working I assume. Does he look up at me? Does he like me sitting here naked waiting for his next instruction? It feels very freeing to have no other obligations but to obey his instructions.

"I need to make a phone call. When I do, I would like you to crawl under my desk, take my cock out of my jeans and stroke me. Then I would like to feel your mouth work its way up and down until I end the call. Do not make a sound."

"Yes Master," I answer, staying in the same position with my eyes cast down. A few minutes later I hear him pick up his phone and start speaking. He sounds just the same, authoritative and all business on the phone.

I take my cue to crawl under his desk, he's pushed his chair back a bit to enable me to rise up onto my knees and reach for his jeans button. Using both hands I gently push the button through its hole and carefully lower his zip. To my surprise he is bare from boxers and hair. I reach into his jeans and pull out his long, hard velvety cock. The head glistens and my mouth waters. Before I peek out my tongue I remember my instructions of stroking first.

Using both hands, I grip the base with one and stroke my thumb over the sensitive skin under the head of his cock as I raise the hand up and down. Watching for his body's reaction, I notice when he lowers back deeper into his chair and despite the conversation continuing above my head, he feels relaxed and pliant—well, everything but the rock hard pole between his legs.

I silently dribble spit onto his cock and use it as lubricant to work him harder with my hands. His thighs begin to shake a little and I take this as an undeniable sign he's enjoying my work.

After I feel I've given his cock enough attention with my hands, I lick my lips. My mouth is already watering, and I lean my head over him and lick from the base to the tip. Once my mouth is lined up, I take him in one deep thrust right to the back of my throat. Aaron goes completely still as well and stops mid conversation. I almost take my lips from him to check he's ok but think better of it remembering my instructions to do as he says.

"Sorry Sally, what was I saying?? I was momentarily interrupted in my office just now. No, no—now is a good time to talk through this."

I move my head higher almost to the tip where I suck and nibble gently and then lower quickly again, loosening my throat and letting his long length fill me up entirely. I hear Aaron let out an almost inaudible shaky breath when he hits the back of my throat once again. I raise up and down and begin a slippery rhythm, saliva begins to pool around my chin but I continue until I hear him wrap up his phone call and say goodbye.

"That, my little submissive, was naughty. You nearly put me off my phone call. Was that your intention?"

I let out a pop from letting go of the suction around his cock. "No Master, not at all. I was only trying to please you." I wipe at the drool at my chin but before my hand connects he pushes it away.

"Did I tell you to remove your saliva from your chin?"

"No Sir."

"Then I expect you to leave it."

"Yes, Sir," I answer, fighting the urge to wipe.

"Finish the job I have given you."

"Yes Master."

I lean my head back over and line my mouth with his cock and thrust down. This time I can feel his eyes burn into the back of my head, I can feel his hips twitch and they seem to be having a hard time not thrusting in. I go deeper down onto him and am rewarded by him stroking my hair.

I can feel his orgasm building, his lean body is tensing up around me. I glance up to see Aaron sit back into his chair and rest his head back on the headrest. His breathing is becoming frenzied and so is mine, I double my efforts whilst trying to suck in air through my nose.

Aaron loses control and pushes my head deep onto him and he spears me to the spot as his come explodes down the back of my throat, gagging me whilst he doesn't allow a millimetre of movement from me.

Once Aaron's orgasm has finished rippling through his body he lifts his hand away from my head and I rise up coughing and choking. I don't wipe my chin or the strings of drool hanging from my chin, I just look up at him for further instruction.

"Clean me up," Aaron directs with his eyes, seeming pleasantly amused that I didn't touch my chin, he approves of my obedience.

I bend back down and suck the last beads of come from his tip and lick up and down his length to ensure there are no pools of my drool left anywhere.

When I rise again to seek my next instructions, Aaron reaches into a drawer and pulls out a tissue. He folds it and then gently wipes at my mouth and chin. The way he's touching me is so different from before, this seems almost like adoration. I feel a little whiplash from him face fucking me, but the desire pooling in my body for more touches and approval is all consuming. No one has ever made me desire someone in such a way. I will literally do anything just for one touch of my chin or rub of my head.

"Put my cock back into my jeans and do me back up."

"Yes Master," I reply and notice he's no longer soft anymore, he's already got a semi and it begins to rise again in my fingers. I fold him back into his black jeans and am careful to do up his zip and button.

"Crawl over to the bed and lie face up with both your hands and feet stretched out like a starfish."

I nod, "Yes Sir," and begin to move following his instructions exactly. I don't look back at him, I just look up at the four poster bed where I'm now lying. *What will he do next?*

In my periphery I can see him walk around to the top right hand corner and I hear a chain rustle. Leaning over the bed

Aaron picks up my wrist and encloses it in thick leather. Moving around the bed he does the same with my ankles and other wrist, pulling each one right to the edge of discomfort. Now I'm stretched open and cannot move or sit.

I watch as Aaron moves back to his desk and opens a drawer lifting out a bag. Bringing it over to the bed he opens it up and lifts a butt plug out with a bottle of lube.

"I enjoy you looking like this for me Roxy. I'll enjoy it even more when I fill you up for my pleasure whilst I work."

Squirting the lube onto the butt plug he applies his attention to my back hole. Drizzling his index finger with the lube, he lines up his finger and slowly enters my arsehole. I try and relax to his intrusion and once his finger is past my ring of tight muscle, I am fully able to be calm and enjoy the pleasure he is giving me. Then he slides in another finger.

Aaron notices my breathing has switched from deep to calm slower breaths, he looks up.

"You like this, my little submissive. You are really going to enjoy this little gift I'm about to give you." Sliding his fingers out, he lines up the butt plug and pushes it slowly inside me. I feel the familiar stretch as my tight ring of muscle opens to stretch around the girth of its bulb but it's not the largest butt plug I've taken—especially not in comparison to my previous playmate job and certainly nothing on my husband's girth. The plug slides in easily and sits comfortably in my arsehole.

I give Aaron a shy smile, I'm utterly open and exposed to him. No shying away from his eyes or his hands. Reaching back into his bag, he pulls out a large vibrator.

He's about to lube up the dildo when he looks more closely at my pussy and can see my arousal leaking from me. I flush deeply when his eyes flick from my centre to my eyes. A smile tweaks on the corner of his lips.

"I bet I won't need lube for this right now?"

"No Sir," I reply both embarrassed and aroused by the admission.

"Good girl." His honey eyes crinkle at the edges and those words spark my clit. I've been hoping to receive this praise.

Carefully, erotically, Aaron lines up the silicone dildo with my entrance and pushes slightly. My slickness gives him no issue as he slowly edges it deeper and deeper allowing my core to stretch around its girth. Aaron is watching the expressions on my face as I slowly part my lips with a small groan. Being filled in both holes by this man is a pleasure that is all mine.

When the dildo hits my cervix Aaron stops the pressure, leaves it where it is and sets his sights on my clit. Rubbing two fingers over the sensitive nub lights my nerve endings on fire. I arch into his touch and he lets out a low chuckle.

"I have some work to do and a brief Zoom meeting. Lie here and be a quiet little mouse for me Roxy." He pauses then adds, "Oh, and be sure to hold that dildo right where it is, I'd hate to have to punish you for letting it fall."

"I will, Sir," I say, peeking over my naked trussed up body. I watch as he sits down at his desk, my naked body in his eye line. I see him run his eyes over my body and halt at my filled centre, he looks pleased with what he sees. I'm completely exposed and stuffed but it feels erotic. I'm open for anything he pleases and right now he wishes to see me restrained on his bed, filled with his toys whilst he works.

I hear Aaron begin to type again. I stay still looking up at the ceiling when a vibration almost makes me shriek. I close my eyes and clamp my lips together to ensure no noise leaves my mouth. My heart begins to thump in my chest. *Where is it coming from?* With both toys so close to one another it's almost impossible to differentiate. The intensity builds and I think it's coming from my butt plug. I clench my butt and my pussy which helps a growing delicious sensation ripple through my body, I begin to pant through it as my clit pulses with pleasure.

I peek an eye open to look over at Aaron and see him watching me. He has a wicked look in his eyes, his head is lowered but his eyes are looking up at me, watching me. I go to ask about the vibrations and then catch myself; I am not permitted to speak. Closing my mouth, I watch Aaron looking over at me and the vibrations stop suddenly. His eyes have lowered, and he resumes typing. I let out a deep breath.

Lying still for a few more minutes time begins to slow, I have no idea how long I have been with Aaron or strapped to the bed. I begin to marvel at how nice it is to not have to work in the café or my business right now. To have no responsibilities or decisions to make. To just be and do as I am told when I am told. It feels liberating. Freeing. I could get used to this kind of existence, even if it is only occasional.

My thoughts are distracted when I hear Aaron start to speak but his tone is not towards me, it's all business and he's facing his laptop. Aaron is having a meeting with someone or a group of people whilst I'm strapped to his bed naked. It's perverse. It's deranged. It's filthy. The thought alone turns me on. I clench the dildo and wish I could move my hand down and rub at my clit, my body is beginning to throb with need. I need a release and not being able to do anything about it is driving me wild.

An intense vibration rolls through my body, catching me off-guard and I let out a squeak. I realise my error all too late. The room becomes silent and then I hear Aaron say, "Apologies, that was my cat. Just one minute."

Oh no, what have I done? I think. *What will he do?*

I watch as Aaron opens a drawer and withdraws a ball gag. He walks to the bed in quick strides. He does not look me in the eye, he only holds the gag up and I obediently open my mouth. Dispassionately, he places the ball in between my teeth, lifts my head and fastens the straps at the back of my head. He lowers my head carefully back down onto the pillow and in two strides is back sitting at his desk, putting his EarPods back in, un-muting himself and continues his meeting like nothing happened. It's as if I'm simply a toy that malfunctioned and he must correct the setting before continuing, but I can only assume there will be a punishment later.

The vibrations are still throbbing throughout my body from the butt plug, and now my mouth is fastened open uncomfortably wide and drool is beginning to pool at my chin. The sensation, the experience, the depravity of it is threatening my very sanity. Pleasure is building, I clench my core and let the sensations run through my body from my butt. I wish Aaron would come off his meeting to push the toy in and out of my pussy, I need more, I need something. Even just one light tap on the bundle of nerves would tip me over into oblivion. And then the vibrations stop and I quiver at their abandonment. A sob leaves my throat but is muffled by the ball gag—if this is what edging feels like, I'm not a fan.

I lie on the bed listening to Aaron making agreement noises to whatever is being spoken inside his EarPods and wonder how long his meeting will run for, how much time do we have left?

Thankfully, I don't have to wait very long to see what he does next. Aaron says goodbye, takes his EarPods out, shuts his laptop and comes to stand over me at the end of the bed.

"Look at you, drooling all over yourself Roxy with that ball gag in after being such a bad girl. Do you like your punishment, or would you like more?"

I can't speak so don't try. He knows I can't answer, he's enjoying watching me blink up at him wide eyed and helpless, just wondering what he's going to do next.

Walking around to the side of the bed, he kneels on my right, gently lifts my head and undoes the strap releasing the pressure of the ball. Pulling it away, a line of drool follows it as it's moved away entirely and placed on the side of the bed.

"What do you say?"

"Thank you, Master."

"I'll ask you the question again. Would you like more punishment?"

"If it pleases you, Master."

"Good answer Roxy." Aaron's eyes crinkle at the corners, he bends his head down close to mine and starts to lap at the saliva that has dribbled from my mouth. I relish his warm tongue licking at my mouth, my chin, under my jaw. It's so intimate and nothing like anything I was expecting him to do. He takes his time, enjoying each taste of me and I melt in his attention. All too soon his lips are pulling away and he's sitting up.

"Let's get you suitably punished shall we? That was an important meeting you interrupted. You almost gave our playdate away." Climbing off the bed Aaron walks towards the bottom of the bed, he reaches for the dildo but before he removes it, he withdraws a little and then gives three thrusts that leave me wanting more. Withdrawing the long object, Aaron watches as my insides clench around nothing and gives a low chuckle at my unashamed need.

"Rewards are given to good girls, my Roxy girl. And you have been bad. Let's get you turned over."

Aaron unbuckles the cuffs at my feet, then my hands.

"Roll over, face down, bum in the air, knees bent. Stay."

I feel the jiggle of the bed as Aaron climbs off. I stay exactly how he left me, straining to listen to what he is doing. I hear a drawer open and close, and feel the bed indent again as he climbs behind me. I feel air shift before I feel the blow against the flesh of my bottom. Air is knocked out of my lungs as a wooden paddle collides with my backside.

Whoosh, another hit and this time I yelp out loud. Another three slaps hit me in quick succession hitting me in the exact same spot and I scream. My bottom is on fire, ablaze with the fury he is raining down on me.

"You can make as much noise as you want now no one can hear you."

Tears start to pool in my eyes before they roll down my face in sobs as more slaps come down relentlessly on my fleshy bare skin. Aaron shifts his angle and hits one cheek and then the other in a painful rhythm until all I feel is pure fire. I stop screaming and just take the punishment, the one Aaron wanted to give me.

And then I feel hands caressing my painful skin. "Beautiful Roxy, so beautiful. Your skin is blooming like a flower in stunning colours. You took your punishment so well," Aaron whispers, I can hardly hear him from my panting and blood pumping around my ears. Aaron sounds like he's in awe. I wonder what my backside looks like right now. How bruised my skin must be.

"I can't wait any longer," Aaron exhales.

I can hear him undoing his jeans and then his zip directly behind my raised throbbing bottom. I then feel the head of his long cock being lined up to my entrance before he thrusts all the way to the hilt. The deep thrust takes my breath away and I cry out. Aaron is rough, his fingers digging into my hips before one moves away and a second later a familiar vibration starts in my arse. I buck back onto Aaron's cock, wanting everything he can give me. I'm desperate to find my release that has been building for what has felt like hours. Aaron must be able to feel the vibrations too, low throaty rumbles are coming from behind me and his movements become frenzied as I chase my climax that is threatening to unleash at any moment. My body is trembling, his body is thrusting wildly, hitting my spot deep within, building me higher until my soul shatters around me and I come so hard around Aaron's cock, my pussy spasms clenching around him prompting Aaron to fall over his ledge too.

"Fuuucccckkk!" is all that comes out of Aaron's mouth as he

stills and I feel his release coat my insides. Coming down off his high. "That was…" he trails off, only letting out a deep satisfied sigh.

Slowly, gently, he pulls out his semi erect cock and I feel our combined desire release and trickle onto the bed. I waiver in my position on all fours and Aaron reaches out his hands to steady my swaying waist, still on my knees with my bottom in the air. The vibrations stop from my butt plug and my body feels like it's floating.

"Hold still, I want to watch us leak out of you." I do as he says, holding still despite my trembling muscles.

"Bare down."

I obey and clench my core and feel more warm liquid seep out of me and onto the bed.

"Turn around and clean me up."

Like a baby lamb on fragile legs, I move around on hands and knees so my head is facing Aaron's softening cock as he kneels in front of me. I lower my head and begin to lick from base to tip, tasting the muskiness of myself and his salty release. I lap and then suck on his cock as it starts to become semi hard once again and then lower my head to lap at his balls, making sure he is clean. I sit back on my heels and look up at Aaron.

He reaches out both hands and holds my face up to look at him, his thumbs gently caressing my cheeks.

"And now the bed."

I look down at the mess that had only just leaked out of me and lower my head to the puddle, making sure to keep my arse high in the air. I flatten my tongue and lap up our juices like a kitten enjoying milk. This is filthy, the dirtiest thing I've ever had to do. But I want to do it, I like tasting us combined and I love feeling his gaze on me, knowing I'll do anything he says. I lick at the wet patch until there is nothing left except my saliva. Sitting back up to meet Aaron's watchful eyes, I see approval and something else. Desire? Hunger?

Aaron's hands reach for my face again but this time they bring my face to his and his tongue reaches out to lick my lips, then a bit deeper, his tongue demanding entry into my mouth. I open for him and feel his body push against mine. His tongue laps at mine, tasting us on my tongue. My nipples pebble against the heat of his lean chest underneath his shirt as he devours my mouth one deep lap of his tongue at a time.

Panting, we break apart, my lips feel puffy and abused. I look back up at his red lips, wanting more but knowing I can't ask for that. I can see on Aaron's face he wants more too but instead of reaching for my face again, he pushes back onto his heels away from me and clears his throat.

"I need to take care of your bottom and help you back into your clothes. It's time, Frank is outside." I see a change in his demeanour, a warmth radiates from him despite a hint of sadness in his eyes. Aaron climbs off the bed and grabs something out of his drawer.

"Lie down on your front please." His tone is soothing, a gentle request that contrasts with his previous demands.

I do as he asks; he pulls my cheeks open and pulls gently on the butt plug and it slides free. He then wipes me down before tenderly rubbing a cream from a tube onto my ferociously sore bottom. "This is arnica, it will help with the bruising. Take this tube home with you and apply liberally after you've showered and before bed."

"Yes Sir, thank you Sir," I reply as Aaron then helps me gingerly off the bed and starts to dress me. First my bra, then my skirt and shirt, doing up each button like he would a child. I notice the thong is nowhere to be found but I don't bring it up. Lastly, he places a shoe on each of my feet and I feel like Cinderella and he's the prince.

This morning has messed with my head if I'm thinking about fairytales. I need to reflect on that later. Aaron opens the bedroom door as he says, "This way," almost in a subdued tone.

I follow him out of the door, back down the stairs and towards the door. I get the feeling he doesn't want me to leave. I also don't want to leave. *Can't we just lie in the bed and snuggle for a little while?* But no, this has to end, I have to leave. The fantasy is over. My job here is done. Sadly.

Standing in front of the door Aaron clears his throat again and says in a raspy throaty voice, "Thank you Roxy, you were the perfect submissive."

"Thank you, Sir, my Master." I don't know what to say without gushing and turning into a puddle right in front of him. Emotion rises in my throat, and I swallow it down. I can't say any more words without my feelings giving me away so I don't.

Aaron opens the door. Just before I step outside, he holds one hand to my cheek and I automatically lean into it. His last touch. I worship this man for his gentle touches and caresses. My eyes betray me as they begin to pool, I smile gratefully and say, "Goodbye Sir." As I step out of the door and head towards Frank.

Inside the blackout windows I look back at the closing door and let the tears fall before I put the blindfold back on and Frank pulls away, turning up the radio as he heads towards my business office.

15

———

Arriving at my office, I thank Frank and say goodbye. I feel completely and utterly drained. An emotional wreck. What just happened to me? I text James to let him know I'm back safe and try to let my work consume me. Only it doesn't. I can't shake how Aaron made me feel. His commanding dominance, his depravity, his caresses. My yearning for more. The need to see him again, be submissive again and to earn his rewards.

I feel a turmoil of loss knowing I may never see him again, I may never feel this way with anyone again. I know these feelings are some kind of come down after such a high but suffering through them is making my heart feel heavy. Every time I sit, my bottom smarts and I remember being spanked by him and then the way he lost control and climbed behind me like a feral animal.

My mind keeps circling around the same thoughts on loop. Over and over again. It's torture. I need to speak to Sophie. I need to speak to her before I leave this office and take whatever I'm feeling home with me. I pick up my phone and dial her number.

"Oh hi Sophie, can you talk?"

"Hey Roxy, sure I can speak. What's up? How was your job this morning?"

My lips begin to quiver and then the flood gates open, "It was so good, too good. I enjoyed it so much I can't now move on from it. The way he made me feel…"

"Oh honey, I know exactly how you feel. I have been there myself. All of us playmates have. The come down after such an amazing experience and connection. It feels like going back to your life is the opposite of what you should be doing. Like following up a first date for a second? But that isn't our world, it's our job to be good and enjoy it, for them to enjoy it and be left wanting more. It means we are human but also really good at our jobs. You had a submissive role this time, you have a beautiful submissive personality, so of course this job was going to hit the mark perfectly for you."

"Oh gosh, I feel like I miss him. How can that even be?"

"Because you just experienced a kink that really suits you, right down to your core. And I'm guessing the club member you worked for today was an excellent Dom? He was commanding but gentle. Made you do things you have never done before. I bet he hurt you but made you feel better, brought pleasure to your body in ways you hadn't experienced and made you come harder than you've ever come before."

"Yes!" I sob. "How can I move on from it, forget about it?"

"Honestly, you don't forget but you learn to move on. It does get easier. You need to see the positives from this. You have found something that you really like, a role you can play that suits your temperament but even better—it suits your bank balance because you get paid well for it. The best way to get over this Dom is to book another job and take your mind away from him. He's just a club member who you may never see again. You are grateful for the experience and for unearthing your true self, but then you carry on with your life. And something else no one has probably told you? That is the first door that has been unlocked to a kink you didn't realise you enjoy so much, imagine what else will be unlocked in your future?"

I let out a breath, she's right. She's talking from experience and I'm not the only one who has felt like this, and it most likely won't be the last time either. Maybe Aaron feels this way. But at the end of the day it was a paid service which is now complete. This is reality and I need to go back to my life with my loving husband and gorgeous children, all of whom I'm doing this for.

"Thank you Sophie, I knew you'd know what this feels like and how to make me feel a bit better about things. Honestly, my mind got caught in some never ending loop from hell like I was some lovesick puppy. I was ready to track him down and offer to be his permanent sub for forever more."

"Roxy, you have no idea how many times my mentor had to talk me off the ledge from doing that too. We are human, we have feelings, and we are allowed to have feelings. Go home to your gorgeous husband and tell him about it and all the things you enjoyed. I bet he'd enjoy stepping into the role of a Dom, more than you think. It just starts with a discussion. Boundaries."

"Thanks so much Sophie, I really appreciate having you as my mentor."

"Anytime Roxy, always. Speak soon ok?"

"Speak soon. Bye."

I hang up and feel a thousand times better than before I spoke to her. I feel like some good sense has been talked into me, but it came from experience and understanding and that has made the world of difference. It's not just me going through it, it is shared and will still happen in my future, I just need to talk about it and learn to handle it.

Feeling lighter, I finish up my work in my office and head home to my real life, my real world.

When I get home, everyone is spread out around the house. I go into the kids' rumpus room and find my daughter who I chat to and ask about her day. Animatedly she talks to me for a bit before I find my son in his room watching some anime. We chat about his day and it warms me that both my children are happy and healthy. I'm lucky, I know I am.

I find James in his office working and walk over to him and rub his shoulders from behind.

"Hi," I say as he swivels around to grab my waist and pull me onto his lap.

"How was being a naughty submissive today my Rose Petal?" He's being jovial but his light tone and smile doesn't meet his eyes. They are looking at me intently, he wants to know exactly what I did today, and in fine detail.

I take in a breath but I'm unsure of how to start. I don't want to gush about the Dom but I do want to gush about how he made me feel in his role. I decide to tell him from the beginning how the morning went in order.

Once I've finished with every last detail James is rock hard below my butt, the heat in his eyes ablaze. He enjoyed my retelling of my morning I can tell. Now I watch him closely to see what he says, he hasn't interrupted me once, just nodded and listened.

Shuffling back on his lap I place both my hands gently on either side of his face and I lean in to lightly dust my lips over his. He feels like home. He smells like home. And home is where my heart is.

"I want to play with you in the same way this member has," James finally says softly. "I would like to learn to become a proper Dom and have you be *my* submissive. Not everyday, but I think there is a place in our life where we should or need to have this dynamic. You crave it and I desire it. I'd—we'd be silly to let this opportunity pass us by without further investigation and implementation."

"Really? You'd like to be my Dom?" I breathe the words out, our lips pulling close again. My core is heating at the very idea of having this kind of dynamic play out in my real life.

"Right now there is nothing I'd rather be. But I need some education first. I know in the bedroom I can be dominating but this is different right? Especially listening to your recount from this morning. I loved every last detail. I want that. I want your submission but I realise there are ways and boundaries and I'd like to explore them properly before we play. I want to go all in for this Rosie, not just muddle through it. I want to be how that Dom was to you, I can see how you lit up retelling the experience, this is your thing. I want it too. It turns me on just thinking of all the ways you will submit to me."

My heart, my pussy, everything flutters. I love this man so much. There is nothing I'd rather do than please him. To earn his rewards and caresses. Butterflies swirl in my stomach at the very thought of crawling for James and being at his beck and call.

What has this job done to us? It's wild. I'm selling my body to strangers and living out other people's kinks, James is sharing me. We are making more money than we've ever earnt and now James might become my Dom? This is more than I could ever have imagined.

Before we can speak any further on the subject my son opens his door and yells out asking what is for dinner. And back to reality I go.

16

———

When I arrive at the Clarendon Club on Monday, Sandy, my manager walks into Café Marion like usual for her coffee but this time she asks, "Hi Roxy, can you pop in my office today at 12? Sophie will be ok to cover you for ten minutes."

"Sure Sandy, is everything ok?" I ask nervously. This is only the second time she's asked me and the first was about my probation finishing.

"Everything is absolutely fine, Roxy. I just wanted to have a catch up is all, and check in on how you are doing?"

"Ok, no problem, see you at noon Sandy."

I serve the members like usual, the club becoming busier as the warmer weather approaches with Spring in Melbourne. I still look around and see if there is anyone I know and try to guess what kinds of kinks they're into. You can never look at anyone and tell of course. It would be amazing if the members could wear different colours to show what they're into, but of course what purpose would that serve other than to put my curiosity at bay.

Sophie hustles and bustles with me around the café, we

work like a team—the dream team as we like to joke. I really enjoy her company and it's what I have been missing in my own little business—colleagues. Coming to work at the Clarendon Club is becoming more appealing than going to work in my own business. Maybe working for myself wasn't everything I'd have wanted it to be. Or maybe it's the best of both worlds, working here and then my own business. But with being a play-mate, do I need three jobs? That is what it is becoming. I file those thoughts away for another time. Right now I have the meeting with Sandy to worry about.

"What do you think she wants to talk to me about?" I ask Sophie when we're finally both in the same spot at the same time with a moment to spare.

"Exactly what she said, she wants to see how you're doing is all. Sandy likes to ensure the staff are happy. Happy staff, happy members. Plus, you've had a few playmate jobs now, maybe she just wants to see how you feel about them?"

"Have you had meetings like this with her?" I enquire.

"Oh sure, every few months—even though I've been here nearly two years. It's nice. I don't mind it."

"Have you or anyone had any meetings about stuff that has been bad, like a client gone wrong or something? What if one of my club members complained about me?"

"Is that what is getting you all knotted up right now?" she asks teasingly.

"Well yes. I hate to think I've done something wrong. I mean I don't think so, but what if I did..."

"You need to relax and have some self-confidence. I know you haven't done anything wrong and I know you would have been amazing. Plus, Sandy would have called you into her office straight away and been much more discreet. Those things don't really happen around here, but if they do I can assure you they are dealt with professionally and in my opinion kindly. Sandy is the best."

"Have you ever met the 'management.'" I say making air quotes.

"No I have not. I've even given up guessing now. That is one secret I have not cracked nor anyone else. I don't even know if Sandy knows them or not."

"Really? This whole place is one giant secret, isn't it?"

"Yes, and I'm ok with that. I don't want my parents or my neighbours knowing about this place. I don't want my real-life colliding with our secret life here. Management probably feels the same. They are probably MP's or owners of huge companies who cannot be associated with any kind of scandal."

"Yeah in fairness, not one of us nor the members would ever like to be exposed so I guess that is why it hasn't come out and likely won't."

"Plus I'm under the impression no one would dare leak anything about this club. So maybe they're mafia running it."

We laugh together. And then a chill runs down my neck making the hairs stand up on end.

"People can leave on their own accord though, right?"

"Yes, yes. No murders or disappearances from here. Well, now there was that one girl before you..."

"Stop." I elbow Sophie. "Unless you're telling the truth?"

"I'm kidding. Nothing unhinged has happened on my watch. Everyone just wants to keep their dirty little secrets a secret. Management has a way of ensuring that happens and everyone is happy. Including me. And so should you."

"Oh I am happy. Imagine if the mums at the school gate knew what I did in my 'other job'." I shudder at the thought of how quickly that rumour would travel around the school like wildfire. "I'd have to move."

"You and me both. So chill. Sandy is a good egg. It's nearly time now anyways."

She's right, I check my watch. Ten minutes to go. "Would

you mind if I dash to the loo before I head up to meet Sandy, I suddenly need a nervous pee."

"No worries at all. I've got everything covered here my friend." And with that Sophie shoos me out from behind the bar and I hurry towards the staff bathrooms before heading upstairs to Sandy's office.

I knock lightly before I hear Sandy's voice answer, "Come in Roxy." I push the door open and enter her bright office overlooking the golf greens. Sandy pats the spot next to her on the sofa, "Here take a seat."

Grateful for the relaxed nature of the meeting, I sit on one side of the comfy beige sofa and look at Sandy expectantly.

"How are you Roxy?"

"I'm well thanks Sandy. How are you?"

"I'm really good, thanks, I hear my intuition paid off when we hired you. You've had three Playmates jobs and all have returned extremely positive and enthusiastic feedback. Management are pleased and I've secretly patted myself on the back. How are you finding the Playmates jobs?"

I blush. Sandy would know the jobs I've taken and the things I've done. I suddenly feel embarrassed and she sees it.

"No need to be shy, Roxy, everyone is a playmate here my love, even me. There is no shame or judgement from anyone. Never. Not on my watch. You can be open with me."

My shoulders lower a hair. I know I have no need to be embarrassed, I have no doubt Sandy has seen and heard it all. I just don't speak to many people about it, only Sophie and my husband.

"I have enjoyed my jobs, Sandy. Each time I have not known what to expect but when I'm there with the club members in their homes I feel at ease like it's a role that comes natural to me."

"Indeed, this does not surprise me in the slightest." Sandy

smiles knowingly at me. "Playing along in other people's fantasies unlocks something within ourselves, something we didn't know was there until thrown into the situation and the fantasy. I speak for myself, but I feel like the kink jobs are a bonus of finding out our true selves and desires. Hidden amongst societal constraints in the outside world but in here we offer a safe place to find out our own truths, whatever shape or form they come in."

"How long have you been a playmate Sandy?" I ask not sure if that is a personal question or not.

"Over ten years"

"And you don't get sick of it?"

Sandy giggles. "Not at all Roxy, the type of people we are gravitates us to the jobs we apply for and then we stay because we like to play just as much as our members."

I nod, I think I'm catching on.

"Has there been a job you have enjoyed more than you were expecting?" she asks with a knowing look.

"Yes." I look down at my hands. "I had a submissive job recently and I had to lean on Sophie a bit after because it shook me to my core how much I enjoyed it."

"Ah yes, the reason we assign a buddy/mentor to everyone. The Clarendon is unlike any other establishment in the world. It's hard to be understood unless speaking to someone who knows exactly what you're experiencing and feeling. I know Sophie will take care of you, she's a beautiful girl inside and out. I had a feeling you'd find your calling with that kink. I hope you find plenty more also. Some of our playmates stick to just their own kinks whilst others explore. There is nothing wrong with either, although I imagine each Dom/sub experience will be different with a new partner and the same can be said with different kinks."

I nod, enthralled by Sandy's words. I am beginning to enjoy

being a part of this secret club and any insight and experience offered I'll lap up greedily.

"That brings me to another reason why I asked to meet with me today. Management believe you are ready to have access to the Amber kinks. When you log in today, you'll see that job board is now open for you to apply also. I hope you have just as much fun if not more with this new selection of kinks and fantasies."

"Thank you so much Sandy. I can't wait to have a look and apply," I say not tempering my excitement this time.

"See you again soon Roxy. Take care. And don't forget to keep up your medical screenings each week."

I nod and say goodbye to Sandy and go back down to finish my last half an hour with Sophie in the Marion. I squeal as quietly as I can when I get to her and whisper, "I'm onto the Amber job board."

"Wow already! That's awesome! I thought you had to do six months, but you must be crushing your jobs."

I clap my hands in glee. "I cannot wait to get to my office and see what jobs are posted."

"Oh you'll have fun seeing them. Eye watering but fun! Just don't take any jobs until you've thought properly about them and spoken to your husband—and me if you need to. Some can be a lot, but nothing near the red jobs. Just give me a shout if you have any questions, okay?"

"Ok, I will do that I promise."

The last thirty minutes are over so quickly and Ava and Thomas turn up to relieve us of our roles so we can leave. I hop into my car and drive to my office where I cannot wait until I can load my laptop up and login to the Playmate Portal.

When I'm online I don't click on the Green job page because the Amber job page allows me to click straight through and there are all sorts of kinky jobs waiting to be applied for and booked.

Wednesday 7pm – 4hrs, MM&MM/FP, DP $5,000

Thursday 4pm – 5hrs, FP/MP&FM, Voyeurism $6,000

Saturday 1pm – 6hrs, MM/FP, BDSM $8,000

Saturday 8pm – 4hrs, MM/FP, Sploshing $4,000

Sunday 5pm – 12hrs, MM/FP, Pet Play $15,000

And the list goes on. Which one shall I apply for next…

THE AMBER JOB BOARD

17

———————

My older sister has just turned 40 and threw one of the best 1920s parties I've ever been to. So much so, I don't actually remember getting home and going to bed. Luckily for me, my parents took my children home with them to have a sleepover so that me and James could continue partying until the early hours of the morning.

I must be in the deepest sleep that alcohol has induced me to be in. You know the one where you pass out and wild horses running past wouldn't wake you up. A classic tequila coma.

I am however having one of the most realistic dreams I've ever experienced. I'm floating on something soft, it's nice and cosy and warm. I'm naked, I can feel something so soft between my legs. Is that the clouds? No, not clouds, it's something warm and wet like someone is lapping between my legs. It feels like the most delicious tongue between my thighs. I move my hips upwards in my dream to reach closer to the feeling giving me pleasure. The devilishly naughty tongue works its way in-between my pussy lips to my entrance and then up inside my lips just stopping for a languishing slow lick at my sensitive bud. Again, and again my dream tongue laps and licks at me like I'm the most delicious ice-cream and they are savouring every single taste of me.

My legs are trembling at each tongue stroke that lavishes my clit, wanting more. This dream is without a doubt the most sensual I've ever experienced but damn I need more. This is hell chasing an orgasm. I can't speak or reach out to ask, I'm too deep in slumber. My body is yearning, screaming for more. *Please dream tongue, lap at me faster or something more.*

My dream gods are listening to my prayers, I can feel something entering me, moving shallow in and out of my centre. That's what I need, the something more. An intensity is building inside of me, it's wracking my body full of tension and pressure. The lapping at my pussy moves up so that it's focused solely on my clit. I don't think I can take any more, the pleasure is becoming too much, my nerve endings feel like they're going to combust. But dream orgasm is close, so close I can almost feel it throughout my entire body, building until I cannot take any more and I combust. Nerve endings fire with pleasure rolling over me in beautiful sensual waves of bliss. I'm floating on the cloud even higher than before as the last licks of pleasure stroke my body.

I feel a warm liquid drip out from between my legs as whatever was inside me is removed very gently. This is without a doubt the best dream I have ever experienced. I breathe deeply in my slumber until I feel something much bigger than before nudge my entrance. It's warm and very slowly edges into my body, each tiny movement makes me consider if I'm dreaming or feeling. Can I feel in a dream? Something is slipping deep inside me; I can feel my body accommodating the intrusion and expanding around it. It doesn't hurt, quite the opposite, it feels nice, really nice.

As I lay on my cloud, I feel nothing else on or around me except a warm rod inside me that is silently edging closer and closer to my cervix. I feel full but completely relaxed. Is my dream continuing? Just as slowly, I can feel the rod gently pull out of my body. Oh no, I feel empty, I don't want to feel empty as my core clenches around nothing.

To my relief the rod enters me again, ever so slowly and gently filling me up to the hilt. I like this feeling; I want to keep this feeling like this as I move my hips to keep the intrusion inside me. It works as the rod doesn't leave my core but moves quicker to reach my centre, a whimper escaping me at the sensation.

I hear someone shushing me from somewhere far far away, maybe I imagined it.

I writhe on my cloud; I don't know what is happening, but it feels so good I don't want it to stop. The rod is now moving gently but faster in and out, wracking my body with a desire I don't know what to do with. What is happening to me? The motion and the fullness is beginning to build something deep in my core, it's making me breathe a little faster, making me tip my hips to meet each quiet thrust. My centre is throbbing with an ache that is sparking the most amazing dream orgasm I've ever experienced. And then it's here, rushing through my bloodstream and filling my body with the most out-of-body orgasm I've experienced. I cry out in a moan that almost wakes me but it's too delicious on my cloud floating and orgasming, I never want to wake up. The rod continues to thrust through my climax, stretching it out to an intensity that only heaven would experience.

And then the rod stills, deep into the depths of my core. It pulses covering my insides with hot liquid and I hear the lightest of groans. A man's voice? Or God himself?

I whimper again, what is real and what is dream? I hear a gentle shhh as the rod is slowly removed and a gush of warm liquid flows onto my cloud. Do I need the toilet? Should I force myself to wake up? I'd rather not, it's warm and cosy in my dream, where only good feelings happen. I'll go to the toilet in the morning. I feel heavy in sleep and floaty in body—now is not the time to wake up. I roll onto my side and feel covers pulled up over me. Did I do that?

When I wake up in the morning, my mouth is dry, my eyes are bleary and my head doesn't feel like lifting off the pillow. What a party. I focus my foggy brain and see two baby blue eyes staring at me and a mop of blond hair.

"Morning, dancing queen," comes the husky voice of my husband James. "How are you feeling?"

"I'm feeling like I danced and drank the night away, that's for sure," I croak as I pull my forearm across my eyes now remembering just how much I had to drink last night.

Then the questions barge into my brain one after the other. *How much did I have to drink? Why did I hit the tequilas? Thank goodness I wasn't sick. Or was I sick? When did we leave? How did we get home? When did we get to bed? Did I even have any water last night? But oh-so much fun. Hopefully I'm not the only one who feels like this...*

I look at James a little closer, he doesn't look half as bad as I feel. "How are you doing right now?"

"I'm feeling ok, I had a near miss with the shots and managed to avoid them, unlike someone else I know..."

I cringe. "Oh god, who gave me the shots? I *never* do shots."

"That would be your brother-in-law. If it makes you feel any better, you were in good company with your sister and all her friends. I stuck to beers all night which I think was a good thing so I could order us an Uber home."

"Thank goodness. Clearly I wasn't getting us home."

"And you weren't sick in the Uber so I take that as a win." James laughs good naturedly. I always spew in the taxi home if I've had one too many—which doesn't happen hardly ever at all now I have my own kids, but I certainly let my hair down last night.

Lifting my head I search the bedside tables for a drink,

James reaches up and hands me one from his side. I groan sitting up and sip tentatively. The movement makes me look down and see I'm completely naked. I side eye James.

"Did I take all my clothes off last night?"

"Yep." He grins. "And I couldn't get you to lift your arms to put your camisole on, so...naked it was."

"Oh gawd." I cringe. After gulping the rest of the water down, I move to place it on my bedside table. It's then that I feel the stickiness between my legs.

"Did we...?" I look at James and he is slightly blushing now.

"Did you have any nice dreams last night?" he asks slyly.

I look at him, he's looking coy. I think back and something nudges at my memory—yes, I did have the most amazing dream.

"Yes, I did have a really nice dream. I had two orgasms in my dream. Since when does that ever happen in a dream?" *Am I asking James or myself?* I question.

"Since when you were not really dreaming," he says, watching me closely to see my reaction.

"I wasn't dreaming?" I reply, confused.

"How good was the dream?"

"It was really good. Too good to be an actual dream. It was you wasn't it?" I say in a playful accusing tone.

"Did you like it?"

I think back, it was one of the most erotic things to ever happen to me. Completely violating and opportunistic. I loved every single second of my incapacitated pleasure. I didn't know James had it in him.

"Did I like it? Hmm let me see. I had the most incredible climax from what felt like someone licking me as an ice cream."

James smirks.

"And then someone oh so gently fucked me until I came again." I am bemused. "What made you do it?"

"You looked so hot last night, I wanted you at your sister's, I wanted you even before we left to go to your sister's. Watching you pull on that tiny thong. I couldn't keep my eyes off your arse as you bumped and grinded all night. You are lucky I didn't fuck you in the Uber home."

"Did you like doing it?"

"Are you kidding? It was the scariest and most exhilarating thing I've ever done to you. I didn't want to wake you; you looked so gorgeous lying there prone and open to take whatever I gave you. Your little moans had me almost coming too soon every time you made a whimper. To take whatever I wanted was one of the most arousing experiences of my life." James looks a mixture of guilty and happy.

"I enjoyed it. I mean it, you can fuck me in my sleep whenever you want to James. It was the best dream of my life. If only they were all like that."

"Whenever I want?"

"Yes, whenever you want. In fact, my body is for your pleasure. You can have me whenever and however you want. Use me, take me, I want to be the object of your desire and pleasure, the very thought turns me on."

"You mean I can bend you over any piece of furniture whenever and wherever I want and take my fill?" James asks, looking at me with hooded eyes, a devious smile creeping across his face.

"I mean what I say James. I want you to. I like it, maybe I *need* you to," I say earnestly. I don't know what is going on with me, but I honestly mean it. Things are changing in my head and the way I feel about sex and our relationship. Ever since my new job as a Clarendon Playmate.

"I have no more questions. It is a deal," says James, his expression looking like the cat just got the cream.

"I'd say it's a pretty good deal." I smile broadly back, then I remember my hangover and headache.

"But first, sleep." I yawn and stretch my arms.

"Before you go back to sleep, can you take the kids to Netball and Soccer not this weekend but the following one? I have a full weekend of Dom training I've booked in for in the city."

My eyes light up. I had no idea he was taking it so seriously. "Do you!?" I exclaim, not able to keep the excitement out of my voice.

"Yes." James eyes me smugly, "I want to get it all right, every detail. So I've booked in with the best. I am going to put you through your paces the minute I'm satisfied I know all the rules and responsibilities to keep your cute little butt in line. How does that sound?"

"It sounds amazing James. I really want you to do it. I want to play with you, I want to submit to you. I couldn't think of a more erotic way to spend my time with you."

"That's settled then. I'm looking forward to it myself."

I lie my head back down on the pillow closing my eyes with the widest grin on my face. If James can give me even a fraction of what Master Aaron did from my first and only experience as an official submissive, things are about to get much more interesting in my household. And I cannot wait.

18

I arrived at the Clarendon Golf Club slightly earlier than usual on Monday. I'm not entirely sure how I managed it after dropping the kids at before school care, especially with a two-day hangover looming over me. I'm not used to drinking so much, and certainly not tequila slammers. The thought makes my stomach curdle as I head into the staff room to leave my bag and jacket. I'm already wearing my uniform of a knee-length black pencil skirt and a white blouse. I just need to add my Roxy badge and I'm ready for my shift.

Opening the door, I see to my delight Sophie is also early today. Since the club hasn't officially opened I know we will be alone and don't have to worry about being overheard and breaking the club's strict confidentiality agreement. Miracles do happen!

"Hey Roxy, how are you? How was your sister's bash?"

"Hi Sophie, oh so good, I had an absolute blast, though I'm afraid the suffering afterwards has followed me into today."

"Oh ouch." Sophie cringes, her pretty pixy face screwing up in sympathy. "Don't worry, I had a quiet weekend and feel fresh as a daisy, so I've got your back today."

"Thanks." I sigh, of course she has got my back, she's always got my back. "So, you didn't get up to much then? No jobs or anything?"

"No, not this weekend, I just spent some quality time with Sam, we went to Prahran Market, took a picnic to Albert Park. It was nice actually. I should really do more things like that. I know we get paid extra well for taking the Playmates jobs but it's nice to take a step back and appreciate the things around us and not always put the extra money we can be making first. Does that make sense?"

I smile warmly, I know exactly what she means. "As my dad always said to me: *We work to live, not live to work,*" I say back to her. "I totally understand what you mean. I try and be present with my kids when I'm with them but when I'm not, I constantly feel like I need to be working, our mortgage and the bills are so high, we would have had to move if I didn't get this job at The Clarendon. I still feel like I need to work more whilst I have the opportunity, our mortgage is so high, I'm talking $980,000!! Just under a million dollars! It was fine when it was 0.1% interest rates, but now..."

"Oh yeah, I can see why you need the extra work then. Working here and being a Playmate will certainly help you pay off that quicker than the average person. Did you look on the Amber job board over the weekend?"

"No." I shake my head, "Why, anything good? You not taking any jobs this week?"

"I have a job booked from the Green board, a Daddy kink for tomorrow night. But the reason I mention it is because there are a few interesting ones you might enjoy."

"Daddy?" I ask not sure if I heard her right. Even on the Green board there are plenty of kinks I'm not familiar with.

"Yes Daddy. The job is to be a naughty teenager," Sophie explains, always happy to help me learn new terms and kinks.

"Well that sounds interesting! Have you done that one before?"

"Yes I have, it's naughty and fun all at once. Like you get taken care of like a child but at the same time you let them play with your body, spank you, fuck you and then say 'Thank you Daddy.'"

"Gosh, that is kind of a mind fuck. But I'm not opposed to it." I giggle, Sophie giggles too.

"Me neither!"

"What jobs are on the Amber board? Any you think could work for me?"

"There are two, and they both have decent payments—in the $4-15k mark. That'll help with your million dollar mortgage."

"Hey, it's $980,000 thank you. And wow $15k!" Sophie said the number so easily. She must be used to bigger paydays but that is without a doubt the highest paying job I've come across. Hearing it sends a bolt of excitement through me.

"Haha, well ok. They will at least cover one or two repayments. Listen, both sound weird but hear me out. I've done both jobs and they are unusual but kinky fun."

"Ok," I say, intrigued with a nervous giggle. I really enjoy hearing Sophie's stories and getting her advice. In my mind, Sophie's opinion is the golden standard when it comes to playmate jobs. She hasn't let me down yet.

"First one is called Sploshing."

"Sploshing," I repeat out loud with a laugh. "Are you making that word up?"

"I am not! Bear with me. It's an actual kink I promise you. See Amber is the job board for unusual kinks. Sploshing is food play."

"Ahhh. Funny name for it."

"It is, but that's ok. Think covering you in chocolate spread and being licked from head to toe. Or having to lick whipped cream from places you never thought you might be licking whipped cream from. Also, I should give a disclaimer—food most likely will be inserted into places that it may never have been inserted before if you catch my drift."

"Ok, yep, I catch your drift. Did you enjoy it?"

"I absolutely did enjoy it. By the end, I was full to the brim of food, and that's not including the food in my tummy," Sophie says with a wink.

I want to ask more, all the details, what kind of food. But we only have 5 minutes before we are due to be on shift.

"You make it sound fun. I'm not opposed to it. More intrigued. What about the other job you mentioned?"

"Look out for the Pet Play one. Now that one is a hoot. They'll dress you up as their favourite animal, tail and all. You have to spend the time being an animal and abiding by their every whim. Sexually I mean. And these pet play guys, they're all deviants I swear. Don't judge me but I kinda get off on it. It's so wacky and unusual, and completely filthy, I dig it."

"You mean you have to crawl around on all fours and actually act like a pet?"

"That's exactly what I mean. Collar and all. And who knows what kind of a pet you might be!"

"You didn't click on the job to see?"

"Nah, not anymore. I used to read all the job posts but I feel like when you've read them a few times, you don't need to read them all the time anymore."

"And you didn't fancy doing this job yourself?"

"Sam is taking me away and that job falls across the dates. Sadly. Otherwise hell yeah, I would likely have applied for it. Look, it's not for everyone. But I enjoy them so I thought I'd mention both to you, especially now you have access to the Amber job board."

"Ah thank you so much, I appreciate the heads up on them. I don't know if I'd have gone for them without having even this tiny insight into them. But if you have done them, maybe I can give them a go. I guess management thinks I can handle it seeing as they've allowed me access to apply for these types of jobs."

"You can definitely handle it. If you have any questions about them when you see them, give me a call," Sophie offers warmly. "Come on, we'd better dash now. You can tell me all about your sister's party whilst we work."

"Despite the fact I had the best time, turns out that wasn't the highlight of my night," I say cryptically as we leave. Sophie raises an eyebrow. "I'll tell you about that little endeavour over lunch," I tease, knowing she'll hate the suspense, and on cue Sophie screws up her face and pouts. Her auburn hair falling around her face as she re-does her high ponytail.

"That's four hours away!" she complains and I laugh.

"I'm sorry! It's not a story for the café but I promise it's a good one."

"Sigh," says Sophie dramatically. "Ok, I can wait. But you had better dish the deets the moment we're in the car, I can't be waiting until lunch is served."

And with that we head into the Marion Café and begin our 4 hour morning shift together.

The morning is busy and flies by, in no time at all Ava and Thomas arrive to take over our shifts and we have lunch together. I put Sophie out of her misery and give her the steamy details of my 'dream' experience. I feel like Sophie is a safe person to confide in about work or home. There is no one I would tell in my *real* life about the way James had sex with me in my sleep. They would be horrified but Sophie wasn't the slightest bit phased. I make a note to look out for those jobs myself, although could anyone else be as good as James?

When I get to my office, I feel heavy. Working for myself has lost its lustre since I first started working at the Clarendon, even more so now I'm a Clarendon Playmate. I took the Clarendon to top up my salary and to keep my little business running. But now, I wonder if that was the right decision. Instead of jumping straight into my orders to pack. I open the Clarendon Playmates Portal and click on the Amber job board and start scanning for the two jobs Sophie had referred to. And there they were:

Wednesday 6pm – 3hrs, MM/FP, Sploshing $4,000 I would like to eat my favourite food from your body. I also have a thing for inserting certain food objects into your body and then eating or sharing them with you. I also enjoy joining in and having food lathered over my genitals for you to lick and suck clean. Things will get messy, sticky and downright delectable. This job is a degustation meal of my desires. Are you ready to be served?

Friday 8pm – 12hrs, MM/FP, Pet Play $15,000 Be my man's best friend for an overnight stay. I will have you looking like my pet dog, acting like my pet dog, eating like my pet dog. You will be at my beck and call like the perfect pet, servicing me as I request. I have a collar, dog bed, pet bath, dog bowl, tail & ears. You will be naked other than the items I give to you. I would like blow jobs when I am eating my dinner. I would like to fuck you whenever and however I want. I am good to my pets, take care of them and love them. Can you be my perfect pet?

I probably shouldn't but all I can see right now is $15,000 for 12 hours. *Fifteen thousand dollars.* What would I do for $15k? Could I allow someone to treat me like a pet? Could I be an actual animal? How hard can it be? It makes the Sploshing job look like child's play. If I did both this week, I'd be able to pay $19,000 off my ridiculously large mortgage. Or at least some and a holiday.

I feel a sense of excitement. Where would I ever get the opportunity to work for 15 hours and earn such a large amount of money? I don't want to miss these two jobs, I want to apply for them immediately. But should I? I still need to run them past James, that was the deal for me being a playmate. But he won't mind this once, especially the money. And Sophie said I'd be fine and would be able to cope. She's done both jobs before and put my mind at rest. I mean, how bad can they be? In the end I decide to screenshot the jobs and text them over to James.

I see the message dots appear and disappear, so I know James received the photos. He's clearly wording a big message. I regret not just phoning him or waiting until I got home. Eventually my phone pings whilst I'm finally packing my business orders, and I pounce onto the phone.

"Sploshing is a new one on me, but you love food so maybe that's a match made in heaven? Pet Play sounds extreme. Think carefully about it. It's a long time to be with someone you don't know, 12 hours. You don't need to do this. Do not think about the money. Think about you."

And that's why I love him. I need to think carefully about being with someone for that amount of time. Using my body. Playing with their body. I'm trying to think really seriously but the money is ringing in my ears, flashing behind my every thought. Maybe this is just one of those things I need to experience and worry about it after. I'm certainly not opposed to being treated like an animal. If I'm completely honest, I'm a heady mix of curious and aroused. *That has got to be a good sign,* I think to myself. I know I should be cautious but how will I know if I don't try? I want to try. And the club wouldn't allow the member or the kink to go ahead if it was bad for me... I reply to James:

"The timeframe is long I know, but the idea turns me on. I want to experience it and do both. I admit the money is also swaying me. But I can do it, I want to do it. For us."

James replies: "It's up to you Rosie. I won't stand in your way. As long as you think you can do it, I'll support you all the way."

I reply: "I think I can stomach it; I want to be able to do it. I'm going to apply. Thanks James. I love you."

"I love you too Rose Petal. See you tonight x"

Heart pounding, I open my laptop to apply to both job applications. First the Sploshing one.

Dear Member 759,

I would like to apply to help you bring all your wildest gourmet dreams to life. I am open and dripping for the main course but can't wait to be your starters and dessert. I have no food allergies and a big appetite to try new things. Whatever you might have planned, consider me your enthusiastic kitchen hand.

Yours sincerely,

Roxy

I hit send and move on to the next application. My hands tremble slightly as I pull up the Pet Play application and begin typing. My heart is pounding just from thinking about the job and money.

Dear Member 465,

It would be my honour to be your personal pet for 12 hours on Friday. Feed me, walk me, pat me and clean me. In return I will be your obedient dog to service you in whichever way my master sees fit. Let me please you, be at your beck and call. Let me snuggle up and comfort you, be there for you and fulfil any desire you so wish.

Yours faithfully,

Roxy

I shut the laptop and take a shaky breath. It's done now. I need to switch my brain back into work mode and focus on packing my orders. The quicker they're done, the quicker I can check to see if I've got one or both of the jobs. I really need to speak to James about shutting this little business down. It's becoming very apparent where my heart lies and running this business is not it anymore. I am no longer the same person who started this business 8 years ago.

I feel sad and happy about that as I muse how different I

have become. My dreams of building this business and hiring staff have dwindled as the cost of living has risen year on year and people's spending is at an all-time low. I didn't want to give up my little dream when I took on the Clarendon job but now I feel differently. I enjoy working at the club, I enjoy being surrounded by people. I really enjoy the Playmates role that comes alongside it and even more—the money those jobs can bring. It's hard to get excited about working for myself now, being on my own for the whole day and earning substantially less.

Being a playmate is opening my eyes to so many sexual feelings and desires, within the job and outside of it with James. I am not getting any younger, I almost feel like I need to make up for the times when the kids were far younger and our time together was much less, certainly my desire to even be touched was very low—sometimes buried under the pile of never-ending washing if I'm truly honest.

As I pack the last order, a sense of calm washes over me. Perhaps this is the closure I need, the moment to pivot and embrace what truly excites me. Every job application I send is a step toward a new chapter, one where my passions align with my work, and where financial stability no longer feels like a distant dream.

Reflecting on these changes, I realise it's not just about the money or the thrill. It's about rediscovering myself and what I want from life. The responsibilities of being a mother will always be front and centre, but it's time to reclaim a part of me that has long been dormant.

I need to speak to James at some point this week. I need him to understand this shift in me, although I'm sure he's already aware. I see a change in him too. Navigating this transition together has been heartwarming, his support in me is unwavering and as always, with every challenge that comes my way he's there supporting and cheering me on.

With a deep breath, I return to my laptop and open the playmate portal. There are two flashing replies waiting for me. Both say the word I was waiting for:

ACCEPTED

Now shit is really getting real. I have a food play job and a pet play job this week. Totalling a whopping $19,000. I wonder if I need to book myself a psychologist appointment for after the Friday pet play session. Instead, I decide to see if Sophie is around for a debrief. She always knows how I'm feeling and what I should do. I flick her a message and smile as her reply is almost instant: "Congrats on the two jobs. Call me any time after them if you need. Enjoy. X"

19

———

I check my reflection in the mirror for the millionth time and assure myself I look fine, lovely in fact and every inch of me has been shaved and scrubbed. My phone alarm goes off giving me 10 minutes to say goodbye and good night to the kids before Frank my driver arrives to pick me up as usual.

The kids are sitting downstairs in the lounge eating dinner, James is with them. The kids don't notice as I walk into the light filled living area, but James gives me a low whistle. I'm wearing a white short sleeved shirt, dark pink mini skirt, pastel pink cardigan and pink high heels. I'm going for the candy look. Hopefully looking sweet enough to eat.

The kids look around and ask where I'm going. I've already told them I have an event I'm working at the golf course for tonight, but they never really listen. I give them both a kiss on the head before James stands and walks me to the front door.

He takes a deep breath of my hair and says from behind me, "You look and smell good enough to eat." He spins me around and then starts to undo the buttons on my shirt.

"James!" I exclaim, "What are you doing?"

"I've just remembered I haven't marked what's mine." And

with that, he undoes a couple more buttons before my bra is on display, he reaches into my bra and pulls out my right breast. He leans his head close, and sucks with force just to the right of my nipple.

"Oh my goodness James. What are you doing to me." It's not a question, I know this possessive bear of a man is marking his territory. The things this action does to me. Liquid heat pools at my core. I can't help my response to his actions, I love it. I love that he wants the stranger I'm about to meet to know I belong to someone else and they're just borrowing my body for a few hours. "You just had to turn me on before I have even left the house," I tease into his ear.

"I want this kinky fucker you're about to meet to know who you belong to and why you are already wet. You're wet for me right now?"

I nod. James knows how to play my body to a fine tune. "Always," I reply.

Looking intently at the purpling hickey he just left on my right breast, he seems pleased that it's big enough. He gently pulls the cup of my bra back up over my breast. The white lace doesn't hide the top of the hickey from peeking out. Then he starts buttoning up my shirt again. Kissing me hard on the lips he says, "Run along my little Rose Petal, I believe your chauffeur has arrived." Cheekily, his eyes sparkling he adds, "Enjoy your meal out." As if I'm going for a dinner with a friend.

I laugh as I open the door and walk down the path towards the blacked out BMW. Turning I wave before hopping into the back of the car. I say my usual hello to Frank, tie my blindfold on and Frank turns Smooth FM up as usual. I settle back into the seat and begin to wonder what exactly I will be having for dinner tonight...

I'm not sure how long we are in the car for when Frank pulls to a stop and tells me to take my blindfold off. I blink trying to focus my eyes to see where we have stopped and notice we are in some kind of underground car park. There are only a few cars in the car park, but they are all incredibly expensive looking. A Lamborghini, Porsche Carrera, Bentley. This time Frank gives me instructions. I'm to walk over to the lift and go up to the penthouse. I say goodbye as I climb out of the car and walk over to the lift. The doors open immediately, and I walk inside clicking on the button that says level 12.

In seconds the doors are opening, and I panic a little when I realise I don't know the number of Member 759's apartment. Looking around I realise I need not have worried; there is only one door and it's just swung wide open. Walking outside to greet me is the most devilishly handsome man I have ever seen. In contrast to James' fair hair and baby blue eyes, this man has jet black hair that forms into tight short curls. His pale white skin and green eyes almost make me stop and gape at his beauty. He's not as tall as James, maybe under 6ft but he's one of the most attractively alluring men I've ever seen. When he smiles at me, the smile reaches his eyes and makes his face look even more beautiful.

"Hi, you must be Roxy?" an Irish lilt meets my ears.

"Yes, I-I am. Hi," I manage to stammer.

Warmly he holds out his pale hand that is covered in freckles and says, "I'm Connor. Thank you for coming. I have been looking forward to meeting you all day."

"I've been excited and curious about meeting you all day too," I answer. Feeling slightly more comfortable with his warm welcome. Connor is more friendly in the first minute of meeting him than all the hours I have spent with my last three job bookings. I take Connor's outstretched hand and shake it politely. He shakes back gently and lets my hand go.

"Please come in. I have everything set up." He gestures for me to lead the way, so I tentatively walk inside the door and am greeted by floor to ceiling windows overlooking the city. What I was not expecting is what I find under my feet. Plastic sheeting is covering the plush carpets. My feet make funny squeaking noises as I walk towards the huge open living space coming to stop at the kitchen island.

I take in the apartment which is perfectly modern and expensive looking. Black marble kitchen countertops and island, black leather designer couches and a black glass coffee table. Beautiful modern abstract paintings on the walls. The apartment is sleek and gorgeous. What doesn't quite fit the look is the inflatable paddling pool sitting between the couch and the marble island where I am standing. I turn my questioning eyes at Connor.

"Paddling pool?"

He blushes slightly. "I gave it some thought and came up with the pool idea for dessert. You'll see. I think you'll enjoy it."

I laugh, feeling a mixture of curiosity and amusement. "Well, I must say, that's a first for me," I reply, wondering what kind of dessert could possibly involve a paddling pool. Connor's eyes twinkle with mischief as he steps closer.

"I promise it will be worth it. But first, can I get you something to drink? Wine, perhaps?"

"A glass of wine sounds perfect," I answer, still trying to wrap my head around the unusual setup. As Connor moves to the kitchen to pour the wine, I take a moment to admire the view from the windows. The city lights sparkle against the darkening sky, creating a stunning backdrop for this intriguing evening.

Connor returns with two glasses of white wine and hands one to me. "To new acquaintances and unexpected adventures," he toasts, clinking his glass against mine.

"To new acquaintances and unexpected adventures," I echo, taking a sip of the light, fruity wine.

Connor leads me towards the seating area, and I can't help but glance again at the paddling pool. "So, are you going to keep me in suspense, or will you share what kind of dessert requires such an...inventive setup?" I push, eager for more details of the evening to come.

With a playful smile, Connor sets his glass down and walks over to the fridge, where he retrieves a small box. "All in good time, Roxy. But first, let's begin with starters. Are you hungry?"

I nod, intrigued and eager to begin his dinner plans for the evening. The city lights cast a warm glow around us along with the dim interior lighting, I feel a sense of anticipation building. Whatever Connor has in store, I have a feeling this will be a night to remember.

Placing the box on the marble counter, he walks towards me. I take note of his navy sweater and tattoos peeking out from the neck. He's wearing beige trousers and navy socks. "First let me help you out of your clothes." Walking behind me, he helps me shrug out of my cardigan. Then circling to face me, his fingers begin to undo the buttons on my blouse. Bolts of electricity fly through my bloodstream when his fingers graze my skin. I blush, being so close to such a physically handsome man is making my knees feel weak. He smells like sandalwood and pine and as he gets closer to unfasten the last button I can smell the mint on his breath.

Connor is looking at my chest like he approves and helps me pull each arm out of my shirt before walking around behind me and unzipping my mini skirt. Slowly he pulls it down over my hips, savouring every inch of me he uncovers. I really do feel like a candy he is unwrapping. Soon I'm standing in my white lace panties and bra and pink heels.

Getting onto his knees, he says, "Allow me," and gestures towards my feet. I lift one at a time and he carefully takes each shoe off my feet. Standing again he calmly instructs, "Unfasten your bra," as he steps back to watch as my breasts fall heavy when their support is removed. If there was one thing I was worried about after having children, it was my breasts becoming flat and saggy. Luckily for me, nothing of the sort happened and I am blessed with a matching set of firm D cup breasts.

His eyes are eating my body up as they peruse up and down, finally he says, "Someone has staked their claim on you I can see. It suits you." Raising an eyebrow at the spot where my hickey is exposed, he just smiles knowingly. "I can understand that," he says with a wicked glint in his eyes. "Your panties next please." His Irish lilt sends shivers down my spine as I hook my thumbs into my panties and pull them down. My last scrap of modesty going with them.

Grabbing a cushion off the sofa he places it on one end of the kitchen island and says, "I'd like you to lie down here so I can eat my sashimi from your body." With my back to the island, he puts both hands around my waist and lifts me easily onto the counter top. The marble is cold underneath my bottom and I shudder. I shift my body into the centre and gradually lower my head to rest onto the cushion.

"Bend your knees and place your feet on the edges." I do as he has requested. I am now completely exposed and open, waiting on his kitchen counter. It crosses my mind to wonder if anyone can actually see into Connor's apartment. If they can, they will surely have a feast for their eyes also.

"Perfect, you look gorgeous like that Roxy, delicious without any food. But let's get the food started and see how much more delicious we can make you."

Walking over to something behind me I hear light classical music begin to play, just like you'd hear in a posh restaurant. Connor opens the box he brought out of the fridge and slowly starts layering slices of Salmon, Kingfish and Tuna across my breasts, down my stomach and onto my bare pubic bone. When he's finished. He takes out a small bowel and fills it with soy sauce which he sits just in front of my pussy, so close I can feel the coldness on my folds.

Taking out a set of chopsticks he picks up a piece of salmon between the sticks, brushes the raw fish past my folds before dipping it into the soy sauce and then lifting it to his mouth. I watch as he closes his eyes and enjoys the morsel. My body feels like it's ablaze with desire. I had never considered how erotic it might be to watch someone eat food from my body. Watching him is making desire drip from my pussy. He too is a feast for my eyes, and I'm glad I'm able to watch him eat.

"Your turn," he says. He picks up another piece of salmon sashimi, brushes it again past my folds and dips it into the soy sauce. As he moves it across my body, small splashes of sauce drip onto my skin. "Here, sit up on your elbows and open for me." I move as he directs, some of the carefully placed sashimi falling lower onto my body and I open my mouth as he delicately lowers the raw fish onto my tongue." Never have I been fed so reverently. He watches me as I chew slowly before swallowing. "Another piece?"

I nod and watch as he does the same with another piece, peeling it off my body, brushing the kingfish along my folds and into the soy sauce before placing it on my tongue. Once I've chewed this second piece, I lie back down and watch as he leans over me and pokes his tongue out flat and licks at the different splashes of soy sauce before sucking a piece of kingfish directly into his mouth from my skin.

"You smell and taste magnificent Roxy." Connor smiles hungrily at me. He's enjoying his first dish of his meal.

Once we have consumed every sliver of sashimi and Connor has licked off every remnant of soy sauce from my body, he goes back to the fridge and takes out a cucumber and some baby tomatoes. My eyes follow him as he moves across the kitchen. He takes away the bowl between my legs and looks at my wet centre.

"You're dripping all over my countertop young lady," he says in a low thick voice like he's sharing a naughty secret. "I think you're ready for a palette cleanser." I move onto my elbows and watch as he takes a red cherry tomato from its box, runs it through my moist folds and pops it straight into his mouth. "Hmmmm," he hums to himself as he eats the tomato like it's the tastiest morsel he's ever eaten. "Would you like to try these tomatoes dipped in your desire?" he asks with a taunting twinkle in his eyes.

"Yes please," I reply in a low whisper. I would happily eat anything this man offers me.

I watch as he picks up another cherry tomato, runs it through my folds and down to my entrance. When he decides it's coated well enough in my essence, he walks over to where I'm perched on my elbows and says, "Open your mouth." My mouth falls open at his command and I'm pretty sure more hot liquid leaks out of me.

Closing my mouth around the cold sweet tomato, I taste the muskiness of myself before the sweetness of the tomato. I have never enjoyed a salad item so much as I watch Connor watch me eat it. Connor goes back to my pussy and we share another five tomatoes dipped in my essence each before the box is empty.

Connor then moves his attention to the long fat cucumber that he begins to unwrap the plastic film. "I think we are both going to enjoy this part of the salad. Especially seeing how drenched you are," he muses.

I watch as he lines up the tip of the cucumber and gently edges it into my entrance. I gasp at the cold intrusion and Connor's green eyes flick up to meet mine. When I give him a shy smile, he smiles back at me and expertly rubs my clit as he nudges the cucumber deeper inside me, twisting it as he goes. Never in my life would I expect this to feel so pleasurable. Maybe it's the person looking on so ravenously as he fucks me with a cucumber. Maybe it's his fingers working my clit at the same time as he thrusts the cucumber ever deeper inside me. The filthiness of the entire situation sparks a climax so quickly I almost try to hold it off. My legs quiver and my breathing is coming in short breaths. I have to give in to it as pleasure explodes through my core and I scream out in ecstasy. Connor looks up at me from between my legs with hooded eyes as he rubs out the last of the tremors from my body.

Slowly, he slides the cucumber out of my pussy and a rush of my juices follow and coat the cucumber. Looking me straight in the eye, he moves the cucumber to his face and licks up from his hand to the tip before taking a bite and chewing. I can see him studying my face for my reaction. I gaze up at him as he takes another long lick and bite. "Would you like some too, Roxy?" he asks, his voice now a little more husky. "Your orgasm is a delicacy you wouldn't want to miss out on."

I watch as he walks towards me and holds out the cucumber. I poke my tongue out and he moves the cucumber so I can lick from his hand to the bitten top before I take a bite myself. The cucumber tastes musky with my cream coating it but crisp and fresh as an aftertaste. Connor holds it up to me to lick and bite again and between us we lick it clean and bite it until it's gone.

"I'm going to help you off this counter now and into my little paddling pool over there. Fun awaits us."

Connor watches as I push myself up to sitting, swing my legs so they dangle off the island bench before he picks me up from my waist like I weigh a feather, my tits in his face for a long moment before he lowers me down onto my feet. "Go grab your wine by the sink, sit in the pool cross legged. I'll get the next dish ready."

My eyes follow Connor around the kitchen as he takes out a large bowl from the fridge and puts it into the microwave. He moves with familiarity around his kitchen whilst I sit cross legged, completely naked sipping my wine. This is up there as one of the most bizarre and hot things I have ever done in my life. I focus on sitting with my back up straight trying to avoid the stomach pouch slouch.

The microwave pings, Connor grabs some oven mitts and takes the bowl out of the microwave and places it onto the island bench. Stirring the contents he explains, "This is a garlic, chilli and tomato spaghetti dish. I haven't overheated it so it shouldn't burn. I'll give it a couple of minutes to settle down. How are you doing?"

"I'm going well, thank you," I smile at his interest in me. "It smells yummy."

"I can promise you it tastes as good as it smells." I watch as he pulls his sweater over his head and his toned abs ripple before my eyes. A tattoo of a phoenix covers his pale freckled hairless chest; his body looks like a true work of art. A pillar of taut muscles, I watch as his thick arms pull down his trousers to leave him in socks and boxers. Pulling off both socks he decides to stay in his black boxers. He opens a drawer, pulls out some cutlery, taps the bowl to check the temperature before walking towards me sitting in the paddling pool sipping my wine. He places the bowl between my naked pussy and folded legs before taking my glass and placing it back onto the kitchen counter.

"You look delectable sitting there naked and waiting for your next course. I can't wait to feed you."

Connor kneels in front of me, spins a fork into the spaghetti pasta and twirls it before me. Lifting the fork he says, "Open for me Roxy."

Obediently I open my mouth and he places the tasty tomato pasta into my mouth. There is too much and I bite down over the dish but the long strands of warm pasta run down my chin and across my chest before sliding down past my pussy. My initial response is that I need to wipe myself clean as I chew the al dente pasta. As I lift my hand to wipe, Connor catches me and says, "Uh uh. Don't wipe. I want you as dirty as possible."

"Okay," I smile, watching as Connor twirls more pasta onto his fork and into his own mouth, not getting even the tiniest rogue line of pasta down himself.

Again, he twirls a large forkful of pasta and feeds me, more pasta slides down my body and ends up pooling between my thighs. I am becoming increasingly dirtier whilst he is sitting there almost immaculate. I don't miss the giant bulge in his boxers and wonder when I will get to play with him tonight.

Once the bowl is empty, Connor places it outside the paddling pool. He lowers his head down and sucks each piece of runaway pasta from between my legs before lapping up the spilled sauce down my chest, across my stomach and over my mound. I am literally being cleaned by his tongue and dear god, his tongue is sending me wild. Every warm swipe edges me closer to a building sensation from deep in my core. He seems to be revelling in the process until I'm wet from his saliva but clean from the pasta sauce.

Satisfied he sits back on his haunches to admire his cleaning work. "I think we are ready for dessert." Standing he takes the empty bowl and leaves it in the sink before opening the fridge and taking out a giant cream cake and large bowl of red jelly. I screw up my face a little. That is a lot of dessert.

Walking back over to me he places the cake next to me in the paddling pool. He gives me a wicked grin and I wonder what he's up to. He walks back over to the large glass bowl of jelly and places that on the other side to me. Now his handsome face looks devilish again. He tucks his thumbs in his boxers and pulls them down stepping out of them. His creamy white, long cock hangs solid and heavy. I gasp at the size of it. No wonder he's been hiding it from me so far. Smirking, he says, "Stand up." Which I do, forcing my eyes to meet his and resist the temptation to stare at his impressive cock.

I watch him carefully wondering what he wants me to do next.

"Stand in front of the cake and face me." I do as he asks.

"Sit on the cake."

"Sit?" I falter.

"Yes." He grins at me. "I want you to sit in the middle of the cake. I want to watch as the cake goes everywhere. In every crease and fold and crevice." Connor licks his lips.

"Okay..." I say uncertainly. "Now?"

"Right now, please. Legs slightly apart."

I do as he instructs, I move my feet apart and I lower my naked bottom until I feel the sponge, cream, chocolate crumbs and jam go into places food has never been before. I keep lowering until my bottom hits the base of the pool and cake is surrounding my hips and lower body. It squishes and squelches and smells delicious.

I look at Connor who is now looking at me, hunger in his eyes. This is what he's been building up to. He prowls over to me and without breaking our eye contact, steps into the pool, gets down on his knees and with one hand reaches for my head pulling my mouth to his. Connor begins to kiss me like he's trying to devour me, his lips moving as his tongue dips further and further into my mouth. Cake is beginning to mush around me, I can feel it pushing further between my folds.

As Connor pulls away for a breath, I look down to see his erection has also been dipping into the cake that is surrounding me. My mouth waters. He sees me looking and nods towards me. "Clean the cake off me, Roxy."

I lick my lips as my reply as I push him back onto his bottom against the side of the paddling pool, his legs spread around me. I peel my bottom from the mushy creamy cake around me and lean forward onto my knees to lick from the base of his shaft up to his tip. The cake tastes like a Victoria vanilla sponge and oh boy does it taste good on him. I lick and suck his bald balls clean, and then continue licking up and down until my face is covered in cream and jam. I lick the beads of pre-come from the tip before sucking him down fully, right to the back of my throat.

He groans out loud and pulls me off his cock. "I'm going to come down your pretty throat if you do that again and I still have plans for you." Leaning forward he takes my face in his hands and begins to lick the jam and cream from around my mouth and sucking it off the tip of my nose. This shouldn't turn me on so much, but the sensations around me and the pleasure from him licking me is turning my insides into jelly like the bowl I'm sitting next to.

"Your turn," is all Connor says before pushing me back into the creamy cake with yet another squelch. Cake is now all up my back as my legs land wide open. Connor licks his lips before moving onto his knees and bending his head down to my pussy. I watch as his tongue peeks out to lick from my arsehole to my clit and I moan.

He pulls up, cream and jam and chocolate flakes stick to his nose and he smiles like this is his happy place. "This is the best way to eat cake, don't you think?"

"Yes," I moan as he dips his head back down and laps at my arsehole again and again before moving his tongue lapping around my pussy but not getting anywhere near close enough to the spot where I want him.

"This cake tastes divine on you. I can't wait any longer to eat it out of your pussy." And with that his head moves back down between my legs and he laps from my entrance to my clit making me buck in surprise and pleasure. His teasing has made my every nerve ending fire with anticipation. He diligently licks out my folds and deep inside me, cleaning me out whilst making liquid heat begin to pool from my core.

I need more and he knows it. He seems intent on licking and sucking everything below my clit until my pussy is clean. He finally moves to my sensitive throbbing bundle of nerves and begins circling his tongue around it, then over it and lapping at it again and again, applying more and more pressure before nipping down on the bud with his teeth and I explode, pleasure ripples through my entire body and I lay back fully into the cake, the moisture of it engulfing me as I float on a high that has me seeing stars.

When my clit becomes sensitive Connor stops licking, lifts his head with a satisfied smile, and moves his body over mine lowering his hard cock to my entrance. With one arm, he wipes his face across his forearm. I tense as he attempts to enter me knowing his size is going to be a big stretch. Seeing my hesitation he says in my ear, "It'll fit I promise, I'll edge it in slowly, like this, see." And I feel my slick inside stretching around him as my walls adjust to the size of him.

With small slow thrusts, I begin to feel the full size of him filling me up. He is being really gentle with me, and I reach out to bring his head lower to mine and he kisses me passionately. We share a moment of just us, connected as one and it feels nice. When we break apart, Connor slowly pulls out and then thrusts deeper, so deep he's hitting the back of my walls.

Connor then scoops out a handful of cake and rubs it into my chest, coating my breasts and nipples in a thick cream and sponge. Holding his weight with one hand, he continues to slowly thrust deep inside me, using the other he collects more cake and rubs it into my neck. Where my head lays on the edge of the pool, he scoops a handful more cake and rubs it over the top of my head. This man is coating me in cake whilst he fucks me. When he's satisfied that I'm suitably coated in cake, he reaches for the jelly, a dark desire emanating from his eyes. He scoops out a hand and rubs it over my stomach, up over my chest and into my neck. Slowly moving in and out of my body as he does it. Scoop after scoop until he's rubbed the jelly into my hair, it's running down my face and down my neck.

Lowering his head he licks at my face and neck sucking off the strawberry smelling stickiness. He's thrusting deeper and harder but still slowly, drawing out his pleasure as the pure depravity of his desires starts to build my own orgasm.

I am a complete mess of cake and jelly, it's coating my entire upper body, face and hair. The cold sensation of the food is then outweighed by the heat of Connor's body pumping into me relentlessly and his hot mouth, licking and sucking at me. When he bites down on one of my nipples after sucking at it mercilessly I fall apart around him, another climax triggering throughout my core. My moans of senseless pleasure tip Connor over the edge and he lets go entirely, groaning so loud I blink my eyes back open to watch him come undone. He stills his throbbing cock inside me and unloads for what feels like forever. Still balancing on one arm, he lowers his head to my neck and breathes into me, "That was incredible."

It feels strange to have this beautiful specimen of a man lying across me having what feels like a more intimate moment than actually having sex with me. It's a bit of a head fuck but I move one sticky hand along his backside and up his back. I'm not sure if I'm caressing his body to bring him comfort or me. But I just try and enjoy the moment because this evening's experience has been heavenly.

Slowly Connor unsticks his chest from my body and pulls his softening cock gently out of me. Smiling down at me he finally says, "You Roxy, are one hot, sticky mess. Come, let me wash you before your ride returns for you."

I watch the thick muscles in his legs as he stands and holds out both hands to pull me up which I gladly take. He pulls me up and I hear cake and jelly falling off my bottom back into the pool. "Now you know there was method to my madness with the plastic floor coverings. Follow me this way."

Connor holds out a hand which I gladly take before I slip on whatever is currently coating my feet. He leads me along the plastic sheeting to a huge bathroom with a double shower. He lets go of my hand to turn both jets on and waits while they both heat up. "In you go, Roxy." And I'm so glad to feel the water rinse down on my gloopy sticky skin. I enjoyed every second of the sploshing sex but afterwards, I'm not loving the stickiness. "Here, let me help you with your hair."

I smile up at him, "Thanks."

"It's the least I can do after rubbing so much of it in your hair." His cheeks turn a light pink as he reaches for the shampoo, moving to stand behind me. "I may have gotten a touch out of control with the dessert, but you looked so beautiful all slicked and caked up. Good enough to eat."

Connor massages and lathers my hair from behind and I work on rubbing off as much cake and jelly from my arms and upper body. Once Connor is satisfied my hair is free from lumps and sugar, he runs conditioner through the ends and goes under his own spray to get clean. I wash the lower half of my body, taking extra care to ensure the water washes away any lingering icing or jelly in my folds, rinse the conditioner out and turn off the tap. Connor points to a towel rail and I pull a giant fluffy black bath sheet around me. It's warm and cosy—the towel rail must be heated. I pat myself dry and then pat my hair down watching the handsome Irishman finish in the shower as he watches me get dry. I go to walk back to the lounge for my clothes but he calls out, "Roxy, your clothes are there by the sink."

I hadn't noticed him carry the clothes in but maybe he did it earlier. I carefully get dressed and am nearly fully clothed as he turns off the shower and wraps a towel around his waist. Water runs down his expansive tattooed chest and drips from the ends of his curly black hair down his beautiful chiselled face. Oh this man.

"Thank you for dinner tonight Roxy, you were delectable. I enjoyed every single course."

"Thank *you* for dinner tonight, it was quite an unforgettable and yummy experience. I'm not sure I'll ever forget it. Or look at a cucumber in the same way again," I giggle.

He grins at me, like a happy puppy. I grin back at him.

"I think your ride will be waiting for you, I tried to make sure you had enough time to be clean and not stick to the seats on your way home."

"And I'm truly grateful for that." I chuckle.

"I'll show you out."

"Thank you, Connor." He leads me out of the bathroom, past the paddling pool filled with cake and jelly and I say, "I will always be reminded of our evening together when I see these paddling pools."

"Me too," he smirks as we get to the door. He holds out his hand, "It's been a pleasure, Roxy."

"It really was Connor. Thank you. Goodbye."

He leans forward and gives me a light dusting of a kiss on my cheek as he shakes my hand.

"Goodbye Roxy. Until next time."

"Until next time." I smile as I release his hand and head towards the lift.

When I get out at the basement level, Frank is waiting for me like clockwork. *If only he knew what I had just been doing 30 minutes earlier,* I think to myself. No one could ever guess.

When I arrive home, I climb the stairs, the whole house is asleep. Which is perfect. I check in on both my peacefully sleeping children. I then get myself ready for bed. James is sleeping peacefully on his back, and I climb in quietly and snuggle up to him. I'm glad James is more relaxed about my jobs now and no longer feels the need to wait up for me. Despite having just spent the last three hours with a dark-haired god of an Irishman, nothing beats getting home to where my heart is. I close my eyes and I'm asleep before he stirs and notices me next to him.

20

———

Two short days later and I've come down from the high of three orgasms with Connor and have been worrying myself into a stupor over my 12 hours of being a dog. I'm sure it'll be fine; I'm looking forward to it. But what if it's awful? He's awful? Common sense tells me he didn't sound awful, and Sophie was the one to tell me about pet play. She has always got my back, I trust her. I just need to get on with it and try and enjoy it. All my other jobs have been mind-blowing and unimaginable but so satisfying. The chances are this one is no different.

I am unsure what to wear seeing as the job description said I'd be naked, so I opt for an all-in-one black romper that is cute and fitted to my curves. If paired with a pair of black ears and a tail, I'd look like a divine cat.

As I pull the zipper up on my romper, I take a deep breath and look at myself in the mirror. The reflection staring back at me seems ready, but inside, a mix of excitement and anxiety churns. Today's experience is uncharted territory, and the anticipation is almost palpable. I grab my handbag, checking I have my phone and a few essentials, and make my way out of the bedroom.

I pop my head into the kids' rumpus room which used to be my home office before I moved into my own office outside of home. There is a computer in one corner facing the window where my son is currently sitting with an iPad to the left of him and a headset on. There is a sofa in the left corner where my daughter is currently lounging with her iPad on her lap and a movie on the TV.

I walk over to her first and kiss the top of her head. I've told the kids I'm going to a work event in the city and staying overnight there. I'll be back in time to take my daughter to netball in the morning. My daughter asks me questions about who I'm meeting so I have to think on my toes but my son happily waves me off with a 'bye mum, have fun' as I hear his friends chatter on the iPad as they all play a Fortnite game together.

I head into our large open plan lounge to find James sitting over his laptop at our dining table. He looks up. "Time to go?" he asks, his eyes warm and knowing when they meet mine.

"Time to go," I breathe out. James reaches out a hand for mine and squeezes it.

"You look nervous."

"I am nervous," I reply

"You are going to be just fine. You have enjoyed all the other jobs so far. This one is going to be no different."

"I know..." I trail off.

"What is your safe word Rosie?"

"Neptune."

"You use it the minute you want to tap out and leave. You owe them nothing. You don't have to do anything you don't want to do. Your well-being is more important than anything. More important than the kinky dude who wants you to be his dog and whatever else he has planned for you ok?"

"Ok." I try and give a reassuring smile. James has said this to me plenty of times since I was accepted for this job. I'm not nervous for the role I will need to play, it's more being there so long. I've never been on a job longer than four hours. Twelve hours is next level and we both know it.

The chair James is sitting on scrapes along the floor as he stands to take me into a giant bear hug. "I love you," I hear him say into my hair. My heart tightens in a vice, am I causing him pain and worry?

"Are you ok with me doing this?" I ask as I pull back and look into his baby blue eyes. His blond tousled hair falls around his face as he looks down at me.

"Yeah I'm fine. It's always you who I hope will be fine by the end of it."

"Me too," I agree. "He won't harm me. I have to keep reminding myself, it's going to be a money can't buy experience. I know I'll enjoy it. I just need to get over my nerves."

"Then take care of yourself and have fun. I'm curious on this one myself. Maybe I could be into a little soft pet play when you return. I'm always here for some pussy play." He smiles down at me and my stomach does a flutter. He's being playful but I know he's also serious. I wouldn't be opposed after I experience the real thing if I enjoy it.

"Is my ownership mark still there?" James asks, his eyes darkening with possessiveness.

"Yes, it hasn't gone anywhere since Wednesday."

"I think I need to give you another one, just to make sure." And with that, he unzips the front of my romper, my breasts hang naked underneath. Picking up both breasts in each hand he squeezes and admires them. "I think this breast needs one too." He bends his head to my left breast and sucks deeply to the side of my left nipple. When he's spent enough time sucking to leave an angry purple hickey, he pulls back to see my pair of matching purple love bites. "You're mine Rosie, and that kinky fucker will now be well aware I'm only lending you out for a night."

I love this side of James, standing there confident, his eyes devouring me, comfortable in his complete possession of me, body and soul. I begin to pull my zip up and cover my breasts back up.

"I think Frank will be outside waiting for me, I should go," I lift my head to brush a chaste kiss on his lips, but James beats me and his lips are on mine. He kisses me hard on my mouth, deepening it with every stroke of his tongue, moving both hands to cradle my head until I am putty in his hands. When it feels like he's sucked out my soul, he pulls back and looks me in the eyes.

"I'll be thinking of you Rose Petal, every minute of every hour you're gone. Be a good pet and come back to me. I love you."

"I love you too," I say almost into his mouth, our heads are still so close. "See you tomorrow." And with that, James releases my head, and I walk towards the door. I turn just before I close the door behind me and see he's standing staring just where I left him.

It's moments like this that make me feel so conflicted. Is this right what I am doing? I know that society would say it's cheating but to me its work, sex work yes. But it's still just a job, one that pays well and helps out our lives.

I see Frank waiting for me at the end of our driveway as expected. I pull open the door and settle into the seat putting my blindfold on as usual. It's 7pm, as I was informed we are an hour away from our destination tonight, so I have plenty of time to reflect on my choices and what I'm about to walk into. I remind myself I do want this, whatever *this* works out to be. I lie my head back onto the headrest and listen to the love songs playing on the radio.

I've just begun to feel sleepy when the car pulls to a stop.

Frank instructs me to remove my blindfold, which I do and I peer up at a barn looking house. There is nothing and no one else around. I can't see street lighting or any other lights to suggest there could be any neighbours around. Only the security lighting from the front door shining a beam of light on the short, gravelled pathway.

I say thanks to Frank and wish him a good night. I know he'll be right here tomorrow morning at 8am. My palms begin to sweat a little as I walk towards the big old oak door with a brass knocker. I'm just contemplating lifting it when I think I can hear deadbolts on the other side. I wait and I am correct, the door slowly opens, and a tall, wide shouldered, red headed, bearded man is looking at me. He beams at me, and I cannot hold back my own smile back at him.

"Roxy, do please come in," comes his deep raspy voice.

"Hi," I say brightly. I know whatever is about to take place will be unusual, but this man reminds me of a friendly lumberjack and almost sets my mind at ease. I know by now you can never have expectations on who has booked your job because they always turn out to be the complete opposite.

"I'm Freddie," he introduces himself and holds out his hand, I place mine in his. He shakes it twice before dropping it again. His hands feel rough, calloused, like he uses them for labour of some kind. He is wearing a checked shirt, rolled up at the sleeves, open at the collar and blue jeans. When I look up at him expectantly, I notice his dark blue eyes and pillowy lips. He reminds me of someone I'd expect to see outside chopping wood or something.

"Please, follow me, let's go into the sitting room." He turns on his heels and leads me through a series of beautifully decorated hallways making me realise just how large this house is. The floors are carpeted, and the ambience of the low lighting and cream carpets makes the house feel fresh and cosy. I follow Freddie into a room with cream walls and mahogany furniture.

Freddie walks up to a three-seater sofa and holds out his hand indicating for me to sit. I do as he suggests and watch as he too sits down facing me.

"Thank you for coming today and agreeing to spend the next 12 hours with me. I just wanted to go over a few things. Firstly, do you know your safe word?"

I nod, "Yes, Neptune."

"Ok great. Please use it if and when you need to. I know how we will spend the next 12 hours will be a role play of sorts and not what you may have experienced before. Frank is only a phone call away and the job will be paid pro-rata to the hours worked/played." I nod, listening quietly as he continues, "I'm sure you're well aware that I would like you to be my pet dog. I would like you to fully encompass being my pet along with some physical and sexual encounters." My eyes follow his movements as he speaks confidently like he's in a business meeting with his hands resting on his thighs.

"As mentioned, I would like you to be naked with some dog adornments. You will be my pet dog and I will be your master. When we get into our roles the dynamic will be simple: I will give you instructions and you obey. You will not speak a word during our time together, excluding your safeword of course. If you need anything, you will bark and do your best to convey what you need. When we get into our roles, I will show you where you will be eating and sleeping.

"When I eat, you will suck my cock under the dinner table until I come. You are to lick me clean once you are finished. When you are finished, you will be able to eat your food from the dog bowls provided. I would like to bathe you and mount you doggy style before curling up to watch a movie before we go to sleep. We will awake early to do a similar routine before we say goodbye. How does that sound to you?"

"I-I think it sounds great," I reply, not knowing what else I should say. I can hardly back out now. Everything he has said so far isn't too far out of the realm of what I had imagined. Maybe not the barking but I can work around that, it sounds like $15,000 of doggy role play to me.

Freddie's eyes smoulder at me, his pillowy lips curl into a wide grin. "Excellent. Let's get started. Please note, I expect obedience and will punish or reward you like any other pet." He smiles at me, the confidence and dominance in that expression clearly representing the authority of his position and what he is expecting in mine. "Please take off your clothes."

My blood heats and my pulse quickens. This is it. I either get naked and be Freddie's dog for twelve hours or I go home. My instincts are telling me I'm safe and I can do it. I remember Sophie's words that she recommends the experience, so I begin to undo the zip down the front of my romper and peel down the sleeves over my shoulders and arms. My breasts hang full and heavy seeing as I didn't wear a bra. I look up to see Freddie's eyes following my every movement sitting back on the sofa with desire written all over his face. I see him take in the hickies James left on my breasts as he looks from one to the other but he doesn't comment on them, only one side of his lips quirk, in approval? I remove my shoes, top half now completely naked. I stand and shimmy the romper down over my hips and pull one leg out after the other until I'm left in just my black silk thong. I pinch the sides and pull the fabric down to expose my naked mound and pussy before bending down and picking up the clothes to lie across the sofa arm.

Freddie reaches down his side of the sofa and picks up a shoebox sized box and lifts the lid off. He stands and lifts a red leather collar and walks towards me. I catch a glimpse of the name tag and am surprised to see my name etched into the shiny gold circle. Without saying a word, he lifts it to my neck and fastens the buckle at the back. My long brown hair is pulled back into a ponytail and he seems to approve.

Walking back over to the box, he lifts out a headband with

two brown perky ears attached, which he turns and places onto my head. Going back to the box he pulls out two mittens and knee pads. "Hold out your hands please, Roxy." I obediently lift my hands up in front of me. He pulls on one thick cotton mitten that has brown fur on the top and fastens it around my wrist before moving onto the next one.

Freddie then picks up a knee pad and bends onto his knees. When his eye-line is just below my breasts he says, "Lift your foot Roxy." I do as I'm told and he pulls the elastic up over my foot, up my calf and settles the padding over my knee. I watch as he carefully does the same with my right leg. This can of course mean only one thing: crawling. Standing once again he pulls out a tube and a tail. "Now the pièce de résistance. Please get onto your knees now Roxy, you will have no need to stand again for the next twelve hours. Lean over the sofa whilst I place this plug in your arsehole. It will fit snugly inside and has a flat base so you can go about the house like it wasn't there. The tail is super soft so you shouldn't have any problems sitting for me." He opens the cap and squirts some lube onto the plug.

I drop to my knees as Freddie requested and lean over the sofa with my forearms. I can feel his hands as they part my arse cheeks and line up the plug to my tight hole. Slowly, he adds pressure to it and pushes it steady and deep until my back hole allows the intrusion and suctions it in with the bulb nestled inside and the tail gently brushing the back of my legs. My face burns, I feel utterly humiliated. *Is this my limit or can I work through this?*

"Now my little pet, your metamorphosis is complete. Please get down on all fours so I can see you."

This is it. I have sunk to the lowest of my depravity. Nothing has ever made me feel so completely naked and out of my comfort zone. I am now this man's pet dog. Can I do this for real? For twelve hours?

I lower myself from the sofa and go on my mitten covered

hands and knees, my butt in the air and the fluffy tail flopping between my legs. I crane my head to look up at Freddie. As my eyes trail up his legs I see the giant hard length in his jeans. I continue up to his face, where my eyes meet his. They are staring back at me, dark and hungry. It pleases him seeing me on my hands and knees.

I try to watch as he walks around me, admiring my naked body. When he's standing back in front of me, he orders, "Sit up." I move my weight onto my haunches and sit back onto my heels with my mitten covered hands like paws bent in front of my chest. "When I tell you to sit up, I would like you to hang your tongue out and pant for me."

Oh god. Is this too far? Can I do it? The utter depravity of sticking my tongue out and panting for him is beyond the humiliation I thought I could handle. I shut down these thoughts, determined to stay positive, *Think of the money, think of the $15,000*. I open my mouth and let my tongue hang out and begin panting. I want to be his obedient pet, I need to act like it. I can do this.

Freddie's smile lights up his dark blue eyes. He reaches out his hand and pats my head in long sensual strokes. "Good girl, Roxy." Every reservation and humiliated thought melts from my mind. His praise courses through me hitting my core and sparking right in my clit. He keeps stroking his large calloused hand from my forehead down to the back of my head where he stops at my low ponytail. I get the feeling this was a test and I just passed. I still have my tongue hanging out and am panting, my naked chest rising and falling.

Freddie's hand stops stroking my head and he tickles under my chin and then bending down himself onto his knees he runs his hand down my chest and across my left breast and then my right. He gingerly strokes and caresses each breast with both hands before moving down and stroking my stomach. Pulling away he says to himself quietly, "Plenty of time to play later." Before standing and reaching for one last item in the box. A red leather leash. He clips it onto my collar where my name tags hangs and says to me, "On all fours Roxy, it's dinner time. Follow me." I lower down onto my knee pads and paw mittens and slowly follow him through the room and out into the hallways.

Never in my wildest dreams would I ever have considered myself being someone's naked pet crawling around their house wearing a tail and collar and being led by a leash. The idea is so wrong, but as I follow my master, something inside of me begins to heat up. The depravity of the whole situation is turning me on like nothing I have felt before. If we are going to dinner, I know I have to suck on my master's cock before I can eat my own dinner.

Freddie walks slowly to ensure I can keep up and we walk together side by side into a large dining room. I look around the sparse room but can only see from all fours. There is only one chair at the head of the table. Freddie unclips my leash. "Sit." He commands and points to where I am currently on all fours. I do as he asks and sit on my back legs, tongue out panting. "Good girl, you catch on quickly my Roxy girl." Again, I am rewarded by him stroking my hair and it feels like the most sensual touch I've ever been granted. I preen and enjoy his strokes before he pulls his hand away and sits down at the table.

I can hear what sounds like a lid being lifted from a plate and I take that as my cue to get back onto all fours and crawl towards him, under the table and stop between his knees. They're open and I run my cheek along the inside of each of his thighs, fully absorbed into my role. I don't just want to be Freddie's pet dog, I want to be the best dog he's ever had. As I nuzzle my face closer and closer to his crotch, I can feel the length of him grow down his right trouser leg. I use my teeth over his jeans and nibble lightly through the fabric and I hear a groan above me at the table. I raise my paws and attempt to undo his button but it's no use. He must have expected this, as he places his cutlery onto his plate with a clink and reaches his hands down under the table to undo the button and zipper, pulling his cock free from his trouser leg.

His meaty, veiny cock glistens at me surrounded by light blond curly hair. I lick my lips and hold it as best as I can in my paws as I lick from base to tip over and over again before swirling my tongue around the underside of his head. I lick up and down just under the sensitive tip like I'm lapping at milk with a flat tongue before raising fully onto my knees and taking him into my mouth. I ease slowly down onto him, raising and lowering as I take in more of his length until I eventually hit the back of my throat. I raise my head up a little before forcing myself back down hard onto his cock and I hear him groan from above me. Up and down I move, working my wet mouth along his length, saliva pooling down my chin and at his base. Every time his cock hits the back of my throat I feel his legs quiver some more. I hear his cutlery placed back down onto his plate again as he focuses on his impending climax. Knowing he is close, I move faster and try and go as low as I can without gagging too much when I feel his big hands move over my head and he holds me still impaled on his cock right up in my throat as I feel his cock throbbing his release down the back of my throat. I feel his body shift in the seat as he arches his head back and groans, "Fucckkkk."

When I feel his cock stop throbbing and his hands move away from holding my head in place, I lift off his cock and begin to lap up the last drops of come from his slit before lapping up all the saliva that has pooled at the base of his cock. Once I finish, I nuzzle my head against his thighs to let him know I'm finished. He understands my signal and tucks himself back into his jeans and does them back up.

"Such a good girl, Roxy, come out from under the table and

sit next to me." I wipe my glistening mouth and chin with my forearms and follow his instructions obediently crawling out from under the table and sitting on my back legs, panting with my tongue hanging out. "That was perfect, my beautiful girl," says Freddie as he lovingly strokes my hair. He reaches from in front of him, lifts the top of a silver cover and below them are two dog food bowls. One with what looks like chopped up food similar to what is on his plate and the other filled with water. Freddie lowers them both to the floor in front of me.

"Good girl Roxy. Now eat."

I eye the dishes and wonder how I am going to go about this. I have no choice but to move back a little, lower down onto my elbows and forearms and put my head into the bowl. The food smells delicious; it's chopped up roast potatoes, roast chicken, vegetables and gravy. I put my mouth over the food but there is no way I can get any into my mouth without sticking my nose in too. So that is what I do. I lower my head, scoop out a mouthful of food with my tongue and sit back slightly to chew and swallow. As I begin to get used to the fact that I'm eating directly with my face in the bowl, it occurs to me I can't hear my master's cutlery moving on his plate. I sit back as I'm chewing and look up to see Freddie watching me, enjoying what he is watching. *Is it my total humiliation he is getting off from or the complete degradation of the situation?* I wonder. Even I am beginning to get off on the situation. I return to my dinner, knowing full well how much food must be covering my face by now. Once I have licked the bowl clean, I shuffle my body over and begin to lap at the water bowl. It's trickier but I manage to suck up the water instead.

Once I have finished my meal and water, I crawl closer to my master and nuzzle up at his leg with my head.

"Good girl Roxy, you ate all your food. You are such a good girl, let me see your face."

I sit up on my heels with my hands bent in front of my chest like paws.

"You messy pup, you have food all around your face. I think it's time to give you a bath." And with that, he stands, picks up the leash from the table and fastens it back onto my collar and begins to lead me back out of the dining room.

This time Freddie leads me down the hallway and up the main stairs. I take my time and end up moving one step at a time climbing the steps. It's been over 30 years since I climbed the stairs like this and I have no intention of making it a repeat occurrence in my future.

Crawling past the first two closed doors, Freddie shows me into a sprawling white bathroom with a huge tub sitting under a large window. From my position on the floor, I can see out the window and up into the night sky. I wonder what my ancestors in the stars would think looking down on me like this. I hope they're watching someone else.

"Please use the toilet over there," Freddie says and points to a white porcelain toilet to the right of the tub. I blush but know I would feel better using it before I'm washed. I crawl over to it and stand for the first time in over an hour. I sit down trying to keep my tail out of the bowl and wish for my body to pee in front of this man. I watch as he bends over the tub to put the plug in and turn on the taps. The sound of the flowing water helps me to release my bladder. It's only when I finish do I realise I cannot grab the toilet roll to wipe myself. I consider my options and decide to whine to grab Freddie's attention. He looks over and I look at him with my best puppy dog eyes and then at the toilet paper. He smiles, understanding and walks over to me.

"Here you go my good girl," he pulls a few squares off and folds them for me. I am about to try and take it from him, when he says, "Up." I do what he says and he pats me dry between my legs. "Down girl." My body reacts before my brain can keep up and I find myself back on my knees. "Crawl over there by the base of the tub for me."

I crawl to the position he has pointed to and sit back on my heels, panting with my tongue hanging out and my paws bent in front of my chest. He walks over to me, bends down and unfastens my collar. Next, he takes off my ears. "Bend over on all fours, let's remove your tail for the bath." I do as he says and gently he pulls at the base of the tail. There is a slight stretch and burn before the plug releases from my arsehole. I look over my shoulder to see him place it on a hand towel and carry it over to leave next to the sink.

I decide it's best to stay in this position until he tells me otherwise, so I remain on all fours, holding my head up to watch as he moves back to the tub and touches the water filling inside. Leaving the taps on, he says, "Sit," and I sit back on my heels. "Paws in front." And I lift my paws out to him. I watch as he unfastens them and then says, "Stand." I do so and he pulls each knee pad down my legs and helps me to step out. "Climb into the tub," he instructs and I do just as he says. I climb in and lower myself down—the water is hot but not burning. The warm water coming up to my belly button.

Sitting down I wonder if I can lie down but decide to stay seated until given my next instructions. It has been an incredibly long time since anyone gave me a bath. I watch this curious red headed man and wonder what is going on in his head right now. Freddie begins to undo the buttons on his shirt and take it off. Underneath I see his incredible torso. A wide chest and strong shoulders, the muscles of a lumberjack. *What does he do when he is not paying someone to be his pet?* I wonder. Something very physical, that is for sure.

"Now let me clean that mucky face of yours," he says as he lowers down onto his knees on the fluffy black and white striped bathmat. Reaching for a washcloth he dips it into the water, squeezes it out and starts to dab at my face. This gesture feels so intimate, my nipples pebble to tight peaks. His face is so close to mine. I watch as he studies me closely to ensure my face is clean. I take in his strong features, so many freckles all over his face, almost joining up to make his skin colour look more tanned then its original paleness. His beard is trimmed but still long enough to call bushy, the colour a mix of red and blond.

Once he's inspected my face thoroughly, his eyes meet mine and hold there. He studies me, looking into my soul. I'm not sure what he sees but I see the lust cross over them, he smiles shyly at me and moves his head closer before tentatively pressing his lips to mine. His lips are soft and feel just as pillowy as they look. When he pulls back, my lips almost follow his. He looks back into my eyes, seeking reassurance it was ok for him to kiss me. I blush and smile back at him. That seems to be enough confirmation for him to lean back and press his lips back to mine, this time peeking out his tongue as I open my mouth to let him in. Slowly his tongue finds mine and our kiss switches from curious to frantic in a breath. Suddenly he's deepening the kiss like he's trying to breathe the air from my lungs and consume me whole.

I'm completely taken aback by the passion I feel igniting between us. His mouth and his tongue begin to devour my own, and my nerve endings blaze with electricity and desire. With both hands around my neck and his thumbs under my chin, Freddie kisses me with a ferocious passion, his chest getting closer and closer to mine. I grab the side of the bath and move to bring myself to a kneeling position to match his on the other side of the tub. My breasts squish against his hard chest. Kissing this man is literally causing my pussy to throb. I want to climb out of the bath and onto his cock but I'm not in control here, he is.

Breaking the kiss Freddie says almost into my mouth, "I need you now Roxy." I look back at him pleading with my eyes that I want that too. I wait for his instructions, not daring to say a word. "Here climb back out of the bath and kneel in front of me." I stand and he helps me climb out of the bath, hot water dripping down my body and onto the bath mat as he helps me kneel with my back to him. I hear his zip and then feel the girth of the head of his cock press hard against my entrance. I don't say a word although in my head I'm screaming, *Do it, fuck me now!*

I'm wet from the bath water and slick with arousal, Freddie slides inside of me and I gasp as my body accommodates the size of him. I know he's not all the way in as I feel him slide out slightly as he readjusts his position behind me before slamming in with the full force of his body, his groans are loud in my ears as his body curves around mine. This man is all muscle, and I feel tiny being encased by him. He begins to rut in and out from behind me, his chest pressed tight against my back, holding me in place—one hand on my hip and the other curved around my breasts as if he's trying to absorb me into his body by osmosis.

I let out small whimpers because I can't hold them in. His hips pistoning his cock in and out of me. Pleasure is building inside me and he can feel it, I lower my head momentarily back to fit in the side of his neck. At that moment he slows and moves his hand from holding my chest upright to lower past my belly button, past my mound until he strums once over my clit with his thumb and my body jerks with pleasure. He does it again and again stroking with powerful strokes until a climax rips through my body and I scream out in a howl of euphoria, my head falling forward as my body becomes jelly. He moves that hand back up to my chest to hold me in place and drives into me, his orgasm peaking mere seconds after mine. "Roxy!" he cries out and stills, holding his huge cock deep inside me as it pulses and releases his come into my core.

Turning his head, he kisses my neck and mutters, "I hadn't

meant to do that here. I was only meant to bathe you and get you ready for bed. But you looked so beautifully innocent, doe eyed and naked, that I couldn't resist any longer. Here let me help you back into the bath so I can at least wash you." I feel Freddie slide out of me, followed by a rush of warm liquid from our combined climaxes. He tucks his arms under my armpits and pulls me up before helping me climb into the bath. This time, instead of sitting alone, I watch as he pulls off his soggy jeans, climbs into the bath and slides in behind me.

Freddie pulls me against him so my back rests on his hard, muscled chest and I'm not sad about that. He reaches for a sponge and squeezes his manly smelling sandalwood shower gel onto the sponge and proceeds to rub bubbles across my chest, over my breasts and stomach and down between my legs. When he's satisfied I'm clean enough on this side he says, "Lean forward Roxy." I pull away from the heat of his body and feel his soapy sponge glide across my shoulders, over my back in warm bubbly circles.

"Lean onto your hands," Freddie commands and I do what he says effectively placing my butt in his face. I'm not allowed to speak so I stay in this position and blush as I imagine the sight he has of me right now. Freddie runs the sponge over my butt cheeks and then between them, dropping the sponge so I feel his hand rub the soap between my pussy to my arsehole massaging between the folds that feels all too delicious and sensual. All too soon he's lowering his hands along the backs of my thighs. "You are now all shiny and clean, my special girl. Let's get you out and dry." Leaving me as I am on all fours, I feel him peel himself from around me, stand up and climb out of the tub. "Here, take my hand and climb out now too." Naked, he stands before me in his masculine beauty holding a fluffy black towel to wrap me up in.

I move into the towel and he encloses the sides around me. I watch as he rubs his arms up and down my body, patting me dry. It's actually quite endearing to watch. *Who is this man and why is taking such good care of me?* Once he's satisfied I'm dry, he points to the sink. "There is a spare toothbrush there, you can brush your teeth." He grabs a towel himself and gets dry. I'm not sure if I'm allowed to walk, so I hang my towel over the bath and crawl towards the sink before rising and brushing my teeth where I'm joined by Freddie who brushes his teeth too.

Looking in the mirror whilst we brush our teeth, we share a moment like we have done this a thousand times before. Freddie finishes and says, "Time to put your tail back in. Bend over the sink and watch in the mirror." I do as he says and watch him squeeze a gloop of lube onto the plug before it's being nudged firmly into my back passage. This time I'm relaxed and it doesn't take long before it slides straight in. "Good job, my Roxy girl." And I feel his hand stroking down my lower back. Seems I don't mind being stroked anywhere this man chooses to touch me.

He reaches for my collar, knee pads and mittens and helps them onto me before placing my ears back into place on my head. "A movie and then bed, let's head to my bedroom." Attaching the leash again, he leads me out of the bathroom on all fours, down the hallway and into the only doorway that is open. I see a huge king bed in front of me with navy bedding. To the right I can see a large cage with a thick dog bed inside of it and know exactly where I am sleeping tonight. This really is an experience.

"Here, climb up onto the bed, good girl." Freddie pats the bed, and I crawl over and awkwardly climb onto it. He pulls on a pair of track pants before pulling back the sheets for me to climb into. "I'd like you to lie on my lap so I can stroke you."

I do as he says, lying down to the side of his large body and resting my head on his thighs as he sits back against the headboard. There is a TV on the wall opposite the bed, Freddie reaches for the remote and clicks on a movie he has ready loaded. Surprisingly it's some romcom I would have chosen myself, how sweet of him? I settle into my position with ease which is unnerving considering I have only known this man for a few hours.

And then he begins to stroke me, just like he would a dog. A feeling of total relaxation flows through my body and instead of watching the movie my eyelids become heavy. He strokes my hair in a hypnotic rhythm, then moves his hand to my shoulders, gently caressing my skin. His warm hand runs down my arm, his fingers lightly grazing my right breast which sends lightning strikes straight to my pussy. Sensing me stiffen from the intimate touch he rubs up and down my curled back, I almost coo in pleasure and I drift off to sleep just like a dog would do curled up on their master's lap.

When the movie finishes, I feel Freddie untangle from me, walk around the side of the bed, lift me up and place me curled onto the fluffy dog bed inside the cage. He closes the door as I awake and realise where I am. "Shhh go back to sleep my good girl." And I do.

21

I wake with a start, trying to comprehend where I am. I'm curled up, naked on a fluffy bed inside a cage. Panic tears through my body before my brain clicks into gear and tells me I'm at Freddie's house on a playmate job. Relief floods my bloodstream as I realise my situation isn't as dire as one might first suspect. I stir my body, trying to get comfortable in the confined space. As I move around I feel the twinge in my bladder and know I need to go to the toilet soon. I can see the form of Freddie's foot peeking out of the large duvet cover and can hear his soft breathing from slumber so I know he's still here with me. Again, relief washes over me.

I can't speak and I can't bring myself to bark. So I make the only sound I can bear to make—I begin to softly whine for my master. I watch as Freddie's foot disappears from my view and I hear movement above me in the bed. I continue to whine and look up at the bed until Freddie's face comes into view as he's shuffled over to the edge of the bed to look down on me.

"Hey there my girl, are you ok?" he says to me, his voice thick with sleep. I have no choice but to whine some more and tap at the locked gate with my paws. I watch as Freddie scratches his beard.

"Would you like a drink?" he asks me and although actually I would like a drink—I have a more burning desire right now. I shake my head and continue to whine.

"Something to eat?" Again I shake my head. "Oh you need the toilet my girl?" this time I stop whining and stick my tongue out and start panting.

"Ahhh there we are. Ok, let's go. We should really be getting up soon anyways." I watch as he stretches his long muscled arms and swings his legs over the bed just in his track pants. He picks up the leash, walks over to me, unlocks the cage and attaches it to my collar. I nuzzle my head against his large forearm and look up at him with gratification. I'm still naked and my breasts pebble at his closeness. As Freddie pulls his arms back, he lifts one hand to rub under my chin and I lean into his touch, yearning for more. His eyes darken at my response to him and he lowers his hand to softly stroke my hanging breasts. The gentle touch drives me wild for more. I try and move forward but my bladder twinges and I remember why I needed him. I move uncomfortably and whine again. That seems to break the spell Freddie was under.

"Right, follow me." Freddie requests. And I do, on all fours. Out of the bedroom, down the hallway and past the bathroom. I stop, wondering where he's taking me. Freddie chuckles, "I have another toilet for you this morning." I frown, but continue to follow him. We arrive at the stairs. Just as I'm about to panic about falling face down down the staircase, he turns around and picks me up in a honeymoon lift.

Slowly Freddie carries me down each step and all I can do is put my arms and paws around his neck to hold on. I inhale deeply as his woody scent fills my nose and nuzzle at his neck. I'm not sure what comes over me but I peek out my tongue and lick at the sensitive part of his neck and I hear him moan. I do it again and realise he has not put me down once we have reached the bottom of the stairs and has continued walking. I lick again with a flat tongue and he moans again.

"I cannot wait for you to do that to my cock at breakfast today, Roxy," he growls at me. I begin to nibble lightly in the place I've been licking and feel his neck shudder in pleasure.

"You keep doing that to me and I won't make it to the bathroom for you."

I pull back and stop, I need to pee, more so than earlier. Then I realise we have reached the kitchen and are standing at the back door. I look up at his face as he turns his to explain.

"We are going for an early morning walk in my garden and you can do your business out here." My eyes widen in surprise. I can't say anything and right now I'm busting so much I'd pee anywhere.

Freddie lowers me to the floor and I get back onto my hands and knees. I look up to see Freddie unlock the door and step outside in the brisk morning air. I shiver in the fresh temperature which is only making me need to pee even more. I whine to convey my urgency. "This way my girl, over here onto the grass." Freddie leads the way and I crawl behind him. The sun has begun to rise but it's still mostly dark. I look around the garden but all I can see is dark trees and bushes. No lights, neighbours or people to watch me being led around this man's garden, naked and dressed like a dog.

"You can pee here." Freddie points at a patch of grass. My relief is short lived when I see him watching me. Not only do I have to pee outside like this, on a leash. I have to do it with him staring at me. I don't even know how to in this position. I decide to sit up on my heels and pee sitting in that position, first ensuring my soft tail is out of the way. I close my eyes and try and relax my body, praying my bladder will finally release. After what feels like an eternity of humiliation, the dam breaks and I sigh into the flow of urine that is seeping into the grass.

"There's my good girl," Freddie praises as he walks towards me. "Such a good girl" he coos in a babying voice just like you would use to a puppy or a toddler. He strokes my head with praise and regardless of how he is speaking to me, his rewarding strokes make everything worthwhile. I shiver again, remember where I am and the chill in the air. Freddie stops stroking me and pulls on the leash, "A quick walk before breakfast."

I'm grateful for the knee pads and mittens covering my hands as I follow him around his huge garden, Freddie watches my every move as we make slow progress and the bulge in his tracksuit pants tells me he's enjoying this little excursion outside. Being outside is a whole new level of humiliation I'm not sure I was ready for but at the same time, seeing the enjoyment on his face and the way he rewards me takes away the shame and replaces it with a need. Maybe I will need therapy after this job but I suspect it will be to unpack why I am in fact turned on from the experience as opposed to any harm it might have had to my mental health.

Despite the fact that my hands and knees are covered, I am relieved to see we've made it to the back kitchen door again. My body is aching, I am not used to moving like this or being in this position for prolonged periods of time.

"Sit." Freddie clicks his fingers and points at me. I obey immediately, sitting back on my heels, paws in front of my chest, I stick my tongue out and start panting.

Freddie opens the door and says, "Inside." I crawl inside the doorway and he follows. He shuts it behind me. Taking a dog bowl of water from the counter, he places it down on the floor in front of me. Grateful I bend my head and begin to lap at the water before sucking down as much as I can.

I don't see Freddie's large frame kneeling down beside me until I feel his hands stroking my head, down my neck along my back and down my backside and then back of my legs. I freeze and lift my head to look up at him, my head tilted as a nonverbal question, but he doesn't catch my eye, only reaches back up to my head and begins to stroke me again. I go back to drinking, hoping he'll continue because I'm enjoying it but I'm also thirsty and need to drink more.

Never in my life have I enjoyed being stroked in the way Freddie strokes me. The caresses spark a yearning inside of me I never knew existed which heats straight in my centre. The touches feel like a tease, I want him to touch and caress me between my legs. Every time his hand runs down my backside, I'm sure they curve deeper inside my thighs. Getting oh so close, but still too far away. I almost whine in frustration.

When I finish drinking my fill of water, my core is a dripping mess running down the inside of my thighs. On his next stroke, Freddie notices. "You like this my girl, don't you. You are dripping down your thighs." He's no longer speaking in a cooing voice, it's now deep and husky, his voice laced with desire. "I am going to need to break my own rules with you Roxy," he whispers in my hair. "I can't wait until breakfast; I need to mount you and fuck you like last night.

With that, he reaches for my paws, picks them up and places them on the kitchen cabinets. He must pull his track pants down because I can feel his hot length against my arse cheeks as he positions my body to how he wants it. The movement of the plug when he adjusts my tail is enough to make me let out another whimper and he pauses to gently thrust it in and out for a moment.

"Roxy, you have been my most perfect dog," he says into my neck as he lines his cock up to my entrance. "I want to mount you and fuck you all around my house," he breathes as he thrusts in one swift move all the way into me to the hilt. I yelp at his deep intrusion, and shudder as he nibbles at my neck the same way I had done to him earlier.

"I. Wish. You. Were. My. Permanent. Pet," Freddie pants

each word into my neck, on every thrust. "You. Are. Perfect." I feel a glow at his words from the inside shining outwards. The feel of his hard body slick against mine, each movement rubbing up against the butt plug as the tail brushes against my back, causes pleasure to radiate from my pussy as he reaches down one large hand and begins to circle two fingers around my clit. I buck between his fingers and his cock, my climax culminating in an almighty crash rushing through my core making me scream out his name, the first word I'd spoken since I was told not to.

"You're making me come screaming my name like that Roxy," Freddie growls in my ear going completely feral, he pounds into me from behind, mating me like a dog. Slapping both hands above my head on the counter top, Freddie roars my name as he thrusts his release deep inside me and stills, his body going slack and he rests his forehead to the back of my neck coming down from his high.

Peeling himself away from my back and sliding himself out from my pussy, warm liquid follows him and drips down my thighs.

He sits on the kitchen floor with his back to a cupboard opposite me, seemingly in a daze. I'm not sure what to do with myself so I swivel around and crawl towards him and settle between his open legs, noticing there's no trace of his track pants on his body. Coyly, I brush my cheek against his. He smiles back at me. I run soft tender kisses from his cheek, along his neck and across his shoulder. I pull back and take in his magnificent naked chest. I run my paws across from each shoulder, over his chest and lower towards his softening cock.

I lift my eyes to meet his, double checking what I am doing I have permission for. He smiles back at me and I take that as a yes. I lower my head and begin to lick my essence and our mixed come from the base of his cock to the tip. I hear his head hit the back of the kitchen cabinet as he relaxes with each lick of my tongue as his cock stiffens to a rock hard pole in my paws. Once I've licked every remanent of our earlier fucking, I stop teasing and lower my mouth over his cock and suck him down my throat. "Fuucckk," I hear him groan.

I move my head up and down, each time his tip hits the back of my throat. I start out in slow glides building up the pace until his resolve gives in and he holds my head over his cock and fucks my mouth until I can feel his abs shuddering on my head and his come shoots down the back of my throat. My eyes stream and I struggle to keep my gag reflex in check. I gratefully suck every drop down and swallow before raising my tear streaked face to meet his gaze, gulping down air.

Leaning forward, Freddie takes my face gently in his hands and kisses me deeply, his tongue finding mine and licking his taste from my tongue. I'm again surprised with how intimate this kiss feels, so much more than two strangers meeting for 12 hours.

"Roxy, you have been everything and more. This morning hasn't played out quite as I had planned." At my worried look, he quickly follows with, "It's been even better than any plans," and smiles warmly while gently petting my head and back.

"Let's get you cleaned up and fed before your car arrives to collect you. Hold out your cute little paws." I do as he says and watch as he unfastens the paws and pulls them off. He pulls me into a sitting position on my bum and wriggles the knee pads off my legs. "Let's keep the collar on you until we get to the bathroom, it suits you."

Holding my forearms, he begins to stand raising me with him off the kitchen floor. He pulls on his navy track pants. Reaching for my hand, he smiles shyly at me and leads me back up the main staircase and into the bathroom. "Lean over the sink and I'll remove your tail." I do as he says and watch as he carefully wiggles and pulls until the plug pops out of me, it's a bit rougher as the lube clearly dissipated overnight but the slight pain is welcome. I thought I'd feel relieved but in actual fact I feel empty.

"Take a shower, I will make us some breakfast, it's not long now before you need to leave. Over there are your clothes, you should dress before coming down to eat." I nod and watch as he walks out and closes the door.

I look at myself in the mirror and realise he forgot to take off my collar. I stare at myself, naked with collar on and see myself in an entirely different light. I have just spent a night with a stranger as his dog. I did it. I enjoyed it. I'm getting paid for it. He said I look cute in his collar, and I'm almost hesitant to remove it. But I would hate to ruin the leather so I unfasten it and begin to run the luxurious rain shower and step in. I try not to get my hair wet but lather my body in his manly smelling shower gel. Once I'm showered, dried and dressed, I put the collar back on and walk down the stairs to find him back in the kitchen serving scrambled eggs on toast with avocados and mushrooms.

He turns to look at me and beams at me, dressed but also back in his collar. "I know I said it before but the collar really does suit you, being a dog suited you too," he says as if that's the most normal sentence you may ever hear. "I guess now you're not really my pet any more you can speak, if that's ok with you."

"Thank you," I reply, my voice husky after being quiet for so long. "Breakfast smells delicious."

"Are you ok to sit and eat here in the kitchen?"

"Sure. You have a beautiful kitchen," I reply looking around at the light wood cabinetry and rounded edges of the marble countertops.

"Thank you. My best friend is a carpenter."

"Lucky you," I say jokingly, "because he's done an excellent job."

We eat in companionable silence for a bit, both lost in thoughts of our experience together.

Pouring out two glasses of orange juice, he hands one to me just before the clock strikes 8am. Just like Cinderella, that's my cue to leave.

I take a couple of mouthfuls of juice before I hop down off the stool, Freddie moving around me. He takes both my hands in his and looks me square in the eyes, "Thank you Roxy, for being everything I have ever imagined and more." I blush at his compliment. "I understand what I like to do is unusual and not for everyone. I couldn't tell if it was your thing or not because you played the part so well. If you're not into it, you were incredible." He smiles at me as his thumbs rub up and down my hands.

"Here, let me unfasten that collar before you leave." Reaching behind my ponytail, he unbuckles the collar, and the air meets my neck again. Without it I suddenly feel bare, more so than when I wasn't wearing any clothes. Walking me to the door, Freddie reaches for my cheek and plants a soft light kiss on my lips. "Goodbye Roxy, I hope we meet again."

"Goodbye Freddie. Thank you for teaching me how to become a pet for the night. I think you have changed me in ways I can't put into words just yet."

He smiles, delighted at my reply. He opens the door for me and I walk out, our hands brush and I wonder if he's going to grab mine but he lets me leave. I turn back as I open the door to Frank's blacked out BMW, Freddie stands by the door, his wide frame almost hiding his front door behind him. I feel a ping of sadness as I give a little wave before climbing into the back of the car. It must be hard to find people with similar kinks when the dating scene is hard enough on its own. No wonder he's a member of the Clarendon Golf Club. I'm glad to have met him.

I place the blindfold across my eyes and Frank pulls away. I lean my head on the backrest and close my eyes.

22

———————

I awake with a start as Frank turns down the music and says my name. Disoriented, it takes me a few seconds to work out where I am again and listen to Frank's words, "You can take off your blindfold now Miss Roxy, you are home."

I slide the blindfold off and blink in the morning light. "Thank you so much Frank, you have a lovely day," I say as I climb out of the car. I retrieve my keys out of my purse and unlock my front door. Inside I can hear the TV on, my son at his computer, voices coming from an iPad and the dishwasher is going. I creep up the stairs and find James rubbing his wet blond hair with a towel around his head.

"Argh," he gasps and jumps in fright.

"Oh no, I'm so sorry, I didn't mean to creep up on you," I chuckle looking amused whilst he looks like he just shit a brick.

"You're home, I'm glad you're home. How was it?"

Smiling, almost wistfully I reply, "It was fine, the guy was nice and being a dog was weird and rewarding and a bit more weird," I laugh. "I'm glad to be home though." I walk up to him, placing my hands around the top of his jeans. "I missed you."

"I missed you too."

"Are the kids ok?"

"They're both fine. Should be getting ready for their games so I need to hustle." But instead of moving away he drops his towel on the bed and snakes his hands around my waist pulling me in closer. "Tell me one thing that got you wet in the last 12 hours before I go."

"Hmm," I muse. "It's hard to choose one thing. I'll go with my top two," I say coyly. "I really enjoyed wearing a collar." James raises an eyebrow at me but lets me continue. "My second favourite was the way he stroked my body. Like a pet, but I didn't want it to end. I can't explain it. Maybe I need my head read."

I feel the length of James grow hard in his jeans where he's pressed up close to my body. Him getting hard turns me on and my pussy flutters at the thought of James collaring me and stroking me like Freddie's caresses.

"I think I would love to collar you and stroke your body all over Rose Petal," James purrs in my ear. That's it, I let out a moan and wish it wasn't a Saturday morning full of sport and kids activities. Rubbing his stiff cock into my stomach James groans, "I have to go but all I want to do is play with you."

I giggle. "I'm sorry."

"You should be, you little minx," he says, smiling good naturedly. "We can continue this conversation later. I need to get our son moving."

"Ok, Sir," I reply and his eyes flash at me. I'm teasing him and he knows it. He spins me and spanks my ass. I laugh out loud as he walks into the walk-in wardrobe pulling on a t-shirt. I need to get changed myself.

"I can't wait for you to do your Dom training next weekend."

"Oh me either Rose Petal, you have no idea," replies James.

"And James?"

"Hmm?" he answers

"Fifteen Thousands Dollars!!" I call out clapping my hands together.

Half an hour later James has left with our son, I've chased down my daughter to make sure her nails are trimmed and earrings are out ready for netball. We have thirty minutes before we need to leave so I take the opportunity to phone Sophie.

Surprisingly Sophie answers on the first ring. "How was it?" she asks.

"Were you sitting waiting for my call?" I ask laughing.

"And what if I was?"

"Were you?" I laugh.

"Of course I was. Now answer the question!"

"It was...an experience," I settle on.

"Did you like it?"

"Yes I think I did."

"It's strange when you do it for the first time I know. But it's bearable?"

"Oh yep it is definitely bearable." I laugh, "For fifteen grand I'll sleep in a dog cage any day of the week."

"What did you have to do?"

"Wear a tail butt plug, a collar, furry mittens, knee pads. I had to crawl, not speak, pant, suck him off at the table before eating out of my own dog bowl. That was weird. But the way he rewarded me..." I trail off. "When he stroked me, I swear I was putty in his hands. It was some kind of witchcraft, that is what it was."

Sophie laughs at me. "Sounds like he knew what he was doing. What did he look like?"

"He was broad, wide chest, red hair, blondish red beard. He reminded me of a mountain man. Does he sound familiar?"

"Doesn't ring any bells with me. I haven't played with him. But he was good to you, didn't harm you in any way?"

"Nope. Not at all. In fact, we had this chemistry. He was washing me—giving me a dog bath, as he was wiping down my face after dinner our connection unravelled him and he pulled me out of the bath and fucked me like a dog from behind right there, couldn't wait. It was hot to see him go feral like that. He made me come, hard. Really, I enjoyed many aspects of my time with him."

Blowing out a breath Sophie replies, "Geesh that does sound hot, I'm going to need a fan to cool me down after this chat with you. So you didn't need to use the safeword then?"

"Not at all. I did consider it when he said I couldn't speak but I could bark. I wanted to balk at that. Then I reminded myself about the money and settled on whining if ever I needed anything."

"Good call, and he was ok with that?"

"Seemed to be. I enjoyed nuzzling into him too. Does this mean I need help?"

"Oh gosh no, I totally understand what you mean. I've done two of these jobs, if you need help, I do too. I think we're fine. It's society that says this stuff is wrong, but I say if it's not hurting anyone and everything is consensual, then get your rocks off anyway you enjoy. Chase the pleasure and the pleasure will find you in abundance."

"Oh words of the wise one," I laugh.

"Listen to the pro here, girlfriend." Now we are both giggling. "Hey, have you heard about the charity job list this year?" Sophie asks.

"What charity job list?"

"At the Clarendon. It's an annual event."

"I haven't heard even a whisper. Should I have?"

"No, it's ok—I can tell you."

"Okay, tell me, tell me!" I exclaim.

"So, every year the Clarendon Playmates run a charity job board. Basically, it's a one off job board where a date is chosen and all the members who want to take part post a job for that one date. However the money they would usually pay to the playmate is doubled. The playmate takes her half, minus 20% which goes to charity, and the other half is donated to charity."

"Ah that sounds like a really nice idea."

"It's really great, I like to take part, well this will be my second year. This year I heard there is a twist. Rather than being just the Green & Amber type kinks, they are allowing Red kinks too. Which will mean crazy shit but oodles more money. I can't wait to see it."

"Can people apply for any of the jobs even if they're not allowed on the Red job board yet?" I ask out of curiosity seeing as I haven't graduated to the Red board yet.

"Yes they would. It's for charity, I know any of the playmates can usually apply for any of the jobs from the charity board. So you would too, if you wanted to. Even if the Red jobs were on there. Ava told me yesterday that the board should be open from 10am today."

I raise my eyebrows. "That's in like 10 minutes?!"

"Yes!"

"Oof, how exciting. I'm keen to see what is on there."

"You and me both." Then Sophie sighs, "I'm going to have to love you and leave you now. I need to fire up my laptop for 10am and see what jobs are on the charity board."

"Absolutely, me too. How exciting. I wonder what there might be."

"Chat on Monday over lunch?"

"See you on Monday. Enjoy your weekend, Sophie."

"You too, Roxy."

"Bye, friend!"

I race to my work bag, pull out my laptop and set it up. I have to leave in 10 mins to take my daughter to netball. Please let the auction board be up and running before then. I log in to the playmate portal and wait.

After pressing the refresh icon ten thousand times, a new job board appears to the right of the Red board that I do not have access to. I click on the Charity icon and the page loads.

Excited, I look to see the different types of jobs flowing in. The longer I look, the more are added. I guess the board is not just open to playmates at 10am, but to members too. My time is running out. I need to leave the house really soon or we'll be late. And then one job catches my eye. I click onto it:

Be our captive for a week. We are a group of 8 male members who would like to keep one playmate to fulfil our ultimate desires whilst the rest of us watch or take part. Not limited to but including:

- *BDSM*
- *Breeding*
- *Shaving*
- *Feeding*
- *Voyeurism*
- *Doctor*
- *Sonomaphilia*
- *Impact Play*
- *Pussy & Anal*
- *Deep Throat*
- *Gangbang*
- *Double Penetration*

Playmate won't have shaved for 4 weeks prior to the week of captivity. Playmate understands that each day will be different and varied. Payment: $250,000

I gasp. Then my daughter walks into the room. I shut my laptop and jump up from my seat. We need to get to Netball.

THE CHARITY JOB BOARD

23

I have the whole of my daughter's netball game to mull over the charity job listing. Luckily, I'm not scoring the game this week. Still, I'm trying my hardest to be present, I love watching my kids play sports despite the fact I have never played any team sport since high school or watched it on tv or in person. There is something incredibly special about cheering on your kid's sports team during a match.

After the match, I drive us home whilst listening to my daughter's post-match debrief on how she thought the game went. I'm listening and nodding and joining in on the conversation but at the same time my mind is whirling about the conversation I am soon to be having with James. I've only just gotten home from an overnight Pet Play job for $15,000, now I'm about to broach the subject of a week's job for $200k. A night is one thing, a week is an entirely different kettle of fish. I don't know what James is going to say when we speak and that fills me full of anxiety. Because I think deep down, I want to do this job, I want to test myself, I have this perverse sense of excitement to find out what all these men would want to do with my body. Would I enjoy it or fear it? To be submerged into a world of kink that I cannot leave for 7 days...

And what about the kinks? Some I'm familiar with like voyeurism and impact play, others not so much. I mean, what is a feeding kink? They like to feed you your food? And shaving, I didn't know that could be a kink, but then again, I'm guessing anything can be a kink if it's sexual and unusual? And doctor, does that mean he likes to pretend to be a doctor or is a doctor? What kind of perverse things do doctors like to do to you?

Despite all the question marks about most of the kinks and the men behind them, despite the intensity of the demands and the extended amount of time, I have an instinctual sense that I can do it, and I want to prove to myself I can do it. I also want to do it for the money, for our mortgage, for the opportunity that we may never get a chance again to pay off $200k in one lump sum. What worries me the most at this point is not the job itself, it's what James will say. How he will take it.

I wait like a cat on hot bricks for James to get home. I start to tidy the kitchen and lounge, keeping myself busy whilst I try and think how I'm going to even broach the subject.

I hear the keys in the door and in bounces my son all hot, sweaty and chatting away. My husband follows, closing the door behind them. I ask how the game went and listen to a blow-by-blow account of exactly how the game went and the number of goals he scored or helped set up. Once his full story has unfolded, he makes himself a drink and goes into the rumpus room.

James then gives me his full version of how he thought the game went and who was there and what he thinks of the current stand-in coach. Once he has finished, he takes a breath and asks how the netball game went, so I give my usual breakdown of, "Yeah she played really well, they won 18-8, it was a good match." Yes I was there, yes the game was great to watch, no I don't remember every detail. I'm not sure if it's because I never grew up watching sports, but I simply cannot retain all the details to debrief afterwards. I'm amazed my husband remembers so much, but he has been playing and watching sports his whole life. That's all I can put it down to.

James eyes me, "What else is going on in that mind of yours, Rose Petal. I can see something else ticking over in there." I'm not sure if it's my furious cleaning of the sideboards or my jittery movements. Clearly, I've given my mood away either way.

"I've seen something on the playmate portal I don't know how to bring up with you," I say honestly.

"Ok, how about you start from the beginning," James replies seriously.

"I phoned Sophie before going to the netball game, she wanted me to call. After telling her that I survived and even enjoyed the overnight Pet Play job she told me about the Annual Playmate Charity Job Board. It's a one-off job board that lists jobs for one date. All the Clarendon Club members can list a job for that date, and it can be for any level—so Green, Amber and Red. Apparently, it's the first year that Red is allowed to be listed. All jobs that are listed are open to all playmates." James nods his head, he's listening.

"The job fee is doubled, half going to charity, the other half goes to the playmate and she or he donates 20% of their payment too."

"That sounds like a pretty cool thing to do. The club members must have some serious cash if they can afford to offer a double fee."

"Yeah I know, right? The charity is split with Beyond Blue and LifeLine this year."

"So what is it that has got you in a pickle?" James asks, he knows me so well, too well.

"Ok, well, I had a peek before going to netball, it launched today at 10am. It's open for a week. There was this one job that jumped out to me and now I can't stop thinking about it. It's a lot of money. But it's also a lot of time."

"What exactly is the job and how much money are they willing to spend?" James asks, he's curious but he knows judging by the way I haven't come straight out with it, it's a lot.

"It's $250k before being doubled. For 7 days." My voice trails off and I watch James' face as he goes through the motions of absorbing what I've just said. His eyebrows come together, then his eyes narrow before blowing out a long breath.

"Who are these people who can spend $500k for one week of kinky fuckery?"

"I don't know," I reply. "I will probably never know even if I get the job."

"If, and I mean if, you take this job, you'd walk away with $200k? That is some serious money. I'm not sure what gets me the most, that people can actually afford to do it or whether they think they can pay someone that amount to live out their sick pleasures."

"I can't help thinking we might never get this opportunity again. To make such a massive dent in our mortgage, I mean."

"Yeah but what the heck would you have to do for it?"

I know James would love to pay off more money on our mortgage just like me. It was only seven months ago we were facing having to sell our home and move somewhere more affordable.

"The job is a group of 8 men pooling their money together. They have a range of kinks, some I've heard of and others I've never heard of."

"What kind of kinks?"

"Impact play, Anal, Voyeurism, Shaving, Feeding, Doctor, Breeding," I say counting them off on my fingers.

"Breeding?" James interrupts my list.

"Yeah, like I say—there are some I've not ever heard off."

"I think we need to search them up before we even consider them, don't you?"

I cringe at his words. I actually would prefer to not look and enjoy the element of surprise. At least then I wouldn't worry so much. Knowing is much worse in my mind. Knowing means I might not apply.

"Yeah I guess."

"You're saying you'd rather not know?"

"To be honest, yes. I don't want a reason to talk myself out of it."

"You're saying you don't want to be prepared or that you'd rather suffer at their hands because you like the element of surprise."

"No, that's not what I'm saying. I'm saying I think it will all be ok, I can handle most things that are thrown at me. I want to do it for the money. If I overthink it, I may not be able to go ahead with it and when else will we ever be able to earn a lump sum of $200k?"

"I know what you mean and where you are coming from, but by not being prepared and seeing what you might be in for, you are setting yourself up for some huge and possibly scary surprises. I mean, shaving? That's weird right? And we don't need $200k, we never thought we were ever going to earn that amount, so it's no loss not getting it. And Christ, Rosie, you earnt $19k just this week. We are practically flying right now. You don't need to do this. Think of your body, of your mental health."

"I have been thinking of them both, I can understand why you're worried. If the boot was on the other foot I would be too. I get it. Who knows what these men will do to me and how I'll react. But I'm strong, I have done some fairly eye-opening things recently, I don't feel like any of them have fazed me at all."

"I know you're strong Rosie, I'm not questioning that. I just don't want you to bite off more than you can chew. And a week could be filled with all sorts of crazy uncomfortable things."

"I know. And in some perverted way, I'm ok with it. I want to experience it and see what these kinks even are. None really frighten me, they pique my curiosity more than anything. It's just the being away from home and the kids for a week which will be the hardest. Being away from you."

"Can you tap out at any point? Using your safe word?"

"I'm sure I would be able to. Management wouldn't let this go ahead if they thought any harm would come to the play-mate. The rules are, no lasting injury or marking on their bodies left from the jobs. They'd do some sort of prorated pay if I had to leave early but I know I'd be able to leave at any time."

"I'm not sure that is giving me peace of mind or not. Are you really considering being locked away for 7 days and being 8 men's plaything 24/7?"

I swallow. *Is this going bad?* I wonder. "Yes."

"I don't know whether you need to get your head read or if this is a good thing," James muses. My shoulders lower a little, I hadn't realised how rigid I had been standing until just then.

"I know it sounds kinda bad; I get that. But I'm looking at it as kind of good. It might be the money aspect for sure but I might even enjoy it."

"If there was one person who could possibly enjoy it, it would be you. I'd put my money on it." James gives me a weak smile. Is he coming around to the idea?

"I want to know my sexual limits. I want to see what they are."

"That's what I'm afraid of. I don't know if you'd tell any one of them to stop, I'm not sure you would be prepared to stop at your limits."

"I think I could. Just because I haven't with you or any of the jobs doesn't mean I won't, it just means nothing so far has pushed me to the edge enough to want to stop."

James presses his lips together. He's thinking. I know he never wants to stop me doing anything or worse tell me what to do.

"I don't want you to make a decision that you might regret, either by doing this job or not doing this job. I want you to consider it. Don't rush into applying. Sleep on it. Speak to Sophie, see what her advice is and then make a decision. How long is the charity jobs board open for?

"A week."

"Good, so you have a week to apply."

"Yes. So you're saying if I come to my own thought out decision, you will be ok whatever the outcome is?"

"Yes, you have my blessing either way. As long as you believe and trust you are making the right decision for you."

I feel a spike of excitement flutter through my stomach, but I keep my body still and try not to clap my hands in delight. Keeping my face unmoved is impossible though. I grin back at James. "Thank you."

"What am I going to do with you, Rose Petal?" he asks playfully. And then in a serious tone, "I don't know how I am going to be not knowing or checking in with you for a whole week." My stomach lurches. That is going to be hard and painful, not calling and chatting. Not checking in that we're going ok. But it'll be ten times worse for James, he'll have to continue his day to day life knowing I would be locked away somewhere with eight men. It's hardly a girls' weekend away to not stress about.

"I'm sorry, I hadn't considered that."

"Rosie, if you think you can stomach what those men might have in store for you and actually go through with it. The least I can do is stomach the worry and get through it too."

24

———

Monday I'm on reception for a change and not working in Café Marion as usual with Sophie. I have to wait the four hours of my shift until I can go to lunch with her. We meet in the staff room, grab our bags and jump into her Land Rover to drive to our favourite lunch spot. After chatting about our weekend and more specifically Sophie's weekend away with Sam, we get onto the subject I've been burning to talk to her about.

"So, the charity jobs. Which job are you going for?" I ask brightly, hoping she is not considering the seven day one like I am. All the jobs are on one day (or at least start on the same day) so we can only be successful in one application.

"I keep looking, there are so many of the usual ones. I was thinking of going for something a bit more outside what I usually try like the Medical Play one. As a backup, I also like the sound of the Shibari job, the guy must be new because I've never seen Shibari listed before."

"What is Shibari? I can guess the Medical Play one, well sort of."

"It's rope bondage, more specifically Japanese rope

bondage. It's an art form and I'm keen to be strung up and see how that feels."

"Sounds interesting. Wonder what he'll do to you when you can't move?" I giggle.

"Yeah, I wonder indeed." Sophie giggles and winks at me. "Did you see that big job for seven days? I read it a few times, but I don't think I'm cut out for that long on a job. I like doing them weekly but to be eight members' kink toy gives me goose-bumps. Eight guys on one booking, sure I can do that. Eight guys for seven days. Ouch. The person who applies to that is going to need a strong stomach, don't you think? Did you see that one?" Sophie looks up at me as she's about to tuck into her avocado on toast. My face heats like a furnace in summertime. My cheeks feel like they're on fire. I am actually embarrassed to admit it. But I don't need to of course, my face gives it away.

"Roxy! You crazy little sex kitten. You are going to apply for it or have you applied already?" she asks as she puts the first forkful of her lunch into her mouth. I haven't started on mine. I feel like I am asking for advice on having sex for the first time. My face heats with a mix of humiliation and embarrassment. If Sophie is not even considering the job, what must she think of me if I am interested?

"I-I am thinking about applying. For the money. Maybe a little for the experience. And a tiny bit to see if I can do it."

"Wow Roxy, you are a special kind of mental. Seven whole days? That is a huge amount of time. There is shaving and feeding involved. I know you have read it. I've never done either kink job, I don't know what they'd be like." Sophie blinks her fiery gold eyes at me as she brushes an auburn hair from her forehead. "Are you sure about it?"

"I think I am. It's literally the only job I clicked on and can think about. It's so much money, it's such a huge opportunity for me to earn that kind of money. Where else would me or James get $200k from a week's worth of work, heck even a year's work. I can't move away from it. It just keeps doing circles in my brain and it feels such a relief to talk to someone other than James about it."

"What does James say about it?"

"He's as supportive as ever. But also, I know he's going to worry about me for seven days. That's the biggest downside for me."

"Not the shaving?" Sophie exclaims flabbergasted.

"Not the shaving. That doesn't really bother me. None of the job description really bothers me. Not now I've done that overnight Pet Play job. Something has shifted in me. I feel different since I took the job, in fact I feel like a different person entirely since I've become a playmate."

"Well now, I can relate to that. I can't relate to the family and mortgage situation, but I understand your motivations. Being a playmate opens your mind and heart for so much more, every day you're more open to doing things you'd never imagined or even heard of. I can see the appeal on the money level and also the challenge. I suspect there is a darker, more depraved Roxy in there somewhere and this job is calling to her. Am I right?"

I blush because I think she is right. Underneath being a mum, wife, small business owner, and employee, being a playmate is peeling me back to my true self, the one I've buried so deep, I don't recognise her and her true feelings.

"You could be right," I decide to reply. I'm being coy, but she knows me well.

"No could be, I AM right," she laughs in reply.

"I think being a playmate is unleashing things about me I've never let anyone else see in me before, even myself."

"I bet Sandy knew they were there. She's got a sixth sense for this kind of thing. I bet she sniffed out your sex kitten desires when hiring you." Sophie laughs and she takes another mouthful of her lunch.

I start on my toasted bagel. "Do you think I can do it?" I ask earnestly.

"I think you can do whatever you put your mind to. Yes ok I freaked out a little when you told me, but now thinking about it more clearly of all the playmates I know, it would be you I'd choose who could actually go through with it all the way."

"Why?"

"Because you are no quitter for a start. But also, you have enjoyed—*loved*, every job you have experienced so far. How many of your friends would be as open as you, do what you have done? Nothing seems to faze you. I know the overnight job concerned you, but you did it, enjoyed it and now you want more. You need more."

"But is more being greedy?"

"Yes," she says deadpan, then smiles. "Joking. No, you are not being greedy. You are saying yes to something you desire. You desire this challenge, this experience. You desire being at the mercy of eight men for seven days. That's the crux of it."

And now the truth is out in the open. The one I wasn't sure I could say out loud. I breathe a sigh of relief. "Yes. I can't believe that is the honest truth of it. Are you judging me?"

"Surely you know me better than that by now. You're my bestie at Clarendon's, I know you, I see you. Don't be ashamed of something you want. Every single Club Member is not ashamed, they're all asking for what they want and getting it. Why can't you?"

When Sophie says it like that, it sounds like the most natural thing in the world. Almost like why would you not want to do this extreme seven day job, not let yourself experience anything you desire? But society says you can't. I have conformed to the rules and regulations of being a wife and a school mum for over ten years. This is the opposite of that life, being a playmate is far away from 'normal' but I've managed to keep that secret well under wraps. I know no one is going to find out about me taking this seven day job if I get it. It's the owning the decision and admitting to myself I'm more play-mate than I let myself believe. I'm more into this life than I realised. I crave it now that I have it. I keep wanting more. More kink experiences, more unknowns, more challenges and more uncovering the true me and my wants from all of this.

A tear tips out the corner of my eye and rolls down my cheek, "Because I didn't think people like me could."

"Oh honey, of course you can. You can chase your desires as much as the next guy. You just need to be brave enough to ask for them."

Another tear rolls down my cheek. Why am I being so emotional? "But it's so hard. I don't want to be judged, least of all by my husband. What would he think if I said the reason I wanted to go for this job was more from desire than the money? I couldn't even admit to James that the idea of someone shaving me turned me on, that impact play is something I've watched in porn..."

"Because it's not the norm, yes. But what if he had desires he never said to you also from fear of being judged. Without having the conversations to start with, how would either of you know?"

"You're right. I still can't get my head around owning up to it. How would I even start such a conversation?"

"Honey, from what you've told me about James, he might suspect you're into more kinks than you've ever said or done with him. But he's learning more about you from every job you take. And what has his reaction been to each of them?"

"He's been pumped when I've returned. He's been inter-ested in what I've done and can barely keep his hands off me."

"Exactly Roxy, his actions are speaking louder than words too. You're both into it. You just haven't said it. My guess is he's learning what he likes just like you are. I bet deep down he's into some stuff that might not be your thing and vice versa. But that's just it. Everyone can have their own kink; doesn't mean you need to ignore it or bury it because it's not for your partner. I would bet every couple has at least one mis-matched kink unless they actually met at a kink club for the same thing or from one of those apps, but even then people aren't usually into just one thing. Everyone has their own desires, their own fantasies, and their own limits. Society just tries to shame us for wanting anything beyond the norm or what is deemed appropriate," Sophie explains passionately.

"Sophie, having this conversation, you have no idea the feelings I am feeling right now. I didn't know I needed to have it, but I so did. I feel like a weight of shame has been lifted off my shoulders. Shame I've carried around my entire adulthood." I feel almost on the verge of tears, just at the knowledge that I'm not alone in this.

"I'm so glad to be able to speak to you openly and honestly like this. It's taken me a long while to own who I am, I am so happy I can help you too. Being a playmate is a journey, heck this life is a journey. It's just nice to finally embrace our true selves and be open with what our true sexual desires are. We are in 2025, not 1925, so to heck with what society says, we should know and own our sexual desires."

I want to stand up and throw my arms around Sophie and hug her tight. But instead, I tame down my gratitude for now by reaching out my hand and squeezing hers. "Thank you, Sophie."

"So, you'll go for the seven-day charity job?"

"I will apply for the charity job. I don't know if I'll get it, but I feel so much lighter about owning the decision. I wonder how many playmates will also apply for it?"

"Maybe a couple, but in all honesty, I doubt most people would want to be cooped up for a whole week. Only the true deviants are into being a captive." She smiles at me wickedly.

"So, I've got a chance then!"

"I'd say you're in with more than a chance! You get applying, girl. Applications close on Friday. We'll find out on Saturday."

"Eeek, what do I even say?"

"Just be yourself. That is after all, all you can be." Sophie looks at her watch, "It's nearly one—you have your next job to be getting to now I think?"

I roll my eyes. My little business is becoming more of a bane then of an escape, something I used to look forward to and now I simply don't.

We both stand and walk back to Sophie's car, before I open the door I give her a big hug. It's hard meeting your kind of people in adulthood so I thank my blessings to have found Sophie. "Thank you again for everything. All your words of wisdom, support and making everything I want feel ok."

"Roxy my darling, you don't need to thank me. It's a pleasure to support you. You are no longer just my buddy at Clarendon's, you are one of my most favourite people."

I smile into her jasmine smelling auburn hair. *How did I get so lucky,* I think to myself.

Before I can do any of my own actual business work and start packing orders, I decide to apply for the charity job and then put it out of my mind.

Dear Members x Eight,

I would like to put myself forward for your seven days of extreme kink and play. It's taken a bit of soul searching to get to this point, but the honest truth is, I think I'd be the perfect captive for you. I'm a new-ish playmate and haven't experienced a wide range of kinks and jobs, but the ones I have, I have gone in with an open mind and submitted wholly to the experience. I enjoy a challenge and more so the element of surprise. I have not experienced

*many of your listed kinks but am interested and willing to try them
and be your personal kink toy.*

*I crave to be at your mercy, would you do me the pleasure of
making me yours?*

Yours, Roxy

The week has flown by, I've not taken any playmates jobs on
account that I took two last week and I'm kind of hoping I get
the Charity one so I haven't looked at the jobs boards this week.
When I got home on Monday evening, I told James about my
discussion with Sophie and that was the perfect intro into a big
heart to heart discussion about our desires. I admitted to James
about actually wanting to be used and abused by eight men
and he admitted he wanted to brand me and own me. He also
mentioned he thinks he's into cuckolding and wants to actually
watch someone else fuck me. I knew he liked to hear about
what other men did to me, I hadn't realised he might even like
to watch. So the conversation was quite enlightening both by
finding out more about each other and also unloading the
burden and weight of keeping my true feelings and desires
from him. It has felt quite freeing all week.

Today is Saturday and I check the playmate portal ten thousand times until I promise myself I'll only refresh one last time
before closing my laptop and heading to my daughter's netball
game. And there is the one word I've been waiting for:

ACCEPTED

25

I am delighted and feel like I could throw up at the exact same time. Reality is trying to hit home but I've got to leave the house now, so I text James one word before shutting my laptop and heading out: 'Accepted.' James replies by love-hearting the message. Oh my, what have I done...?

When we are all home for lunch after the kids' sports games, James tells me he's arranged for our babysitter to come over later this afternoon to watch the kids. We have a date to attend. This is news to me; we never have surprise dates to attend. *What is going on?* I wonder; it must have something to do with me getting accepted for the charity job. The charity job that starts four weeks from today.

A few hours later climbing into Jame's car, I ask, "Ok husband, now you have me, where are we going?"

"That is for me to know and you to find out, Rose Petal," he winks at me, not giving me anything to go on.

"Ok man of mystery. I can wait. Tell me, is it a nice surprise?"

"No clues." He reaches over the seat and pulls at my long brown hair. I didn't know what to expect so I've thrown on a cute black see-through blouse with a lacy black camisole underneath it. And paired it with black heeled boots and dark blue skinny jeans. My aim was dressed up casual. Not sure if I managed it but here we are. James insisted I didn't need casual comfy shoes at least.

We drive to PrahrPrahranan and I'm surprised to be here; we used to live here before we had kids, opting to move to the sleepy suburbs. I raise an eyebrow at James but he remains tight lipped and raises both eyebrows back at me as if to say 'What?'

Once we've parked the car, James takes my hands and we walk down past some cafés and shops before turning into an alleyway. I slow down a little, "Where are we going down here?" I ask. We've never been here before, I'm sure. Melbourne is full of hidden alleyways and secret bars.

"Just up these stairs," James says as he turns right where there is an open doorway and leads me up the stairs. I look around and the whole staircase is covered in graffiti art. Not the trespassers type of graffiti, this looks commissioned.

At the top of the stairs James pushes open a door and leads me into a waiting room which is clearly the waiting room of a tattoo artist.

"You're getting a tattoo?" I guess.

"You're getting a tattoo," James counters or was that commands?

"I'm getting a tattoo?" I repeat. "What tattoo am I getting?"

"You're getting what I want tattooed on you."

"Okay…" I trail off wondering if he's lost his sweet mind. "Where?"

"You'll see where."

"Why are you being so cryptic?"

"Because I don't want you to bail. If I keep it a surprise, you like surprises."

"Why in the world would I bail?" I ask, my brows furrowing now.

"You might not. I own this beautiful body of yours, Rosie. I am about to have my branding on your body for everyone, including the eight men who are buying you for a week, to know who you belong to," James says darkly in a low voice. He's still holding my hand. We never hold hands. Does he actually think I'm going to run?

Before I can ask any more questions, a thick set man with tattoos covering 80% of his body comes out of a room at the back and walks towards us. He's wearing jean overalls and a shirt rolled up at the sleeves. His head is shaved, and he has at least five piercings in both ears. "Rosie?" he enquires.

"Hi," I reply, unsure what to say. I didn't know I had an appointment until I turned up.

"Hi, I'm Bronson, lovely to meet you. And you must be James?"

James holds out his hand to shake with Bronson, who then turns and shakes mine also.

"Ok, if you're ready, follow me, I have your designs ready to go."

I look over at James who smiles coyly but gives nothing away. I have two choices right now. I can dig my heels in and make a fuss to find out exactly what and where I am getting a tattoo, or I can give in to this absurdness and allow James to have his way and brand me. I am leaning towards option two because honestly, I want him to brand me, I want to see what he has chosen for me. This side of him makes my pussy flutter and my clit tingle. I like James in his possessive mode, I don't see it very often, certainly not out in public.

"Ok Rosie, if you can hop onto the bed and remove your top and bra please." My eyes flick over to meet James' who has found himself a chair by the side of the wall. The tattoo chair is in the centre of the room.

"Here, you can place these over your nipples if that makes you feel more comfortable." Bronson passes me over two nipple stickers. Is that really going to make me feel better?

"I'm good thanks, unless you'd prefer I wear them?"

"I'm happy with whatever as long as you're comfortable."

I undo the buttons on my blouse and pull my arms out, I throw it over to James. Then I pull the lace black camisole off over my head and throw that to James. I sit perfectly still, naked from the waist up. My nipples pebble despite the warmth of the room. I feel exposed but not uncomfortable. Bronson is easy going and seems all about his job. It's James whose baby blue eyes seem dark and hooded as he watches me.

"Ok I have the first one here ready. Rosie, if you can lie down with your right arm above your head, rest it up there on the headrest, I'm going to lower the seat so you're lying down almost flat."

I lift my arm as Bronson directs and feel the chair flatten out. I glance up to see the outline of a rose on a transfer before it is stuck on the side of my right breast. *That isn't so bad* I muse and lie back and watch Bronson work over my body, remarkably close to my nipple but never brushing it.

The tattoo hurts a little, but not too bad. It's been a long time since I last got a tattoo. After thirty or so minutes Bronson seems to finish and straightens. "That's the first one down."

I raise my eyebrow at James.

"I've cling-filmed this, you'll need to try and keep it dry for a few days and put some cream on, which I'll give you before you leave. James can help you put your tops on before we move on to your lower half."

Whilst Bronson's back is turned as he gets the next tattoo ready I assume, James stands up and whispers in my ear, "You look fucking beautiful over there, getting my name tattooed on your breast."

"Is that what it is, a rose with your name?"

"Wait until you see it. It looks fucking perfect. Lift your arms," James commands and I do as he asks. He lowers my lace camisole gently over my arms and head and then down across my body. He then helps me into my blouse before doing up the buttons on the front. He most certainly brushes my nipples, on many occasions. "Stand up."

I swing my legs over and hop off the bed. James begins to undo my jeans' button, then the zip and then pulls them over my hips and my bottom before pulling them off each leg. I look at him questionably, but he doesn't say a word. He stands, throws the jeans over his chair and pulls my thong down. "James!" I cry out.

"You need these off for your next tattoo."

"Why, where is it going to be?"

"On your pussy."

"What?!"

"On your pussy lips to be exact."

This answer renders me completely speechless. Behind me Bronson has covered the chair with a long tissue covering like they have at a doctor's. I don't know whether to be turned on because of James' behaviour or mortified that I have to lie back and let this stranger see and tattoo my most intimate parts.

"Hop back onto the bed again Rosie. This time you can sit up but I need you to bend your right leg at the knee so you're open towards me." To my horror, he's holding a razor and begins to shave my right pussy fold. I go to close my eyes but decide to instead glare at James. This was a mistake to look over at him because the heat in his eyes is molten. He is enjoying watching this man shave me. I can't be turned on by this, I don't want my desire to leak out of me. I have to look away from James and instead try and focus on what Bronson is doing.

He's finished shaving me now, he puts the razor down and picks up another rose on transfer paper. He sticks it to my skin before gently pulling it away and leaving a blue ink design of a rose and now I see James' name along the stem. I watch as Bronson reaches for the tattoo gun and begins working on me. Never in my wildest dreams did I imagine James bringing me to a tattoo parlour and insisting I have his name branded onto me, on my *pussy*.

Thirty minutes later Bronson has covered over my second tattoo and James is helping me back into my clothes. I am flush with emotions I don't really know what to do with. Am I happy or angry? They are both warring in my brain. I'm fine about the tattoos, turned on even. It's just the full exposure that has got me in knots. It wasn't even a bad experience. It was just an unexpected one.

James helps me carefully step back into my jeans and I shimmy them back up over my butt and hips. Bronson is tidying up and then gestures for us to follow him back out to reception where James pays him. Bronson hands over some cream to apply on the tattoos which James snatches up. "I'll be applying this lotion, thanks Bronson." I blush and say thanks to Bronson. I'm not sure if I ever want to see him again or not. I follow James down the stairs and back into the alleyway. I am about to ask James what that was really all about when he turns to me, pushing me up against the wall and holds onto my chin, angling my face up to his. "Now every mother fucker who pays for your body knows exactly who you belong to. You are mine Rosie Bell and now you have the branding on your body to prove it," James growls the words into my ears, his voice is husky and dripping with possessiveness.

Has the Charity job tipped him over the edge? I wonder.

"Who do you belong to Rose Petal?"

"I-I," I stutter.

"Who!" James demands.

"You, James, I belong to you."

"Good girl," he purrs in my ear, his face so close to my face I wonder if he's going to lean in and bite me considering the intensity in his expression. "Now I no longer have to leave hickeys over your body to lay my claim. You looked fucking stunning open wide for that guy whilst he tattooed you. If I thought he'd allow it, I would have got my cock out and stroked it watching him tattoo your pussy and when he'd finished I would have come down the back of your throat to brand that also.

"James," I say as he grinds his stiff length into my stomach. Despite the unusual circumstance of getting two new tattoos, I would do it again if this is how James reacts and makes me feel.

"I would lift you up and fuck you now if I hadn't just got your pussy tattooed," James whispers in my ear as electricity courses through my body straight to my clit. I actually wish we could do it right now. Instead, he leans even closer and kisses me with such ferocity my head bangs into the wall behind me. Pulling back he says, "Instead, I need to calm down with the knowledge my name is now on your body and we have a table booked around the corner for dinner. We may as well make the most of the babysitter whilst we have the chance."

I breathe deeply trying to catch my breath from our kiss. I am all kinds of flustered and horny. I'd prefer to grab a hotel room right now but that is likely not the best move now I have two tattoos I need to look after. So instead, I pat my hair down, take James' hand and together we walk back out of the alleyway and towards a nice dinner for just the two of us. "We should do this more often," I say as we get to the Italian restaurant.

"Tattoo your pussy?" James smiles as I gasp and elbow him in the ribs. "Because I'm down for it any day of the week. Although I think I really do need to find someone who will let me fuck your mouth whilst they tattoo your cunt." And with that, he pushes open the door and I'm flustered as I make my way inside, hot and horny all over again.

26

───────

It's been four weeks of working, healing my tattoos, not being a playmate, not shaving and organising two kids' birthday parties because my little angels were born two years and two weeks apart. Life is busy, chaotic and normal. The only thing missing is the worry about paying our bills. I should be thinking about my impending Charity Job, but I have decided to push it to the back of my mind until the time is upon me. I decided not to take any other playmate jobs in the lead up, I wanted to spend more time with my family and I was about to earn more money than my wildest dreams. And the fresh tattoo meant I'd had to take a break from sex even with James. Plus, I was hairy everywhere and it didn't feel very sexy.

Frank is collecting me and driving me two hours away at 7am. I have been tossing and turning all night. My dreams are filled with disjointed conversations and worries. Every time I wake up, I fall back to sleep and another nightmare enters my subconscious. At 5am I decide to start just waking myself up and mentally preparing myself for the week ahead. I'm excited and nervous, I've been trying to keep both emotions under wraps but they are now strumming through my mind and body.

My stomach gurgles and my heart pounds. What will happen to me? Will I cope? What will they look like? Will they be kind to me? Gentle? Will they push my limits too much? Will I have to use my safe word?

I slowly climb out of bed but James' arm reaches out and pulls me back. "Don't go Rosie, stay and snuggle, I want to make the most of you before I give you up for the week." I smile at his sleepy tone and climb back into bed. I lie my head on his chest and curl around the side of him, he rests his arm around me and holds me close. "I'm going to miss you, Rose Petal."

"I'm going to miss you too." My voice fills with emotion.

"You're going to be fine. More than fine. You're going to have the time of your life, I bet," James says into my hair.

"I hope so. I've been trying not to think about it."

"Me too."

"But I'm nervous now though James. I think it's hitting me."

"Everyone and anyone would be nervous, just breathe through the nerves. Breathe them in, breathe them out. Exchange the nerves mentally for excitement. I wish I could watch all the depraved things they are going to do with your body. Remember you are in control. You can stop the scene at any point. They need you. I know you want the money, but we don't *need* the money. Always remember that you would be letting absolutely no one down. Every single person, even those men, have their limits. You are human and they are human."

I sign and relax my tensing muscles as I feel lighter from his words. "You always know the right thing to say."

"It's just one of my many talents," James jokes.

"Indeed, it is one of your ever extending talents," I agree. "Will you be ok this week with the kids?"

"Absolutely. You have nothing to worry about. The kids will be fine, I will be fine—we'll all be fine including you."

I close my eyes and try to absorb the feeling of James' body under mine. The movement of his chest rising and falling and his heart beating below my ear. I love this man. I am going to miss him. I drift off in the safety and comfort of James' arms before my alarm goes and it's 6am. I jump with a fright and this time I do climb out of bed to take a shower.

Fifty-five minutes later, I'm clean, dressed, fed and hugging James goodbye. Both kids are still asleep but that's ok as I said goodbye to them the night before. Saying goodbye this morning would be much harder for me and them. Why does saying goodbye to your kids feel like someone is tearing out your heart?

I look into James' eyes. My lip begins to quiver and my eyes pool with water.

"Hey, none of that. You're going to have the best time."

I nod, incapable of finding words.

"I love you. Be safe. Remember your safeword. Use it if you need to. I'll pick you up from the moon if that is where they have taken you."

I smile as the tears break free and tip down my cheeks. "I love you. See you in a week."

"See you in a week, Rose Petal." James kisses me gently on the lips.

I open the door, make my way down to Frank's waiting car with blacked out windows and climb in, before I shut the door, I smile and wave up at James who is smiling and waves back at me. *See you in a week my love*, I say in my head. I tie the blindfold as usual and rest my head on the headrest. I try to relax and focus on my breathing. I'd love to get some more sleep because who knows when I can sleep alone again. Frank turns up the radio, his favourite Smooth FM is playing love ballads and I focus on them and not my impending job. I really don't know what to expect.

It must be two hours later that I startle awake as I hear Frank repeat my Playmate alias. "Roxy. We're here. Don't take your blindfold off. I am going to come around and help you out.

Then you will be collected and walked towards the house by one of the club members."

"Ok Frank, I understand," I answer. When I hear the door open, I swing my legs out and reach for a hand. Finding Frank's warm outstretched hand, he helps pull me out of the car and I pull my overnight bag along with me. I had no idea what to pack, so I packed light. The description was captive, so I'm guessing there won't be much need for heels and a dinner dress. I have plenty of different underwear sets, plus my toiletries and nightie. Frank leads me slowly along a path and I hold onto his hand for dear life. Panic is rippling through my body as shit is about to get real, oh so very fucking real. Frank stops and I hear another male voice speak to him.

"Thanks Frank, I'll take her from here. See you next week," comes an easy-going voice as I feel Frank's hand drop mine and another warm slender hand take hold.

"Lovely to meet you Roxy, I'm Dr Jack and I'm going to lead you into the house. I just need you to keep your blindfold on a little longer. We can walk nice and slowly. I'll take your bag."

I feel as he tugs the handle from out of my hand and pulls me slowly along towards wherever I'm being led to.

"One small step here, Roxy."

I lift my foot. I feel like Bambi walking on new feet. I never realised how hard it is having your sight taken away and walking with no bearing as to where you are. I walk a couple more steps and the floor changes under my feet to what sounds like tiles.

"I'm going to lead you towards some steps. There is a rail, you'll be able to hold my hand and the rail," Dr Jack says soothingly, like I'm a child he's guiding.

We walk for a few minutes slowly until Dr Jack stops. "Ok, here is a banister rail," he places my hand onto the rail. "We are going down some stairs now. There are about 20. Take your time."

I hesitantly reach out my foot and lower until I can feel the step below. Ever so slowly, I take one step at a time, and I realise I'm beginning to sweat. I have a horrible fear of falling, stairs being one of them.

"And we're here. Let me take off your blindfold." I feel Dr Jack standing behind me as he unties the fastening. When the covering falls from my face I blink in the dazzling artificial light that greets me.

I am standing in a basement that reminds me of a cellar in a winery. The brick walls are painted, and the underground room is expansive. What takes my breath is what I am looking at in the centre of the huge room. With all the lights on, it looks like a glass room. Or should I say, a glass box. On the inside of the room is a giant bed against the far wall. A pile of books, an old leather brown armchair and a padded wooden chair underneath a small table with a speaker on it. There is also a glass door on the other side of the room that I hope leads to a bathroom. It's eerie, and it reminds me of the X-Files or an observation room. My skin prickles and I realise I'm being watched.

For the first time, I turn and look straight into the warm green eyes of Dr Jack. He's a young man, in his mid-thirties like me and only a touch taller than me. He reminds me of the boy next door although he's too old for that now. He has floppy light brown hair that is ruffled on his head, he's wearing simple blue jeans, a shirt and a long white overcoat exactly what a doctor might wear in a hospital. Seems odd that he'd need to wear it in here.

"Hi again Roxy, now you can actually see me."

"Hi," I reply shyly and give him a smile.

"I'd like to show you around your lodgings for the week. Come this way." He playfully curls a finger at me, and I can't help but laugh and follow him into the glass box of a room. When we are through the door, I'm surprised to realise the glass is one way viewing, I cannot see outside of the glass like in a police interview room. I'm not sure how I feel about this. A goldfish comes to mind. As Dr Jack closes the door behind us, the door doesn't make a single sound. There is a big rug covering most of the floor, the room is soundproof, and I can't hear a single thing now we're inside. It makes me shudder.

"Here is your room, I think we have everything you might need. Through this door is a bathroom." Dr Jack leads me through the large room and opens the glass door at the back. I can see through this door, but he opens it for me anyway. It is a lovely modern bathroom with a shower, tub, toilet and sink. There are pink fluffy towels hanging up and matching pink bathmat. "I tried to make this room a little more cosy for you," Jack says a little more shyly than his earlier easy-going tone. I warm to him instantly. "I also brought some products I'd—we'd like you to use whilst you are with us."

I smile at him. "Thank you. Where are the other men?" I enquire as Dr Jack leads me out of the bathroom. Dr Jack sits down on the large bed with plump white bedding and pats the space next to him for me to sit. I do as he asks, both our bodies are facing each other, our knees almost grazing.

"They are all here. We decided to not all visit you at once and overwhelm you. We have arranged a little schedule for you so you will meet each of us very soon." He smiles at me warmly.

That makes me feel a little relaxed. Dr Jack seems nice; I wonder what his kink is. "Are you really a doctor?" I enquire.

"Ah no, but I know enough about medicine."

"Oh, yeah of course." I stare at him realising I can't ask personal questions, so I bite my lip as to not follow it up with any more questions. Instead, I decide to hold my tongue and wait for Dr Jack to continue.

"And I know enough to take care of you, rest assured."

That makes me pause—why would I need a doctor exactly? Then it hits me, this is his kink. He has a doctor kink and I relax my tense shoulders again.

"We have put together a loose plan for you, you have no idea how excited we all are to finally have you here." Dr Jack beams at me. "Our plan for you this week is: Every morning you will shower, Carl will shave you all over and moisturise. Gerry—who we affectionately call Cook, will bring you your meals. He also likes to feed, so he will be feeding you. Tom likes to watch, so that chair over there," he points to the brown leather armchair, "that's for him. He doesn't say much, so don't worry about him too much. Darcy likes to play with you whilst you're sleeping. You'll be his real-life sleeping beauty." He winks at me.

"Will I meet him at all if he only likes to see me when I'm sleeping?" I ask, genuinely curious as it'll be a first to have someone touch me who I've never met or seen before.

"Yes, you'll see him at some points during your stay, don't you worry about that. Bet it would be nice to put a face to the body that will be playing with you during the night." He chuckles.

That almost sounds unhinged, I think.

"David likes his impact play and was born to dominate. He has his own toys he's bringing to play." Dr Jack's eyes twinkle. "And then there is Blake and Jake. I think you'll like them. They're together but Blake is the top and the Dom, Jake is the bottom and submissive, he's looking forward to being a top this week."

I nod, that's seven men. "And you're into being a doctor then?" I ask.

"Yes that's me," he answers casually but again, there is that glimmer of something else under the surface of his demeanour. *Wasn't it Sweeney Todd who managed to murder so many women because of his boyish good looks. Is that the same as Dr Jack? I wonder.*

"Ok, we have put together a few rules for your stay," Dr Jack removes his phone from his pocket. "Are you ready?" I nod for him to continue.

"One: No clothes unless any of us gives you something to wear. Two: You eat what you are fed, all of it (that's Cook's rule). Three: Unless you use your safe word, which is Neptune, anything you say will be taken as part of the scene. You can use your safe word for the scene, and everything stops but you can stay. Or you can use your safe word and leave here entirely, you are not a prisoner. We want you to enjoy yourself as much as we know we will. Four: Don't speak to Tom. Five: Use the products I've provided for you to use. Six: We are all tested and received our clear results this week. We all want to come inside you. We know it's club policy for testing anyway but I just wanted to reassure you and confirm we are all looking forward to having you with nothing between us." Dr Jack looks up from his phone at that, a wicked gleam in his eyes that I almost miss. He blinks and his expression clears to soft and warm again. A smile wide on his lips. I smile back at him. "Seven: Expect lots of sex, we all want to fill all your holes." Again, he looks up and this time his smile is darkly unnerving. There is no shame behind his eyes and his words, he means them wholeheartedly. I admire that. And I was expecting nothing less. "Eight: If you wake up when Darcy is with you, pretend to be asleep, he likes that. And that's the list. Do you have any questions?"

"Um, not really. Will someone be with me all the time?"

"No you will have breaks, I think you'll need them," he says coyly, with a twinkle in his eye. Something tells me he enjoyed putting together the schedule and knowing what everyone has planned for me. He then continues, "We have a speaker over there that will play music most of the day. And you probably spotted the pile of books by the bed. We didn't want you to go stir crazy when you're resting."

"Thank you, that sounds really great. You have thought of

everything," I say, "Are you allowed to tell me what I have planned for today?" I ask.

"I think that's allowed. Carl is coming in to shave you first, Tom at the same time to watch. Then Cook will bring you lunch and dinner. Beware, Cook makes the most delicious food you've ever tasted. It will be a toss-up of who enjoys it more— you for eating it, or him for feeding it to you."

My eyebrows furrow. That's an interesting thing to say.

"You'll see. I bet you've never come across a feeder before. I hadn't until Cook. It's going to be an experience this week, that's for sure," Dr Jack chuckles.

"Have you ever done anything like this before? All of you together I mean," I ask, feeling more relaxed around him the longer I'm in his company.

"Nope. Never. We had this room specially built just for you. We have enjoyed planning our time together. It's going to be unforgettable. I wouldn't be surprised if the guys are all watching us right now. So, if you don't have any more questions —let's get started."

"Sure," I reply, wondering what is going to happen now.

"I'd like to remove your clothes now."

"Okay," I reply demurely.

"Please come here and stand in front of me."

I do as he commands. I jump down from the bed which is higher than I'm used to and stand in front of Dr Jack.

"Closer," he directs.

I take a step closer so I'm standing between his legs. Dr Jack reaches for the buttons at the top of my shirt. Carefully he undoes the top button, and his fingers graze my skin. I feel every nerve ending where he's touched, my body becoming very aware of our proximity and the way his fingers are moving down my body, one button at a time. He pulls at my shirt and untucks it from my jean skirt. My breathing has become shallow, my heart has doubled its pace. Dr Jack is taking his time;

he looks as if he's unwrapping a present. He reaches for the fabric on my right shoulder and slowly peels it down before doing the same with the left shoulder. Carefully, he pulls the shirt down my arms and off my body.

Placing the shirt on the bed next to him, he says, "Turn around with your back to me."

I do as he asks, and I feel his fingers undo the zip on my jean skirt and feel him tug at it over my hips and past my bottom. It drops to the floor and I step out of it and move to bend down to retrieve it.

"Stop. Leave it there. Back to where you were standing."

I rise and am taken aback by his commanding tone. It doesn't sound like the same person who just showed me around. I move back between his legs, and he pulls me closer so my back is now rubbing on his crotch, and I can feel just how much he's enjoying undressing me. He unclips my bra and slowly moves each strap down my arms before pulling it off completely and putting it on the bed.

"That was for the boys," he whispers in my ear. I look at the glass walls in front of me, but don't see anything. They must be on the other side. Watching. "You can take that tiny piece of fabric off from between your legs please."

I do as he asks, hooking my fingers into my red silk thong and pulling it over my hips and bottom until it drops to my ankles, and I step out of it. This time leaving it where it is. It feels strangely erotic to be standing naked in front of a glass wall not knowing who is watching and how many eyes are looking back at me.

I feel the lightest of touches as Dr Jack runs his fingers from the back of my neck, down my back and over my butt cheek. It sends a shiver down my spine. It's then I realise it's warm in the room. Cosy. But being naked, watched, and touched is messing with my temperature gauge.

Dr Jack keeps me standing where I am and puts both hands

on the back of my neck before running them down my spine again. The movement feels revered like he's touching a woman for the first time, soft and gentle, sensual. I begin to relax, and my shoulders feel like they lower two inches. Taking his time, he carefully runs his hands over my heating skin again, along the curve of my neck sending tingles down my back. His touch is mesmerising, and I lean into the direction of his movement.

Dr Jack leans in closer to me so I can feel his chest pressed up against my back, his breath skitters across my shoulder. He moves my ponytail away from my shoulder and presses light, slow kisses from behind my ear, down the sensitive part of my neck and across my shoulder, his right arm begins to snake around my waist and lightly strokes at the hair on my mound. He is barely touching me with his lips and his fingers, but my body comes alight with each glancing contact, he's making me crave for more. He's teasing me. Raising his head, he begins the slow descent of feather kisses from behind my ear, this time his right hand moves up my navel to stroke the underside of my right breast. I tip my head back slightly and moan at his touch. I can feel his mouth move into a smile against my shoulder.

"You are putty in my hands Roxy, I bet you'd let me do anything I wanted to you right now, wouldn't you?" he asks in a low voice that might sound menacing if I wasn't so horny right now. He's right, I am putty. He's turning my insides into molten lava which is being pumped right down to my pussy, my clit is throbbing for something, anything.

"Yes," I breathe in response. "Do what you want with me."

"All in good time my precious, all in good time," he whispers into my ear before nibbling at my ear lobe. "I can't keep my fingers and my lips away from you. I promised Carl I wouldn't have come leaking out of you before he's shaved you. I'm finding that promise increasingly difficult to keep."

27

On that note there is a knock on the door.

"Clearly he doesn't trust that I will keep my promise either," he says louder now so that the man entering the room can hear.

"Roxy, please meet Carl. Carl, please meet Roxy."

I turn, very aware of how naked I am, to see a beautiful, dark eyed man entering the room. He walks right up to me. I watch in curiosity as he doesn't say a word, his face unmoving, his eyes focused and intent on my face. He reaches out a hand and cups my face, looking unnervingly into my eyes. Not a handshake. I take a breath as he drinks me in, the only movements are his eyes moving from left to right.

Instead of speaking he leans in and kisses me softly on the lips. He pulls away a millimetre before kissing me again so deliciously I'm caught off guard. He deepens the kiss, this stranger. I feel his tongue searching for mine, I can't help but give it to him. He tastes of coffee and caramel and kisses me slowly, taking his time to savour me. I melt into his kiss wanting to feel closer to him. I move my hands to curve around his waist and press my body closer to his. It's then that I feel the huge bulge in his trousers. Satisfaction courses through me, he is enjoying our introduction as much as I am.

Just as I begin to wonder if he is going to let go of himself and have me, he pulls away and holds his forehead against mine. "I can see why Dr Jack was getting carried away Roxy, you are intoxicating," he says in a deep husky voice.

I look into his eyes but don't say a word. He is in control now, I know what he wants.

"I would very much like to shave you now, and then come back to your lips."

"I am looking forward to you shaving me, Carl," I reply. Carl's eyes light up and I know I've said the right thing.

"Let's get you in position then."

Carl pulls away and I miss his body heat immediately. I watch as he walks into the bathroom and comes out with a huge, light pink bath towel which he lays in the middle of the bed. He then walks back over to the door where I see a large bag he's left there. A movement catches my eye to the left of the bed, and I gasp in shock. Sitting in the brown leather chair is a hulk of a man. He has a shaved head with a blond beard and a stacked body. He is wearing a black t-shirt that is stretched across his wide chest and tattooed arms. He looks relaxed, one leg crossed over the other like he's sitting in his living room watching his favourite show. Tom, it must be him. He's looking at me with a bland face and fierce eyes. I can't read his expression but it's not warm and welcoming. The rules were I'm not to speak to him so I turn my attention back to Carl who is now in the bathroom filling up a bowl of water which he carries in.

"Lie down on the towel please, Roxy." And I do as he requests. With my head on the pillow, I can see Tom on my left and Carl on my right. Dr Jack must have slipped out of the room. Carl looks deep in his head now, this is his time, he must be in his element. I won't say anything further now unless he speaks to me. It feels strange though. Here I am, naked in front of two strangers. Everyone is acting as if it's completely normal. Tom is watching on with rapt attention. Carl is busying himself in preparations which I can only assume is something he fantasises about often.

Carl places a bowl of warm water to the right of my thigh and then kneels next to me on the giant bed. He has laid out a bar of creamy coloured soap and a razor on the towel that I'm lying on. He dips his hands into the bowl with the soap, rubbing it slowly in his hands and then he lifts my right arm and begins rubbing the softly scented soap down my arm. I can smell shea butter, I think. I watch as he then picks up the razor and runs it down my forearm from wrist to elbow. I was born very fair, it's only as I've grown older that my hair colour has changed to a light coppery brown. The hair on my arms and legs has stayed fair. I've never shaved my arms so it'll be a change that they'll be as smooth as my legs for once.

Carl puts barely any pressure on the razor as he runs the blade down my forearm, carefully over and over again. Then he lifts my arm to rest it above my head and soaps up the bar of soap before gently caressing the skin under my arms. I flinch and giggle. It tickles. I don't think anyone has ever touched me there in such an intimate way. Carl glances down at my face and his sweet smile could light up a thousand cities. It's a mix of joy, shyness and happiness. He then picks up the razor and I can hardly feel the strokes as he runs it under my arm. He's shaving me like a porcelain doll who might break. And I'm totally fine with his gentleness seeing as he's very soon going to be shaving me somewhere I'd prefer to keep my skin 100% intact.

I watch as Carl hesitates for a moment, his attention caught by my right breast. He's noticed my new tattoo. He reads the name at the stem, his eyes flicking to mine knowing I've been branded. I look back at him. We share a conversation with our eyes. I try to convey that I am happy with it and don't feel any shame or pain. He gives me a subtle nod and turns back to his razor and shaving me.

I can feel my body loosen into the experience. When he is done, he moves to the other side of my body with the bowl of warm water and carefully soaps my left forearm and shaves it before raising my left arm and almost reverently he shaves under my armpit. Once he's finished, he moves down the bed and kneels between my feet. I watch with relaxed eyes, in awe of this man in his light beige trousers that have splotches of water on them now, his light grey t-shirt equally sprinkled with water flecks. Carl picks up my right foot and lifts it to bend my knee and places my foot back onto the bed. He then picks up the soap and this time dips it into the bowl and runs his hands and the soap up and down my right calf. If anyone was watching, like Tom right now, you would think I have been in a relationship with Carl for years because the careful tenderness he is showing me would only be expected of someone who loves me.

Once my calf is sufficiently lathered up to my knee, he puts down the soap and picks up the razor, diligently shaving in overlapping lines to ensure not one hair is missed. Carl looks like he's performing an operation that requires the full intensity of his attention. He soaps up my thigh almost up to my hip and shaves me again in low slow swipes. In all honesty, I could get used to having someone shave my body like this. If it weren't for the full exposure and the voyeur in the corner, I could almost be at a spa right now. Lowering my right leg, Carl lifts my left foot and begins the whole process again until that leg is completely hairless.

There is only one place left to do. Carl turns his attention to the apex of my legs. I haven't seen him take even a glimpse at it until now. His eyes seem to widen slightly as he takes in my mound, my folds and the four weeks of hair that has grown through. Usually, I go hairless, so it's been a challenge to not wax it.

Carl lifts both my feet, one at a time to bend my legs at the knee and place them wider apart than earlier. I am spread wide and open for him now, my folds parted and ready. He reaches into the bowl and soaps his hands before gently rubbing at the hair on my mound. I want him to look up at me, I want to see into his eyes but he doesn't even blink at me, his sole attention is on rubbing his soapy fingers into my curls before lowering them down each side of my pussy and lower closer to my back hole. No one has ever shaved me, or even soaped me down there in the way he is doing now. It feels sensual, a luxurious treatment you might receive and hope you get a massage too, and a happy ending.

I feel blood pumping through my body as my heart rate picks up, it especially starts to pump down to my pussy where I start to feel the building sensation of pleasure trickling through me. Carl looks happy with his soaping efforts and puts the soap down in place of the razor. Gently he strokes a line from close to my back hole up over my folds and up across my mound in one slow and steady movement. His hand has a tiny tremor now which I assume is because of the delicate location he is shaving. Or maybe he's excited to be shaving me there. He works with one hand holding my folds taut and running the razor blade up and down with the other. It feels like an erotic tease, the slower and longer he takes, the hotter and hornier I feel.

Carl takes in a breath when I know my other tattoo has been revealed. I watch him take it in, he places the razor down and runs his thumb tentatively over the rose. It's completely healed but I know it must be an unusual find for him. Wondering if he's shaved many women and ever seen a tattoo there. Most likely not given his attention to it. He appears to like it, the corners of his mouth twitching. He doesn't say a word and I wonder what is going on in his head.

I can feel liquid desire begin to leak out of me and as he turns his attention on my left pussy lip, he too notices what is leaking out of me. He sucks in a breath and looks up at me wide eyed. "Do you enjoy me shaving you here?" his deep husky voice sends a shiver down my spine.

I crinkle my eyes, and the corners of my lips turn up in a slow smile, something tells me this man needs care and gentleness in return for his, "I had no idea how good it would feel, Carl." And that is the honest truth.

Pleasure ripples across his face as he answers, "I have waited a very long time to do this." Before turning his attention back to my pussy. He begins to shave me carefully and I trust him. When he pulls back to admire his work, I see once again the bulge in his trousers. He then dips a washcloth into the soapy water and gently wipes away any remaining soap across my body.

Moving off the bed, Carl takes the bowl, razor, soap and washcloth to the bathroom and returns with a small bottle of oil. When he opens it, I think I can smell camomile as he dabs a drop on his hand before closing the lid and then begins to rub the oil delicately into my right arm, then my left. Another drop later and he's massaging my legs better than any massage I've ever experienced. Maybe it's because I'm naked and turned on so much, I could burst into flames. Rubbing up and down my legs, getting close to my pussy and then further away again. I'm enjoying the massage so much but it's also killing me that he's not touching me near my clit which has almost got its own heartbeat.

Finally, he tips another drop of oil into his hands and rubs it into the folds of my pussy. He works upwards just like he did with the razor, even my back hole wants the attention of his magic fingers. Carl's massaging fingers edge closer and closer to my clit and I wonder if he's avoiding it on purpose or oblivious to it. I get my answer instantly when he swipes three fingers across it, and I can't contain my moan. One side of his mouth crooks up and he does it again, and then again. I'm so far gone on the edge, it's the fourth stroke that has me arching my back and screaming out his name as he continues his swipes until the pulsing of my orgasm has depleted and I begin to shudder at its sensitivity.

Carl looks in awe of what he just did or maybe how I just reacted. In a blink his eyes turn hungry, he undoes the buttons to his trousers, pulls his stiff, hairless cock out and lines it up to my entrance. Without a word, he slowly slides between my folds and edges inside of me, my legs still bent and open. I can see he's on the edge himself as I wrap my legs around his waist and my hands around his face, a couple of thrusts until he hits the back of my walls and he's coming undone inside of me. I feel his body shudder and his cock pulses deep inside of me.

Looking down at me with questioning eyes, I offer the reassurance he needs immediately.

"That was the most incredible experience I've ever had Carl, thank you," I say, trying to convey in my voice I mean every word.

"I'm sorry I was so quick. I nearly came twice when I was shaving you, especially after I found your second tattoo," he blushes.

"I thought I was going to self-combust when you were shaving me too," I giggle.

Carl gently pulls out his softening cock and goes to tuck it back into his beige trousers before thinking better of it. Instead, he chooses to leave it out and lie next to me on the bed. "Thank you for allowing me to shave you like that. It was everything I dreamt it would be and more."

"It was my pleasure Carl; I felt like I was at a sensual spa with a happy ending." I giggle as I turn on my side to face him.

"You took better care of me than any massage or treatment I've ever received," I smile at him. I lie with him and enjoy the afterglow we both share before soft music begins to play on the speaker. I frown at him questioningly and he groans.

"That's Cook's music, it means my time is up for today. But I'll be back to shave you every morning. And I'll be around and watching."

"I'm looking forward to seeing you again already, Carl." I'm surprised that I do genuinely mean that too.

He leans in and kisses me deeply, our tongues reuniting for one last kiss before he pulls himself off the bed, cock hanging out of his trousers as he walks into the bathroom to clean up. He returns with a washcloth and carefully spreads my legs, dabbing it between my folds before we both look up and see a man coming through the doorway in front of us. He smiles widely, creating dimples in both cheeks. This must be Cook. He's slim with cropped blonde hair and black rimmed glasses and deep dimples in his cheeks. My guess is that he's in his early forties.

He nods to me, then to Carl and Tom. To Carl he says, "We enjoyed watching you shave our Roxy here, I've had a stiffy since Dr Jack undressed her."

I sit up and cross my legs on the bed seeing as I no longer need to lie down.

"Hi Roxy, it's so nice to finally meet you in person," Cook says as he bounds up to me holding out his hand. I take it and he shakes it softly. I smile back at him. "I hope you're hungry," he says teasingly.

"I think I've built up an appetite being so well looked after by Carl," I say as I watch Carl head towards the door. He turns and smiles shyly at me.

"See you tomorrow, princess," he says as he walks out of the door.

28

———

"I can see you are quite the hit Roxy, so please, come sit over on the chair," Cook directs in a cheerful voice. I swing my legs and hop off the bed. "I am going to wheel in the trolley with your lunch on it."

"Ok," I answer. Cook returns pushing a two shelved silver trolley with many dishes covered with silver covers, to keep the food warm I suppose. Or a surprise?

"I'm just going to grab another chair." Cook goes back out the door and returns with a similar wooden chair and I wonder for a moment if it was just on the other side of the glass being used by one of the men. I take a moment to consider the people I have met so far. Aside from Tom who hasn't said a word, the first three men have been much more friendly and welcoming than I had imagined. I don't know what I was expecting. After all, what kind of men pay to keep a woman captive for a week to fulfil their every kink fantasy—not normal people I had assumed. And now I'm beginning to realise I've been proven very wrong.

Cook lowers himself onto the chair in front of me and

pushes his glasses back higher onto his nose again. From his rolled-up sleeve I see he has a tattoo of a huge kitchen knife of some kind on his forearm. He has a navy striped apron on, which has a few spots and stains that seem recent. *Maybe he is an actual chef in real life*, I muse.

"I have prepared a few dishes I hope you love. Forgive me, I may have over indulged a little, but I see it as a celebration having you here, so let's get started. First we have oysters." He lifts the covering from a small dish and lowers the plate on the table, we both sit opposite each other, our knees almost touching, the table on the left of us and the trolley to the right. Enclosed in. It's a bit odd to prepare to eat a meal while not facing the table. To my surprise, he lifts an oyster and angles it so I have to tip my head back before it slides swiftly down into my mouth.

My taste buds are on high alert as the salty, fleshy deliciousness attacks my senses. I love all seafood, yet I hardly ever eat oysters. I smile gratefully at Cook, who takes that as a prompt for the next one.

The next dish is raw kingfish, and I gasp, "Oh that is my favourite."

Cook smiles widely, "It's mine too," seeming pleased at the coincidence.

The next plate he uncovers is a crab pasta bisque which is mouthwatering. Cook curls every piece of pasta onto the fork and lowers it into my waiting open mouth. It feels strangely intimate to be fed like this, least of all because I'm still completely naked. Memories of my time with Connor come back to me but in contrast he loved to make a mess of me and slopped pasta all down my body to eat and lick off me but Cook is careful and precise as he feeds me, not allowing me to drop even the tiniest morsel. Cook drinks me in, watching with a satisfied contentment as I carefully eat each forkful of pasta he offers.

I begin to feel full and start to rub my tummy, "I'm not sure I can eat much more, I'm getting so full now."

"You are doing so well baby girl. I think you can finish these last two forkfuls for me." I glance down at the bowl, *they would need to be two very big forkfuls,* I think to myself. But he manages it, and I manage to chew the delicious pasta down.

I rub my stomach again. Cook watches with glazed eyes as I rub circles around my bloated stomach. "Here, let me," he says, as he moves the chair closer and puts a hand on my stomach and begins to rub. It feels oddly soothing. Here is a grown man feeding me and now rubbing my stomach. He begins to rub large circles, and his wrist brushes the underside of my breasts making my nipples pebble.

"I'm looking forward to watching you grow in front of my eyes," Cook says and I tilt my head to the side a little. Before I can ask what he means by that, he asks, "How are you feeling now, would you like a sip of water?"

"Yes please," I nod. And he hands me a glass over. I sip the ice-cold water and do feel slightly better like I've washed some of my lunch down.

Cook takes a moment to properly take me in, his eyes move from my closed knees to my stomach and up over my breasts where they stop at my tattoo. One of his eyebrows twitches up but he doesn't say a word as his eyes continue to roam across my chest and rest on my smiling face.

"Are you ready for dessert?" he asks and I realise there is another covered plate left.

"Um." I'm about to say no, I'm not sure I can fit another morsel in when I remember the rules. Number two, was it? Eat all of Cook's food. Shit, this is what they meant. What will happen if I don't? I don't want to upset or offend him on my first day. So instead, I nod and he looks delighted as he opens the lid and I see a wickedly thick chocolate mousse. "How'd you know that's my favourite!?" I exclaim, forgetting for a minute how on earth I'm going to fit it in.

"I figured all women enjoy chocolate," he replies, smiling broadly.

I laugh, "Indeed you are right. I do!"

"Open wide baby girl, you deserve this desert for eating all your dinner for me." I do as he asks and feel a tingle between my legs. What was it about that sentence that has got my clit sparking? As he lowers the spoonful of rich chocolate mousse onto my tongue, I can't help my gasp of joy as the sweet yumminess fills my taste buds and I close my eyes in heaven. This mousse tastes just as good as it looks and smells.

Spoonful after spoonful Cook lowers into my mouth, he is rapt at my obedience and enjoyment, but I do begin to slow down. My stomach is becoming full and distended. I'm rubbing it again and he leans over to rub it too. "My baby girl can finish her mousse for me can't she?"

"I think so, I have to take a minute to let it go down." I breathe and he passes me the glass of water to help wash it down.

"Open wide, three more to go," commands Cook, and I open my mouth.

When I have swallowed the last one, I groan, "I think I've made it to Christmas full."

"Christmas full?" Cook repeats, brows furrowed.

"You know the type of full where you eat so much delicious Christmas dinner that you are filled up to your chin," I offer as an explanation.

"Ah, I see. So you're Christmas full. I'll have to remember that one. You look so beautiful when you've eaten so well for me. Here, let me help make you feel better now. Follow me."

Cook stands and walks towards the bed, he fluffs the crisp white pillows and puts them one on top of each other. He strips down to his boxers, showing me his lean pale body. He climbs onto the bed, sitting up, he leans his back onto the pillows and pats between his legs. "Come sit here and I'll make you feel better."

I don't understand what he means but I climb onto the bed in front of him as he guides me to sit with my back to his chest and I lay against him, my head just to the left of his neck, resting on his chest and shoulder. Cook begins to rub slow circles around my full and extended stomach. It feels odd at first but the more he caresses my skin, the more I sink into his warm body. Every now and again, he brushes against my breasts and my focus begins to shift from the fullness in my stomach, to the intermittent touches he leaves against my breasts. Making me want more of those kinds of touches and less on my stomach. We lay there for what feels like 30 minutes at least. I start to feel drowsy from all the food, the warmth of his body and the rhythm of his heartbeat and his motions. As my eyelids start to become heavy, I see a slight movement to my left.

It's Tom still sitting in the armchair, cock in hand, just stroking. He is stroking himself watching me being stroked and I wish I was being stroked somewhere else too. Cook seems to notice too. He reaches his right hand down between my folds and dips his fingers into my wetness. He groans too. "You are dripping baby girl," he growls into my ear.

"I am," I moan in reply. Raising two fingers from my entrance to my clit, he begins to circle around the bundle of nerves I so need him to touch right now. I look over at Tom and his eyes are now trained on Cook's fingers. It doesn't take long before that familiar pleasure is building higher and higher with each circle around my clit. Tom is stroking faster now, as Cook puts a little more pressure on his stroking of me. Tom groans loudly, the first noise I've heard from him as lines of hot come pulse out of him onto his hand. And that's all I need as I moan out Cook's name and he tips me over the edge of my own electrifying orgasm.

"You come so magnificently for us, Roxy," Cook says as he dips his fingers into my hot release. He then lifts them to his mouth and sucks, one finger at a time until they are clean. "You are a better delicacy than I could ever prepare. Tom you need to taste our girl."

29

To my utter surprise, Tom rises from his seat and tucks himself back into his jeans. He's already wiped his hands on a tissue. He walks to the front of the bed, his eyes solely on my core, climbs on and leans his face into my pussy, taking a deep breath before using his tongue to take one deep swipe from the bottom of my pussy lips all the way up and finishing at my clit. I shudder at its sensitivity and also the depravity of this man who has been watching me get shaved, fondled, fucked, fed, and fingered and now he's here tasting me.

He lowers his head and does it again, deeper and my eyes roll into the back of my head as I moan, leaning into Cook. I feel fingers reach for my nipples and begin to pull and stretch them. It's Cook's arms that are moving but I raise my head to see Tom look up with me, his beard glistening with my release. He stares at me, his eyes so intense I wonder if he likes or hates me. Not saying a word, not changing his facial expression from openly glaring at me, I watch as his eyes look down at Cook's fingers playing with my nipples. One corner of Tom's mouth twitches up, he looks behind me at Cook and they seem to exchange something between them before he lowers his head and laps at my pussy again from the bottom to my clit. Intense pleasure begins to build as Cook puts more pressure on my nipples which shoots electricity straight to my clit. And then Tom assaults my clit with pressured licks up and down until my legs are shaking around his head and I'm close, I'm almost there with another climax. Tom senses me pushing closer to the edge and I feel two fat fingers enter me and caress my g-spot as I explode around him, arching my back off Cook's chest and moving my hips closer to ride out the pleasure on Tom's tongue. What is happening right now?

I lower back down onto Cook's chest and from my high, I feel utterly boneless and floaty. After all the food and orgasms, I could nap right here right now. As my eyelids flutter closed, thick hands pull me from Cook and then flip me over, manoeu-vring me onto my hands and knees. My eyes flutter open to see Cook's stiff cock glistering in his hands and I feel Tom's thick cock prodding at my entrance. In one swift move, Tom's cock pushes deep inside me to the hilt as he presses his hand on my back to lower my head over Cook's cock.

I lower my mouth quickly down onto Cook's cock who groans loudly from above me. Tom fucks into me hard. *Is he hate fucking me*? He sets a rhythm from behind for my head to bounce up and down Cook's cock.

"That feels incredible baby girl, you're sucking me whilst Tom fucks you hard. He thinks you've been a naughty girl for selling yourself to us. But I think that turns him on even more. Isn't that right Tom, you are loving watching our girl be used and pleasured. You couldn't help yourself to join in rather than just watch."

I hear a gruff, "Fuck you," from behind me. The power from this hulk of a man is hitting me exactly on my sweet spot and Cook's words are all I need to hear. I'm in heaven with my mouth around his cock as he begins to move my head in tandem with Tom's thrusts.

"Roxy is loving being spit roasted right now. You deep in her cunt and me deep down her throat, both of us about to unload at the same time and painting our girl with our brands. She is ours for the taking this week, aren't you baby girl. Take my come right now, drink it down that hot throat of yours."

I feel his hot salty come at the back of my throat which is all I need to make my core begin to spasm around Tom's cock and I hear him behind me roar, "Fuck." His cock is deep inside me as he stills, and I feel it pulse his release.

Now I am completely and utterly boneless. Used to an inch of my energy, I have nothing left. I sway and Tom catches me as he pulls out of me and lifts me into the air and onto his lap where he's kneeling. Concern crosses his face but he doesn't say a word, just looks at my face trying to read me.

Cook leans over and says, "I think we have rung our girl out. Let's get her cleaned up." Nodding, Tom holds me on his lap whilst Cook moves off the bed and I hear him in the bathroom. Then I hear taps running and know he is running me a bath. Exactly what the doctor ordered.

"I am going to get you something to drink and hydrate, Tom is going to put you into the bath. I will be back shortly." And with that Cook is gone and it is just me and Tom, looking at each other. Expressionless. Naked.

After a few minutes, Tom places me onto my bottom on the bed, climbs off and turns off the taps. I can smell vanilla coming from the bathroom. I follow him in after a minute and find him bending over the tub, swishing the water around amongst the bubbles.

"Would you mind if I use the toilet?" I ask, hoping he leaves the bathroom. He turns his head from where he's kneeling, nods and stands. Leaving me to myself in the bathroom. Relief washes over me, and I pee in privacy, well as much as I can—the door is still see through, he can still see me if he wanted to watch but I don't see him at the door so maybe it's not his thing. I finish up and head over to the bath. I touch the water which is a nice toasty temperature so I climb in and lay back into the sweet-smelling water. What a way to start my stay here. If my first four encounters are anything to go by, I'm going to need all the food Cook is feeding me just to keep some level of stamina between them all.

There is a knock on the bathroom glass door before it opens, Cook enters carrying a Gatorade. "Will this be ok?" he asks earnestly.

I smile back at him, "That is perfect, thank you."

"I'm going to leave this with you, you take all the time you need in here. I will be back this evening with dinner. See you later, baby girl."

"See you later," I reply and I'm grateful for this moment to myself. I also feel a twinge of anticipation to see him again soon and of what he is going to feed me next. I lie back and focus on breathing. I've been fucked by two men in one day. I guess that has happened before, but one of them was James. And then guilt squeezes my heart. *James.* I'd been so wrapped up being here, it's only now I'm able to actually take a moment and think of him. It sounds silly but I send him hugs with my mind and my heart. I wonder if he's thinking of me as I think of him.

I stay in the bath for what feels like over an hour. I keep topping up the water with more hot until it's simply too high and I have to pull the plug and get out.

I climb out and wrap one of those fluffy pink towels Dr Jack chose for me around my body. I pat myself dry before hanging it up and walking into the bedroom. No one is in the room, Tom is not in his seat so I walk over to the stack of books and scan the titles until I see one that looks vaguely familiar and pick it up. I walk over to the bed, fluff up the pillows and then sit back on them with my knees up. It feels weird to have not put any clothes on, I wonder if anyone is watching on the other side of the glass. But I can't tell so I relax back and begin to read.

30

———————

I lose myself in the book I'm reading and almost forget where I am. Hours must have passed and I've snuggled myself in the bed now reading. I don't remember the last time I had this much time to myself to relax and read. Seems almost wrong that I am being paid to do this but then I remind myself of what I have done so far and what is likely to come in the next seven days.

A knock at the door draws my attention and a bustling Cook enters the room with a delicious smelling trolley laden with food. My stomach growls. I can't believe I'm hungry again after everything I ate for lunch. Cook must hear it too and chuckles, "Just in the nick of time by the sounds of it. I don't want you starving, baby girl. Let's get you fed and rested back in your bed for tomorrow's boys," he says with a knowing smile. He must know what everyone has in store for me. I blush a little.

"Your trolley of heaven smells divine, Cook," I say and he gives me a full smile, his eyes twinkling behind his glasses.

"I can't wait to feed you again Roxy."

"Are you allowed to tell me what's on the menu for tonight?" I ask.

"It would be my pleasure. To start we have a Parma ham & melon entrée, for main you have an organic fillet steak cooked medium rare with hand cooked chips twice fried and for dessert, a handmade chocolate fondant cake."

My mouth waters. I just hope I can squeeze it all in. Just like earlier, Cook feeds me every bite. I feel almost too full before I've even made it to the dessert. Rubbing my stomach, I sit back in my chair.

"Oh gosh, I need to get used to your portions. Usually, I wouldn't manage a dessert if I've had a starter."

"But for me, you'll make the exception?" he replies, teasing but I hear a command in there laced with playfulness, hinting at the rules to finish all of his food.

"Of course, although I'm going to need to take the fondant slowly."

"Baby girl, you take all the time you need. If you like, we can sit back on the bed like we did before, I'll rub your stomach as you eat the cake. How does that sound?"

"Sounds like a perfect idea," I reply, maybe him rubbing my stomach will help the food go down, or at least alleviate the stretch and over-full feeling I'm experiencing.

Cook climbs onto the bed fully clothed, I climb on and lower with my back resting on him and the fondant and spoon in my hand.

"Here you go now baby girl, start eating like a good girl, I'm going to make you feel all better."

Despite not wanting to eat any more food, I spoon in the first mouthful of dessert and moan at the deliciousness of it. Chocolate fondant is another favourite and the texture to this one is just right. It's not too dense but not too light either. I feel slightly better as Cook rubs his hands down my sides, and then around my stomach, making circles—each hand taking it in turns. His hands do bring me comfort and I try to continue eating more. I'm halfway finished when I have to start taking deep breaths to try and make more room.

"You can do it baby girl, every last spoonful. It's going to make you big and strong and beautiful for me."

I take another spoonful.

"I wonder what will look bigger in a few day's time. Will it be your breasts, your hips maybe or this beautiful stomach."

Oh god, the calories I'm ingesting just in this dessert I can feel go straight to my hips. It's a good thing I could do with an extra kilo or two. But I think I might be gaining one each day at this rate...

After a few more words of motivation, I manage to scrape the bowl clean. Never have I felt Christmas full twice in one day.

"You have been such a good girl. I'm going to let you settle in for the night, but I'll see you tomorrow morning for breakfast." With that Cook climbs off the bed and reaches for my bowl. Then he piles the plates back onto his trolley and he happily leaves me to myself.

I can see why people say they fall into a food coma when they've eaten too much, that is exactly how I feel right now. But I drag myself up from the bed and go brush my teeth with the supplies Dr Jack bought for me. I use the toilet and look at myself in the mirror above the sink. I stand there for a moment and really look. I know I'm the same person, I look the same and I feel the same, but what I have done today is not something I would have done a year ago. Yet it surprises me how totally unchanged I feel. I'm not repulsed or remorseful, I'm not upset or sad that I've sold my body to get ahead. I'm not even fussed that I stand here naked as the day I was born. Something has shifted, but maybe that's acceptance of who I am and what I choose to do with my body. I'm a big girl and I can take ownership of this decision I have made. I have enjoyed today.

More than I ever imagined. Maybe not every day will be like this, I have met only half the men who are paying for me. But at least for today, I can look myself in the eye and know I'm being true to myself.

Leaving the bathroom, I climb back into the bed and begin to read before my eyelids become heavy and I put the book aside. It's then I wonder who might turn the lights off. Thankfully, the moment my head hits the pillow, they change to barely there dim lights. It's not pitch black, but this I can handle, as well as the reminder that I'm constantly being watched. It's been a big day; my body feels heavy. Surprisingly, I drift off to sleep like I'm at home.

31

———

I awake to soft music coming from the speaker on the table. The lights are still dimmed, and I wonder if I have awoken because of the music or because I slept all night. I have no way of knowing what the time is, so I try and gauge how I'm feeling and if I still need more sleep. As I take stock of my body, I feel something wet between my legs. I pull the covers back and sure enough, there is something sticky on the inside of my thighs. I frown. Did I do that? No, it looks like semen. But I didn't have sex with anyone last night. Surely, I would have woken if Darcy had come to visit me? I know I am a heavy sleeper, but who sleeps through having a visitor in the night? Maybe we didn't have sex, maybe he just came on me. But that doesn't make much sense.

I climb out of bed, trying not to make a mess as I pad off to the bathroom. After using the toilet, I remember Dr Jack's instructions. Shower, then shave, then eat. So, without knowing what the time is, I turn on the shower and climb in.

Once I'm clean, I have a drink of water from the taps and brush my teeth. As I'm drying my hair with a towel and walking out of the bathroom, I startle to see Carl eagerly sitting on the bed and Tom in the corner, looking relaxed in his armchair.

"Good morning you two," I smile cheerily. "How are you today?" I glance at Tom but rest my eyes on Carl who I assume will be the only one who answers my question.

"All the better for seeing you right now," Carl answers brightly but still looking a little twitchy as though he's nervous. I try and break the tension with a silly comment.

"I'm sorry you have caught me getting dressed. Oh wait, I don't have any clothes," I say with a self-deprecating smile.

Carl walks up to me and pulls a wet strand of hair that is stuck under my chin and places it behind my ear. "Clothes wouldn't suit you princess." There is a twinkle in his midnight black eyes. Up close he looks so much younger than he seems, his skin is flawless and freckles scatter across his nose. He leans forwards and kisses me softly on the lips. "I've been looking forward to seeing you since the minute I left you." Then he leans back in and kisses me more deeply, that familiar taste of coffee and caramel invading my taste buds. I find myself absorbed in this man, his mouth, the way he gently pulls me closer to him and holds one hand around my neck and the other around my bare waist. There is something so unassuming and gentle about him, this beautiful, tan man who likes to kiss me like a delicate flower and shave me like it should be a service offered in a spa. Caressing his tongue with mine, it's me who wants to push deeper, take more and give more to him. But I have to catch myself. I need to be how he wants me to be. I need to give and not take, I'm happy with whatever he chooses to give to me.

Pulling away only to look into my eyes, I feel his warm breath on my lips as he says, "I can't wait to shave you again Roxy. Are you ready?"

"I can't wait to have your special treatment and you all to myself again Carl."

He gives me a shy knowing smile, I liked his style of kink and I want him to know it. Pulling away, he repeats exactly what he did the previous morning. He retrieves the towel, asks me to lie down on it, and brings in a bowl of warm soapy water along with the soap, washcloth and oil. I relax back and enjoy the way he makes me feel, pampered and cherished. I enjoy watching his reverence as he carefully shaves all the tiny, minute stubble away from my arms, legs and between my legs. I breathe deeply as he rubs that slippery, sweet-smelling oil into my skin finishing up at my folds. I move my hips to the rhythm of his rubbing, hoping he'll rub his slippery fingers on my clit too. He seems to take the hint and begins rubbing three fingers in slow languorous circles, his eyes tipping up to mine for the first time since he began shaving me.

Watching Carl shave me has been a test to my restraint as each swipe of the razor to my pussy, each swipe of the oil on his fingertips has sent my core into meltdown. I'm barely hanging on by a thread. And then that thread ruptures into a thousand pieces as pleasure pulses through me and I ride the wave that the climax is delivering to me.

"That was beautiful," mutters Carl, "Will you rub the oil into my dick now?"

"It would be my pleasure," I reply in a slow blissed out voice. "Here, switch places with me, lie down on the towel."

He does as I suggest, I unclasp the dark jeans he has on today and pull those, and his boxers down his thighs and then off completely. I squirt a couple of droplets of the oil into my hand and then kneeling in between his bare legs, I begin to work my slippery hands up and down his stiff erect cock. There is no hair to dip the oil onto. I use one hand to massage his balls and then seek lower to his taint.

Carl looks like he's caught between absolute pleasure and something else, I think he's trying to hold on to his climax. "You can let go you know Carl; I can do this every morning if you would like me to?" I ask in a low voice. "Or you can have me any way you like every day, especially after you shave my pussy so well."

Hot ropes of come spurt up towards his belly button and he groans in euphoria. I gradually stop stroking him and instead lie down against his side. He turns his head, and smiles shyly again, "Thank you."

"You're welcome." I grin back at him.

"You are perfect."

"So are you," I reply warmly.

"I should go get cleaned up."

"You should, I think you got your t-shirt," I say playfully.

"Yeah, I think I did." And with that, he sits up, trying to catch the come as it dribbles back down his stomach and walks into the bathroom. It's then I look up to see Tom staring back at me, a mixture of emotions fighting on his face. He wants to speak to me maybe or join in? But he's angry at me for doing this, is that what Cook said yesterday? I don't know. I feel something radiating off him. Anger? Jealousy?

Carl comes back into the room, finds his trousers and starts pulling them on. I want to ask him a thousand questions about himself, but I know we're not allowed to unless they offer. Instead, I say, "Will you be here all day or do you leave now?"

He looks up and grins, "I'm staying here. I don't want to miss a minute of your time here."

"You were here yesterday too?"

"Yes. Just on the other side of this glass."

"Really." I frown a little, "With anyone else?"

"Indeed, I was with most of the guys, all patiently waiting their turn and plotting their time with you."

"You were? And do you like watching?"

"Yes. Not as much as I like shaving you but it's enjoyable watching the others with you."

"Do you know my plans for today?"

"I do."

"Are you allowed to tell me?"

"You have David visiting this morning."

"He's the impact guy?"

"Yes, BDSM is his thing."

"And this afternoon? Will I meet the other three men?"

"Blake and Jake are playing with you tomorrow. And I think you'll meet Darcy soon enough." He winks.

"He came to visit me last night?" I ask, trying to confirm if my suspicions were right. Confused how I did not hear, or feel, a thing.

"Yes, I think he might be visiting you every night, it just depends on if you wake up whether you will meet him sooner or not."

"Did you see him visit me?"

"Yes."

"How did I not?" I ask, shuddering at just how deeply I must have slept. I can't believe it; how did I not feel him?

"He's a magician, if you wake, you will find out," he teases, not willing to let me in on the secret clearly.

The classical music that has been playing quietly in the background changes to an upbeat jazz tune and Carl takes that as his hint to leave. "See you tomorrow princess," he says as he bends down and kisses me softly on the lips.

"See you tomorrow, Carl." I smile sweetly at him knowing he'll be seeing me sooner then I'll be seeing him. I watch as he opens the door and walks into the dark room behind him.

My stomach grumbles and I confirm it must be breakfast time. I become very aware of the glass surrounding me. Looking out through it like a caged animal wondering who is looking back at me.

There is a light knock on the door before it silently swings open, and the delicious scent of bacon hits my nose. Behind the trolley is Cook, his wide smile denting his dimples on either side of his mouth. "Good morning baby girl, you are looking incredible this morning. Did you sleep well?"

"Good morning, Cook. I sure did. But you knew that didn't you?" I reply playfully. If Carl knew Darcy visited me in the night, he would too. He was probably watching. "Did you sleep well?"

"Sleeping is for when I'm dead," he chuckles. "But you are right, I did know you slept well." He chuckles again. "Now come over here, let's get you fed up like a good girl," he says pointing to the chair.

Cook happily feeds me a full cooked breakfast with juice and tea. It's bigger and a heavier meal then I would usually start the day with, but it's delicious nevertheless. Cook does what I now come to expect, rubbing my stomach as I eat. I have to stop and start because it really does feel like a lot of food. When we're finished, he packs up his trolley ready to leave.

"I'm going to leave you alone earlier than I would like, you need to let your food go down because David is coming to visit you shortly. I'm going to leave you some sandwiches over here for when you get peckish and will be back with your dinner. Enjoy yourself, you are in for quite a treat today."

"I don't know how I feel about you knowing what is going to happen to me before I do," I shrug. "I guess I do like the element of surprise."

"This will be a good surprise baby girl; you can take it, I know you can."

"Yikes, that sounds ominous."

"I think pain and pleasure can go hand in hand if given by the right person," replies Cook before he runs the backs of his hands down my chest, brushing my nipples and they pebble under his touch. He palms both my breasts and looks me in the eyes. "I'm looking forward to seeing all of you this evening."

"See you this evening."

And with that, he's left a covered tray on the table and is

pushing the food trolley back out of the door. Tom stands and follows him out of the room also, not saying a word to me as I've come to expect. I feel full to the brim. I walk into the bathroom, use the toilet and brush my teeth. When I'm back in the bedroom, I make the bed and sit cross legged on top and begin reading my book again.

32

The speaker that has been playing light jazz music in the background switches to something classical again. I look up and wonder if this is the signal that David is coming. I think it must have been over an hour since I ate, my stomach no longer feels so full and uncomfortable.

A light knock sounds at the door before a polished man wearing light grey tailored trousers, and a matching waistcoat over a crisp white shirt enters the room. He has salt and pepper hair, a stern looking face and a narrow chin. His presence feels serious and strict—nothing like the shy and sweet Carl, bubbly Cook, or even the cheerful Dr Jack.

I put my book down next to me on the bed and swing my legs over to get down but in a few swift steps, David is standing in front of me. "No need to get down yet, we need to set up in here." Reaching out a hand, he offers, "I'm David, lovely to meet you today Roxy," speaking in a well-mannered clipped tone.

"Pleasure to meet you too, David. It's so nice to put a face to the name," I reply in what I hope is my usual voice. I want to ask what he needs to set up, but Tom saves me by entering with a wooden cross structure which he places in front of the bed.

"Excuse me for a moment," David says and with a few long strides he's opening the door and leaving with Tom before a moment later they return carrying what looks like a miniature padded picnic bench. The bench just barely squeezes in through the door and I almost laugh out loud. When they set it down on all four legs, I was not far off in my description. The piece of furniture, equipment I guess it is, really is like a small picnic bench but the top part is padded red leather and the seat parts are also padded leather. I've never seen one like it nor the wooden cross that has leather cuffs hanging down from the top.

"Thank you, Tom," I hear David say once they've settled the bench piece to my right. Tom nods and takes his seat in the leather armchair. He's wearing light grey track pants and a white fitted t-shirt today. If he wasn't so gruff and intimidating, I would like to walk over and climb on his muscular lap and see what he tastes like. But fear keeps me in check. Also, Dr Jack's rule of 'don't talk to Tom' comes back to me.

David leaves the room once more and returns with a small black suitcase on wheels.

"Roxy, I think we have everything we need," he says to me as he approaches the bed again, this time he perches on the side to face where I'm sitting. "Have you ever had someone tie you up and use paddles and crops on you?" he asks so directly I squirm.

"No David, this would be my first. Is that ok?" I enquire, unsure if having more experience would please him more.

"On the contrary, that is perfect," he smiles brighter than he has so far. "I like to play with untamed bodies and minds. And you are exceptional in both, from what I've viewed so far."

"T-Thank you," I stammer, unsure how I should follow that compliment up.

"Do you remember your safe word?" he asks.

"Yes, Neptune."

"Excellent. And you know you can use it at any time, and I will stop immediately. You have the choice of stopping just the scene or stopping the scene and your entire stay here. No one here is willing to force you into anything you are not comfortable doing."

"Yes, I understand thank you. Dr Jack explained everything to me when I arrived. I'm unsure what you are about to do to me, but I'm intrigued also. I'm not afraid."

"And nor should you be. What I specialise in is a certain type of pain but also pleasure. My pleasure is in your pain, and I reward your pain with pleasure. Does that make sense?"

"Yes, I think so," I smile into his dark blue eyes and notice his clean-shaven face, his greying eyebrows and a small scar under his left eye. His face looks stern along with his demeanour. He's sitting straight and rigid next to me despite just perching what should look casually next to me.

"I am going to use a number of instruments on you today. Please rest assured, I have many years of experience using them and can read reactions to gauge limits. I expect you will react in ways I'm familiar with but as always, use your safe word if you feel the need. Are you ready?"

"Yes, I think I'm ready sir," I reply, almost like I'm speaking to a schoolteacher. His smile reaches his eyes, and they almost look like they glimmer.

"Indeed, you can call me Sir for our scene here today. Hearing it from your lips pleases me immensely. Let's get you in position then." He reaches for my hand to help me off the bed and leads me over to the bench.

"Yes Sir," I say, trying to be everything that pleases him.

"Kneel on here please, one leg on either side and straddle your body over the top, I would like to start with your beautiful behind."

I do as David instructs, placing my knees on the padded

benches on either side, then lean my body over the padded tabletop onto my forearms in a bracing position. I feel stable and supported with plenty of space for my knees on the wide benches, but also exposed, my arse spread open slightly and my breasts hanging freely.

"Look at that pretty arse Tom, doesn't it just scream to be reddened like our specially made bench here?"

I turn my head towards Tom who slowly nods his agreement. Him watching me in this position should feel unnerving, but instead his dark brooding eyes set me alight before David has done anything to me. I wonder for a minute whether I'm into people watching me. I must be, or is it just Tom? Though I admit the idea of the other men watching from behind the glass only adds to the building heat.

I feel David's warm hand rub over my butt cheeks from the tops of my thighs to the small of my back and then down again. After a couple of strokes, his hand edges towards my inner cheeks and rubs from the small of my back, down between my cheeks and his fingers graze my pussy lips. I suck in a breath. *Is he going to touch me properly there?* His hand stops and he runs one long finger through my folds before pulling it away.

"I think you're already enjoying being open and on display for me, Roxy."

"Yes Sir," I admit honestly.

"Open your legs wider on the bench please. Wider. I want to see your pussy wide open for me. Good girl, like that," continues David as I carefully slide my legs to the edge of each bench. "I want to feel your flesh under my palms first."

Standing behind me, David lifts his right hand and slaps my left arse cheek which feels like a warm up strike. I brace my full body for the blow, every muscle locked in tight and ready but breathe out as I can easily tolerate the pressure of the slaps he begins to rain down on me. Gradually they begin to build up, I hardly notice the difference in pressure with his clever, well positioned strikes until David lifts his right hand and slaps my left arse cheek with such force, I almost front roll off the spanking bench. The pain sears through me, feeling like I've just been branded with a hot iron, not one man's palm. He moves to the side and slaps me just as hard on my right arse cheek. This time I'm more prepared for the impact and try to stay where I am, anchoring myself heavier on my knees and forearms. I can feel his handprint ablaze on my cheek. His hand must be sore too, the noise alone was loud enough.

David runs his knuckles over where he's just slapped me, "Pinking up perfectly Roxy, you should see it. Tom, look how lovely her skin blooms," says David who sounds pleased.

"A couple more should do the trick," David raises his hand and lets it fly, the hand hitting with such ferocity, I can't hold myself in place.

I can't hold still, jerking forward as I squeal, "Ouch," unable to keep it in. This seems to spur him on, he hits me hard, on both my cheeks two more times. The burning is evoking a fight or flight reaction in me and between trying not to scream, I'm trying to fight my body to stay exactly where David told me to stay.

My body is smarting, but the slapping has stopped. I raise my head from where it's hanging low over my forearms and look around to see what David is doing now. David is bent down behind me—my backside is lower than his eye level. He places both hands on my cheeks and rubs them up and down my burning skin. His hands feel nice, they're gentle. He's very close to my centre, I suddenly feel very exposed and self-conscious. I dare not move though; his gentle caresses seem to indicate his sincere enjoyment of the moment.

Standing, I hear him move to his open suitcase and pick something up. "This one will have a different impact feeling, Roxy. I wonder which one you will prefer."

I hear something move through the air before I feel a flat

wooden paddle slap my arse cheek in one quick blow. I lower my head and suck in a deep breath. I'm not sure if it hurts more than his hand because it's wood or because my arse cheeks were already burning hot, but this is a lot of heat focused in one spot. Moving from left to right, David does not hold back on paddling my backside. Sometimes in the same spot, sometimes just under my arse cheeks. I can't help myself; my body moves involuntarily after each painful slap. These slaps are bruising. I feel like their impact is hitting on a deeper level, each one building on an intensity—demolishing a pain threshold I thought I had and reaching new levels I've never experienced before.

When the blows stop, I try and collect myself. Can't be much more.

"Stunning, Roxy. Your arse is a deep red and purpling now. One last set with my crop here and your bottom will be done for now. Can you take the crop for me, Roxy?" he asks me sternly.

"Y-yes Sir," I croak out, "If it pleases you."

"It will please me a great deal, Roxy. You are doing so well. We are going to build up your taps. Here we go."

I hear a swoosh before my head has got around what is about to happen. Lightning strikes me just below my right arse cheek and I actually howl. David waits a beat for me to recover my senses before I hear the swoosh again and the lightning pain hits my opposite cheek.

"Shhhh, my good girl, a couple more taps and you are going to be floating."

I don't have time to look at him before the next strike hits me square on my arse cheek, then another and another. Black spots begin to fill my vision, and the pain begins to merge into one hot fiery beast, a pulse is raging from my arse cheeks, but the pain is subsiding into a feeling of numbness. I'm no longer howling at the lightning strikes; silent tears are running down my face but my body is still, pliant, obedient to the punishment raining down upon it. My head clears slightly and my body begins to feel light, floaty. The whipping noise of the crop has stopped, I realise the impact has stopped too. David has walked around to the other side of the table; he lifts my tear-streaked face from where it's now resting on my forearms and looks into my eyes.

I see satisfaction in his eyes and a hint of hunger as his dark blue eyes stare back at me. "I have one more thing planned for you Roxy, can you stand?"

My body is shaking but he helps me unfold myself back onto my knees and then holds out a hand so I can steady myself as I stand up. David leads me over to the large wooden X in front of my bed, positioning me in front of it, facing the room. "Hold up your arms to each corner, Roxy."

I do as he says and watch as he buckles my wrists into the leather straps.

"Legs apart now please," David gets down on his knees and buckles in my ankles so I'm completely immobile and at his mercy. David pours a glass of water and brings it up to my lips, "Here, have a sip, Roxy." And I do as I'm told, grateful for the moisture going down my dry throat.

"Thank you, Sir," I say. *What can he have in store for me now? I wonder.*

"I am now going to slap your beautiful breasts in the same manner as your beautiful backside. Are you ready for me, Roxy?"

"Yes Sir," I reply, wondering if I really am ready.

David does not hold back, he slaps my left breast with his left hand with so much force, my initial reaction is to fold in on myself but that is impossible with both my hands and feet cuffed in place. He uses his right hand to hit my left breast from the other side and I yelp out. The slap is still ringing in my ears when he takes aim at my right breast, raining down two blows in quick succession. My breasts jiggle and fly in different directions as David lets go of apparently all restraint and hits me in all directions. Hitting up, then down, from left and right. My breasts are two hanging pieces of meat he is enjoying beating. The burn begins to subside into numbness as I take what I'm given, and I watch this serious man take apparent joy from his abuse to my skin and flesh. I wonder if he's gone into a zone that he won't be able to pull himself out of looking at the intense focus of his eyes on my breasts.

My breasts must be quite the colour by now but I'm afraid to look down when suddenly David takes a step back and folds his arms. "Stunning Roxy, your breasts are stunning. All red, purple and blotchy. They bring out the rose on your right breast beautifully." The tent in his suit trousers is unmistakable.

I look down, he's right—there is an array of colours emanating from my skin. My breasts hang heavy and battered, burning heat radiating from them but I'm not in agony. I'm reminded of the last time they looked like this with Greg and the way he touched me for the first time. Both of these men are so different and similar at the same time. I love that I get to see and enjoy this side of them.

Unfolding his hands, he walks back to me and pinches my nipples before twisting them hard. I gasp in surprise, but the sensation sends a spark down to my clit and I feel moisture dripping down my thighs, surprised I hadn't noticed how wet I was under the intensity of the pain until now.

Watching my face David says, "You like this, don't you? Your sensitive breasts are now aching to be made to feel better. Tom, come here and play with our girl's tender nipples, I have some rewarding to do."

I watch as David pulls up his trousers slightly on his thighs before lowering onto his knees in front of me. I feel in a daze, my brain is not firing on all cylinders. David cups his hands around my sore arse cheeks and takes a long, ludicrously slow lap of my pussy.

I look up to see Tom to my left, his head bending down before I can see his face and he latches onto my left nipple and sucks, reaching up with his hand to tweak my other nipple.

So many sensations all at once from two hungry mouths. David is toying with me with his slow laps, Tom is sucking deliciously earning a groan from my throat. Tom pulls away to look at me, his face a mask of unreadable features before he goes back to my nipple. David languidly laps at my entrance before finally making his way up to the bundle of nerves that are screaming from every pore in my body to be assaulted.

"Please," I whimper, "please stay there Sir."

Tom stops sucking and moves around to my right nipple, pinching my left with his thumb and forefinger. David holds his mouth over my clit and starts sucking with the same pressure as Tom. It's too much, these sensations coursing through my body from my nipples to my clit are overriding all senses, they're all consuming on every level of my being. I can feel myself building to a peak of near explosion before Tom bites down on my tender nipple and I scream "Yessss!" as my climax rips through my core and leaves me panting and quivering. David continues to suck the orgasm out of me, Tom removes his fingers and then his mouth before looking back at my lolling head as the endorphins engulf my body.

When I open my eyes again, I have two sets looking back at me. I smile shyly back at them, feeling relaxed and groggy.

"Thank you, Tom," David says, dismissing him from where he's standing. Tom lingers for half a second looking like he's going to say something but moves away and back to his seat, hunger written all over his face.

David busies himself un-cuffing me, rubbing my wrists and then my ankles before bending down and picking me up around my sore bottom and carrying me over to the picnic bench furniture. David puts me down on the top, places one foot on each of the lower benches. He pushes me down so that my back lies flat on the bench, the pressure of the bench against my bruised arse is both distracting and arousing. I lie back, completely open and waiting for him. I hear his zipper being pulled down before I feel his hot cock nudge at my opening.

No words are needed as he slowly enters me and then pulls out, then in a bit further and out. Teasing me, teasing himself, and also teasing our audience as I hear Tom groan from his chair. I move my head to look over and he's stroking himself watching as David impales me, fully sheathing his cock in my warmth. My body is thrust up and down on the tabletop. David grabs my hips to hold me in place as he sets a brutal rhythm of thrusting deep inside me.

"More," I manage to breathe out to David or Tom, or anyone listening really. David slows his pace a fraction and releases one of my hips but before I can even whimper in complaint he brings two fingers to rub over my clit turning my building orgasm into a soul shattering one as he continues to thrust deep inside me. I cry out, "Sir!" as I come around his cock, sparking a frenzied pace of him fucking me into the table until David shudders and holds his cock deep and pulsing inside of me. I hear a groan from Tom and know he's found his release too.

I float back down into my body and raise up onto my elbows to watch as David pulls his long cock out of me, liquid splashing onto the floor. David looks at me, his serious demeanour more relaxed and ruffled, his shoulders look slack, his face pink from exertion and coming.

David's eyes lower to my breasts and then back to my mouth where they linger. I sit up higher, inviting. He almost reacts but instead takes a step back. "I'll get us cleaned up," he says, almost to himself. I watch as he leaves me sitting, open and dripping. I look over at Tom who is wiping himself up.

David returns with a damp washcloth and begins to dab me clean. He holds out a hand, "Let me help you down Miss Roxy," and I take his hand, gingerly unsticking my sore bottom from the table and climbing down.

"Lie on your front on the bed if you can, Dr Jack will be in shortly to fix you up."

"Ok," I reply. Then add, "Sir." I am disappointed David is going already. I feel like there is something unsaid or left undone. But I don't want to push him or do anything that might upset him, so I school my face to hide my emotions and allow David to help me get settled on the bed.

David bends down and kisses the top of my head. "You were incredible, Miss Roxy. I will see you again soon."

And with that he picks up his suitcase and leaves the room. Tom does not follow, he stays exactly where he is, still, relaxed and unspeaking.

33

———

Lying on my front with my head resting on my pillow looking at the glass and wondering whose eyes I might be looking into; I don't hear the door open and footsteps approach. It's only when Dr Jack's frame comes into view that I startle.

"Hi sweet girl, how are you doing?" Dr Jack asks as I continue to lie still on my front. His boyish good looks staring back at me.

"I'm going okay thank you, just a little sore," I reply with a relaxed smile.

"I have come to take care of you."

"You have?" I reply brightly, but I still dare not move.

"Yes, I have lots of creams and ointments to get you soothed and healed in no time," he replies in a soothing doctor's tone.

"Thank you, that would be appreciated," and I mean it. I have sores and pains in places I've never hurt before. "Did you watch?"

"Sweet girl we *all* watched. Watching you succumb to David has been quite the highlight. There wasn't a dry dick in the room, you were spectacular," he replies enamoured.

My heart flutters. This warms my core. I want to make sure everyone is getting what they paid for.

"You enjoyed it," I glow.

"Oh baby, we all did. Every spank of your beautiful, bruised arse, every line made by the crop, every slap of your gorgeous breasts. We felt them, we loved them, every single one," he says wistfully, remembering them. "I didn't think I would be into impact play as much as I was earlier. I think we all agreed, watching that was something we unexpectedly enjoyed more than we initially thought."

Dr Jack puts down a large toiletry bag down next to my hip that I hadn't noticed he was holding. I hear him unzipping it.

"I know you are sore, sweet girl, but you took your impact play so well. I'm going to make it feel all better now. First, I'm going to run you a bath filled with Epsom salts to release those tense muscles of yours, then I'm going to treat any sores and bruises. You will feel good as new in no time."

Relief washes over me. I am in a bit of a state, I didn't know how I was going to recover in time for whatever else they have planned for me. "Stay here sweet girl, I'll be back when I'm ready for you." He runs the lightest of touches over my sore bottom up towards my waist before he takes his hand away and I watch his back disappear into the bathroom. I laugh to myself, he is wearing his white doctor's coat again.

Lavender floats to the bed on clouds of steam as the tub is being filled. I would use lavender myself at home, it's just another sweet touch I know is Dr Jack's. He appears back in the doorway, his white coat off and his arms appear damp. "Can you roll on your back for me?" he asks gently.

"Yes," I reply and begin to move in slow motion, squeezing my eyes shut and biting down a squeal of pain as I roll so I'm lying face up. Dr Jack bends his knees and scoops me up into his arms and walks me into the bathroom where he lowers me into the steaming lavender-scented water. I let out an audible sigh, "Ahhhh." The water feels like a warm hug but the few sores I must have prickle and sting like stinging nettles throbbing across my skin.

"Give the bath time to soak your muscles and the stinging will eventually stop too. Just lie back and relax now."

I lie back and rest my head on the bath, closing my eyes, ready to let the bath do its magic. I feel fingers at my scalp, my eyes opening in surprise as Dr Jack begins to massage my head. What a delight it feels to alleviate pressures I hadn't realised I'd been holding onto. Tingles float down my spine and pleasure erupts in my core. I close my eyes again and drift away as his clever fingers caress my scalp. I never want him to stop.

I have no concept of time, but I feel Dr Jack's fingers eventually stop moving, and then notice they are no longer on my head. I open my eyes and see he's grabbed a pink fluffy towel. "You'll be a shrivelled prune unless I get you out now," he chuckles at me. My eyelids feel heavy and I fake a scowl up at him as he offers a hand for me to take. I take his hand, and he helps me to stand up slowly as I begin to feel my head rush and I sway.

"Easy tiger, I've got you," he drops the towel and reaches for my other hand gripping them both tightly. "Ok, one foot at a time now," he instructs, and I do as he asks. When I'm standing safely on the bath mat, he wraps me in the towel carefully before patting me down gently. I do feel remarkably better and even my sores are not smarting half as much as they were.

Dr Jack leads me over to the sink and I look at myself, all pink and blotchy from the bath. The bottom of my dark hair dripping from being in the water.

"Bend over and rest your arms on the sink, I am going to rub antiseptic into those couple of sores from the crop and then arnica lotion into your bottom. Deep breaths."

I sure need the deep breaths as the antiseptic is gently

dabbed onto a few places on the back of my thighs and then a few on my bottom. I whimper but don't move a muscle.

"There, there, all done my brave girl. You did so well. Let me make it all better for you now." I hear a jar being opened before I feel cold lotion being carefully applied to my arse cheeks. This time I don't whimper but let out a sigh of relief as the lotion soothes into my bruised skin. Bending over my body, I can feel Dr Jack's heat and the stiffness in his trousers brushes up against me. "Stand up and let me check your front."

I straighten and spin to face him, looking up to his boyish face. He lowers his eyes and runs them down my neck and to my purpling breasts. "I'm going to need to make these feel better," he says as he runs his thumbs up from the underside of my breasts up to my nipples and circles them gently. I close my eyes and lean into the sensations he's creating in me. When I open my eyes, he's rubbing the arnica lotion into his hands before carefully stroking them across my breasts, one at a time. Not once does he add pressure or hurt me in any way. It's such a featherlight touch, I look down to check he's actually rubbing the cream into my skin.

"Cook will be in shortly with an early dinner, then rest. Doctor's orders," he smiles at me.

"Yes Doctor," I reply, my voice low and throaty. Dr Jack's pupils dilate, he suddenly looks like he's about to pounce on me before he straightens up and takes my hand.

"Say that to me again when you've healed and see what happens," he threatens. Both fear and excitement make my heart pound in my chest. Dr Jack can look scary at the flick of a switch. Why does that turn me on so much? "Let's get you settled before I let Mr Hyde loose on you." *He doesn't mean Cook, is he talking about himself?* I wonder.

My eyes widen at that. So, he does have two sides and he's very much aware of them. I can feel one bubbling under the surface, but I haven't seen it unleashed yet. Should I be worried? The heat between my thighs says I want to know for myself, sooner rather than later. Once I've healed a little at least.

Pulling me into the bedroom, Dr Jack walks me toward the bed. Before I begin to contemplate sitting down, he reaches for my face and kisses me softly. He tastes of mint and cinnamon. When he pulls away, he says, "I've wanted to do that since I laid eyes on you. I need to step away before I lose control. I'm going to give some arnica cream to Carl for tomorrow. You should feel much better in the morning. I'm not saying it will perform miracles but also, that is some special cream. Good night sweet girl, see you very soon."

"Thank you for taking care of me," I say in a small voice as he turns to leave. I squeeze his hand to emphasise it. He turns, torture in his eyes—he's fighting himself to leave me right now to recover. I hope he knows I do want to play with him, very soon. I hope I heal overnight.

When he opens the door, I shuffle myself back on the bed but this time my movements don't feel so stiff. The bath has done wonders for my body. Even my sores don't feel so angry. Feeling brave, I sit on my bottom and reach for my book. Settling back, I begin to read and lose myself in the book for I don't know how long—hours?

When a light knock comes at the door, I almost jump out of my skin. For a moment, I had truly forgotten where I was, so deep into my story. In bustles Cook holding one large smoothie with a straw. It's then that I realise Tom isn't in the room, neither is the wooden cross frame or picnic table. He must have left when I was put into the bath. I wonder if I'll see him for the rest of the evening.

"Hi baby girl. I saw your session with David, I've made you a protein shake for dinner so you can stay exactly there and drink it, no touching from me tonight." Then on a side note he adds, "We want you rested and strong for Blake and Jake tomorrow who are really looking forward to finally meeting you in person."

"I am really looking forward to meeting them," I declare, smiling up at Cook's friendly face as he hands me the drink. "I'm really grateful for the smoothie, thank you."

"My pleasure," he beams and sits on the other side of the bed companionably. True to his word, he doesn't lay a finger on my creamed-up, healing skin. And strangely I miss his touch. I almost associate eating with him caressing me in some way. How quickly new habits can build. Once I have sucked down the creamy chocolate smoothie, he takes it from me. "Are you going to be ok sleeping tonight? Would you like some pain killers?"

"That might be a good idea, just in case I move in the night."

"I'll go fetch some, be back in a tick." I watch as he slides off the bed with my glass, walks to the door and returns a few minutes later with a glass of water and a box. "Here you go baby girl, take two and then go back to your book until your eyelids feel too heavy." I take the two tablets and swallow them with the cold water.

"I will, thank you Cook."

He leans over and kisses me on the lips tenderly before saying goodnight and leaving me to my evening of reading. It isn't very long after he leaves me that I feel my eyelids drooping and place the book aside. I venture off the bed for the toilet and to brush my teeth before gingerly climbing back in and laying my head down on the pillow. As they did last night, the lights immediately dim, and I send James and the kids my love before closing my eyes and I'm asleep.

34

I awake to soft classical music just like I did the morning before. I also feel the stickiness between my legs before moving a muscle. *How?* I wonder. Then I remember the day before and try to move, which I do far easier than I was expecting.

I shower and wash my hair, and although my sores sting at first, they're not as needle-like as they were yesterday.

Sweet Carl comes in to shave me and is extra gentle with me, even though where he is shaving hasn't got a bruise or sore on it. Though once he's finished he rubs the arnica cream into my arse and breasts before spreading the oil on my arms and legs. He rubs my pussy with oil so deliciously I come hard, and I massage his dick just like I promised.

Cook brings me porridge topped with honey and berries, barely touching me other than kissing me gently before leaving again. I know today is Blake and Jake's turn and wonder when they will visit and what they will be like.

I'm sitting on my bed finishing my book when I hear a knock on the door. I look up to see two handsome men enter. I smile up at them and they both smile warmly back at me, making quick work of reaching my bed.

"Hi," they both say in unison.

"Hi, you must be Blake and Jake?" I ask looking between the two. If I could think up two polar opposites, these men would be it in colouring.

"I'm Blake," says the broader and taller of the two with dark skin and dark eyes, holding out his hand for me to shake. I take it and look into his deep brown eyes and catch my breath. His beautiful square jawed face looks back at me intently, his eyes are telling me a thousand things he'd like to do to me as I watch his tongue peek out and lick his lips.

"And I'm Jake," says Jake, breaking me out of my locked gaze with Blake. Jake is softer spoken and his pale grey eyes beam at me. He has a slender face with short cropped white-blond hair. His eyes are rimmed by long beautiful blond eye-lashes, he's so fair he could almost be albino. These men are night and day, and I wonder if they can see what I'm thinking cross over my face as I look between them.

"Really lovely to meet you both. I've been looking forward to putting your faces to your names," I say conversationally.

"We wanted to meet you sooner," replies Blake petulantly.

"But we had agreed to stick to a schedule, so we have had to watch until now. Although don't get us wrong, you have been spectacular to watch," says Jake playfully. He seems the warmer out of the two.

"I'm happy you feel that way. What do you have planned for me?" I ask Jake but then switch my gaze over to Blake who has an air of authority to his personality in contrast to Jake's playfulness.

Blake puts his hand on the back of Jake's neck possessively before running it down his spine. "I'm going to be directing Jake here with you, he doesn't get to be a top very often," he says wickedly. "And I'm going to fuck him whilst he fucks you."

I draw in a breath. "That sounds like the hottest thing I've ever heard."

"Oh Roxy, you have no idea how much Jake here wants to feel you around his dick. And I cannot wait to watch you two together," says Blake, smiling darkly looking between us.

Jake beams at me again and picks up my hand. "It's been a long time since I've had any pussy. Yours look sensational," he says as he runs a hand up my naked arm to my shoulder.

Blake walks over to the armchair that Tom usually sits in and it occurs to me he's not here. He's always here and watching so I wonder if he's on the other side of the glass.

Sitting back in the chair, Blake directs, "You can kiss her now, Jake."

I turn my gaze from Blake in the armchair to Jake. He pulls me gently at the waist so that I'm sitting with my legs over-hanging the bed and he steps in between my legs.

"Pretty lady, I have wanted to taste this mouth of yours for days," he says, his crystal eyes shining brightly at me as he lowers his lips to mine. When they meet mine, they are soft and caress gently over my lips. He takes his time deepening the kiss as his hands move up my arms and meet at my neck, tilting my head upwards towards his. Slowly, sensually I feel his tongue move into my mouth, finding my tongue. Peppermint bursts into my mouth and my taste buds fire as he kisses me leisurely. I fall into the kiss; I feel like I'm being savoured and devoured all at once. My skin is heating up and my core is becoming liquid lava. This man knows how to kiss. I lift my hands to snake around his waist and pull his body to mine. I can feel him hard between my legs, my bare centre sitting flush against his cock that I can feel straining in his trousers. He groans into my mouth as he presses his cock harder into me.

I want this man just from the way he kisses me alone. If this is the way he kisses me, what would fucking me be like?

Jake pulls away and moves his mouth to my ear, "Pretty lady, you are driving me wild. I can't wait to be inside you." He begins to nibble on my earlobe before he scrapes his teeth down the sensitive part of my neck and nibbles there too. My head falls back as pleasure is pulsing desire throughout my body, my back arching and my breasts thrusting forward.

I hear Blake from the seat command, "Suck her sweet nipples into your mouth Jake, I want to see them red and puffy by the time you're finished."

Jake looks at me, heat clouding his crystal eyes as he lowers his pink lips to my right nipple and sucks it into his mouth deep and I moan, "Jake."

Pinching the other pebbled nipple with his hand, my clit begins to pulse at the sensations wracking my body. Jake sucks deeply at my nipple and I want this feeling to last forever. He lets go of the suction with a pop and I look down to see the elongated peak red and puffy.

"Good boy," comes Blake's voice from the chair. "Now the other one."

Jake moves his attention to the other nipple, and I couldn't be happier. Sucking it deep he simultaneously plays with my other nipple which is a thousand times more sensitive now. I run my fingers through his soft blond hair and moan at the delicious pleasure he is giving me. I want to play with myself and come undone, but I don't. This is their fantasy, I'm just a doll for them to use as they please.

After what feels like endless minutes he lets go of the suction and releases my puffy nipple, purpling around the edges.

"Beautiful. Did that make you wet, Roxy?" asks Blake.

"Yes," I breathe.

"Check for me Jake, tell me what you see."

Jake pulls back a little and lowers his eyes to between my legs. There must be a wet patch on the bed because I have been dripping since he kissed me.

"She's dripping, Blake."

"Show me," Blake commands, "Dip your fingers into her pussy and show me."

Jake runs two fingers between my folds, pulling back glistening fingers and holding them up for Blake to see.

"Put them in Roxy's mouth," instructs Blake.

I open my lips obediently so that he can slide his fingers in, leaving them there whilst I suck my desire clean off his fingers.

"Good girl, Roxy. You enjoyed the way my Jake kissed you and sucked your nipples?"

"Yes," I reply.

"Jake, taste our girl on herself."

Jake's lips quirk up, he reaches one hand for my neck and laps his tongue in my mouth. Then his tongue intrudes deeper, trying to taste every last drop of my desire on my tongue. He feels like he's eating my face but that only makes more desire leak between my legs as I give into his hunger for tasting me.

Pulling back, Jake licks his lips which are red and puffy like my nipples. My lips must look the same.

"Now taste her from her pussy."

It's like Blake just handed Jake the golden ticket. His eyes widen with lust as he falls to his knees immediately and pulls me into his face. No seconds to think about it, he's on me. One full lick from seam to clit and I'm almost bucking. I lean back onto my forearms and watch Jake's head bob between my legs. The way his tongue moves and laps at me is pure perfection. I'm teetering on the edge.

"Look at me Roxy," commands Blake.

I raise my eyes to find him staring reverently from the chair, he's removed his cock and is slowly stroking his full length. My mouth is open as I pant through the building orgasm.

"More pressure around her clit, Jake," Blake directs. "Eyes on me, Roxy."

My eyes lock with his as Jake laps harder and faster at

exactly the right spot and angle that I come undone. I quiver and buck as Jake licks out my climax until I'm a quivering mess, my body lying flat on the bed and my chest heaving for air. Jake pulls his hot, powerful tongue away and stands to look over my naked body, desire emanating from his expression. He moves his gaze from my eyes across my breasts and to my pussy. Then he looks up at Blake, a pleading look in his eyes.

"Take your trousers off, Jake," commands Blake. I lean up on my forearms to watch him pull his trousers off. "Now your t-shirt." Pulling his t-shirt off in one move, I take in his physique, he is fit, impressively athletically fit. "Now take off your boxers and show Roxy your cock."

Looking at me Jake pulls down his black boxers and his cock springs out to attention. It is thick and the head looks swollen and glistening.

"Rub your cock along the seam of Roxy's pussy but don't enter her until I say so," instructs Blake. I am enthralled by their dynamic and the way Blake commands the room.

Jake holds his cock and takes a step closer to me. Holding himself, he guides his cock through my folds up and hits my clit making me arch into his body. I ache for him to be inside me already. I see the look reflected on Jake's face yet he obeys Blake perfectly. He runs his cock back down through my folds slowly before his meaty head is tapping my clit again.

Being dominated by Blake is hot as fuck. Watching Blake command Jake is firing all sorts of erotic signals to my clit. Blake stands and removes his clothes, watching Jake stroke me with his cock, teasing us until we teeter on the edge of losing all control. I am a breath away from pulling him inside of me when Blake walks over to us on the bed, a tube of lube in one hand as he squirts it into the other.

"You can fuck her now," is all Jake needs to hear and he's inside of me in one slick, hard shove. I gasp at the sudden delicious intrusion. I have wanted his cock since the minute he kissed me.

Jake moans, "Fuck Roxy, you've clasped my cock too good, you are going to milk me dry."

"Not until you have milked me dry, Jake," comes Blake's voice from behind me. Jake pauses his thrusting and stills inside me; he lowers his body over mine allowing Blake to slide into his arse from behind. "So tight when you're fucking pussy Jakey," Blake murmurs desire thickly lacing his words as he moves closer into Jake who moves even deeper into my pussy. I clench at the pure lust I see in Jake's eyes. He's fucking into me as Blake is rutting into him, Blake's body setting the rhythm of Jake's thrusts.

Heat begins to bloom from my core, with the way I'm laying down Jake's cock is rubbing hard against my g-spot and I'm not going to be able to hold my building climax down for much longer. I hear Blake say, "I have never wanted to fuck you so much as when I saw you lick out and begin to fuck Roxy's pussy. You were made to take my cock up this arse whilst you fuck Roxy, look at what you're doing to both of us, feel her cunt wrap around you and squeeze your come straight from your balls. That's it, take my cock, take it deep up your arse because she's going to make us both come undone any minute now."

"Jake!" I scream as I bear down on his cock, my inside walls contracting around him as I arch into an orgasm that keeps on giving as Jake continues to plough into me as he is being ploughed into from behind. Jake lets go and roars as his release rips through his body, spurring Blake to push harder and tipping him over the edge and into oblivion. Jake stops moving, Blake stills as he comes deep inside Jake's arse. We all stay locked into each other like puzzle pieces we didn't know fit so perfectly together. Blake moves first, pulling out of Jake. I watch as a sated Jake stands and pulls slowly out of me, not taking his eyes off where we are joined.

35

———

Once we have all untangled, we make our way into the bathroom and shower. Giggling and messing around like teenagers. I barely notice the warm water hitting my few healing sores or my bruised backside. My mind is consumed by these two attractive men and soaping up their bodies and their dicks. In turn, they enjoy soaping up my body and each other. We make an excellent throuple. Jake climbs out of the shower first before handing me and Blake a towel. As we bustle back into the large bedroom, we see someone (presumably Cook) has pushed in a trolley with trays of sandwiches, fruit and champagne.

"Are you staying with me? You don't have to leave straight away?" I ask, not bothering to hide my delight.

"Yes, pretty lady," smiles Jake warmly. "We've waited long enough; we get you all to ourselves today."

I look at Blake who nods his head in confirmation. "Well now, that is wonderful," I exclaim.

Blake comes up behind me pulling me back into him, he leans his head down and says into my ear, "You didn't think I'd finished playing with you two, did you?" I shudder at his dark commanding tone.

"I-I was hoping you hadn't," I reply before turning my head to look up into his strong, serious face. His eyes are pools of dominance, the side of his lips curls up before the moment is broken by a loud popping noise.

We both turn towards Jake in surprise who has just popped open the cork on the champagne and is now filling up three glasses. "Let's get some sustenance in you Roxy, we have some fun planned this afternoon." I can see he means it, his wicked dark eyes staring back at me.

One of the others also brought in another chair so there are now three chairs around the table. Jake and Blake have their towels tied around their waists; I keep mine tied around my chest. It seems appropriate whilst we have an impromptu lunch together. When we sit down Jake holds out his glass of bubbles in a cheers motion, so me and Blake follow suit. "To the best week of our lives," he says, and we repeat it smiling happily at each other toasting the champagne. I take a sip and muse how much I do actually mean that. It's not my wedding week or having the kids. But it's already been such a crazy adventurous week where I've been stripped down to my soul both physically and mentally. Giving myself over for these men's pleasure which in turn is my own pleasure. This really is a week I will never ever forget.

I want to ask how long the two men eating lunch with me have been together, but I remember the rules and sit silently until Jake asks me how I'm enjoying my stay here.

"More than I could imagine in all honesty," I reply, meaning it. "I miss my real life of course but I feel so far removed and preoccupied here, I know I should make the most of this experience and my family will be fine and will be waiting for me when I return."

"And that's why we all chose you, Roxy," says Blake. "You

have taken each of us in your stride. Nothing and no one has been too much for you. You are so open and willing; you have been stunning to watch and even better to play with so far."

I feel my cheeks turn pink and I brighten at his sweet words, "Thank you Blake. I really want to give you all an experience you will never forget and make sure you get what you have paid for. But also, I am enjoying myself beyond my wildest dreams. I realise this might not be for everyone, but for me—right now, this is everything. I feel my body yearn to be played with and used. I am getting pleasure from that *plus* the pleasure of many many orgasms. Which I'm getting paid for. Even if I wasn't being paid, I'd want to be here. I wouldn't change a single thing." I hope my voice conveys the pure truth of those words. They surprise me but I mean them. I do yearn to be here and to be used, there is something very freeing about having no responsibilities other than pleasing the men that have brought me here.

"You are without a doubt our favourite toy we've ever played with," says Jake sweetly.

"And we cannot wait to play again," Blake adds, smiling wickedly.

"Eat up pretty lady, you are going to need your energy for what we have in store for you this afternoon," says Jake cryptically.

"Is that so?" I reply playfully.

"Oh don't you know it." Jake winks and reaches his hand under the table to squeeze my knee. As he does, he begins to take a detour up my inner thigh and stops just before my centre.

I smile darkly back at him. He gives me a *What?* look.

"I see what you are doing Jake, did I give you permission to touch Roxy?" Blake speaks in a low menacing voice to Jake. Jake's hand freezes where it is. He looks back at Blake sheepishly. "Remove your hand and let her finish her lunch."

Looking like a naughty schoolboy who had just been caught playing inside the classroom, Jake slowly glides his hand back down my leg and places it back on the table.

I giggle into my bubbles. The dynamic of these two. They're adorable but incredibly hot. I'm enjoying spending this time with them.

Once we have eaten all the finger sandwiches, strawberries and blueberries and finished the bottle of champagne between us, Blake clears his throat. "I think it's time we get a little more comfortable on the bed.

"Playtime!" Jake quips as we all stand up, drop our towels where we were sitting and make our way over to the bed.

"Kneel in the centre of the bed Jake. Kneel facing Jake, Roxy," Blake instructs. We both climb onto the bed and do as he has asked us, then we both look over to him as he stands to the side of the bed waiting to be told what to do next.

"Stroke his cock Roxy, feel him between your fingers. Look him in the eye whilst you're stroking him."

I look down at Jake's length pointing almost directly at me, stiff and leaking in anticipation. I move closer so we're only the length of Jake's cock apart. I sit back, lowering onto my heels and reach for Jake's cock as I look up at him. He groans as my warm fingers clasp around his heating rod between us and I begin to run my hands up and down. He's so smooth. Jake is looking back at me with all kinds of desire emanating from him. He leans himself into my hands further as I rub his pre-come down his length.

"Spit on his cock," Blake commands. I don't need to be told twice; my mouth is watering for a taste of him. I lower my head until my mouth is almost touching and I dribble as much saliva as I can gather onto my tongue. The liquid helps me slide easier up and down his long shaft.

"Are you enjoying the way Roxy plays with you Jake?" asks Blake.

"Every second of every minute," groans Jake.

"Would you like her to suck you deep into the back of her throat?"

"Oh God yes," comes Jake's throaty reply.

"Roxy, be a good girl and suck Jake down your pretty mouth."

"Yes Blake," I reply obediently, I keep my eye contact with Jake's as I lower my head and begin to slowly suck him down. My desire for this man is building up higher, coiling into tight knots—teasing him is teasing me.

"Deeper," commands Blake.

I move my head into position and take him whole, hitting the back of my throat in one deep thrust.

"Oh my god," is all Jake can say as my lips slide up and down, each time allowing him to touch the back of my throat. I can feel his legs begin to quiver as he approaches his building release.

"Stop," commands Blake and I freeze in motion. Looking up at Jake, my mouth full of him—he looks like he's in pain.

Blake climbs onto the bed, onto his knees next to Jake. He's fisting his own dick. "Remove yourself from Jake, Roxy," he demands, his eyes searing into mine. "Do not wipe your mouth. Slide that hot wet mouth over my cock. Jake is not to come unless it's deep in your cunt."

I slide off Jake but before I move only slightly to the left for Blake's cock, Blake grabs my jaw and holds my face up to look at him. He places his thumb into my mouth and presses down making me open wider. I stare up into his sardonic eyes, my mouth held open. I am hyper aware of this commanding, dominant man, my skin tingles at the way he is holding me and his thumb in my mouth. It's degrading, his treatment of me, but I crave it deep in my soul. He rubs his thumb further into my mouth, reaching my throat where I almost gag before he removes it and pulls my head towards his engorged cock. His cock is thick and veiny, an angry, pulsing rod he then shoves into my mouth.

"Suck me like a good girl Roxy." And I do. One swift glide and he's fully seated down the back of my throat. Just as I'm about to slide up and back down, he pulls out from my mouth and gestures to Jake's cock. Grabbing the base of Jake's stiff dick, he feeds me onto it. I slide down Jake's cock and as I come back up his shaft, I feel Blake grab my chin and pull me onto his own once again. I understand what Blake is asking of me and switch between the two in tandem, as I pop off one cock, the other is waiting and thrust down the back of my throat. I stop thinking about whose cock is whose, I just suck them and suck them—the depravity of being used in such a way is overwhelming, my pussy clenching needing something to fill it.

Blake's legs begin to quiver, "Stop," he commands, and I don't suck down Jake as I pull off Blake. "What do good girls say for the pleasure of sucking our cocks?"

"Thank you," I say looking up into their hungry eyes.

"Good girl," Blake reaches out and strokes the hair away from my face, the gesture feels more like a sign of ownership than an attempt to bring comfort.

"Lie down on the bed Jake, I think it's time Roxy received her reward."

I watch as Jake lies on his back, his head resting on the pillows. "Climb onto his cock Roxy, it's all yours."

With delight I climb onto Jake, it does feel like a reward, my core aches for this man and the release he can help me achieve. Jake holds his erect cock and looks at my body like he's starving for me. I lower slower down, edging deeper and deeper watching Jake's face as bliss takes over his features and he takes in a shuddery breath.

"That's my girl," Blake says from behind me. "Ride his cock like the paid whore you are for us." His words bite. I *am* a whore. I want to ride Jake like the whore he paid for. I willingly move my hips and feel the deepness of him, I am almost teetering on the edge of an orgasm.

I hear a cap of a bottle close from behind me and then a lubed finger rub up and down my back hole. I slow my thrusting rhythm to turn and see what Blake is doing. He is pumping one lubed hand up his cock and the other lubed hand over my back hole.

"That's right Roxy, you'll be taking both of us. Are you ready?"

My eyes bulge at his meaty cock, *Am I ready? Can I do this?* I don't trust my voice so instead I nod my head.

"I want you to look at Jake when I enter you," instructs Blake. I've stilled with Jake fully seated inside of me, I feel Blake push me down so my chest almost lies on Jake's and then feel him nudging at my arsehole. "Hold our girl in place and help her relax Jake, there's a good boy."

Jake reaches for my worried face and smiles warmly before pulling my mouth to his. He kisses me gently as I whimper into his mouth. Blake is so big, I'm not sure I can relax enough to let him enter, especially with Jake already inside me.

"Shh pretty lady, you can take it," Jake says into my mouth. "Relax into me, focus on my lips as Blake slides into you. Don't clench, I can feel you around my cock." I try and do what he says as he begins to kiss me more forcibly, his tongue finding mine. He kisses me like I know he wants to fuck me; I can feel it with every stroke of his tongue tangling with mine. I lean into the kiss and meld into him, our two bodies combining into one. I know it's enough for Blake to edge past my tight ring of muscle, then I loosen up even more as Jake kisses me like his life depends on it. Further into my arsehole Blake slides, Jake still seated in my pussy.

"I can feel you inside Roxy," groans Blake from behind me.

"I can feel you too," replies Jake, pulling away from my mouth to answer.

Blake pulls out a little and then pushes in further and further, the depth of him switches from a burning sensation to a pleasurable stretch.

"There we go Roxy girl, you are taking us both like a good girl. I'm fully seated up in your gorgeous arsehole, you are taking us perfectly. We are going to start moving now, you are going to enjoy this part."

Jake kisses me reassuringly as Blake begins to move in my arse, thrusting in and out slowly. I rise higher off Jake's chest, Blake's thrusts move me along Jake's cock. Jake grabs hold of my hips, "Stay there pretty lady, we are going to fuck you so good just like this." Holding me in place, Jake moves me across his cock as Blake moves from behind me, they work in a rhythm of thrusting, and I let go. I uncoil between them and relax into the sensation of being filled in both holes at the same time by these two strong, delicious men. I begin to feel euphoric as the pressure of my throbbing centre starts to take over my entire body. Shaking, I try and pant through what is about to combust inside of me.

"She's going to come," breathes Jake as he feels me begin to clench around him.

"Come for us Roxy, all over Jake's cock. We want to feel you pulse over our cocks as we plough into you deeper than you've ever been taken before."

Fireworks ignite from my core and explode throughout my body, and I scream, "I'm coming, I'm coming, you're making me come so hard, I—" I lose the ability to speak. This spurs the boys on, and they go feral as they move inside of me stretching my orgasm out as I pulse around them.

It's Jake who falls over first, mere seconds before Blake finds his release, they both cry out my name as they still and pulse into both my holes, filling me to the brim with their come. Jake is still holding me up but gradually lowers me to rest onto his chest, still fully erect and filling me.

Blake slowly pulls out from behind me, and I feel the familiar rush of liquid follow his retreating cock.

Blake doesn't move off the bed, he climbs over Jake's leg and lowers his head to mine. Moving my damp hair away from my face he begins to press light kisses along my neck and shoulder. It's the most care he's shown me, and I lap it up for what it's worth, he's showing me how grateful he is. I smile sleepily up at him depleted and fully fucked as I lie flat on Jake's heaving chest.

"You were epic, Roxy," Jake praises in my ear. "Never had we ever imagined it would be that good. Not even in our wildest dreams." I close my eyes and breathe in our sticky scent and relax knowing that they enjoyed it as much as I did. Blake lies on his side next to us and runs circles on my back as we all catch our breath and take in what we just did together. This moment in time is so intimate it feels like we've done this a thousand times before. I'm lying on and between these two attractive men who have just used and abused my body in a way it has never been before. It's an experience I will never forget for as long as I live.

We stay cocooned for a little while longer before Blake gets up and walks into the bathroom, returning with a washcloth that he sweeps over my back hole. He then lifts me off Jake's softness and lays me down on my back, wiping between my legs as the proof of our pleasure leaks from me.

"You sure are a sight Roxy, leaking us out from both your holes." Blake stays between my legs wiping delicately between my folds for several long moments before walking back to the bathroom. My eyes follow his movements but I'm floating in a haze of endorphins, unable to move or speak. When he returns, Blake curls into me and Jake does the same on the other side, we all lay snuggled together in a pile of damp naked limbs, smelling and tasting of sex and orgasms.

I awake with a start when Cook pushes in a trolley of food for dinner. I smile back at his beaming face.

"I bring sustenance for you all after that beautiful show," he winks back at us, and I see the boys rouse at Cook's voice.

"Thank you Cook," I reply sleepily. "Will you join us?"

"No, this is the boys' time. You all take your time and enjoy each other and the food."

"Thanks, Cook," the boys say in unison.

We stay curled together for a little longer before the glorious aroma of spaghetti and meatballs can't be ignored any longer. The rollercoaster of emotions I'm experiencing right now is sure making me hungry. We all clamber off the bed and sit around the small table as we had earlier. No champagne with this meal, but a bunch of different sodas to choose from.

We all have an afterglow and eat together companionably, flirting and talking about tv shows and movies and enjoying each other's company like a first date.

I try and stifle a yawn once I've finished my bowl of pasta.

"You young lady, need to get your rest. It's been a fun day, but you have more fun coming and you'll be needing your energy for what's ahead," Blake tells me with a wink.

"It's been a pleasure pretty lady," says Jake, kissing my knuckles. "I am already counting down the minutes to be inside of you again."

I blush. His words make me melt, I feel the same way, but how can that be when I've only known him and his partner for a day?

The two men stand at the table, I stand too. It's Jake who comes around to my side first and wraps his warm arms around me, naked along with me and Blake. "Pretty lady, we'll see you really soon," he says as I look up into his crystal eyes. Then he kisses me gently on the lips. Not opening his mouth but pressing his lips to mine and holding them against mine so that I feel his goodbye. "Ok?" he looks at me with concerned eyes.

"Ok," I reply, feeling a sadness tug at my heart that they were leaving me.

"We'd stay, but that wasn't what we all agreed upon," says Blake, coming up to the side of us. Jake pulls away as Blake pulls me into his fit frame and kisses me on the lips too. I startle in surprise as he hasn't kissed me once since we've been together. Looking down into my eyes, his eyes pools of darkness, they crinkle at the sides and he looks less like a Dominant and more like a departing lover. "We'll be watching, we'll be with you always." He drops one last lingering touch to my lips before the men are pulling their clothes back on and filling the empty food trolley and pushing it out of the door.

For the first time I feel sad to be alone. I enjoyed this couple, both their personalities and their dominant and submissive sides. There was something so likeable and relaxed about being with them. I'm not sure what I should do with myself as I sit and feel a little lost on the bed.

After looking at the glass walls and wondering who was looking back at me, I gather myself up and walk into the bathroom for a quick shower. I decide to get ready for bed and read until my eyelids close on me.

36

———

I awake with a start, but it must be earlier than I usually wake, there is no music to wake me. Maybe I fell asleep earlier than usual. The lights are low, and I lay still under the covers. And there it is, that familiar wet feeling between my legs. *Do I really sleep that heavy?* I muse.

I lie still a little longer and reflect on my week so far, the men I have met and how they are taking care of me and the sex I've been having. It's unfathomable what I have been doing yet here I am. I feel a connection with nearly all the men in small or bigger ways. Tom is unreadable but even he doesn't seem threatening. No one has made me feel wretched or like an actual whore. They've done the opposite and made me feel wanted, enjoyed and valued. I know going into this experience I had no idea what to expect, but these men are a thousand times better than any preconceived idea I could have had. They simply just want to be free to do their thing. And I get that. Up until I was recently made a playmate, when have I ever felt comfortable asking for what I want, or even acknowledging what I want. Not even to myself. I thought those kinds of things happened only in porn or brothels. So far away from my reach it's almost laughable where I find myself now.

Nothing has been done to me I haven't enjoyed. These may not all be my own personal kinks, but I am enjoying them just the same. The new experiences make me wonder what more is out there and how much farther and deeper can I go in the world of kinks? All the way? And what way is that?

Then my heart pangs and I think of James and my children. They're in my heart always. I know the kids are perfectly fine and James is looking after them so they're safe and happy. But who is looking after James? Who is there to hear about his day, help with the kids and tell him I'm ok. Is this time away tearing him apart from worry or has he managed to compartmentalise and is able to rest knowing the club wouldn't allow anything bad to happen to me?

I ache to reach out to him and let him know I'm fine. To give him an update and reassure him. He is such a wonderful man inside and out. I am lucky and I know it. Even more so with the most recent events leading up to today and where I am. Who else's husband would allow this? Who else would really be on board with me becoming a playmate, I haven't even told my best friend or my sister. I mean, he's so into it, he's taken two weekends of Dom training this month. Not as if he's let me in on what he's learnt and what he's like as a Dom yet, just teasing me and promising to share all after this week. I cannot wait to see this side of him just as he's watched and enjoyed seeing me change and become a playmate.

Becoming a playmate is so far outside the realms of normality, I fear the kind of backlash my stomach can't handle. And once it's out, I can never go back. Living a double life is not hurting anyone, it's protecting my children and ensuring everyone continues believing we're living the status quo just like every member of the golf club and the playmates. There is a very good reason for the secrecy, proven by tabloid after dirty tabloid story. We haven't reached a time yet where sexual freedom is accepted and it's unlikely in my lifetime. But what I know is, it's happening just like it's likely happened for generations: people from all walks of life finding their safe place through underground secret clubs and memberships. I'm thrilled and thankful it found me, or I found it. It's been very freeing to say the least and with the support of the man I love, what more in this life could I possibly want? I have a husband who supports me, two healthy, happy children and a job that not only pays incredibly well but allows me to unleash a side of me I had no idea existed.

I contemplate getting up when the music begins to play softly, and I know for sure it must be time to get up and showered, ready for Carl. A bolt of delight goes through me to see him and that's all I need to pull the covers back and make my way into the bathroom to shower and brush my teeth.

My morning events go just like the previous two. Carl shaves me to perfection, moisturises my skin like I'm a delicate flower and then flips me over in a first and takes me gently from behind.

Cook feeds me well with fruit and porridge again but with a twist of maple syrup dribbled along his cock. That was a sticky, delicious mess.

After sweetly saying goodbye to Cook and him not giving me a hint of what is in store for me, I settle on the bed with a new book and anticipate what the men have planned. There have only been two men who haven't played with me properly, Dr Jack and Darcy. But I'm pretty sure Darcy plays with my body every night. So that leaves Dr Jack unless Tom hasn't had his way with me yet in the manner he would like. I find it hard to concentrate on reading as I mull over in my mind who will be walking through the door next.

When the door does finally opens, a smiling, white coated Dr Jack enters with Tom behind. Tom wears his usual mask of unreadable features and makes his way directly over to the brown armchair, I affectionately think of it as Tom's armchair now. He sits, relaxes back and folds one leg over the other as his eyes finally land on me, staring intently at my nakedness. Only Tom makes me truly feel like I'm exposed. Why is that?

My attention is quickly taken by Dr Jack who is carrying a briefcase and has a stethoscope around his neck. I hold in a giggle; he sure does look the part today.

I smile warmly up at Dr Jack and say a bright, "Hello handsome Dr Jack, it's lovely to see you today."

Dr Jack's eyes flash at me, his boyish good looks make my insides melt into a puddle as his grin lights up his face and he replies, "Hello to you too. I've missed you, sweet girl."

"I'm glad you're here doctor. Have you come to give me a check-up?"

"I sure have. You have been fucked by many men in the space of three days. It's time you had a check-up to make sure you are fit and healthy to take the rest of us," he winks at me. "Ordinarily I would ask you to strip, but you are the perfect patient and have already taken all your clothes off for me." Another wink and I almost swoon where I'm sitting.

"Tom, wheel in my patient bed, would you?" he asks over his shoulder but doesn't take his eyes off me.

From my periphery I can see Tom stand and leave the room. Moments later he pushes in a medical looking bed that I recognise from the stretching playmate job I'd had. *Where do men buy these from?!*

"First, I'm going to give you a breast examination. Please come and stand in front of me." Dr Jack has sat on my bed, so I shuffle off it and stand fully nude in front of him. Reaching out his hands he begins to press down with his fingertips on a flat hand down on different locations on my breast, seeming like he's checking for lumps. He does this to both.

Moving back to my right breast, he squeezes with both

hands, and I whimper at the sudden change of pace and pain. Dr Jack doesn't seem to notice as he focuses on squeezing, both hands circling my large breast and keeping them there whilst it bulges and begins to turn an angry red. I squirm under his firm grip. He doesn't seem to notice and continues to squeeze even harder, seemingly fascinated with the colour my poor breast is turning, which is almost purple right now. I begin to whimper and move from one foot to the other trying to stay still but unable to command my body not to move. "Ah there we go; would you look at that. I'm going to let go now and make sure that your circulation is pumping as it should." Dr Jack lets go and relief flushes my body as blood flow begins to seep back in.

Dr Jack moves his attention to my left breast, squeezing just the same if not harder until my breast turns a deep shade of purple, seemingly unbothered by my shifting and the whimpers I can't contain. When he finally lets that one go, he reaches for both nipples with each hand and pulls. "As beautiful as these perky little nipples go, I have a special test to see how long they can go so we can measure. One moment please."

I watch as he opens his briefcase and from a glance I can see an array of objects and tools. He lifts out two small cylinders that appear to have screw tops. "Let's get you onto the bed first." Taking my hand, Dr Jack leads me over to where Tom has left the medical bed and stands aside as I climb onto the white sheets and lay down on my back. The bed is between my bed and the door. Tom has angled it so that when I lift my head I can look straight at him.

Lifting one of the small cylinders I watch in fascination as he places it over my left nipple and begins to screw the top which suctions my nipple longer and longer until it reaches the top of the cylinder. He walks around to the other side of the bed and does the same with my right nipple. I lie still and look down at my chest, both nipples elongated, stretching painfully inside the tubes. It's a strange view and feeling, but I like the pull and the stretch. I've never experienced anything like it before.

Snapping out of whatever role Dr Jack was in, he strokes his hand along down the side of my face, rubbing his thumb over my bottom lip. "I'm going to leave these here whilst I take swabs. I have a special instrument to open you up wide for me, ok sweet girl?"

"Ok Doctor," I reply demurely. "Whatever you think is best." There it is again, his eyes flashing, hinting at something or someone else hiding beneath his boy next door demeanour.

Lying back on the bed, I watch Dr Jack walk back to where his briefcase is resting open on the bed and picks up a metal speculum. *Is it larger than usual or is that my nerves?* I hear Tom shift in his chair, and I move my attention over to him. He's lowered his leg and is sitting forward in the seat with almost as much anticipation as I feel.

I'm all too aware of my nipples, screaming for attention as they stretch and ache deliciously in their tiny prisons. Dr Jack walks over to the end of the bed, unfolds two stirrups on each side and lifts one leg at a time, positioning them into their new placements. The bed is tilted so I'm lying down but not completely flat with my legs wide open, completely exposed at my centre. With the way I'm placed, my open pussy is perfectly in Tom's line of sight, as well as anyone who may be watching from behind the glass.

"Let me see how wet you are before we begin," says Dr Jack, peering hungrily at my core.

I can feel the liquid heat building inside of me, I don't need Dr Jack to tell me.

Dr Jack runs one finger through my open folds and into my entrance only entering the tip of his finger before pulling it out dripping with my desire. He looks up, his eyes burn into mine, "Sweet girl, you are dripping. Are you enjoying the attention of a doctor right now?"

"Yes," comes my throaty reply. I can't deny, this is the most turned on I've ever felt being examined by a doctor.

As he lifts the finger to his mouth, something catches his eye, he taps two fingers together and a string of moisture sticks between them and stretches out. Dr Jack's eyes widen. "You are ovulating, Roxy. Baby making time in your calendar. Can you imagine if your birth control failed you whilst you were here because you have been fucked so thoroughly and regularly. Imagine one of us sowing a baby into the depths of your womb? You have no idea how much I would want that to be me. I am going to fuck you so hard once I've taken all your swabs that there would be no denying if you were to fall pregnant it would be by me."

My mind suddenly freaks out at the slim possibility at the same time my clit sparks with lightning bolts of desire. Having a baby fucked into me by one of these hot, incredible men turns me on even more and hot liquid begins to seep out of me. Dr Jack looks from my flush face to my dripping desire. He dips his finger back down and this time sucks the liquid off his finger. "You want us to fuck a baby into you too, your pussy just gave you away," he says so darkly, he almost sounds nothing like himself. *Why is this turning me on so much, since when do I have a breeding kink?* Since now?

"Let's get to work sweet girl. We have tests to run, and your thirsty pussy is needing her medicine quickly."

Dr Jack picks up the speculum and he nudges it towards my entrance, and without any lube it begins to slide in easily. He pushes it slowly and my body opens to accommodate the metal object as it reaches my cervix. When fully seated, Dr Jack begins to screw it open, stretching my walls wide. The stretching feeling grows until I'm certain the speculum has reached its maximum diameter, I can only imagine the view this must offer to Dr Jack and the others. Just knowing they can see into my very core causes the heat to build and I'm sure I must be dripping onto the table.

"Beautiful, sweet girl, I am just going to collect a sample with this spatula, and we're almost finished with your vagina." I feel a light tapping on my cervix before Dr Jack withdraws the spatula and fastens it into a test tube. I feel the metal device inside of me shrink as Dr Jack screws it closed and gently pulls it out.

"We need a sample from your anal cavity now," says Dr Jack holding the speculum up. "Now have your juices coated this instrument enough or will we need some lube?" My eyes bulge in concern at the size of it entering my rear entrance. I open my mouth to request he please add some lube when he continues, "I think a spot of lube will help smooth the process, we need your anal cavity in good working order now don't we. Don't want a speculum having all the fun." I sigh in relief at his crude words.

Dr Jack squirts a healthy portion onto the metal speculum and moves it towards my tight rear hole. "Easy now sweet girl, this is going to be fast and painless, relax now."

Taking in a deep, shaky breath I do as he asks and feel the metal end nudge gently at my arsehole. I repeat the words *Just relax* over in my mind as I feel more pressure nudge harder and I take in Dr Jack's focus. His deviant demeanour and the obvious pleasure I see there at the depravity of what he is doing and is about to do to me, helps me relax. I know it shouldn't and for millions it wouldn't, but for me this is erotic and all kind of messed up logic. My doctor is doing what he wants with my body and I'm letting him shove a speculum up my anus.

I've relaxed enough for the speculum to enter me, passing my clenching ring of muscle. I feel the wide uncomfortable burn as Dr Jack pushes it further into my anal cavity. "There we go, a little more until it's fully seated and we can open it up. You're being such a brave girl Ms Roxy, look at you taking a speculum so far up your arse. I can't wait to see you gape open for me."

His soothing yet crude words are making me feel light-headed with desire. Dr Jack is building a burning passion inside of me whilst he defiles me in such a delicious perversion of the usual safe medical setting. And then I feel it, he's turning the screw to open up the speculum inside of me, I can feel the pressure on my walls.

"Here we go, a little more and I'll be able to see right inside you to take our sample."

More pressure and I wonder how much further he is going to open me up and how much more I can take. I clench my fingers into balls, a movement that catches Dr Jack's notice. He leaves the device open, exposing the depths of my arsehole to Tom and whoever else is watching outside, and walks to the top of the bed. Stroking the few flyaway hairs away from my forehead gently, he looks down into my eyes before he bends over my mouth and catches my lips with his. Moving a hand to cup the back of my neck, he kisses me reverently sending prickles of pleasure rippling down my skin.

My tongue meets his in a slow and gentle tango opening his mouth wider for our tongues to dance further. It's an all-consuming sumptuous kiss, I forget where I am, I forget what has just been done to me and I embrace everything Dr Jack is giving me. So many sensations are pulsing through my body from his kiss, the tautness of my nipples, the stretching of my arsehole. They're building me up high, into a tight ball of near combustion.

Dr Jack pulls away and looks at me like he's teetering on the edge of madness himself. "One more sample and we're done. I need to hold it together for one last sample," he says, though I'm unsure if he's talking to me or himself?

Walking back down to the end of the hospital bed, he takes a specula and slides it inside of me and I feel a strange prodding sensation deep into my anal cavity before it's gone and Dr Jack is screwing it into a test tube.

He moves his stare from my open back entrance to my face with heavy lidded predatory eyes. "I'm not going to unscrew the speculum; I'm going to pull it out gradually at its current girth and watch you gape at the end when it slides out."

I nod as words fail me, I can only look on from my pillow and Dr Jack begins to slowly tug with rapt attention. It doesn't burn, just a soothing release of pressure follows the instrument as it leaves my body. I pant through it and my nipples bob a little at the movement reminding me they're still trapped and aching with pleasure.

"And there it is, stunning," Dr Jack whispers hoarsely, he has one hand on my arse cheek helping to hold me open longer whilst the other hand is holding the wide speculum he's just slid out from my arsehole. Dr Jack bends his head down and places his tongue over my closing ring of muscle and I let out an involuntary moan as does Tom who I had completely forgotten was in the room.

One stroke of my clit and I would come a thousand orgasms at once. I need something right now; I need him now. Dr Jack removes his tongue from my arsehole, lifts his head and he looks like a different person. His face is contorted with hunger and need. In quick, jerky movements, he lifts my legs out of the stirrups placing them back on the bed and folds the stirrups back under the bed. He walks to my side, places his arms under my body and lifts, carrying me bridal style to the large bed before placing me as close to the centre as he can.

He tugs off his doctor's coat, pulls off his grey t-shirt and tugs down his jeans and boxers in quick succession. He's moving so fast I can barely make out his toned body, the prominent V pointing down to a very prominent erection. He climbs on the bed in a flash and he's on me, unscrewing my right nipple and then my left. Pleasure and pain course through my beasts at their freedom. Dr Jack sucks one elongated, sensitive nipple all the way into his mouth, I gasp at the hot wetness and the suction which has just replaced the previous suction. Pain filters through me as blood tries to flow back into my nipples.

I feel giddy with need, running my hands through his soft hair, rubbing my legs on any part of his flesh they can come into contact with. I want this man beyond anything I have ever wanted in my life. He pinches my other smarting nipple, and I yelp at the sudden slice of pain firing straight to my clit. "Doctor," I moan, "I need you."

Moving from sucking my nipple up my body, Dr Jack kisses me feverishly across my chest, up my neck—nipping and sucking as he goes. When he gets to my mouth, our teeth clash as he delves into my mouth lapping like a man possessed. I can feel his hard length stabbing into my stomach as he straddles over my hips.

Dr Jack runs his hands up my nape and holds my head in place as he devours my mouth. I melt into him, giving over to his hot mouth and rocking my hips upwards hoping he'll reward me soon.

A sharp pain has me jolting as I taste blood on my tongue from my lip. Dr Jack sucks my bleeding lower lip into his mouth and my eyes roll into the back of my head. I need to come *now!* I try to rub myself on his body but he's too high for friction.

Dr Jack moves back down my neck, sucking and biting harder than before, marking me, branding me. His hips are now above me, he's moved his legs inside of mine and I open wider, inviting. He rears up, his eyes wild as his cock finds my entrance. And when his length ploughs inside of me straight to the back of my cervix I erupt around him, my coil bursting and obliterating. I have never needed to come so much in my life and Dr Jack thrusts inside me, stretching out the orgasm as I arch into him, screaming and moaning wildly whilst he ruts into me fervently.

"I'm fucking my seed into you now Roxy, I can't hold back any longer. I want a piece of me and you combined forever. You are perfect, you will look perfect stretched and bursting with our child. Your breasts leaking for me to suckle. I want to fuck my seed into you over and over again."

I come undone again, another orgasm ripping through me as he roars into the air and buries his stiff cock to the hilt and freezes, coating my insides with every last drop he has to give. Dr Jack lowers himself to lie over me, his head resting by my face, he's panting heavily, our bodies slick with sweat, still intertwined.

We lay there panting together and take in what just happened. It was perfect, so many feelings are coursing through my body but I feel relaxed and lightweight, I gently stroke circles on his back with the hand he's not lying on. A soft intimate gesture that I want to give him and myself if I'm honest. I want to touch him and feel close to him. He stays still, his head still buried in my neck, he makes no move or sound, just lies depleted and still on top of me. I breathe him in, the fresh clean masculine smell of his hair and his body.

After a few long moments I feel him grow harder inside of me, I stroke up his strong back and he eventually lifts his head and rests his upper body onto his right arm. Wordlessly he looks into my eyes, and he looks every bit of the boy next door again, doe eyed and earnestly looking back at me. Without a word he gently lowers and kisses tentatively on my lips, worlds apart from the way he was just kissing.

Dr Jack kisses me lovingly, slow sensual kisses as he begins to move slowly inside of me again. He's making love to me; I can feel it in every ember of my body. His delicate kisses and his gentle caresses of my face and neck... I writhe in the change of pace and this delicious sensuality. Long, lingering strokes of him inside of me have me offering up every last piece of myself for him to take. Right this very second I'm lost to everything except this man making love to me. I hear and see nothing but him, I feel claimed and ravished and now loved. He nuzzles into my neck as I feel heat flow down to my core and slowly begin to build a fire inside of me. He's fanning the flames with each stroke angled just right, hitting the perfect place as he whispers hoarsely in my ear, "I want my seed to grow inside of you, I want to plant it in you over and over again sweet girl, now I've had a taste, I want nothing and no one else. I am going to paint your insides every chance I get."

And that's my undoing, "Doctor," I moan into his ear as my pussy clenches around his cock, ripples of ecstasy pulse from my core, sending shivers throughout my entire body. I feel him reach his climax alongside mine as he paints the inside of my cervix with his seed again. He stills himself inside of me, lifts his head up and looks deep into my eyes and we hold that moment for a lifetime. Words unspoken and an intimacy unmatched. I may never be able to walk away from this man. And yet I must.

He must be thinking something similar as he lowers to my lips and kisses me tenderly before pulling away. I see him pull himself away from me emotionally in that moment also. Pulling out from inside of me, he climbs off the bed.

Standing beside me, he's back to his cheerful playful self again. "You, sweet girl, look thoroughly fucked. A glass of water and a shower for you, doctor's orders."

I grin back at him, appreciating his light tone and change in pace again. This one is much easier to navigate. Dr Jack reaches out a hand which I take as he helps pull me up to a sitting position and then off the bed. Warm liquid begins to run down my inner thighs which makes me move that little bit faster to the bathroom to clean up.

Dr Jack takes care of me in just the way he does. He hands

me a glass of water, runs the shower for me, washes me delicately and pats me dry. Dr Jack rubs a cream into my bitten lip and also into my neck where I know there are small bites and hickeys. When we are back in the empty bedroom—Tom seemingly has left us again—he gets dressed. I watch with melancholy as he pulls on his clothes and hides away his beautiful body.

Turning to me, he strokes a strand of hair away from my face, "I'll see you again very soon, sweet girl. Thank you for this morning, it was better than I could have imagined."

"Thank you for my check-up doctor, it was the best one I've ever had or will ever have," I smile back at him. "Let me know the results when you have them," I smile widely at him.

"Oh, I will do sweet girl, now get some rest. Doctor's orders."

I giggle and place my legs under the covers in bed sitting up. My new book on my right. Dr Jack picks up his briefcase, places the swabs inside and walks towards the door. I realise Tom must have pushed the bed out when we were in the shower. Dr Jack gives me one final nod farewell at the door and then I'm alone again.

37

I try and take my mind off Dr Jack with my book until Cook comes in with lunch. His sunny face instantly makes me brighter. I may never get over this feeling of being appreciated to be here, it's like I have seven doting boyfriends and one fantasy one whom I've never met but is behind the glass somewhere.

Cook feeds me mouthfuls of sandwiches and talks about watching me with Dr Jack. The way he recalls so many details, it feels like he was in the room with me. I ache for Dr Jack but Cook's hungry eyes tell me I won't need to ache for much longer, he'll be taking my mind off Dr Jack very shortly. He goes easy on me with the lunch, not as much as usual as I've yet to get used to the volumes he's been plying me with. He raises one hand up for me to bite the sandwich but uses the other to stroke down my neck, along my chest and down one breast, tenderly, lovingly.

"I have a different dessert, but can I ask you something first?" he asks almost longingly.

"Of course, Cook, anything," I reply, offering him my best

reassuring tone. I reach out a hand and rest it on his thigh which is easy as we're sitting so close together.

"I've watched every single one of the men fuck you in every way. My cock weeps for you almost 24/7. May I come inside you, as dessert?" He follows with, "Seeing you with the Doc, it just did things to me that I can't shake out of my head. The instruments, your stretched nipples, the way he mounted you. I just want to feel you clasped around my cock, not just your wet mouth. Your pussy too.

I adore this man, the way he's been feeding me, the way he strokes me, the way he takes care of me and fills my mouth with his cock. I want him too, I want to feel him inside me, find out how he tastes and how he likes to fuck. He need say no more as I stand from my seat and climb onto his lap. "Cook, I've been waiting for my time with you and am thrilled that time is right now."

Cook is fully clothed, apron and all. I am fully naked as I thread my hands around the nape of his neck, brushing his blond cropped hair. Being mindful not to knock into his glasses, I lower my mouth to his and kiss him tentatively. I don't want to be too forward.

Apparently, that was all Cook needed as he heatedly kisses me back, his tongue delving into my mouth tasting like black cherries. We stay this way until I break away gasping. He stands from the chair, lifting me wrapped around his body and walks us both to the bed when he gently deposits me. He begins to tear his clothes off like they're on fire. I stifle a giggle. He catches me, "I'm going to make you pay for that baby girl," but his dimples give away his playfulness as he smiles back at me. "You need to shuffle up the bed now before I come before I've even entered you."

I do as he asks and shuffle my body up to the top of the bed as he prowls after me on his knees. I giggle again but don't try and hide it. My giggles are replaced with a loud groan when his hot mouth lands directly on the bullseye, straight on my clit. "Cook you devil," I groan again as he adds his tongue and then two of his fingers slide in and curve up. "Oh god Cook, what are you doing to me?"

Cook releases his mouth only long enough for the words, "Catching you up with me right now."

His fingers are caressing in just the right spot inside when he adds more pressure and circles my clit with his tongue. I manage to say, "Lick me, just there, harder." And I'm coming all over his clever fingers. Cook works his fingers inside me long enough for me to ride out my climax before he's replacing them with his cock. In one swift move, he's completely on top of me and sliding inside, my own release coating him and allowing quick and easy access.

My internal nerves are all firing from my climax as I accommodate his size as he begins to rut into me. There is no holding Cook back, whatever fuse was lit as he enjoyed Dr Jack's time with me, it's now burning quickly as he chases a climax of his own buried deep inside me.

"Baby girl, the way you feel around my cock—so hot and juicy, I'm not going to be able to hold on for much longer. I want to plant my seed so deep Dr Jack's has no chance. I love to feed you and watch your stomach extend and stretch, your breasts and your body are already growing deliciously in front of my eyes, it's impossible to keep my hands off you and now the last of my restraint has broken. Picturing feeding you pregnant, full in stomach and in breasts, that's it!" he roars into the room, his words and his pulsing cock tipping me over the edge of my own orgasm.

Breathing heavy, Cook looks down at me and smiles wickedly, dimples and all. "I think I have unlocked a new kink today."

"You and me both," I giggle back. "It turns me on too, I had no idea."

"Oh boy, you have no idea. It got nearly all of us when we were watching the Doc with you. Be warned, I wouldn't be surprised if they're not all queuing up for you this afternoon. I certainly couldn't keep myself out of you. Wild horses may have struggled to keep me away."

Cook pulls out of me and rolls onto his side next to me, then leans forward and places a kiss on my nose.

"Thank you for dessert baby girl, I promise to bring a proper one with dinner. I need to get moving, I wasn't supposed to lose my control just then, but it was worth it." He winks at me.

"Oh so worth it," I wink back at him. "You can lose control whenever you want around me, Cook. Your mouth and fingers," I give him a chef's kiss motion, "are simply divine. Now go get on with what you were meant to do, you deviant, before you get into trouble with the others."

Chuckling and chef kissing me back with a raised eyebrow, Cook climbs off the bed and leaves me on my back, thoroughly fucked for the second time today. What a day in what a week. *Can someone pinch me please?*

Cook pulls his clothes on a lot slower than he tore them off. I lie back and watch the reverse strip show. He leans over the bed and kisses me gently on the lips. "See you tonight baby girl." And he's gone.

I pad into the bathroom to get cleaned up before picking up my book and sitting in Tom's leather armchair to read. Makes a nice change sitting up on a chair. I settle in for what feels like an hour or two.

38

———————

There is a light knock at the door, and I look up from my book. To my surprise it's Tom. He usually watches me when one of the other men is playing with me. I wonder why he's here. I'm curled up on his chair, this should be interesting, I wonder if he'll talk to me. *Am I allowed to say hello or is that breaking the no talking to Tom rule?* I wonder.

Tom walks directly over to stand in front of me and I clamber up out of his chair like a naughty child. Clearly my instincts will have to guide me when it comes to Tom. He's massive in comparison to me, he dwarfs my slim 5ft 5 frame. He's stacked with muscle upon muscles. Even his muscles have muscles by the way his arms flex his tight t-shirt.

I am about to slide past him and go back to my bed when a thick hand grabs my arm roughly just below the shoulder. I grind to a quick halt. I look at his hand gripping me tightly and then follow it up his tattooed arm into his heated angry stare. *Is he angry that I was sitting in his chair?*

"I'm sorry, I won't sit there again," I babble in reply as my heart begins to thump loudly in my chest.

Tom narrows his eyes, and I get the impression it's not the

chair he's angry about. His eyes lower to my mouth and back to my eyes again. Energy bristles between us and I feel the atmosphere around us darken as if it's sucking in a breath in anticipation. There is no movement on Tom's face, he wears a mask of stone half hidden with his beard—only his green eyes stare back at me and that's enough for me to draw in a breath of fear. *What is he going to do now he's touching me?*

As though reading my mind, Tom guides me back to the bed, his hand clasping painfully around my arm. I bump into the bed with my thighs when I get there, and he spins me to face the bed and pushes my face into the covers. Not a word or a single sound comes from him. Today he watched Dr Jack give me a check-up and Cook lose control. Has he lost control also?

I dare not look but I can see in the reflection of the one-way glass as Tom pulls his black fitted t-shirt over his head to reveal a torso covered in tribal tattoos. I hear his belt buckle open along with a zip and he must be pulling off his jeans and boxers. Then I hear the very familiar sounds of the lube bottle and feel a thick finger nudging at my back hole. I clench initially, *Is Tom going to hate-fuck my arse?* Will I need to use my safe word? Can I trust him?

Although the finger is thick, it is gentle even as it forces its way past my tight muscles and up to the knuckle as another one joins the first. Tom plunges his fingers in and out of me languidly, slowly enough that it actually feels nice. Nothing like how his eyes conveyed their anger. Was it passion I mistook for anger?

I begin to moan as I relax into his fingers that are filling my back hole so well. I reach down under my body to roll my fingers over my clit, making Tom's fingers feel a thousand times better. I move my arse back onto his fingers, silently asking for more. Tom reads my movements and gently withdraws his fingers. I feel the loss of him and begin to turn my head when I feel the tip of his meaty cock replace where his fingers had just been.

He's not going to fit, I begin to panic; *he's going to tear me in two.* Tom reaches around and picks up my hand and places two fingers over mine, joining me in rubbing slow circles around my clit until he can feel my body relax against him and he uses the other hand to hold his cock at my back hole. I am tight and it takes all the focus in the world to relax and not clench my arsehole to avoid his entry. But a part of me wants to do this, wants to let him have me like this. He's making me feel good and not once has he done anything to hurt me.

He slides a fraction further into my arse, the burn overwhelming as I hiss in a breath. He continues to hold his fingers over mine, ensuring I continue rubbing my clit as he nudges inside of me, gently but confidently requiring me to let him in and accommodate the girth of him. When I guess he must be halfway in, he leaves my massaging hand alone and places his onto my hip for leverage as he begins to oh so gently move in and out, only fractions at a time but they begin to feel good, good enough for more.

"Yesss," I moan, a sign he takes to put a bit more pressure behind his hips and delve deeper into my depths. I remember now why I love anal sex so much. It feels so fucking good being filled like this. So dirty and wrong, but it sparks my clit like nothing else.

Tom is bending his legs to fit into me, I am on my tiptoes pressed down against the bed. I can feel my orgasm building as I work my clit furiously. I decide to risk breaking the rules and turn my face to the side to say, "Will you come in my arse Tom, fill me to the hilt with your seed? I want you to come so deep I feel you for the rest of the evening." At that thought, his thrusts and my rubbing, tip me over the edge and into an oblivion. "Tom!" I gasp as I come undone and shiver around his cock.

He lifts my hips higher forcing me to take my weight onto

my forearms feeling the burn in my core like I'm planking as Tom unleashes with ferocious fucking, deep into my arse before he detonates and says the only words he's spoken so far today, "Fuck Roxy, fuck your arsehole is milking me for everything I have got for you!" I can hear the intensity of arousal in his gruff voice and I feel him pulse as he holds me still until his orgasm has subsided before gently lowering my feet to the floor, bending his knees behind me and slowly sliding himself out as a gush of wetness follows him.

He doesn't leave me as I expect. Instead, he places butterfly soft kisses along my shoulders that send a flurry into my core. *Who is this complex quiet hulk of a man?* I wonder. "Stay," he mutters into my ear before moving away and into the bathroom.

When he returns, he wipes up the come dripping down my thighs and then I hear a lid and some cooling cream being applied to my back hole soothing it so much it makes me purr. I look to the side and see him screwing the cap back on a jar of Happie Holl which makes me giggle.

Tom then tenderly flips me over and lays me down in the centre of my pillows, his cock at full mast again as he uncaps a bottle of clear liquid which he squirts into his palms, situates himself near the bottom of the bed and begins to massage my feet.

So help me god, have I died and gone to heaven?

I must have nodded off because when I open my eyes I'm alone in the room. *How long was I asleep?* I wonder. I didn't get to say goodbye or thank you to Tom. I look over to the table next to my bed and see a single red rose.

Having no idea of time, I use the bathroom and climb back into the chair to read, the slight twinge in my arse causing me to smile as I sit down. When my stomach starts to rumble, Cook enters the room as if he were listening out for it. He feeds me and strokes me and lets me lie on his chest as he rubs the food down in my stomach. His clever hands give me one more orgasm before he kisses me slowly and leaves me to get ready for the night.

I fall asleep easily, closing my eyes and thinking of all the men I've had today and all the men I'll take tomorrow. *I could get used to this kind of life... Couldn't I?*

39

I awake like I've had the best night's sleep of my life. It's day five and the fourth morning I've awoken with something sticky between my legs. I lick my lips because they feel dry but a familiar taste fills my mouth, semen? Surely not... But it tastes so similar... What was that Darcy up to last night? And how on earth have I managed to sleep through our—or should I say *his* —interactions. I cannot wait to meet this mystery man and find out what he gets up to after dark.

My morning breezes past in a delicious array of men, shaving, fucking and eating. Not in that order but my morning routine is already something I look forward to. Carl and Cook are sweethearts in their own ways. I'm not sure what the men have planned for me today, I imagine they are watching the clock as time is now ticking. Day five means only two full days and then I leave. There comes that melancholy feeling again. I'm over halfway now. I've been fucked two ways to Sunday and have enjoyed every single interaction. I can't even fathom going back to real life, how will I cope shaving and feeding myself? Not to mention going without the string of men seeing to my every sexual need and desire, even the ones I didn't know I had.

I am delighted to spend the morning with Blake and Jake ending our time together in a triple fucking session with me on the bed, Jake inside me and Blake inside Jake. I get off watching the boys interact and crossing swords, there's a new kink unlocked for me.

I spend the afternoon with Dr Jack and Tom playing cards and then fucking them both. They did not cross swords but were more than happy to alternate and spit-roast me. Twice.

After being fed so thoroughly, Cook kissed me goodnight and I fell into a wonderful warm sleep. But not a deep sleep like usual. Maybe it was something I ate or a loud noise or the temperature changing, I have no idea but for the first time since I slept alone in the glass room, I awake. I lay still, not moving a muscle as my mind wraps around where I am. I am lying on my back, my head on the pillows as usual but I don't have any covers over me like I did when I fell asleep. *Where did they go?* I reach for them, but they are not in reach, not on any part of my body. I open my bleary eyes and try to focus on my surroundings. The lights are dimmed like every evening, but I can always see around the room and as my eyes focus and I look down on the bed, I see there are no covers on the bed. I frown in confusion and am about to sit up when a slender man with black curly hair walks from the bathroom towards my prone naked form.

Fright consumes me for a minute before I realise this must be Darcy. Despite never having met him, curiosity has me stifle any noise that was about to come out of my mouth as I remember the rule to play asleep if I wake up. I close my eyes and hope my fast-rising chest and breathing haven't been noticed yet. I try my hardest to calm down and relax. My heart is thumping so loud in my chest it's hard to hear what Darcy is doing.

A chill runs down my spine and I suspect it was the temperature that cooled and woke me up. Lying still and pretending to be asleep has just turned into my life goal of acting. I am not sure I can pull off pretending to be asleep. Staying immovably still feels impossible. Already I have an itch and a deep desire to move a limb. I don't think I am going to be able to do this. My heart rate begins to spike again as I fight myself to keep control and stay still.

I feel the air around me move and then with the lightest of touches I feel the pad of a finger circle my left nipple. The touch is featherlight, almost there but almost not. It's arousing, makes me want to lean into the touch but I know that would break the rules. I wish I could open my eyes to see how Darcy is looking at me.

After minutes of Darcy's feather-like touch circling, I feel his mouth gently replace his fingers. He doesn't suck or apply pressure, he simply holds his warm mouth over my nipple and gently laps his tongue, so gentle it's a barely there movement that has my core building up to an inferno of desire. Speaking of heat, I don't feel so cold anymore. In fact I feel warmer without the covers suddenly. Have they been playing with the heating to ensure I stay asleep and comfortable when Darcy visits me each night?

Lying deadly still, my mind focuses solely on Darcy's mouth. He makes almost no noise and certainly no big movements. When he seems to have had his fill, he lifts his warm mouth but no cold air hits my nipple from the wetness, it's simply warm enough in the room not to notice.

Like a burglar in the night, I feel Darcy slide himself gracefully off the bed and he must move around to my left side as I feel the air move slightly but see and hear nothing. He must climb onto the bed next to me and again I feel the pad of a finger circle my now pebbled nipple. He plays with this one for an eternity, seemingly having all the time in the world, or all night as he usually would. He removes his finger once again and places his soft lips, encasing my nipple. Shocks of electricity spike down to my clit. He is being so sensual, and it almost feels like such a waste that I miss out on this every single evening. I would prefer to know and feel, but I guess that is not what turns Darcy on. He likes me unmoving and unaware. That is both absolutely appalling and unbearably hot at the same time. Clearly, I need my head read but ever since James fucked me in my drunken haze of a deep sleep after my sister's 40th, the idea has turned me on endlessly.

I have zero idea of what the time is and in all honesty, there is something very relaxing about a stranger playing with your body so secretly, I could actually fall back asleep. But I'm too curious, I want to know what happens next, what will he do?

Eventually Darcy's warm mouth moves off my nipple and silently the bed dips only slightly around me. I don't move but the bed moves near my head. My head is facing to the right towards the bathroom. I haven't moved a muscle since Darcy walked out of the bathroom. I feel something soft and velvety run along the seam of my lips. A barely there touch but over and over again I feel the lewd act of Darcy's cock run along my lips. I want to open them; I want to run my lips around his head and then suck him down. Fighting myself to stay completely still or ruin his pleasure, I relax my breathing and facial muscles and pray he hasn't noticed I'm not breathing as I should when I'm asleep.

When I don't feel the featherlight touches along my lips, I feel the bed move lightly by my head and then a few moments later at the end of the bed between my legs. Then I feel the feathery caress of fingers along my folds. They feel teasing and I yearn to be touched, no matter how softly, on that one ball of nerves that must be erect and sitting to attention right now as anticipation racks my body. Not seeing and only hearing and feeling is heightening my arousal to a breaking point.

Darcy must feel similarly because I hear a light groan and then I feel something thicker gently rub along the seam of my pussy. It's warm and velvety and I know that feeling very well. He's barely touching me with his cock, but I feel it on every nerve ending shooting through my pussy. Need bristles through my body, the need to reach out and touch, the need to draw him in and fuck me, the need to come. My body is ablaze with need, and he doesn't know because he's enjoying my sleeping body. Does he enter me whilst I'm sleeping? The answer presents itself when I feel warm ribbons of come coat my pussy, they dribble down my mound and down my folds, hot sticky creamy goodness he could have left inside of me. I want to move and tell him but it's too late and I remind myself that this is what he enjoys, not the actual sex part.

Darcy taps the tip of his cock lightly leaving the last dribbles on my skin. I feel the bed move slightly and then again near my head. Then I feel a delicate finger pad rub a warm liquid along my lips so gingerly I question whether I'm feeling it at all.

As if in denial I peek out my tongue and swipe my lower lip and the burst of salty flavour hits my tongue. I slowly open my eyes to see hazel ones looking back at me encased in long dark lashes. We stare at each other, reading each other and I build up the courage to say, "Stay with me tonight."

I don't know whether I have just upset Darcy, I know I've broken his rules but there is something in his eyes that emboldened me to ask. A yearning perhaps?

His lips press together as if he's thinking and then quirk upwards in a small smile and he replies simply, "OK."

He moves off the bed where I watch his dark, toned body disappear into the bathroom. When he returns, he cleans me up so I'm no longer sticky, pulls the duvet back onto the bed and lies his head down on the pillow next to me, facing me. Darcy has his hand splayed out in front of his chest on the bed and I put mine on top of his. We just look into each other's eyes until mine begin to feel droopy and sleep claims me again.

When I awake again it must still be early, there is no music, the lights are still dimmed low, and I hear the light breathing of the gorgeous man sleeping next to me. He's moved onto his back and an idea creeps into my mind. If he likes to do things to women whilst they're asleep, how would he feel if things were done to him whilst he was sleeping?

Gingerly I slide myself off the bed, walk around to Darcy's side of the bed and peel off the duvet cover from over him. Then I walk to the end of the bed and climb on moving slowly just like I felt him do last night. Barely breathing, I slither myself up the bed and in between his legs trying my hardest not to touch them. Finding his flaccid cock lying between his legs I begin to place featherlight licks on and around the head. Barely there wet touches of my tongue up and around the underside of his head until I notice blood flow inflating his cock to half-mast, creating more length for me to lick. I dribble a line of spit onto his growing erection and swirl it softly around with my tongue until it's sitting fully erect below my face. Delicately I lower my mouth and slide it down over the head of his cock, so that just the head is encased in my mouth. I don't move another muscle, I just softly swirl my tongue around the sensitive underside and then up and over his slit. I can taste the pre-come as I sweep across. I'm trying so hard to be as featherlight as he was to me but now he's fully erect and in my mouth, I suspect the game is going to be up very soon.

I suck very gently as he begins to stir and opens his eyes to meet mine looking up at him, my lips wrapped around his erection. Now he's awake, I no longer need to be featherlike and soft. Keeping eye contact, I take him fully into my mouth and suck him down hard. Darcy lets out the most delirious moan that sends heat rushing to my core. He allows me to pump my mouth up and down a few times before he grabs me under the arms, pulls me towards his chest so I'm lined up for him to thrust inside my sopping pussy.

Darcy pushes me down as he thrusts up inside of me and we groan in unison. Keeping eye contact, I begin to ride him gently, feeling every single inch of him moving past and rubbing my g-spot and then hitting that delicious spot deep at my back walls. As we move together, we both pick up the pace, a frenzied movement of my hips until I sit upright on him, fully impaled and riding him quickly to chase my climax.

Holding my hips, he moves me forward and back, over and over again. My breasts wobble, my nipples feel like tight peaks, and I pull at them looking for that one last nudge into paradise. Darcy pulls me back down across him, reaches his head up and takes one nipple in his mouth and bites down. I cry out from the pain and the ecstasy all at once as endorphins flood my core and my climax tears through me. I whimper as I quiver through my orgasm, clenching around Darcy who thrusts deeper, ploughing up into me and stretching my orgasm along too.

Rocking me harder and faster, his eyes boring into mine, Darcy holds me still and unloads so deep, I know his seed is shooting straight into my cervix. He lets out the breath he was holding onto and blissed out pleasure fills his features as they relax and look softly back at me.

Taking in his appearance, he looks possibly early forties, maybe Arabian descent. All dark skin and beautiful. I can't believe I have finally met him and actually fucked him. Just in the nick of time seeing as it's now day six of my stay with these men.

I pull off Darcy and slide to lay curled facing towards him how we'd fallen asleep the previous night. He curls in towards me too, "Thank you for that wake up, I have never experienced anything quite like it. I always thought it was just playing with sleeping women's bodies that got me off, but waking up in your mouth is something I wish I could do every morning."

I glow at his words. We haven't even had a proper conversation until now so as an opener, this is music to my ears. It makes my heart puff out and glow. It's exactly what I want Darcy to feel because I want all the men to get what they have paid for and more. "I'm so glad you enjoyed it. I wanted to return the favour for last night. You know, I wish I hadn't slept through all our other encounters knowing what you were doing to me, it was hot, like lava hot."

"You were awake longer than when you opened your eyes?" he enquires, surprise raising his eyebrows to his forehead. I did good on my acting.

"Yes, and it was the most erotic and sensual thing I have ever woken up to."

"I guess I know that feeling now myself." He smiles brightly, like he's just had his first orgasm all over again.

"Tonight, will you suck a bit harder and actually fuck me so I can feel it? I won't make a sound or move; I might even be in a deep sleep anyways. I just don't want to miss out on you one last time."

He grins and I can see him thinking behind his handsome face. Finally, he says, "It would be a deal. But you have a busy day today, you might not be able to take one more fucking in your sleep."

"Will you be a part of it?" I ask earnestly.

"Yes," he smiles warmly back at me, "I wouldn't miss it for the world."

All I can do is smile brightly back at him, like I've been asked out on a first date. That's how it feels in my stomach. Like good things are coming, they're happening.

"I'm so glad," I reply as soft music fills the room. "That is my cue to have a shower," I say.

"I know," he replies cheekily.

"Have you been watching me?" I raise an eyebrow at him playfully.

"Always," is his only reply as he gets out of bed, picks up his clothes and walks confidently towards the door. "See you shortly, my sleeping beauty." And he's gone. Leaving me in a puddle of lust and desire.

40

———

It's day six and once Darcy leaves my morning is like every other one since I've been with the men. I'm not sure how I will adapt when I can't start my days with such luxurious attention and care.

Carl shaves me so deliciously but doesn't fuck me. Cook feeds and strokes me but doesn't so much as stick his cock in any of my holes. I read for hours and am beginning to feel a tinge of loneliness when Cook brings me an early lunch.

"Why has no one been with me this morning?" I ask, trying to keep the hurt out of my voice. Clearly I have gotten used to the constant attention and need and always being used and appreciated.

"Baby girl, it's not because we don't want you. We are all saving ourselves for this afternoon's events. That's why you are having an early lunch, we cannot wait a minute longer."

"What do we have planned?" I ask, brightening up.

Cook taps his nose playfully, his dimples indenting deeply as he grins back at me. "That, baby girl, is for me to know and you to find out."

"Oh a secret. When will I be let in on the secret?"

"In about half an hour. When you've finished eating and your food has gone down. That's when the show begins."

"Show?" I reply.

"Figure of speech."

"Ok, well thirty minutes isn't so far away."

"Exactly. I get to enjoy you all to myself for thirty minutes. All these heavy breasts and puffy pussy. You eating so well has put good meat on your bones, you are looking even more delectable than when you arrived," the lust is clear in Cook's voice and his eyes as they seem to devour every inch of me.

I blush, I have certainly been fed very well. I've never eaten so much food in my life, clearly, it's had an impact on my curves. It pleases Cook so it pleases me. I don't mind some extra flesh for my men to hold on to. *My men.*

I'm lying on the bed with Cook rubbing my stomach after a huge smorgasbord of luncheon delights was fed to me when the music changes pace and Cook takes that at his cue to leave. "Go hop into the bathroom baby girl, use the loo and sit on the lid until one of us comes to get you. We are just fixing up the room for an afternoon of playtime."

I turn to face him on the bed, "Sounds mysterious," I chuckle, "No problem. I'll go brush my teeth and pee. See you soon?"

"See you sooner than soon."

Cook tweaks both of my nipples and I shriek in painful delight, "Cook, you devil!"

I climb off the bed and hear his cheeky retort, "There's plenty more where that came from." Smiling to himself, he moves off the bed and begins to push the food trolley out of the room as I walk into the bathroom and close the door.

I don't know how long I've been sitting patiently on the loo. *I should have grabbed a book before dashing inside,* I scold myself.

But I listen hard and think I can hear a few voices and some movement. But the music has been turned up and really, I don't know anything about what is going on inside there. Should I be worried? I don't think so, these men have been nothing but gentle and caring, even David who spanked and paddled me hardly left any marks.

A light tap comes on the door and Dr Jack pokes his head around to find me sitting waiting on the toilet lid. "Hey sweet girl, are you ready to come out and play?"

"Hey yourself handsome. And heck yes, I am ready to play. I have been working myself into a tizzy wondering what you are doing in there."

Dr Jack walks through the door wearing just his black boxers and holds out his hand, "Let's put you out of your misery then. Come this way Roxy darling."

I take his outstretched hand and follow him through the bathroom door into my room, giddy with excitement. I'm startled to see it looks different. Mirrors line the glass walls; the bed is covered in silk black sheets and bedding. The lighting is dimmed down. There is a table laid out with toys and floggers, there is a drinks trolley with champagne on ice along with other liquors, mixers and glasses. To the left of the bed by Tom's chair is a tall square wooden frame with metal loops around the edges.

What stands out the most is the eight men, almost all of whom are nearly completely naked waiting for me. All eager eyes and stiff heavy cocks, except David who is wearing trousers. Even Carl is standing by the drinks trolley looking edgy but sweet. I feel like it's my birthday and everyone came to my party.

"Ah, the girl of the hour. It's a pleasure to see you again Roxy, you have made splendid viewing since we were last together," says David standing by the table of instruments.

I beam brightly at David, "Thank you Sir. It's so lovely to see you again too, and everyone." I look around the room at all the muscular and athletic men looking back at me. I smile warmly at Blake and Jake standing by the bed, Tom in his armchair, Darcy at the end of the bed standing next to Cook who is looking at me with pure excitement in his eyes. I take a moment to digest the sight in front of me. All these beautiful men paid money to spend time fucking me for a week when they could get any woman in the world. There is so much testosterone in the room, their male pheromones fill my nose and I pretty much swoon.

Dr Jack, who is still holding my hand, leans in close to speak in my ear but says it loud enough for everyone to hear, "We wanted to get the party started with the drinks, but David suggests we play a bit now and drink a bit later. Would that be ok with you?"

"Sure, that's fine, what do you have planned?"

"What does *he* have planned shall we say? David is in charge of tonight's festivities. We have all given our blessing to be directed by David. We trust him."

"Even Blake?" I ask, a bit surprised the Dom would be up for that.

"Even Blake," replies Blake with a growl.

Dr Jack snickers. "Yes, even Blake. Excellent, that's settled then, David the floor is yours," Dr Jack says to David.

"Thank you, Doctor. Roxy let's get you fixed up," says David.

"Sure Sir," I let go of Dr Jack's hand and walk up to David. I'm now accustomed to being completely naked with eyes on every inch of my body.

"Blake, would you tie this twine around each of Roxy's breasts. Tight," David hands Blake some twine and I shudder in anticipation. I remember the way they felt the last time they were tied up tight, my pussy tingling at the memory.

"Jake, take the clamps and attach them to her folds. Then you are to attach the twine through the clamps and around under her bottom to hold her pussy open," instructs David and I take in a breath. He's getting serious.

"Cook, please help Roxy's ankles and wrists into cuffs and then attach them to the corners of the frame. We want her to be nice and stretched out for us."

"No problem, David," replies Cook like a good boy scout, jumping into action.

There are now many hands on my body. All three men bustle with their jobs. Jake places what look like document clips on my pussy folds, he lines three up on one side and then three on the other. They bite into my skin like a clothespin, making me yelp with each one, and I wonder how I'm going to tolerate the pain, let alone when they're tied to my legs.

Whilst Jake is bending down, kneeling directly at my core, Blake has knotted a piece of twine tight around my right breast and is now coiling the twine around it creating a solid bulbous circle of flesh that is my breast.

Cook joins us. "Right wrist please," he requests almost jovially. He looks to be having the most fun right now and has no intention of hiding it. I feel on edge, heat is pulsing through my body, raising my temperature as so many hands work my body and so many more watch and wait for their instructions. I hand Cook my right wrist where he fastens a thick leather cuff. He moves on to my left wrist and then my ankles. Meanwhile Blake has moved to my left breast and they both begin to throb and ache in unison. Looking down at them, they're changing colour before my eyes and looking more of an angry red. Jake has managed to tie the twine around my left leg and through the holes on the top of the document clips. When he pulls the twine, my folds move open and my entrance is almost completely exposed along with my clit.

"Arms up now, baby girl," coos Cook, and I do what he says and watch as he fastens my arms just below each of the corners of the frame. "Now legs, sorry Jake—won't be a minute."

Jake moves back from running twine around my left leg to allow me to stretch my legs out and for Cook to cuff me to the corners of the frame. I'm fully exposed as Jake finishes tying the document clips open on my left side and Blake ties off the last of the twine around my breasts.

"Excellent boys, doesn't she look a picture." I hear them all agree from different parts of the room.

"Dr Jack, will you do us the honours of placing one of the butt plugs on the table of your choosing inside Roxy's anus?"

Dr Jack's eyes flash, "Certainly David, that would be my pleasure."

The table is in front of the frame so I can see all the toys lined up. There are so many different shapes and sizes of dildos, butt plugs, floggers, paddles, feathers, lubes, clips, and even an eye mask and ball gag. Dr Jack strolls over to the table and picks up a decidedly larger butt plug on the table and a bottle of lube.

I'm strung up like an offering as he walks back to me. He runs a finger down the contours of my face, "You can take it Roxy, I know you can." He walks around to my back, trailing a finger down my neck, over my shoulder and down my spine sending chills in its wake. With my legs fastened open, it's easy access for him. I hear the pop of the cap and then feel a finger rubbing up and down my back hole before I feel his finger nudge easily and slip inside.

There is a groan coming from Tom's chair as he has the best view of my behind. Turning my head to look at him, I can see he's stroking himself whilst watching the show.

"Look how nice and relaxed you are Roxy, accepting a finger into your arsehole so easily. This plug is going to have no problems slipping straight in," says Dr Jack who is kneeling behind me.

I have never been so turned on for eight men to have me. I have never wanted whatever David instructs the men to do to me more in my life. I have no doubt Dr Jack will have no problem pushing anything into any hole because I am a willing and ready recipient. I relax my muscles and feel the plug press in, I breathe deeply and focus on that one spot as it burns, then feel the pressure of the large butt plug enter inside of me before my tight muscle suctions it in and seals it in below the base. "Now there's a good girl taking her butt plug so well and easily," says Dr Jack before taking a nip of my arse cheek before standing.

All four men have finished their jobs and step back.

"Carl, why don't you come over here and kiss Miss Roxy, get her all warmed up," instructs David.

Without saying a word, Carl walks over from the drinks trolley, and stands in front of me. We're eye to eye. He doesn't look down at my body, he just steps into me, placing his hands gently around my neck and his lips on mine. His own flavour hits my taste buds as his tongue tentatively begins to massage mine. I relax my arm muscles and melt into him, my trussed-up breasts rubbing against his naked chest. I ignore that niggle of pain as I enjoy this intimate moment with the man who takes such good care of me every morning.

When Carl stops to catch his breath, I know our time is up as David says, "Thank you Carl, you can sit on the bed now." Carl nods his head at the instruction but places one last lingering kiss on my lips before he does.

"Tom, please can you pick up a flogger of your choosing."

Tom nods, rises from the chair and walks over to the table. He selects a brown leather handled flogger with long leather tassels. He looks up at me, face a mask hiding whatever might be going around in his mind. Out of everyone in this room to flog me—he is either the very worst choice or the best. He seems the angriest but has proven he can be so gentle.

"Tom," David addresses him when he's standing behind me. "I know you had a few reservations about sharing Roxy, I think this might help you to get those reservations off your chest and punish her and her whoring ways."

I gasp in surprise. I blink around the room and see surprise on Jake and Cook's face also. Surely, he's the worst person to be handed any torture equipment for those reasons. My legs begin to quiver as I take in shaky breaths. "When you are ready Tom."

I stare unblinking at Dr Jack, pleading with him to save me. David has got this wrong, Tom is going to hurt me and there is nothing I can do about it. Or there is one thing. My safe word. But I don't want to ruin what they all have planned for me tonight. I can't do that to them, I can't do it to me. I want this. I need to handle whatever Tom is about to dish out and hang on. The men won't let him hurt me badly, I just have to trust in them and believe Tom won't tear me to shreds.

Blocking out the fear, I begin to relax my arm muscles and try to stand a little straighter.

I can feel the air move behind me, I look to the mirrors and can see Tom raise his hand and whoosh, blazing hot pain fires through my skin as the first lash of the flogger makes contact with my upper back. Tom is not holding back. I don't think I'm bleeding, maybe it's the shock of the first hit. I raise my eyes back to the mirror and see him raise his arm again and another blaze of pain rips through my back. My legs begin to shake violently but despite the pain, I'm able to still hold it together. Before I look back up at the mirror to see when the next lashing hits, I look at the men sitting or standing by the bed in front of me, rapt to attention, nearly all except Carl are stroking themselves. Dr Jack has lost his boxers at some point. They are all enjoying the view of me getting flogged so wickedly. There is something about that which makes heat coil in my core. They are getting off on this torture.

"Tell Roxy what you think of her every time you flog her Tom," requests David

"You're a whore who sells her pussy to the highest bidder."
Swoosh.

"You love to be shared and used by people you don't know."
Swoosh.

"You enjoy being fucked by countless people, especially more than one at a time." Swoosh.

"You get off on everyone else's kinks, you have more kinks than any of us." Swoosh.

"You are begging to be taught a lesson and even this you are enjoying." Swoosh.

The pain plateaus into a heated numbness. I feel dazed as I listen to Tom's reasoning for being angry with me, all of which are true statements about me. I can't disagree with any of them, but I also can't find it in myself to agree with his anger. He is here too; he is buying my body also.

"Thank you, Tom, hold back for one minute would you please," commands David. "Darcy, would you get on your knees and lick Roxy's pussy between flogs.

"Certainly," Darcy practically pounces off the bed and is kneeling before me in the blink of an eye. My pussy is stretched wide open vulgarly. I am open but not ready for his hot mouth to place over my entrance. I am in a heady headspace and his mouth is conjuring all kinds of sparks up to my clit. Darcy pulls off just before another swoosh and I sag forwards. Darcy, laps straight to my clit and I cry out from the sensitivity and pleasure. I hadn't realised how much I ached for a release, focusing so much on the pain of my back.

Darcy's licks stop and another swoosh hits my back and I sag again against the pain. This time Darcy laps longer at my sensitive bud, I am so very close right now. I'm teetering on the edge before he's gone, and another stinging flog hits my back. Darcy's clever tongue laps with more pressure this time and it's all I need to tip over the edge into oblivion. I whimper out my climax as it shudders through me, and I hang from the cuffs holding my body up.

"Thank you Tom. Do you feel better now?"

I move my head to see him walk in front of my hanging body, fire blazing in his eyes. Darcy is still between my legs licking up my release but Tom pays him no mind, standing to the side of him, he reaches for my neck and brings his mouth to mine, crushing his lips on mine. He opens his mouth to make the kiss deeper and hungrier as he devours my mouth with everything he has. Our teeth clash as he kisses me feverishly. When he pulls away there is pain and passion behind his eyes as he says to me, "I didn't mean to hurt you Roxy."

Something in my heart ruptures. "You didn't hurt me Tom, you said it yourself—I enjoyed my punishment," I say in a croaky voice hoping I convey to him that I am ok. "Are you ok?"

He nods and that's all the reply I receive before I hear David's voice from behind me.

"Dr Jack, would you come over here and fix up Roxy's back. Cook, suck Roxy's nipples—see if you can make them stand to attention despite them being so engorged."

Both men hop into action, Dr Jack walks over to the table and picks up a jar of lotion and moves behind me. Cook walks over to me, his eyes glistening with mischief. "I have wanted to touch these breasts since Blake strung them up. Look at them so thick and hard. Just like my cock right now."

I look down and he isn't wrong. He's rock hard and his head is red and angry, weeping at the tip with pre-cum. He leans in to kiss me on the mouth before trailing kisses down my neck, down my chest before lowering his hot mouth to my nipple. He sucks in hard and I moan, liquid pleasure pooling at my core.

From behind me Dr Jack rubs lotion into his hands and places them palm down onto my skin. I jerk at the coolness, but Dr Jack is shushing me. "Shhhh, sweet girl, this is going to take the sting straight out of your heated skin. Let me make it feel good for you. There we go," he coos as he gently slides his hands in circle motions from my shoulders down to my buttocks. I breathe a sigh at the relief the cream and his hands are giving to my heated skin.

I roll my head back at the thrill Cook is creating, tormenting my nipples with his hot mouth. So many sensations pulsing through my body from my chest to my back. I moan Cook's name forgetting I have an audience.

"There we are sweet girl, all better now. Do you feel better Roxy?" asks Dr Jack.

"Yes, thank you Doctor."

"Thank you, Doctor," comes David's voice from behind me. "Blake, come here and remove Roxy's cuffs please."

"Certainly," is all Blake says as he climbs off the bed and reaches to unfasten my wrists from the hooks. Cook is still sucking at my throbbing nipples, I'm glad he hasn't stopped. When Blake lowers each arm, blood begins to pour back in, and I roll each shoulder to bring back some movement into the stiff joints.

When I am free from my restraints and cuffs, David instructs, "Thank you Blake, Cook. Roxy, kneel for me."

I turn to face him and lower to my knees.

"Crawl over to Tom and thank him for your punishment."

I nod and move one hand and knee to crawl over to where Tom is sitting in his usual chair, my breasts bulging and heavy in their restraints. I feel the butt plug and the stretch of my pussy lips as I slowly make my way to sit between Tom's thighs. The view from behind me when I crawl must be a scene with the butt plug sitting snuggly and my folds tied open and exposed.

When I reach Tom I sit back on my heels, placing my hands on each of his thick thighs. I run my hands down his thighs before stopping and saying demurely, "Thank you for my punishment, Tom." His cock hangs thick and heavy between his legs, but I don't reach far enough to touch it.

"Show him how grateful you are for your punishment, Roxy."

I do as David instructs, licking my lips and crawling closer so my body is now tightly between his thick thighs. I look up at Tom who is glowering at me, desire and turmoil in his eyes as I lower my mouth and lick at the pre-come leaking out of his tip. Slowly, I lower my mouth down around the girth of his head and slide down inch by inch as far as I can go. I raise up, swirling my tongue around the underside of his cock before lowering down further and hitting the back of my throat. Tom groans from above me as I begin to work up and down his shaft with my mouth.

"That's enough Roxy," David instructs, and I freeze. Surely Tom doesn't want me to stop. I lift my head up and off Tom's wet cock.

"But I haven't finished, Sir," I reply to David, still staring at Tom.

"Do as you're told Roxy; I don't expect you to speak back to my instructions." I blush at having been told off but don't go back to sucking Tom off.

"Crawl to the end of the bed and then sit on the edge. Carl, use the safety shears and cut the twine around her thighs. Darcy, uncoil the twine around her breasts."

I look up once more at Tom's chiselled bearded face before dropping a sneaky kiss on the top of his cock and backing out from between his strong legs and crawling the short distance to the bed where I stand and sit on it. I feel pressure in my butt from the huge plug, but I can still sit. It's my thighs and clamps that feel awkward like this.

Carl is at my centre with a pair of safety scissors as he snips the twin around my legs and my folds move back to cover my entrance. I wince and whimper a bit as he removes each of the six clamps and blood flows back into the flesh. Carl hears my whimper. He stands and goes to the table, bringing back some lube, he squirts it on his fingers and begins to slowly massage my pussy which is painful at first and then extremely pleasurable. I breathe into the feeling, noticing Carl doesn't swipe even the tiniest bit close enough to my clit.

Darcy sits to my right and finds the knot Blake left and unwinds the twine. My breasts are purple and when the twine is off the first one, it's covered in indented lines as it hangs heavy, aching and throbbing with the renewed blood flow. Darcy moves to the other side of the bed and does the same again whilst Carl teases me to the edge of insanity.

"Cook, massage her right breast whilst Darcy uncoils the left," instructs David.

Cook grabs some oil off the table and sits to my right, he squirts the oil into his palms before rubbing them over my tender breast. I have three men's hands on me and I feel one more come up behind me. Dr Jack sits on his knees behind me, pulls my ponytail off my shoulder and nuzzles into my neck planting delicious kisses along the sensitive part of my neck. I feel Blake finish uncoiling the twine on my left breast and Darcy hands him the oil.

I am in heaven. I must be. "You guys, what are you doing to me?" I whisper as desire builds in my core.

"Dr Jack, lay Roxy down on her back and take out her butt plug. Thank you, Darcy, Blake and Carl."

"With pleasure," is Dr Jack's reply, and the other three men move aside as he lowers me onto my back. Dr Jack moves quickly to hop off the bed and is at my back entrance and applying pressure to pull out the plug. "Relax Roxy, let me pull it out nice and slowly for you. Easy, here we go, that's right it's coming." I feel the burn and then it's out of me. I look up at the ceiling and to my surprise I'm looking back at myself. There is a mirror on the ceiling.

"Carl, you take her pussy first. Jake, Blake you get her hands and Tom, you get her mouth so she can finish the job. Let's start there." I watch as they take their places like a military operation. Tom picks up a pillow and places it under my head which I'm grateful for.

I look around at all the men in their positions with a smirk and say to all of them, "Give it to me boys."

And that's all they need to hear as Jake and Blake thrust their cocks into my left and right hands, Tom angles my head and then feeds me his cock. Carl, who is standing in front of me at the end of the bed, spreads my legs open letting my knees bend to the sides, he pulls my pussy towards him by my hips and then he enters me in one slick motion. I moan around Tom's cock in my mouth and try to focus on keeping some kind of rhythm with my hands. They must realise that it's a losing battle as Jake and Blake hold their hands over mine and help keep the steady pace on their cocks.

Tom holds my head as he begins to fuck my face, Carl groans and comes inside of me.

"Darcy, take Carl's place," David instructs.

As Tom fucks my mouth, I feel Carl slip free and Darcy steps between my legs at the end of the bed and then nudges at my slippery entrance. I almost choke on Tom's cock as Darcy ploughs deep all in one hard thrust. Darcy rubs two fingers over my spot as I've been craving for what has felt like hours. I begin to see stars as he fucks me into an oblivion and Tom's cock blocks my airways until I shatter around Darcy's cock and Tom shoots into my mouth. I choke for a moment but manage to guzzle his come as it slides down the back of my throat before gasping for air as he withdraws it. A moment later Darcy finds his release and I feel him pulse inside of me.

"Blake, you take her mouth, Jake you take her pussy, Cook & Doc, you take her hands." Movement happens all around me, I just lay there, a used-up, dripping mess.

Cook and Dr Jack hold my hands over their cocks and help to guide my fingers as Jake lines himself up and nudges gently inside of me. Blake places his cock on my waiting tongue and feeds it into my mouth. Dr Jack pinches at my nipple and Cook gropes my breast as they help me to wank them off. Jake finds his release at the same time as Blake withdraws a little and spurts onto my waiting tongue.

"Cook, lie down on the bed. Doctor, place Roxy onto his lap. You can take her from behind," instructs David. I look up and see them both smile at each other before lifting my hands from their cocks. Cook moves down the bed and lies down with his head on a pillow, Dr Jack helps me up and then into position, literally lining me up so I can slide onto Cook's cock. Come dribbles down from my leg and I slide easily down the entire length. Cook pulls me down onto his chest as Dr Jack lubes up his dick and nudges at my back entrance.

"Nice and slowly Roxy, we got you baby girl," Cook whispers into my hair.

I relax enough to feel the burn as the doctor enters my back hole. I whimper and begin to take deep breaths. "He's going to make it feel nice for you any minute now. The Doc always takes care of you now, doesn't he?"

"Yes," I croak as the doctor feeds his cock deep inside me, his gentleness and the excess of lube bypassing the burn and reaching the pleasure of what fullness brings.

"There we go, sweet girl," coos Dr Jack from behind me. "I'm going to start moving now, ok? Here we go."

I lift my body so I'm being held up by the two men as they start a rhythm of fucking in and out of me.

"Fuck, I can feel your cock against mine," says Cook to Dr Jack.

Dr Jack just grunts in reply as he's close. "I'm too wound-up Cook, I'm going to blow any second now. Roxy, are you close?"

"Yes!" I scream as I feel a climax rip through my body as

Cook and Dr Jack pick up their pace and explode one after the other, stretching out my orgasm that feels like a never-ending train of euphoria.

Collapsing in a heap, I'm sandwiched between two sexy sweaty bodies, my holes still filled with both men.

"That was quite the finale, you three. Let's get you cleaned up Roxy and we can pop open the champagne," commands David.

I smile, boneless on Cook's chest and reply sleepily, "That sounds amazing." Dr Jack pulls out and it's Tom who pulls me off Cook and carries me into the bathroom. A tub has already been filled and he lowers me into it carefully like a precious child. I look up at his strong muscular body and huge chest. He makes me weak at the knees just looking at his body. But his eyes are trying to tell me a thousand stories.

I lie back and just stare into his green eyes looking back at me. Without moving his gaze, he lifts a sponge and softly runs it over my body and delicately between my legs. We hear Dr Jack walk in and he gets into the shower, followed by Carl, Jake, Blake, Darcy and Cook. The entire time it took all six of them to shower, Tom stayed to wash and be with me. When Cook gets out of the shower last, Tom says one word to me, "Up." And I stand up as he helps me out of the bath. He wraps me into a towel before leaving me with Cook and taking his turn in the shower. Cook leads me back into the bedroom where the rest of the men are nibbling on food and drinks. I guess the party just started. *The naked party,* I correct in my head.

41

—————

Dr Jack hands me a glass of bubbles when I fold my towel over the chair. Cook has prepared a huge grazing board, so I load up a plate one handedly. I don't know what the time is, but I am really hungry. Having sex with seven men will do that for you.

We eat and chat about the week and be merry. Everyone is naked, getting loose and many hands touch and stroke and squeeze me during conversations. It's fun, I imagine this is what an orgy would be like. *Maybe this is the definition of an orgy, or is this more of a gangbang?*

I'm sipping my second glass of champagne when Dr Jack comes up behind, "I have a scenario to run past you sweet girl, something I think would be hot. A final showdown of the week."

I turn and smile into his boyish good looks, all pretty and bright eyed, "Ok, I'm listening. Tell me," I reply with piqued interest.

"Well, there's no way we're all going to be able to keep our hands off you shortly. And I think you deserve a departing gift."

"Okay..."

"I propose we all fuck you from behind and fill you up with our come. Breed you like you were ours. For tonight. Maybe one of us will make you theirs, maybe we won't. But, and I think I speak for all of us," he looks around at the men who have stopped talking to listen in on Dr Jack's proposal, "we would all enjoy sowing our seed in you one last time, especially if it meant breeding you."

I look around at the hungry eyes around me; Dr Jack wasn't lying, they are all looking at me like they could pounce.

"Is that so?" I ask coyly. "Carl, would you like to breed me tonight?" I ask.

"Yes," he replies without hesitation.

"Tom, you have a breeding kink too?" I probe, assuming he out of all of them wouldn't.

"With you, yes," comes his gruff reply. I raise my eyebrows.

"I was not expecting you to say that, Tom." And I wasn't. Surprised doesn't even cover it. The mere idea makes my blood heat at the thought of Tom wanting to fuck a baby into me. "David?" I ask in a near whisper of desire to the last man who I assume would want this.

"I am going first," is his reply. Again, my eyebrows shoot up. I glance around and all the others are nodding their heads, some with smirks, some with more gentle smiles but all of them have a matching hunger in their eyes.

"Ok, I guess that's settled then."

"You'll do it? You want to do it?" asks Dr Jack.

"For you, and for all of you boys—I'll do whatever you want tonight. Take and give me what you want. I'm yours for the taking.

"Drink up boys, the night is still young," is Dr Jack's reply as he throws his head back and takes two large gulps of white liquid, screws up his face and sets the glass down. He turns me into him so he can kiss me deeply, vanilla vodka fills my taste-buds. My mind swirls, *what did I just sign myself up for?*

Pulling away for a breath Dr Jack tells me, "Drink up butter-cup, I cannot wait to see you filled and dripping with all of our come." I nearly snort out the champagne as I was taking a sip. "If I could have it my way, I'd be branding you tonight. Leave my mark on your breast and pussy lips too." Darkness is clouding his features at his admission.

"You are a dirty boy tonight," I say emboldened by the bubbles and the heady feeling of what's about to happen.

"Every night with you, sweet girl."

"Jake, be a good boy and go help Roxy relax whilst she finishes up her champagne before she has an evening full of being fucked," instructs David.

"Yes sir," comes Jake's reply. Dr Jack steps to the side in amusement as Jake gets to his knees right in front of where I am standing and delves his tongue straight into my pussy.

"Oh, my goodness, Jake," I cry out in delight and woozy amusement. I reach out the hand not holding my champagne and find Dr Jack's forearm and grip tightly as my knees go weak at his delicious intrusion. I take a gulp of my champagne and then nearly spit it out again as I feel someone else nudging at my arse from behind. I swallow and look around to see Cook on his knees behind me spreading my cheeks. "Cook," I murmur but it's too late, I feel his tongue swipe at my back hole and this time Dr Jack has to hold me in place.

Carl, Tom, David, Darcy and Blake watch as I quiver where I'm standing as both holes are lapped at. I begin to lose focus as raw desire pumps through my veins. Carl moves off the bed and walks to my other side, he moves my face to meet his and he kisses me all consumingly. I lean into all the feelings from every hole. Carl kissing me, Cook rimming me like I'm his favourite food and Jake moving up to lap at my clit before circling it just as I like, all with Dr Jack still helping to hold me in place. I pull away from Carl just long enough to say, "Don't stop," before Carl reaches for my lips again and devours my mouth with his wickedly talented tongue.

I hear Dr Jack over the thumping of my heart say, "She's close boys." Then Cook roughly spreads my arse cheeks and presses his tongue into my arsehole and I come undone, crying out into Carl's mouth as Jake continues to lick me through my orgasm.

"Finish your champagne Roxy, you are ready for us," says Dr Jack whose demeanour has changed. Gone is the sweet, boy next door looking man, now stands a brooding man who is a heartbeat away from snapping.

Jake stands in front of me, mouth red and glistering, Cook stands behind me and playfully bites my shoulder. "T-thank you Jake, Cook. That was amazing," I say, not finding any better words for that mind blowing experience.

"Anything for you," replies Jake as Cook leans into my neck and sucks hard.

When he pulls away, he replies, "I would do that every day for the rest of our lives if I could."

I take the last gulp of my drink, and my glass is whipped away from my hand by Dr Jack.

Then it's David who is moving, standing in front of me. "On to the bed Roxy, in the centre on all fours. Face towards the door."

"Yes Sir," I reply and walk past him and climb onto the bed and in position. David pulls down his trousers and boxers and stands with his impressive cock hanging heavy between his legs. Everyone in the room watches as he climbs onto the bed and behind me.

"If anyone is going to be breeding you tonight, Miss Roxy, it's going to be me." David lines himself up to my wet, waiting hole and slowly nudges inside, savouring every inch as he moves deep inside me. I groan at his delicious intrusion.

Darcy walks in front of me, stroking himself. I look up at

him as I'm being fucked by David and watch as he gently strokes the full length of himself. I lick my lips, and he knows what I'm saying. He climbs onto the bed, and I lower my mouth over him. David fucks me onto Darcy, and I suck him down deep. Darcy groans, "You're too good at this, I'm not going to be able to hold out if you continue deep throating me." I pull up and look up at him from hooded eyes.

"You want to breed me too."

"No question."

I feel David shudder and pulse inside me.

"My turn," I hear Darcy say as he makes his way behind me, "Roxy nearly had me blow—I'm so close as it is."

David pulls out of me but I try to keep my butt in the air, holding in the seed he just deposited deep inside me.

Darcy lines himself up and slides straight to the back of my walls in one hard thrust. He pounds into me until he comes undone and roars my name.

Carl is ready and waiting as Darcy slides out and his cock is replaced by Carl's who fucks me slow and steady. He doesn't last very long either and I'm filled with my third deposit of come.

Cook takes Carl's place and he hits me at just the right spot, angling himself and leaning a hand under me to rub at my clit. That is all I need to come on his cock as he rides me through my orgasm to find his.

I look around and see all the men stroking themselves, even Darcy, Carl & David. I've already taken four cocks when Blake climbs onto the bed. He's the only one who hasn't fucked my pussy since I've been here, preferring to fuck my arse and Jake's. I am a sopping wet mess of a hole when he slides into me and moans. Jake lies on the bed next to us, stroking himself as he watches Blake fuck me. I can see in the mirror that Blake is watching Jake as he fucks me and it's so hot I could come again with just the right position, but before I can get there Blake is coming inside of me. Jake gets up and leans in to kiss Blake who is still inside me. These two drive me wild seeing them together.

Blake pulls out of me with a splash, and I try and hold all the come up inside of me. Jake leans down and sucks Blake's cock clean as we all watch on. Then he too is behind me, the squelching noise coming from me is lewd and degrading, but the thought of one more load of come inside me turns me on and I clench around Jake's cock. That pushes him over the edge and he moans my name as he releases his seed inside of me.

That's six cocks and two more to go.

Dr Jack nods to Tom who wordlessly accepts it's his turn, clearly Dr Jack wants me last. Tom runs his huge hands down my back before grabbing my hips and impaling me onto his cock. He ruts into me making me cry out as he hits the right spot over and over again. Cook climbs onto the bed and takes one of my nipples between his fingers and pinches down hard. I scream in pain and ecstasy as I come again around Tom's cock and he comes deep inside me. I am almost a quaking mess as Tom slides out and Dr Jack comes behind me.

"Roxy, if only you can see how erotic my view of your creaming cunt is. It oozes everyone's come and soon it'll have mine too. Breeding you tonight would be the ultimate ending to what has been the most incredible week. Are you ready to take one last cock and suck my balls dry with your pussy?"

"Yes, do it," I reply hoarsely as I prepare to take my eighth cock.

Unlike the last few men, Dr Jack enters me gently and he fucks me slowly. David and Darcy stand in front of me, rubbing themselves enthusiastically—despite both having come only a few minutes before they are impressively hard. David climbs onto the bed and I open my mouth for him knowing exactly what is coming.

"Good girl Roxy," David says as he places his cock on my

tongue and comes in my mouth, there's less to swallow but he seems to have enjoyed the orgasm as strongly as before.

Dr Jack continues slowly fucking into my sopping hole, stringing out the pleasure for as long as possible whilst Darcy climbs onto the bed in front of me, I open again and he pushes into my mouth and comes down my throat. I drink back the salty liquid as Dr Jack pants, "Anyone else wanting to come down Roxy's throat before I come, and we're done?"

We look around the room and it's just Tom that has his cock in his hand, he walks towards us and climbs onto the bed. Dr Jack picks up his pace. Surprisingly, Tom doesn't stop at my face; he reaches under me and strums against my sensitive clit, lighting a spark of a fire inside me. He circles two fingers and adds just the right amount of pressure whilst Dr Jack fucks into me that a fire begins to build until I'm bucking and losing control as a burning explosion of pleasure tears through me. Tom rubs himself a few more times until I feel warm streams of come land onto my back and Dr Jack roars into the room as he finally unloads the last of the eight men's come into my pussy.

I lower onto my forearms and rest my head onto the bed, keeping my bottom held high, come oozing slowly down my legs and stomach.

Dr Jack lifts his dick out of me panting, when he catches his breath he says to the room, "Come check out this view before Roxy collapses."

The rest of the men climb onto the bed behind me to see. The depravity of the situation is crude and degrading. But I'd be lying if I said I hadn't enjoyed it and didn't find it erotically filthy.

"Bear down now Roxy, let's see how much you've taken."

I do as Dr Jack asks and feel a long line of thick creamy liquid leak out of me and onto the silky black sheets. On and on it falls out, I guess this is what eight loads feels like.

I feel a cloth run down my back and then feel it mop up the

remaining come from my aching pussy. "Roxy my love, you can relax now. Come here, lie back onto Cook's chest," says Dr Jack. Tom helps me to manoeuvre onto my bum and then into the waiting lap of Cook who strokes me so lovingly, whispering words of praise into my ear as I lay out on him, completely depleted of any energy.

After what could be twenty or thirty minutes, Carl hands me a Gatorade and I take it appreciatively. I sip it and begin to feel a bit more human again. "Let's get you showered whilst we change the sheets and get set up for the night," says David as Blake and Jake appear in front of me and help me into the shower. They carefully help wash my body down and only dab gently at my pussy with a sponge knowing how much I have taken this evening.

The boys wrap me up in the pink fluffy towel Dr Jack brought for me and dry me carefully. When we return to the bedroom, there are fresh sheets and two fold-up beds on either side of my king bed and a few mattresses on the floor. It looks like we are having a sleepover.

I climb into bed sleepily and lay between Tom and Darcy. Jake and Blake are on the camping bed on the left and Dr Jack is on the right. David, Cook and Carl are sleeping on single mattresses on the floor in front of the bed. This would make an interesting evening if I wasn't so thoroughly rung out and tired. The lights dim and I fall asleep almost instantly nestled between the two warm bodies wrapped around me.

42

———————

I awake to the smell of fresh coffee and see Cook has set up a breakfast station for everyone. It's adorable. I'm lying on my side, curled into the hulk of Tom and can feel Darcy wrapped around my back. I can hear movement around the room but only from bodies under duvets. Cook walks to the end of the bed and places my folded-up shirt and jean skirt and winks at me as I move my head to watch what he's doing. I guess naked times are over.

My heart plunges into the depths of my stomach. The week is over, I will never wake up like this again. I will never be shaved by Carl or fed by Cook. I won't have special check-ups by Dr Jack or nighttime visits by Darcy. No one will make impact play feel as good as David, Tom won't be watching me. Jake and Blake won't be there to share me. Sadness wells in my heart as I imagine never seeing any of them again. I *won't* see them again. This will never happen again. The pain tears through me like an open wound. I always knew this week would be difficult in some way, but I never considered the hardest part would be saying goodbye.

Frank will be collecting me at 9am so I'm guessing there is

no playtime on the menu this morning, not as if my body can take much more. I'm pretty sure I pushed my limits yesterday by taking all eight of them.

Darcy nuzzles my neck and whispers, "Good morning gorgeous," into my hair and I can hear his smile. His morning glory pressing into my back, I ache to ride it. Tom shuffles next to me and moves to his side to look at me on the pillow, his beard almost touching my face. His sleepy eyes crinkle at the sides and the smile in his eyes lights up his whole face. This complicated man is stunning when he's waking up and relaxed. I wish I could do it every morning. But I need to wake up. This is not real life; I have a real life waiting for me at home. I have James. My heart plunges again. *James.*

The men rouse around the bed, pulling on their boxers and making their way over to the breakfast spread and the coffee.

I don't want to move. I don't want this fairytale to end. The minute I sit up and put my clothes on, it will all be over and my bubble will burst. The end. Tom reads it in my eyes, my sadness. He raises his hand and runs it down the side of my face. I try and smile brightly but it probably looks pained. I feel Tom's eyes go cloudy as he sees the pain behind my eyes which makes my eyes well up. I'm trying to hold it together but I'm hopeless at saying goodbye and right now the last thing I want to do is leave them all.

"It had to come to an end," Tom whispers gruffly but his features form into worried lines.

"I know," I reply as a tear breaks free and runs down my cheek. "I hadn't considered how fond I'd become of you all."

"I don't want to let you go," comes Tom's reply and his eyes tell me he means it.

"How can I go back to real life after everything we have done, after yesterday..." I sniffle.

Hearing our whispers Darcy speaks into my hair, "We have to. It was part of the deal. This is always how the Playmates work, none of us want it to end but we have to. Believe me I've thought of every scenario where I keep you. But you have a life to get back to and so do we. Whatever they look like, we have to go back."

Dr Jack leans up onto our bed, "Sweet girl, don't cry. You have given us one of the best weeks of our lives. We will all cherish it forever. Even weddings and births won't touch the time we have spent here with you."

Cook brings over a mug of black tea and reaches up the bed to hand it to me, I sit up and take the mug and say thank you. Everyone must be listening in on our conversation. David hands me a tissue which I take gratefully.

"I'm sorry, I don't mean to cry when these are our last few hours or minutes together. I just can't believe I won't see you all again. It's just hurting thinking about it."

"You don't need to say sorry to us," Cook says kindly. "I am one blink away from crying myself. Baby girl, we all feel what is currently reflecting in your eyes. It's why we all stayed over last night. We're here for you now like you have been for us all this week. We adore you and you have graciously taken all of us just as we are, kinks and all. You have let us live out our wildest fantasies without fear of judgement or reproach. Your acceptance and sweetness makes us yearn to find someone like you for ourselves. But we know we can't keep you. It's the deal we made, and we will stick to it. It might not be goodbye but hopefully more of a see you later."

"Thank you Cook," I sniffle. "I couldn't have wished for a more perfect group of eight men. I'm humbled you chose me, and you let me love you all, even if it was only for a week. I mean it when I say, I'm going to miss you all like a hole in my heart."

Walking over to sit on the bed in front of me, Carl rests his hand on my ankle and says softly, "Thank you for being the best thing to ever happen to me Roxy. I won't ever forget you."

"I won't forget you, Carl. I'll miss you in so many ways and will always be reminded of you when I shave," I say kindly.

Jake and Blake walk up to the bed too, "Thank you for being the only person to join in our relationship, you made being a throuple effortless," Blake says, voice warm but serious.

"I know it's hard now, but we know all good things must come to an end eventually. And this is the best way we thought we could do it, by having yesterday and this morning. Roxy, what you have given us has been a gift, know in your heart that we all love you in our own way," Jake speaks up. "We will all say our goodbyes and we'll chalk this up as a once in a lifetime. And move on. Go back to doing what we usually do on a Saturday morning and then a Sunday and Monday—you get the picture."

I nod my head. It hurts but he's right. I'm allowed to feel the feelings. I am human as Sophie always says. "Thank you, I am incredibly sad but also wildly happy this happened to me, and I got to be your captive for a week." I dab up my tears and try to shake the impending doom I'm feeling right now.

"Here put your clothes on, I'll hold your tea. It will help acclimatise you to wearing clothes and going back to reality very soon. As sad as I am to say goodbye to your gorgeous tits, it will also help the raging boner I'm struggling to keep down," Darcy says, a hint of frustration and lust in his pleasant tone. I giggle, *he's right.*

Darcy takes my mug, and I climb off the bed. Carl runs one finger over the rose on my breast in a gentle caress. *James,* I'm putting my clothes on and going back to James, my husband, my love, my family. I feel pain to leave these men but I feel pain to be away from James. So many feelings, my mind floats away with them until Carl holds out my blouse and I put my arms through and continue to get dressed. He does each button up. There is no bra or thong, apparently Dr Jack doesn't know what happened to them. Carl holds out my skirt for me to step into and then he zips up the back.

"Let's get you eating before Frank arrives," says Cook.

"Eating without you won't be the same," I say to him, grief threatening to strike again.

"I enjoyed every single meal you had, baby girl, that will keep me going for some time," he replies cheerfully.

I sit back on the bed with the pillows behind my back, Tom hands me my plate and I lean in a little closer to him as I take a bite and look around at the eight pairs of eyes that are on me. I try to memorise every feature on their faces and bodies to store them away and mentally write them down, so I never forget a detail about them.

When I finish eating, Darcy hands me back my tea which I sip contentedly until David says the words I have been dreading, "Miss Roxy, it's almost time for you to go now."

I look over at him in horror, sadness flooding back into my soul.

"None of that now Miss Roxy, you are a brave girl. You will be fine," he says sternly but his face is soft, and his eyes are not piercing, they look sad like mine. "Come here, you can say goodbye to me first."

Darcy takes my mug and plate as I shuffle down the end of the bed and hop off. I walk over to David and look up at his strong face and his greying eyebrows. "Goodbye David, it's been a real privilege to meet you," I say and mean it.

"Roxy, the pleasure has been all mine. You were incredible this week. Do take good care of yourself. Maybe our paths will cross in the future."

"I hope so David, that would be wonderful," I reply hopefully. David leans down and brushes a kiss on my lips before pulling away. He gives me one last long look before turning and walking out of the door.

Carl comes up to me next, he says nothing but kisses me so

sensually, my toes curl. He really does have a talent. He and Jake might have tied for the most sensual mouths, I only wish I could experience them both at the same time. Pulling away, he kisses me on the nose. "Thank you for everything, Roxy. I'm going to miss you."

"Thank *you* for everything. I'm going to miss you too." I go onto my tiptoes and kiss him on his nose too.

He smiles widely before saying, "Goodbye Princess."

"Goodbye Carl," I reply as he squeezes one of my hands and turns and walks out of the door.

Jake and Blake walk over to me next, "Goodbye Roxy, we will always take you as part of our future throuple if life doesn't work out for you in the future," Blake teases, though with a solid core of earnest truth, and I giggle gratefully.

"If life takes a turn for me, I would be honoured to join your beautiful relationship. You'll take good care of each other, won't you?" I look at the two of them.

Blake leans in and kisses me on the lips, then he says to Jake, "Be a good boy and kiss our girl properly goodbye, I want to watch you one last time together."

"It would be my pleasure," chuckles Jake who takes my face in his hands and leans in to kiss me slowly and erotically, his tongue gently finding mine and lapping against it as if we have all the time in the world. Being allowed to share Jake like this feels like a gift and I know if life was ever different, I might enjoy being a part of their dynamic. When Jake pulls away my mouth misses his. "Goodbye Roxy, until we meet again," says Jake soberly.

"Until we meet again," Blake echoes and leads Jake out of the room.

It's Cook who wraps his arms around my back and squeezes me. I lean back into his slim frame and breathe him in. "I'm going to miss you so much Cook."

"Me too baby girl, me too. My glasses are fogging up. I need to say goodbye before the dam breaks." He spins me into his arms and kisses me hard on the lips. "Eat well baby girl, goodbye for now."

"You too," I splutter as I begin to well up again. Cook lets me go and swiftly heads towards the door and then out of the room.

Darcy walks over from the bed, "Farewell sleeping beauty. I loved playing with you. Being with you exceeded all my dreams. My only wish is that I'd slept next to you every night as well."

"I wish that too, but I'm glad I did wake up and have the true Darcy experience. It really was a highlight of my time here."

"As was waking up to you sucking me off," he chuckles wistfully.

I giggle, "Goodbye Darcy, until we meet again."

"Until we meet again." Darcy lowers his head and gives me a kiss on the lips before turning and walking out the door.

Tom walks up to me next, bends down, lifts me up by my waist and I wrap my legs around him instinctively. He presses his forehead to mine. This man, this solid, complicated, gentle man of muscle. We stay there for a few minutes before I move my head back then lean in and kiss him gently, he allows me to lick my tongue along his lips before letting me kiss into his mouth. He kisses me just as gently as he cradles and holds me.

Dr Jack clears his throat, and I know time is running out. "Goodbye my gentle giant. I'm going to miss you," I say with my eyes filling and my lip beginning to tremble. I'm not sure what this connection is that we have, but I feel it and it hurts to let him go. Slowly he lowers me to the floor, pulls me in for a tight bear hug, kisses my hair. He pulls away, his usual stoic mask now etched in pain as he takes one last look into my eyes and then walks out of the door and possibly out of my life forever.

Turning to Dr Jack, the last man left here in the room with

me, he smiles at me sombrely. "I always hate saying goodbyes but saying goodbye to you is by far the hardest thing I've ever had to do," he says grimly. "You were amazing from the minute you arrived and took your clothes off. I thought of nothing but you for an entire week. I feel like part of me has died letting you go now. My entire body is screaming to keep you all to myself, hide you in my basement and make 10 babies with you. But I know I can't."

I laugh, "Ten babies?"

"We can compromise?"

"In another life, that would have been perfect Doctor. I'm sorry I have to go. You have been so thoughtful and caring, looking after my every need here. Looking after me. I'm going to miss you, but I'll always hold you in my heart." I trip over the last words as a lump forms in my throat.

"I don't want to upset you," Dr Jack leans in and kisses my eyelids as fresh tears begin to fall. "I never want to upset you." Then he kisses me with every emotion running between us. I feel his love, his care, his passion for me. It takes every ounce of strength not to tear my clothes off and climb him again. I can't be here any longer, I have my children and husband to get back to. I have my life.

I pull away and look into his watery eyes. "Here are your shoes," Dr Jack holds out my shoes, he also has my bag next to him on the floor. "Put these on and then I have to place the blindfold back on you."

I slide into my shoes that I haven't worn for a week. Then Dr Jack ties the eye mask behind my head. Taking my hand, he slowly guides me out of the room, up the stairs, through the house and out the front door. I hear a car door open and then Dr Jack helps me lower into the back seat of Frank's car and places my bag next to me on the seat. When Dr Jack has buckled me in, he leans in and kisses me hard on the lips and whispers "Goodbye sweet girl." And he's gone.

"Morning Miss Roxy," comes Frank's familiar voice. "You'll be home in two hours."

"Thank you, Frank," I sniffle back to him. The next two hours my mind swims with memories. It was an experience I will never forget, for so many reasons but mostly because of the men I shared it with.

43

———————

"You are home Miss Roxy."

Home, I think. Am I ready to join real life again? I have to be. I unfasten the mask, open the door, climb out and pull my bag out too. As I close the door, I hear my front door open, and a familiar tall blond man comes striding out. Frank pulls away and James lifts me into his arms and spins me around. I shriek in delight and all tension loosens from my muscles. I'm *home.*

James carries me along the path and through the front door, where he holds me up against the wall and kisses me deeply. I lean into him and the kiss, letting it roll over and through me, familiarising myself again with my husband. I'm home and he loves me, he's missed me. As I come up for air I see a suitcase at the bottom of the stairs.

Breathing deeply I ask, "Where are the kids?"

"They're with your parents."

"Why?"

"Because we have a long weekend away booked."

"We do?"

"We do."

"How come?"

"We need to get reacquainted," he says kindly but I feel a tinge of regret weighing down on his words. They feel heavy on my heart.

"Ok," I say uncertainly. Not sure if he is upset with me or where we stand right now. Has everything now changed between us?

"It's been a big week for you, for us. I'm not losing you to eight men. You are mine, Rosie and I'm going to spend the next three days reminding you of just that."

My eyes fill and I look into the haunting eyes of my husband. He knows what I am feeling and what I am going through. How? I don't know. But I'm grateful he sees me and understands me.

"Where are we going?"

"Daylesford."

"When do we leave?"

"Now."

"Yes Sir," I dole each word out slowly, smiling up at him. His eyes flash and I know I am finally about to meet the real Dom in James.

THE SECRET JOB

Next in the Clarendon Playmate Kink Series coming in 2025.

Following Rosie's Charity Job of captivity, James whisks Rosie away for a weekend of romance and reconnection. Something she doesn't expect is unearthing James' new array of kinks.

Astonishingly Rosie is granted early access to the Red Job Board and takes a deliciously painful job along with a role play job that pushes her to her very limits.

Between playmates jobs, Rosie's personal life takes an interesting turn when someone close to her is invited into her bedroom in the most unexpected ways.

And then, there is the **Secret Job**—one with red flags and a lot of money. Will Rosie take it? Can she afford to walk away from it? How far into the depths of depravity can she go before she looks into the eyes of a sadist and craves every drop of pain he's ready to inflict on her?

THE SECRET JOB - SNEAK PEAK

We sit in the car in silence for a few minutes as James begins the drive to Daylesford, a sleepy town of hot springs and countryside and then we both speak at the same time,

"You go first," I say.

"No sorry, you speak," James replies looking at me with a longing in his eyes I have never seen before. They are asking me to choose him, not the eight men still cramming into my brain and my heart. I knew it would be an experience spending seven days with eight men, but not once did I ever consider the pain of saying goodbye to them. It's not that I don't want to go back to James, it's just that there are a lot of feelings raging through me and I don't know how to deal with them or what to make of them. Where does that leave me and my husband when there are currently eight other men in our relationship?

"How was the week with the kids, did everything go ok?" I ask almost sheepishly. I don't want to talk about my time away, not yet, I'm not ready to explore those feelings with James yet and judging by the look in his eyes, he knows that.

The 1.5 hours' drive to Daylesford passes with light chit chat about the kids, James' work, our families and just about anything other than what I have been doing for the past seven days. It feels like a cloud is hanging low over our heads, the air feels thick with a tension neither of us is trying to break or even acknowledge. When James pulls up to a cute, white-brick Victorian house garnished with beautiful flowers and bushes, I know this is exactly where I want to be.

I open the car door and eye the pretty house before climbing out as James climbs out and pulls our weekend bags from the car boot. I follow James' lead, and we walk through the iron gate and up the cobblestone pathway. Keying a code into the lock, the shiny green door opens, and I follow James inside the quaintly decorated house and close the door behind me. There is a long, chequered rug that runs the hallway but I don't make it two steps from the door when James turns and the look in his eyes startles me still.

"Take off your clothes," he says in a low, almost choked voice. His eyes burn into me and I startle at the heat blazing in them. Is it pain or desire I'm staring into?

I go to speak, open my mouth to say, "Jame—"

"Now," he cuts me off.

ABOUT THE AUTHOR

A few personal details about me: I have a wonderful husband, two children, and a dog. I live in Melbourne, Australia. I work for myself during the day and write for you in my spare time—fitting it in around home life, kids' sports, dog walks, movies, and dancing with my friends after a few glasses of Prosecco.

First, a quick thank you to you, my dear reader. Thank you for taking a chance on an unknown author. I really hope you enjoyed the story that has been living in my head rent-free for the past year. I know I'm no literary genius, but I've got a wicked imagination—which helps, right? If you did like it, I'd be so grateful if you could leave me a review. Every single one I see—even if it's just pretty stars—makes me do a little happy dance and send you boundless amounts of good karma in return.

My second thank you goes to my husband, who wisely said, *"You read so much smut, why don't you write your own?"* To my own James, thank you for nudging me in this direction but never pressuring me to let you read it. While I hope you never read this book or see this thank you, I want everyone who has read this book to know how grateful I am for your support—it's led me to where I am today.

www.RubySkyeAuthor.com

ALSO BY RUBY SKYE

The Clarendon Playmates Kink Series

The Secret Job - Book Two

The Secret Proposal - Book Three

The Secret Stalker - Book Four - Standalone

The Secret Beginning - Book Five - Standalone

The Women in Warehouse 13 - Standalone

The Hucow Hotel - Standalone

* 9 7 8 1 7 6 3 8 5 3 5 0 8 *